Inkpot Gods

BY THE SAME AUTHOR

Deadlands: Boneyard
Dusk or Dark or Dawn or Day
Dying with Her Cheer Pants On
Laughter at the Academy
Letters to the Pumpkin King
Overwatch: Declassified: An Official History of Overwatch
Strixhaven: Omens of Chaos
The Proper Thing and Other Stories
Velveteen vs. The Early Adventures
What If . . . Wanda Maximoff and Peter Parker Were Siblings?

THE OCTOBER DAYE SERIES

Rosemary and Rue
A Local Habitation
An Artificial Night
Late Eclipses
One Salt Sea
Ashes of Honor
Chimes at Midnight
The Winter Long
A Red-Rose Chain
Once Broken Faith
The Brightest Fell
Night and Silence
The Unkindest Tide
A Killing Frost
When Sorrows Come
Be the Serpent
Sleep No More
The Innocent Sleep
Silver and Lead

THE INCRYPTID SERIES

Discount Armageddon
Midnight Blue-Light Special
Half-Off Ragnarok
Pocket Apocalypse
Chaos Choreography
Magic for Nothing
Tricks for Free
That Ain't Witchcraft
Imaginary Numbers
Calculated Risks
Spelunking Through Hell
Backpacking Through Bedlam
Aftermarket Afterlife
Installment Immortality
Butterfly Effects

THE GHOST ROAD SERIES

Sparrow Hill Road
The Girl in the Green Silk Gown
Angel of the Overpass

THE ALCHEMICAL JOURNEYS SERIES

Middlegame

Seasonal Fears

Tidal Creatures

Inkpot Gods

THE WAYWARD CHILDREN SERIES

Every Heart a Doorway

Down Among the Sticks and Bones

Beneath the Sugar Sky

In an Absent Dream

Come Tumbling Down

Across the Green Grass Fields

Where the Drowned Girls Go

Lost in the Moment and Found

Mislaid in Parts Half-Known

Adrift in Currents Clean and Clear

Through Gates of Garnet and Gold

Seanan McGuire's Wayward Children, Volumes 1–3 (boxed set)

Be Sure: Wayward Children, Books 1–3

THE INDEXING SERIES

Indexing

Indexing: Reflections

AS A. DEBORAH BAKER

THE UP-AND-UNDER SERIES

Over the Woodward Wall

Along the Saltwise Sea

Into the Windcracked Wilds

Under the Smokestrewn Sky

AS MIRA GRANT

THE NEWSFLESH SERIES

Feed

Deadline

Blackout

Feedback

Rise: The Complete Newsflesh Collection (short stories)

The Rising: The Newsflesh Trilogy

THE PARASITOLOGY SERIES

Parasite

Symbiont

Chimera

Rolling in the Deep

Into the Drowning Deep

Overgrowth

Final Girls

Kingdom of Needle and Bone

In the Shadow of Spindrift House

Square³

Unbreakable

SEANAN McGUIRE

Inkpot Gods

TOR PUBLISHING GROUP
NEW YORK

This is a work of fiction. All of the names, characters, organizations, places, and events portrayed in this work are either products of the author's imagination or used fictitiously.

INKPOT GODS

A Tor Book
Published by Tom Doherty Associates / Tor Publishing Group
120 Broadway
New York, NY 10271

www.torpublishinggroup.com

EU Representative: Macmillan Publishers Ireland Ltd., 1st Floor, The Liffey Trust Centre, 117–126 Sheriff Street Upper, Dublin 1, D01 YC43

The Library of Congress Cataloging-in-Publication Data is available upon request.

ISBN 978-1-250-33932-4 (hardcover)
ISBN 978-1-250-33934-8 (ebook)

First Edition: 2026

Printed in the United States of America

10 9 8 7 6 5 4 3 2 1

For Manda, one of the finest alchemists I have ever known.
And for Pippa, who is her own alchemical language.

When last we came together, you and I, we spoke to each other of middles, which are vast and tangled and sticky. They can cling to your feet and drag you down, such that you find yourself eternally wandering in the center of a story, trapped with no way back to where you began, and even less hope of a way forward to the finish. We spoke of beginnings and their commonalities, and indeed, we had a beginning together, side by side as we set off into story, following a path that exists only for the reader, and not for those already standing inside. This is only fair. They have access to roads that we do not; the world would be out of balance if they could reach for all of ours.

But that was then, in the dark and distant country of the past, where you and I can never go again, no matter how much we might desire it. Time is a road that only runs in one direction for all save a very fortunate few, and none of us is counted in their number. We must go onward. We must leave the middle behind, as once we left the beginning, and continue toward the high, looming cliff of the conclusion. We are almost to the end, my dears, and once we reach it, there will be no further road to follow. This story will be finished. You can go back to the beginning, should you desire, and begin anew, but as time will not start over with you, you will not see the journey the same way. You will know things. You will understand things. Only be aware that knowing and understanding may change the way you feel about the beginning, the middle, and the end. Traveling through the same story a second time is a form of alchemy. The story you have already experienced will never be available to you again. That tale is ending.

As we are approaching the last time we will be able to speak together for the first time, it seems like a kindness to remind you of what has come before, what obstacles we have overcome and what wonders we have seen, all in the reaching of this place. We are still in the country of once upon a time, after all, and it would be best to remember that as clearly as we can. . . .

—From *Under the Smokestrewn Sky*,
by A. Deborah Baker

BOOK I

Tin

I am no prophet—and here's no great matter;
I have seen the moment of my greatness flicker,
And I have seen the eternal Footman hold my coat, and
snicker,
And in short, I was afraid.

—T. S. Eliot, "The Love Song of J. Alfred Prufrock"

Circles standing in holy ground
Stone rings follow the seasons round
Roofless walls rise in graceful arches
Secret doors lead to these far marches.

—Talis Kimberley, "Ancient Sky"

Wisdom

TIMELINE: 12:00 A.M. ET, JANUARY 7, 1865.

The news that Elisabet Turner is with child takes most who hear it by surprise, for it has long been understood that Elisabet Baker has never known, *will* never know, the touch of a man. Even the village drunks have been seen to pale and turn away when she approaches, refusing to meet her eyes for fear she might use a moment's glancing contact to somehow make a claim against them, might find a way to call herself defiled and hence force them to her bridal bed. The chances might be slim, the likelihood low, but such is the reality of Elisabet Turner's existence. Her own mother was ill while she was with child. It seemed all but impossible Elisabet should be born, even less likely that she should see adulthood.

Yet born she was, and grown she is, and from the swelling of her middle, pregnant as well, even as none might name the father. She is no witch. They are civilized people, living in a civilized time, and they no longer believe in such nonsense as women who dance with the Devil and set their names to his book in exchange for power. But if the Devil were to truly exist, and if he were seeking his brides as the old stories said, well. Elisabet Turner would no doubt be the first such recruit to reach for the pen, trading everything she was in the hopes of being repaid with some better circumstance.

Instead, she walks the world alone. Her parents are long since dead, and even if they had been among the living, she is an unmarried woman of twenty; she would only have been a burden upon their house. She is ugly by any standard, not blessed with pleasant or uniform features, with a comely voice or with a pleasing silhouette; to these early misfortunes she has sadly added two bouts with the pox, the second more violent than the first, leaving her complexion pocked and scarred. Port-wine stains that have been hers to bear since birth blotch the few patches of smooth skin which remain between the heavy scarring, and her right eye is a reddened, rolling horror, her brown iris floating in a sea of bloody sclera, pupil never fixing long on anything.

Her limbs are weak and twisted inward, making her unfit for farming or most forms of labor; her back is hunched, her mouth a ruin of snarled scars and missing teeth. She is ugly, without question, and those who would say ugliness is not a sin are first to sneer and turn away when she draws near, setting their eyes against God's will. Her parents were farmers, and she was born a farmer's daughter, destined for a life tithed to the land, but her mother's brother lives in Boston, the distant, dazzling city; when her parents passed, he sent word that he would be glad to have her join him, to trade her muddy boots for dancing slippers and her planting tools for needle and thread. He would have made a lady of her, and gladly, in his sister's memory. She sent her refusal not two days before her first bout with the pox, and by the time her strength returned, it was clear that the opportunity had passed.

They are civilized people, living in a civilized time, and still, no one likes to bring reminders of sickness into their home. To remember what the wind might carry is to invite it to blow in your direction, to kindle the embers of plague in the bosom of your own family. Her uncle's invitation was rescinded before she had fully recovered.

And so it has been for all of Elisabet Turner's life. One door closes, and two more follow in quick succession, while she stands and complains that she cannot leave the room. When she began to show the first signs of her condition, no one could believe it, and now, some three months on, they still can't believe it, but neither can they deny it.

Perhaps Elisabet Turner is a witch after all.

She walks the village streets during the day, pays for meat and milk with coins scrabbled from what little remains of her family fortune, and sets her eyes toward the horizon, watching the sky as if she seeks to steal its secrets for herself. She sighs longingly at the sight of clouds, but says nothing to anyone that might answer why. The villagers watch her and mutter among themselves, trying to figure out whether she understands her condition, whether she knows why her body is changing. Only the village priest is brave enough to approach her directly, and afterward, he claims not to remember their conversation in any true detail, only to know that Elisabet is under no circumstances to be troubled or forced into accepting charity.

"She is serving in an older story than her own, and how she has the telling of it will determine all our fates and futures," he says, which seems queer indeed coming from a man of the cloth. The villagers whisper about it behind closed doors, but they're far enough from the city that finding a replacement is all but unthinkable: he's their priest, he keeps them in the eye of God, and he will keep them so until the end of everything.

They ask no more questions. Elisabet Turner is with child. She will bear her infant when the time is right, as people have done from the beginning even to the end of time. This will not be changed by questions, and so her neighbors fall silent, forming the hush before the sermon, and they wait for the miracle to arrive.

* * *

Elisabet Turner is no witch. She has never signed the Devil's book, never held his pen beneath the summer moonlight, never shed her clothing to dance around the fire. She would have done all those things, had she been but asked, but no one has ever thought to ask her such a thing. She is a living afterthought, a woman well accustomed to being ignored by all around her. She has no powers beyond those natural to a young woman raised in the farmland of Massachusetts, her back to the wood and her face to the sky.

She knows herself well enough that certain sentinel truths are etched firmly in her mind: she knows she is not lovely, that any chance she may have had at loveliness fled forever when she fought her first battle with the pox. She knows a third bout would kill her, without question. She is lucky to have survived the first, much less the second. The scarring she carries runs far deeper than the skin alone. The secret, hidden parts of her body are just as riddled with the damage done by the disease, and they will fail her if forced to face another challenge.

She knows God has no plan. Because despite everything she's been through, everything she's survived, she is not yet a bad person. She speaks no lies against her fellows, commits neither crime nor sin, save perhaps for the crime of ugliness, which some seem to fear as the greatest sin of all. If God had a plan, if her suffering were to serve some grand design, she would surely have seen signs of it by now. There are a thousand tiny signals before the spring. A quickened egg will show a venous system when held before a candle. But she watches the world she walks through, and she sees no signs of God's design, nor indications of His existence.

She has seen other signs, however, signs that would surely see her condemned to death by hanging, were she to speak of them in another's hearing.

She has seen women who walk through the woods in the deepest part of winter, their arms bared and their hair so full of ice that it gleams like a cloak of diamonds across their backs. She has seen men who walk in summer, their heads bare to the sun, trails of flowers growing bright and shining in their wake.

She has seen the people stepping out of the sea with scales across their chests and webs between their fingers, and seen the women who ride down on shafts of moonlight when the moon is full and true and centered in the sky. She has seen the smooth-limbed, sexless youths who dance by starlight, their steps so light as to not disturb the evening dew.

Elisabet Turner is nothing particularly special. Just a woman who has survived her share of hardship, who has tried to cling to her virtue as she walks the long, inescapable road between birth and dying. But as some people who are pushed to the outskirts are wont to do, she has learned to pay attention, and she has seen more than she was, perhaps, intended to see.

She isn't sure that she believes in God, but she believes in gods. She knows they walk the world, pagan things from before the Bible was set in stone.

She knows one of them came to her in the guise of an early winter storm, and when he shook the lightning from his hands and the thunder from his voice, he was a handsome man to look upon, his skin smelling of petrichor and the electric burn of static, his body no more clad than any other storm. She knows he looked upon her ugliness and didn't shy away, didn't behave as if she were anything other than a woman, as if he were anything other than a man. He took her in his arms and took her to the bed she had always known as lonely, but would forever after know as a place of love and delicacy.

He loved her gently, carefully, as a man may love a woman, and when his lightning pierced the flesh of her form, the storm was all. She had never in her lifetime feared the rain. After that night, after those hours in the arms of that storm, the rain is a sacrament to her, as holy as any communion.

She knows he was gentle, and that when he left her where she lay, he left a storm cradled in her womb, where it sparks and stretches still, wind and rain and lightning all growing together, bound in flesh and silence. She will be a mother, and all because a storm took pity on her and came down from the heavens to claim her as his own. She will no longer be alone.

All she has to do is wait.

* * *

The second day of July is wading through the golden hours of morning, and Elisabet labors in her agonies on that same bed, holding tight to the ropes which bind her wrists and keep her from keeling forward, unable to find another ounce of fight in her fragile skin. The midwife is a stranger to their village. She rode in three nights prior with a caravan of traveling folk, and while her hands are gentle, her voice is strange, thick with an accent Elisabet doesn't know.

Not that she's been listening to the woman's voice much for the last fistful of hours. She pushes when she's told to push, she breathes when she's told to breathe, and she screams when she's not told to do anything at all. She knows something is wrong.

Then, without warning, the woman is at the head of the bed, her mouth near Elisabet's ear. "We told him, when he found and fancied you, we told him your body was not as strong as it would need to be to survive the cost of his attention. We told him *you* would not survive. But he has never been one to listen to those he considers less than his equals, and he took you for his lover all the same."

"My . . . storm," gasps Elisabet, catching the midwife's meaning. "Not . . . sorry."

"Ah, good. That is better, then, if only by a small degree: it means you may not regret the price you pay." The woman leans closer still, her dark eyes fixed on Elisabet's. "The labor does not go well. You know that, yes?"

Elisabet is no fool. She's known for hours now that things are not proceeding as they should, that her child is not to have an easy entrance to the world. She nods, saving her breath for another scream.

"I came at your lover's request, because those who labor are my domain; it is my duty to do for you what little I can. But at this stage, what I can do is *very* little. I can save one of you. Both is beyond me."

Elisabet gasps, struggling to breathe, fighting to understand. "Which one?"

And the stranger smiles, sorrowful as a Sunday, and inclines her head, dark hair falling around her features like a mourner's veil at a funeral. "That, my little love, is for you to decide."

Elisabet gasps again as she understands the choice before her, the offer that has been made. "Why?"

"That question could have a thousand meanings, and we don't have a thousand years. Why did he choose you? Because he could. Because he knows our time is over, fading into antiquity and shadow, and when he finds the strength to appear before a comely maid, he feels compelled to do so. Why did he leave you with child? Because such encounters will always birth new life. Why should you choose to live? You are young, Elisabet Turner, and the world is wide. You could have a marvelous future, and leave this place so far behind you that it echoes only in the deepest of your dreams. You could be happy. I know that doesn't sound real right now, but I swear on my mother's name, you could be happy. You could shine like a star, if you chose to live."

Elisabet is past speaking now, her throat stopped with pain, her breath committed to moving sharply in and out as she struggles to keep living. Still, her eyes plead with the stranger, who sighs and nods.

"Why should you choose to let your infant daughter survive in your stead? Because you have always wished to be a mother, and if you choose her, you will die knowing that your dream came true. Because she will be exceptional, bright and brilliant and blazing.

Children of storms always are. She will change the world, Elisabet. Not in the same ways you would, but in ways that it will never forget." She pauses, then adds the words that she knows will seal Elisabet Turner's fate: "She will be remembered."

Elisabet nods fiercely, and manages her final word, a question: "Name?"

And the stranger, who could interpret that word in two directions, chooses the easier answer. She has been speaking hard and terrible truths since her arrival, even if she can't control how Elisabet will hear them: this time, this last time, she will speak the softer truth, the one which changes nothing at all.

"Ilithyia," she says, and moves back to the foot of the bed, resuming her position.

Elisabet's labor, which began upon the stroke of midnight, ends at the stroke of noon the following day, taking her life with it into nothingness after twelve hours of agony. Her daughter, newly born and still wet with blood and amniotic fluids, wails her existence into the air as Ilithyia extracts the placenta from Elisabet's cooling body and separates the infant from the organ which sustained her until this moment.

In other villages, at other bedsides, she might hurry, might even flee at this stage, aware that someone will be coming to point a finger and seek someone to blame. Here, now, she attends to the body of a woman barely shy of accusations of witchcraft, misliked and likely to go unmourned by her neighbors. The only question is the baby. She can leave her here, count on these people to do the right thing by the girl, or she can claim to have lost them both and vanish into the wilds with the child swaddled in her own arms.

There is temptation in the thought of taking the child as her own. The girl has as yet done nothing wrong, has had no opportunity to grow into anything more than a squalling infant, made entirely of possibility and unspent potential. Ilithyia told only the truth when she said Elisabet's daughter would change the world, that she will be remembered: she has never once lied to a mother in childbed, and she won't allow this girl to change that fundamental part of her. The girl *will* change the world. But if Ilithyia takes her now, that change will be kinder, will claim fewer lives.

So much hinges on this choice. She reaches for the child, is on the verge of lifting her from the mattress when someone hammers on the door, and the voice of the village priest calls, "Elisabet? I heard the silence. Are you well?"

Ilithyia looks over her shoulder in surprise, and when she looks back to the child, the future where Ilithyia took her is gone, replaced by a single shining road of iridescence and impossibility stretching into the unvarying future.

"Very well, then," she says, and swaddles the baby with quick, well-practiced motions, lifting her and carrying her to the door, which she opens easily.

The priest looks at her with wary grief. He knows, already, in some terrible way. He knows, and she knows the village will take his acceptance of the dead woman's child as proof that he broke his vows. He'll raise her for seven years, then send her to her uncle's in a vain attempt to restore his honor. It won't work. It never does.

"I was unable to save the mother," says Ilithyia, and hands him the girl, who quiets at once when he pulls her to his chest. She stares at him with her unfocused eyes, and he stares back. Ilithyia wonders how much of his future he sees in that child's gaze, and whether it changes anything.

She rather thinks it doesn't.

She walks away, and no one stops her. No one ever does. The afternoon is young, and she has very far to go to make it back home to Olympus.

Logic

TIMELINE: 4:18 P.M. ET, JULY 11, 1872.

It has been seven years since the death of Elisabet Turner. Most unmarried women who died in childbirth would have been forgotten long since, or mythologized into cautionary tales to offer to the youth: *See?* they say. *This is what happens when you sin. This is how the Devil claims his own.*

Most unmarried women were not Elisabet Turner. She had never once even hinted as to the identity of her child's father, and had been so unfortunate to look upon that the thought of a passing hunter or Frenchman down from the Canadian territories forcing himself upon her had been simply beyond consideration. The only man anyone could remember her spending much time with was the village priest, Father Clemence, and he had always been a man of unshakable faith.

Then she had passed, and he had taken in her daughter as a foundling, even giving her his own surname to carry—as a man might do when faced with his own bastard. The whispers grew louder after that, and only continue to swell year after year. Floretta Bearse looks nothing like her mother. She looks nothing like Father Clemence, either, but people seem content to overlook that as they murmur about whether the priest's ward might not be his child by blood as well as by baptism.

She is straight of spine and long of limb, tall for a girl of her age, with a face like the flower that is her namesake, ever turning toward the sun. Her features are sweet, her voice melodic, and despite the questionable status of her birth, more than a few of the village sons have begun to look at her with approval. Perhaps that, atop everything else, is why so many have begun to gossip about her origins.

It might be a kinder world if she were to be allowed to remain Floretta Bearse, a copper-haired child picking wildflowers in the shadow of the Massachusetts forest, unaware of storms that walk like men, of midwives who appear from nowhere and offer impossible choices. She would grow up clever but ordinary in the shadow of those trees, would marry and have children in the common way, and all the changes she was destined to force upon the firmament would go unmade.

But Ilithyia would be a liar, and if there's one thing gods can't stand, it's being turned into liars. The future is seen: the future is set. Some things, once set in motion, cannot be turned aside.

Floretta is running through the fields when a half dozen of the village men come to her adoptive father in his office, forcing their way past the closed door with claims of concern for his spiritual health. He is the spiritual center of their community. If they worry that there might be rot at the root, it is his duty to soothe them, and so he welcomes them inside.

At first they speak in vagaries and pleasantries, skirting around the subject they have all come here to discuss. None of them wishes to be the one to bring up the true reason for their visit.

"If you'll forgive me, I have a sermon to prepare for this weekend—" begins Father Clemence.

"The girl is wild, Father," says one of the men, almost frantically. "I was never one of those who thought Goody Turner guilty of witchcraft. She was a simple soul who never did anyone any harm."

And yet you use an archaic title for her, a title most commonly associated with tales of witches, thinks Father Clemence, and holds his composure.

"But the girl," continues the man, and the others nod, murmuring their ascent. "Her mother was sickly, yet she has never ailed a day. She runs wild when not at her lessons, with no woman to teach her the proper way of things. She lures our daughters from their chores into the fields."

"She means no harm," says Father Clemence, voice hot and tight with anger. He isn't any louder than he would normally be; his control is better than that of the men before him. But he's lived with the girl for seven years, and he knows her better than he knows anyone else in his parish, knows her fears and her fantasies. He knows these men are here out of fear and concern mixed in almost equal measure, which forms a slurry of something similar to but not entirely like love. And he knows he's going to lose this battle. He was expecting to lose it years ago, is lucky to have gotten nearly seven years.

(He is also, although he doesn't realize the true relevance, the only one of them to know the truth of Floretta's parentage, or at least to know that he is not, could not be, in any version of this world, the father. He chose the priesthood out of both a true higher calling and a distaste for the company of women; were he stationed in a larger city, he might have betrayed his vows by now with one of the lithe and laughing boys who haunt the taverns and the public houses. But here, in the tight tangle of a small village, he's been able to remain pious and pure. Elisabet Turner was no temptress, and even if she had been, he would have been above temptation. No, he took the girl out of a feeling of obligation not because he had sired her, but because he had somehow allowed one of the most vulnerable among his flock to be led astray. *Someone* got Elisabet Turner with child, and her halting, incoherent confessions of sin and selfishness had only left him afraid that his stewardship had allowed her to be preyed upon by something far beyond his ken.)

"Now," says one of the men. "She means no harm *now*. But Father, surely you can see that the child of an unmarried woman will present an unfair temptation to our sons as they grow. She cannot be compromised, cannot be defiled, for she is already marked by the circumstances of her birth."

Father Clemence is distantly relieved that the man has avoided the word "tainted." Once they begin to speak of taint as if it were something that could truly be carried by a child, there is no defense he can offer. Not as a man of the cloth, and not as the moral center of this village. "What would you have me do?" he asks instead, and his words are a thin film of earth and root above a great muddy sinkhole, a hidden horror into which children can tumble and be lost forever. He sounds hollowed out.

"Her mother, Goody Turner . . . she had an uncle," says one of the men, and the future is set.

God help them all.

* * *

John Baker is precisely the sort of man Boston was constructed to create, a hard-pressed diamond formed from good New England coal. He's everything Elisabet was not, tall and strong and straight as an arrow, with a spine that could easily have been sculpted by God himself. Despite his age—he must be in his early sixties by now—his hair is still thick and lush, a dark copper shade that mirrors without quite matching Floretta's. The resemblance between them is stark enough to illustrate their differences.

This is not a man inclined to smiles and softness and the gathering of wildflowers. And while it might seem reasonable that a grown man would have different interests than a little girl, there are men who walk in the world with an air of wonder about them, a softness which says they *would* pick wildflowers, were that an option. There are men who have clearly remembered how to dream.

There are also men who have remembered but conceal that knowledge behind a veil of hardness, a shale crust spread across their wonder and their whimsy. John Baker is not such a man. He has pressed himself into the shape he wanted to wear, has molded himself like marble, and there is nothing left of him that does not serve a proper purpose.

He looks around with cold eyes as he steps out of the carriage that has brought him here, to this small village in the shadow of the Massachusetts trees, where his sister lived her short and difficult life before she was consigned unto the soil, where his niece did the same. He is here because he has been summoned—summoned, him, like a common assistant! No one here should have any authority to call for him, and yet they did, and so he has come, out of curiosity as much as pride. He would like to know why they think they have the right to interfere with his business, before he burns their bucolic little hamlet into ashes.

John Baker was never a man who took easily to being challenged or presumed upon in any way, and the slow death of his entire family has only reinforced his desire to be the master of his fate in all possible ways. He does not want to be here. The letter he received, from the village pastor no less, did not properly explain why he was needed, or why it should matter that he appear in person. Elisabet is dead. He knows that much, was sent the news some years back: there is no good reason for his presence.

He closes the carriage door, the sound sharp and foreign in this miserable place, and waits for someone to come and tell him why he's been disturbed.

A door opens, and a thin, sandy-haired man in clerical vestments steps out, squinting in the thin sunlight that manages to break through the clouds overhead. Between the weather and the trees, John's not sure these people have ever truly seen the sun. It would explain the obvious poverty of the land, the way the fields lie half-fallow in the autumn air.

(The true explanation would be harder for him to understand, or to accept. Gods have always walked the world, have always spread their seed where it may not have been wanted, and have always abandoned the gardens they plant in such a manner. Elisabet's storm had no more loved her than a mountain loves a songbird. He had seen her from a distance, the broken, ugly girl who saw more than most of her kind would ever dream, and he had desired her, and then he had taken her, and that had been enough. Had she lived, he would not have magically returned to be a father to her child; he was always going to leave her. Her daughter, though . . . her daughter was a different, even older story.

Elisabet Turner was the lover, for a night's duration, of a god. Her daughter was the child of one. Floretta would always be special in some regards, always be watched by distant, questionably approving eyes. The sky had been clouded almost since the moment of her birth, her father's domain watching over her. Those clouds saw every slight she received from the villagers around her, every moment of rejection, every cruel comment delivered to a child too young to fully understand them. The storm did not punish, not directly. But the clouds blocked the sun and the rain did not fall, and the crops withered on their vines. The land had been sour since Elisabet Turner's death, and because a storm is not properly a father, the god who had sired her child didn't understand that all he was doing was making things worse for the girl he was trying to protect.)

John stays where he is, impatient but unwilling to approach the priest, unwilling to seem like the petitioner here, when he has been summoned. Still, he's relieved when the priest sees him and turns in his direction, moving with reasonable speed across the cracked and oddly muddy ground. How it can be dry enough to crack and muddy at the same time is a small mystery, one that must remain unanswered evermore, for the priest is growing closer, a look of strange reluctance on his face.

"Mr. Baker?" he asks, and his voice is suited to his figure, slight and weaker than it seems like it should be.

This is their man of faith, the spiritual center of their community? This is the man who sent for him?

John Baker sticks out his hand with a strongman's confidence. "Father Bearse?"

"Most call me Father Clemence," says the priest, taking the offered hand and shaking with surprising strength. "But yes, I am Clemence Bearse."

"And I am John Baker."

Silence falls between them, less companionable than inevitable. Father Clemence recovers his hand, shaking it as if to restore feeling to his fingers.

"I wrote to you," he says. "I was hoping you would answer my invitation."

"Is that what you call it? It sounded more like a summons as it was written."

"It wasn't meant to be," says Father Clemence, uncomfortably. "I was hoping to catch your attention, sir, and knew I would need a compelling argument to draw you from Boston to our little village. None has seen you here since—"

"Since my sister's death, I'm well aware," says John, brusquely. "I had no intention of ever returning to this place. I still don't understand what drew her to settle here, so far from everything she'd known."

"She was a pious woman who raised a pious daughter. You should be proud of her, and find joy in her memory."

"I find joy in her memory, but not in her choice of habitat. Why am I here?"

"Your niece, Elisabet—"

"Is as dead as her mother. I remember that as well. I am not so callow a man as to forget my losses, even as I was unable to attend her funeral. I sent money. If this is about some unpaid debt Elisabet left behind, I have already done my duty by the girl."

"She did leave something behind," says Father Clemence, with deep and evident discomfort. "It was not a debt in the material sense, but in the spiritual sense, for do we not all owe faith unto our families?"

"What are you on about?"

"Your niece died in childbed."

John Baker goes very still. Someone happening upon the scene might be forgiven for thinking the priest was in conversation with a statue, and not a man of flesh and blood.

In his stillness, his resemblance to Elisabet is easier to see. They have the same coloring, and his handsome features are a more refined version of hers, which were never beautiful, but had a certain striking harshness to them, one which translates better to a man's face, unkind as they might be for the world to say. The world has never been particularly focused on kindness. Nor has it been particularly focused on reality, and while there is no true reason that the shape of a brow or the angle of a nose should be more suited to a man than to a woman, people often see them that way, and their seeing is often enough to reshape the world.

Father Clemence looks at John Baker's stillness and is relieved. The man's obvious distress is not showy or loud, but he's been a priest long enough to have seen grief in all its many forms, from the keening wail of a mother burying her son to the quiet weeping of a husband burying his wife. He knows sorrow when he sees it. He sees it now, and that seeing awakens a small kernel of hope in his heart, a belief that his dear Floretta will have a safe harbor waiting for her in her uncle's arms.

He would be horrified if he could see John Baker's heart. John's stillness is not sorrow, but calculation, the frantic freeze of a man running numbers against the future and coming up with answers he doesn't fully understand. Any grieving he was going to do for Elisabet was concluded years ago, when she refused his invitation to Boston. In his eyes, she had died long before her body ceased to be the house where she dwelt.

John takes a breath after what seems like an interminable time, and says, in a voice like a tomb door slamming shut, "The babe died with her, of course, or you would have called me long since. Have you found the man who defiled my niece? She would have invited me to her wedding, had she enjoyed one." Unspoken is the fact that any celebration larger than a roast chicken and a honeyed cake would have been funded by his accounts: he had never subsidized Elisabet's hardscrabble days, but he knew his duties as her closest male relation, and he would have fulfilled them, had he been called upon to do so.

Father Clemence shakes his head. "No, Mr. Baker, I'm afraid the father of Elisabet's child was never identified. She refused to say, even unto her deathbed."

"I see."

"As to the babe, we did send word." Once, by post, in an unremarkable envelope which had gone mysteriously astray before it reached its destination. Gods can interfere in more than rain, and in the beginning, Elisabet's storm had been content to see her child stay in the shadow of her mother's bones. "You never replied. I assumed, at the time, that you didn't have an interest. I apologize if I was mistaken."

John's gaze sharpens. "The child lived?"

"She did." The admission is simple, small, and drops like a stone into the still waters of a well, sending ripples swinging wide but making not a sound. "I have sheltered and kept her these seven years. She has her letters, reads both English and Latin with reasonable skill, and can do her sums well enough to keep a household, when the time comes for her to set out on her own. She is a biddable child, clever if a bit wild, and has been one of the great joys of my life."

"I see." John scowls at him a moment, making it clear without saying so directly that he believes the man is lying when he claims to have sent notice of the girl's survival. He won't question the word of a man of the cloth, but he can say it with his eyes. "Then why, if you thought I had no interest in my own kin, have you chosen to contact me now?"

"Well, Mr. Baker, she is approaching seven years of age, and some among my congregation begin to question the appropriateness of her dwelling in my household."

For the first time since this conversation began, John is startled enough to bark a quick, sharp laugh. "You mean they don't like their priest living with a girl he's not related to? Might tarnish your holy virtue?"

"She's not old enough yet for anyone's virtue to be at risk, but yes, there are some who would prefer I avoid even the impression of impropriety," says Father Clemence, stiffly. "Floretta has been a great comfort to me in these hard years. The harvests have been lean, you see, and the village suffers so as our larders run bare—"

"Floretta? Did Elisabet name her that?"

"No. My housekeeper did. Floretta Bearse is the only name she has ever known or answered to."

John wrinkles his nose in evident distaste. "We'll fix that soon enough," he says. "No niece of mine will face the schools of Boston with a name like Floretta."

Father Clemence droops, even as relief blossoms on his face. "You'll see to her care, then?"

John scowls. "Of course I will. She's my niece. She should have been with me from the beginning."

"Indeed." Father Clemence nods. "Then we see the world set right."

Knowledge

TIMELINE: 7:07 P.M. ET, JULY 21, 1872.

For Floretta, a summons to the dinner table is nothing unusual. She doesn't eat with the good father every night; he's often busy with parish business, sitting by the bedsides of sick villagers or blessing newborn babes. She isn't generally invited to these visits, and if she understands that her exclusion is partially due to a vague belief that she might bring bad fortune in her wake, she's young enough that she's managed not to let the knowledge sour her disposition. Nor has she complained about it where anyone could hear her. She knows what's expected of her as a priest's daughter.

She also knows that there's a difference between a preacher, like the man who sometimes rides his cart and buggy through the village on his way to Boston, Bible in his hand and hellfire on his lips, and a priest, like her own Father Clemence. Preachers marry rarely, but they *do* marry, and those who do have children in the normal way of things (young and somewhat sheltered she may be, but she's also a child in a farming village—she knows the ways in which children happen, assuming humans work the same as cows or barn cats). Priests, on the other hand, don't marry, and they don't have children. But her priest did, and she definitely exists.

Various adults have tried to explain to her where she came from. She knows she had a mother once, and she knows her mother's body is in the churchyard, resting peacefully. Everyone she speaks to seems to have their own mind as to where her mother's soul has gone. Some say up to God and the angels, and some say down, to the other place, and since they seem to be equally divided, she assumes her mother's soul is with her body, sleeping in the earth. Father Clemence scolds people who tell her that her mother's gone below, ordering them to speak more kindly to a child. She loves him for that, for his kindness to the mother she never knew.

The village is equally divided on whether he's her father by blood as well as by care. Some of them say he is, and that her mother was a fallen woman, while others say he's barely short of sainthood for taking in the bastard daughter of a simple soul who'd been led heartlessly astray. Floretta has long since come to the conclusion that no one knows for sure, perhaps not even Father Clemence, and so the truth must be whatever she decides it should be.

The truth *should* be that he's her father. That the man who has brushed her hair and eased her fevers should belong to her, as she belongs to him. Every night in her prayers, she asks God—who is good, who can do absolutely anything if He only decides He should—to make Father Clemence her father in every possible way, so that she will never be asked to leave his house, as some of the village women have implied she'll one day have to do. It's a small and selfish miracle, but if God can make the heavens and the earth, she assumes He can handle the requests of children. She wants this so badly, it would be a blasphemy *not* to ask him to make her wish come true!

She's been down by the river all afternoon. An arrogant name for a muddy trickle of water that barely seems to aspire to the status of creek most days. Still one of her favorite places for all that it puts on airs about its status. She loves the ripples on the water, the quick, shy flashes of silvered fish below the surface, the occasional frog brave or foolish enough to stray into sight and find itself scooped up by her quick young hands. Father Clemence has long since abandoned scolding her for muddying the hems of her dresses, for pruning the skin between her toes. It brings her joy, and joy is in short enough supply in the village.

She bangs through the front door, running through the house without hesitation. It's not large, just two bedrooms and a kitchen sprouting off from a central sitting room that serves as dining space and visiting area for villagers with problems smaller or more personal than the ones they air in the village church. She knows Father Clemence used to live in the small apartment attached to the church itself; the house where they live belonged to her mother, and to her grandparents before that. It is the only home Floretta has ever known.

And today she runs into it to find a stranger sitting with her beloved Father, his back straight and stiff as a black oak tree, his hands folded over his middle like the village schoolmaster preparing to deliver a lecture she doesn't feel she deserves. A chill runs down her spine, and a feeling like the one she gets every autumn when she sees the first leaf fall, every spring when she sees the first dandelion going to seed. Something is changing. Once it's changed, she won't have the strength to change it back.

The stranger's eyes flick over her, taking her measure, from her muddy hem to the reddened scratch on her shin where she got too close to a thornbush. It feels like he weighs her in that look, finding her entirely wanting. Any flicker of interest in those eyes is outweighed by the disdain, and she can't imagine him wanting anything more to do with her.

Father Clemence looks at her, at first the way he always has, and then, when the stranger makes a small, disapproving noise, with widened eyes, like he, too, is seeing her for the first time, seeing all her flaws with the eyes of an authority figure, rather than a father.

"Floretta," he says, his tone breathless and oddly rushed. Floretta feels something in her chest curl inward like a fern escaping from the sun, delicate and bruised and shying away from his unfamiliar rejection. She doesn't think she can take him looking at her like that for very long, thinks it might sink into her skin like a poison and rot her away from the inside out if she tries.

She turns her own eyes away, and finds herself looking at the stranger, who stares unflinchingly back at her. His eyes are a clear and somehow layered blue, like river water running over stones. Her own eyes are the same, and in that moment, she knows that God has never listened to her prayers. He may have heard them, but He didn't *listen*, thinking that all she wanted was a father, when what she was asking was that He make sure her life would never need to change.

She doesn't want this. But still, she is a biddable girl, if somewhat wild, and she knows what's expected. So she bobs the shallowest of curtseys, her skirt held firmly in her hands, and says a polite, "I'm sorry, sir. I didn't know we were expecting company."

"Floretta, this isn't company. This is—"

She knows what his next words will have to be, and thinks they might well strike her dead, that it might be better to be struck dead than to be forced to face the reality of another father.

"—your uncle, come to visit us from Boston," he finishes, and Floretta blinks at him, struck silent by the denial of her expectations.

Her silence stretches out for too long. John begins to frown, judging her apparent lack of manners, and she knows, in the dark, sinking part of her heart, that any chance she has to win his good regard is slipping rapidly away.

She isn't sure she *wants* his approval, not really: Floretta has always been a sweet-natured girl, eager to charm the people around her, fully aware that the questionable reality of her parentage puts her at a disadvantage. There aren't many people for her to charm in their little village, but she's done her best, flirting and flouncing and laughing her way through life. This man, though, with his connection to the mother she never knew and his roots in faraway Boston, which might as well be the moon for all the distance there is between them . . . this man may be too dangerous to charm.

Or too dangerous not to.

Floretta smiles, wide enough to make a dimple appear high on her left cheek, and bobs a deeper curtsey, this time putting some respect and effort into the gesture. "A pleasure to meet you, sir," she says. "I am Floretta Bearse, and I am grateful to make your acquaintance."

Her voice is clear and carrying, her words well formed and easily understood. John doesn't stop frowning, but does acknowledge, silently, that she might not have been entirely destroyed by her country upbringing, by her early privation. Oh, he'll have his work cut out for him, he can see that clearly enough to have no question, but the work no longer seems insurmountable.

"We'll have plenty of time to get to know one another in Boston," he says crisply, decision made.

Horror flits across Floretta's face, there and gone so quickly that it could easily be mistaken for a shadow cast by the nearby trees, for the sun passing momentarily behind a cloud. "Boston?" she asks, voice quavering, eyes darting to Father Clemence.

And Father Clemence, beloved Father Clemence, guardian against nightmares, provider of safety, comfort, and warmth, does the unforgivable: he looks away.

"Your uncle was not properly informed of your birth when it occurred," he says, and his voice is a pit leading to perdition, deep and empty and echoing. "Now that he is aware of your existence, it seems only right that he should have the custody of you. He will see to your care and education, and he will be able to do a far finer job than I could ever have achieved."

"No," gasps Floretta. She all but flies to Father Clemence, scrabbling for his hands. "No, you can't do this to me, no. This is my home! I have as much claim to this place as you do! Who will sweep the hearth and light the fire? Who will sing to Mother's bones?"

"Quiet yourself, child," says her uncle sharply. "These things are not a child's burden to bear. You will come with me, and I will shape you into a proper lady. I will grant you the life you should have lived from the beginning. You would have no such qualms if things had been done as the law demands, and you had come to me as your closest living relative." He rises, and he's so tall, he's tall enough to eclipse the sun, to blot out everything else in the universe.

(Later, of course, she'll realize that he's just a man of slightly more than average height, as Father Clemence was a man of slightly less. He only seemed so tall because she was a terrified child, and once both those conditions have changed, he'll dwindle in her eyes until he becomes something more surmountable, something she can overcome. But that day is far in the future, and by the time it arrives, Floretta Bearse will no longer, for all intents and purposes, exist.)

In the murky, unpleasant present, she shies away from him like a wild creature, shooting one last desperate glance at the man who has, up until this point, been the final authority in her world. "Am I to have no choice in my own future?" she asks.

Her uncle shakes his great, implacable head. "You are a child, and a female child beside; you should count yourself endlessly fortunate that I'm willing to take on the burden of caring for you."

Floretta wants to scream, wants to tell him that if she's such a burden, he can leave her here where she's familiar and comfortable and safe. She doesn't. She can see by the way he's looking at her that such an outburst would do her more harm than good. Her fate is set. The ink is dry, and she is leaving home, leaving the place where a storm touched down and a woman died to bring her into the world.

She looks upon the future, and she is afraid.

* * *

Her uncle has a name—John Baker—and as his coach rattles along the road between home and Boston, she learns that she has a name as well. Not the name she's worn for her entire life, no: that name belongs to Father Clemence, and is no longer hers to carry.

Floretta Bearse leaves the village where she was born, and Floretta Baker arrives in Boston a full day's drive after their departure, bones aching from the unfamiliar motion of the coach, eyes aching from her desperate attempt to take in the entire world outside their windows, soul aching from the loss of everything she's ever known.

Her uncle is a cold man, and barely spoke during their drive, instead taking the time to study and catalog her with his eyes, making note of every flaw and imperfection as if he had every intention of repairing them, making her over into something more suited to his glittering life in the glorious city. Floretta squirmed under his regard, and she squirms still as the coach pulls to a stop in front of a great brick house, so large that it seems barely smaller than a castle, more fit for a fairy-tale queen than a little girl in a dirty, tattered dress and her unsmiling uncle.

She looks, quickly, to Uncle John, waiting for him to tell the driver that they've stopped in the wrong place, that they need to continue onward to their actual destination. Instead, he huffs a great sigh and picks up his valise (which she has not seen him open yet, not even once; whatever it contains is still a mystery to her), as he climbs out of the coach. He pauses then, looking back, and asks a question she wishes he'd asked upon their meeting:

"Are you coming?"

Floretta Baker is a biddable child, if not as biddable as Floretta Bearse once was. She climbs out of the coach and follows him without complaint, allowing him to lead her through the gate and up the stairs to the grand oak door into his impossible house. The hall on the other side is paneled in mahogany and feels like it should be flooded with a honeyed sunlight at all times, even now, with the hour slipped well beyond midnight and all the stars alight in the sky. She clutches her own small suitcase, which contains everything she has any right to call her own, and looks around with awestruck wonder, so dazzled by the dream of absent sunlight that she doesn't even notice the woman in the white cap and apron who stands in a narrow doorway to one side, watching them.

"Deborah," snaps her uncle. The woman steps into the foyer, reaching out to take his valise, sparing only a half-curious glance for Floretta. Uncle John ignores it, continuing in the same aggravated tone: "This is my great-niece. She'll be staying with us for the foreseeable future. Please see to it that a room befitting her station is prepared for her, and ask Miss Cottingsly to order her a whole fresh wardrobe."

"Yes, sir," says Deborah, casting her eyes toward the floor. "Everything, sir?"

"Bows to toes," says Uncle John. Floretta glances at him, startled. The rhyming is the most playful thing he's done since she met him in the parlor of her—of Father Clemence's—home. Perhaps he's not going to be so terrible after all.

But then he continues: "The dress she's wearing is a horror. Burn it once she has something suitable to wear. Burn it all. None of it is suitable for a daughter of this house."

"Yes, sir."

"Take her now. Her company is a tedious thing, and I do not wish to see her before breakfast tomorrow." Unspoken was the command to clean her up and prepare her for polite company, a herculean undertaking for anyone, but especially for a single housemaid who looks barely old enough to be working outside her parents' home.

Deborah nods and bobs a curtsey, then gestures for Floretta to join her. "Come along, child," she says, encouragingly. "I'll show you where you can get something to eat, and then meet Miss Cottingsly. She's head of the house staff, and she'll need to measure you for your new wardrobe."

"Yes, ma'am," says Floretta, moving to her side. She glances back at her uncle and, out of an abundance of civility, says, "Thank you, Uncle," before she can be led away.

Deborah waits until they're both halfway down the hall and out of his hearing before she says, in a tightly clipped voice, "Never speak after you've been dismissed. It only encourages him to continue perceiving you, and that will end poorly for you if it occurs."

"Ma'am?" asks Floretta, voice gone small.

"You're to be a member of our household now. From your attire and demeanor, I'm supposing this was as much of a surprise to you as it is to me?" There is no deference in her tone.

(Deference would come later, when Floretta had completed her transformation into the ward of the master of the house, rather than the in-between creature she was now. Deference would come when there were no other choices to be had. It would not be enough. Nothing, once the wheels had been set into motion, could have been enough.)

"Yes, ma'am," says Floretta.

"How old are you?"

"Seven," says Floretta.

"Do you know your letters? Your numbers? Can you do simple sums?"

"I can read well enough to sound out the scripture, and do simple maths with sufficient ease to relieve some of the household pressure on my guardian," says Floretta, with careful politeness. "Am I needed to handle the household accounts?"

"Good Lord above, girl, no," says Deborah, sounding shocked. "You are a *child*. You will be expected to comport yourself as a child does, to attend your lessons and mind your manners. Do as you're told and we'll have no problems."

Floretta frowns. "Is there to be no time for . . ." She trails off. She doesn't know how describe the life she's lived up until this point, or how she's spent the majority of her days. Does Boston even know the value of wildflowers, or the need for wandering in the woods between lessons and chores? Do wildflowers grow in Boston?

She has never felt so small, or so alone.

"The master is a good man. He will see to it that you're fed and clothed, and elevated to the heights to which your birth entitles you. Don't look so glum, girl. You've landed in a fortunate position here, and whoever—whatever—you were before, you're Mr. Baker's ward now. Appreciate what you have, and forget what you haven't. It doesn't matter anymore."

Floretta nods and says nothing.

It doesn't feel as if there's anything left to say.

* * *

Miss Cottingsly seems too old by half for the title she carries; Floretta has never seen a "miss" old enough to be her grandmother before. The woman's face is seamed with wrinkles, and her hair is white as cotton and cut short enough to curl in on itself, like a lamb's wool. She wears a simple dress and a white apron, perfectly tied around her admirably thick waist.

She looks at Floretta as Floretta looks at her, taking in the child's measure with a quick, calculated motion of her head, eyes slightly narrowed as she considers the job in front of her. The girl's hair will need to be cut and styled, her face washed, and her dress replaced by something more suitable, yes, yes, but these are the superficial aspects of what must be done.

Everything about the child screams "provincial." She is a creature of forest and fen, the mud under her fingers so deeply engrained that it may as well be a part of her, immutable. There are wildflowers in her eyes. It will need to change, every bit of it, before she can be a respectable daughter of a respectable household.

And Mr. Baker keeps a respectable household. The woman he calls Miss Cottingsly could no more explain his profession or the source of his funds than she could the movement of the heavens; she is a simple soul, employed for her discretion as much as for her skills, and she has never once inquired after things that are not hers to know. He pays her wages, provides a roof above her head, and so she allows him all the secrets he desires. She was well trained in the household she served before this one. She knows how to practice discretion.

"Stand up straight, girl," she says, and her voice is as matronly as her appearance, and utterly devoid of warmth. "I want to see you."

Floretta is exhausted. In any kind household, she would already have been shown to her room—a room which Deborah is no doubt frantically preparing, having dropped her charge with her superior and run off to fulfill her employer's commands. But this is not a kind household, and so she fights to stand straight when her body yearns to droop in place, squaring her shoulders and lifting her chin while she silently recites the scripture to herself, commanding obedience, biddability, all the other things she has been ordered, over and over again, to be. She must be without flaw. If she is perfect, perhaps she'll be sent home. Perhaps they'll see that her guardian up until this point has been the right one to make her the best possible person she can be, and they'll let her go. She'll remember her uncle, and his grand, cold house, in her prayers for the rest of her life, if only they'll let her leave.

So she stands rigid and unblinking as Miss Cottingsly looks her over, a small frown tugging at the corners of the older woman's mouth, and when Deborah comes back into the kitchen, she finds child and matron staring at each other, locked in a silent battle of wills.

"Ma'am?" asks Deborah.

Miss Cottingsly jerks upright. "Don't sneak up on me, girl," she half-snaps. "Is the room prepared?"

"Yes, ma'am. Do you have her measurements?"

"All that I need," says Miss Cottingsly. "I'll have to contact the seamstress in the morning. It's too late in the day to do it now. Still, she'll have a whole new wardrobe by the end of the week. I'll consult with the master as to my budget."

"He said—"

"I'll have him say it to me himself, rather than risk the consequences of any misunderstanding."

"Yes, ma'am," says Deborah, wilting slightly. "I'm sure you know best."

"I always do." Miss Cottingsly returns her attention to Floretta. "I'm sure you're thinking of running away, urchin that you are. Think you can return to the dirty farm that produced you."

"I wasn't raised on a farm," says Floretta. "My guardian was a priest. He taught me everything I needed to know. I can milk a cow if I need to, but we didn't have any of our own. We survived on the good grace of the village folk, and they saw to us."

"You'll not need anyone's good graces here, girl, save for your uncle's, and he must have those for you in plenty, or he'd never have claimed you," says Miss Cottingsly. "See to it that you give him no cause for regret."

"Yes, ma'am," says Floretta, voice going very small.

Then Deborah's hand is on her shoulder, and she's being led out of the kitchen and back down the hall to the stairs. When she glances into the room where she last saw her uncle, he isn't there; the space is empty and dark, a void waiting to be filled with light.

Then she's being guided up the stairs to the landing on the second floor, and down another hall to a closed door, which Deborah opens, revealing a bedroom almost as large as the entire house where Floretta has lived up until this point. She holds the door, waving the room's new occupant inside. Floretta looks to her for confirmation, eyes wide, then steps over the threshold, staring at everything around her with rapture.

Any other girl raised to her new social status would see the marks on the walls where pictures have been removed, would notice that the furniture is large and heavy, made of dark wood, designed for adult guests rather than a child. Floretta sees none of those things. She sees only the space to dress without twisting or bending uncomfortably, the bed large enough for her to sprawl and stretch her limbs out as far as they will go, never touching the sides of the mattress. For the first time since her uncle appeared in her parlor, she looks around and understands why someone might want for Boston, might wish for more than their fair share of everything.

"It isn't much of a view, I'm afraid," says Deborah, gesturing to the room's single window. "But you can see the moon at night when it passes overhead, and the light it casts will help to give you sweet dreams. Your clothing's in the wardrobe, and I've added a few things from the household stores. It's been some time since there was a child living here. I hope you'll find them to your liking. Is there anything else I can do for you, miss?"

Floretta turns to her, and blinks in sudden confusion. The housemaid is almost glowing in the darkness that pools around the room, glowing a pale, lambent silver, like swamp fire in the deep forest. Like moonlight.

"Your skin—" she says, and stops herself, swallowing the next words before they can come. If the master of the house decides she's lost her senses, she's more likely to be bound for an asylum than she is to be returned to her village. To win her freedom, she must seem perfect. So perfect that he can deny her nothing, and will grant her clear desire to go home.

"My skin?"

Floretta shakes her head. "Nothing. I'm sorry. I was . . . I'm very tired, I was seeing things."

"Your nightclothes are in the top drawer of the wardrobe. We can draw you a bath in the morning. For now, you should change, and sleep. The household had dinner several hours ago. The master may call for something light before he turns in, but understands that you'll not be up to dining with him until you've had time to rest and recover your senses."

"Thank you," says Floretta, with deep and obvious relief. "I am not trying to be . . . that is to say, I would rather not . . . but I'm not accustomed to . . ."

"I understand," says Deborah. "He will too, once he's had time to reflect on the events of the day. He's a powerful man, and a willful one, but he means you no ill, and he loved his sister. He asked your mother to come here and live with him when she was scarcely older than you are now, and he always regretted the fact that he was unable to convince her, unable to save her. He'll save you if you let him. He'll be an anchor you can use to hold yourself to ground when the storms blow through, and he'll never ask for more than you can offer."

Floretta is young and scared and very far from the only home she's ever known; she's been fighting to be brave since the afternoon. Words desert her, and she bursts into tears.

Deborah is there almost immediately, gathering her close, making soothing noises that aren't motherly, but more like what Floretta imagines an older sister might do, a loving relative. Her skin is still glowing a faint silver, but Floretta doesn't comment again, only closes her eyes, leans close, and cries until she feels wrung out, as dry as a dishrag after the last plate has been put up and the water has been tossed out the back door to soak into the ground.

Deborah releases her then, guiding her first to the drawer where her nightclothes have been folded neatly away, then to the bed. She draws the curtains as Floretta sinks into the pillows, and calls a soft "Goodnight" before leaving the room.

Floretta swears to herself that she won't go to sleep in this strange place, that she'll stay awake and plan her escape until morning.

She doesn't even notice her eyes closing, and then there is sunlight streaming around the edges of the curtains, and the distant song of birds, and her war is lost before she could begin to fight it. Everything that comes after will come, whether she wills it so or not.

Education

TIMELINE: 8:25 A.M. ET, JULY 22, 1872.

Floretta awakes in such softness that for a moment, she questions whether she might still be dreaming. It feels like she's sinking into a cloud. She stretches languidly, feeling the delicious clench of the muscles in her back and legs, then rolls onto her side, eyes fluttering shut again. It would be so easy to go back to sleep, and for a moment, she considers it. There is no rooster crowing in the distance, no hand hammering at the door and demanding she rise for her chores—

And just like that, her eyes are open and she's sitting up in the middle of her confectionary snarl of blankets and pillows, staring at the wall, which is covered in a dusty blue wallpaper patterned with small white flowers like stars. She's in Boston. She's in Boston, and home is so far away that she can only think about the distance if she measures it in hours rather than miles, and Father Clemence must be sick with worry for her. He's never liked her to be out of his sight for more than a few hours. What will he do without her?

She slides from the bed, digging her toes into the soft plush of the rug, and wonders what she's supposed to do now. Uncle John and Miss Cottingsly both mentioned new clothes, which seems to imply that they don't like the dress she was wearing when she arrived here: would one of her other dresses be more suitable? She has three, which is an embarrassment of riches none of the other girls in her village can boast. One was her mother's, and the other two were provided by Father Clemence, who said that she had to meet certain standards if she was going to be seen in public with him. All three are patched and worn, tattered at the hems and stained on the bodices, but they're the finest things she's ever needed.

She looks down at the nightdress she was coaxed into the night before, and understands that her definition of finery will have to change while she's living here. The sleeping gown is purest white, unstained, and there are no signs that any part of it has been torn or mended. Looking at it makes her feel grubby, like she has no right to be touching something so fine. She tugs the sleeves down, covering the scratched and scabbed backs of her hands, and moves toward the wardrobe. Even if nothing she owns can be good enough for this house, she can't wear this nightgown any longer. She'll dirty it with her presence, and that feels like a sin. She's always struggled not to be a sinner. It seems unfair to subject the nightgown to her failure.

The cleanest of her dresses is hanging in the wardrobe, front and center like an offering. Floretta would be happier if she could bathe before putting it on, but she doesn't know how to go about asking for a bath, and she doesn't want to leave the room so immodestly dressed. She pulls the nightgown off over her head and pulls the dress on the same way, doing up the buttons on the back with quick, practiced fingers. It's been years since she needed to see in order to get dressed. Father Clemence always said it was inappropriate for him to help her with her bows or buttons, or anything that might show more of her skin than her dresses themselves exposed. The thought of him sends a spike of sorrow through her heart, and she finishes getting dressed with grief slowing her fingers, moving through it like she's swimming through molasses.

There is a knock at the door as she fastens the final button, and she turns, struck silent by surprise. Seconds tick by, and the knock is repeated. Floretta swallows, mouth gone dry, and finally calls a hesitant "C-come in?"

The door opens, and Deborah is there, looking perplexed. "Did I wake you?" she asks, stepping inside. "No: I see you're dressed. Miss Cottingsly won't like that dress, but until we have something newer for you to wear, it'll have to do. Did you rest well?"

Floretta cannot speak. Her mouth is a bone lost in the desert: her heart is the vulture come to carry it away.

Deborah sees her silence for the terror that it is, and sighs. "This is all too much for you, isn't it? Poor child. Your uncle has breakfast set out in the parlor downstairs; he's asking for you to come and join him. I don't recommend making him wait. He's not a very patient man, your uncle."

"I don't know anything about him," protests Floretta. "How am I supposed to know what kind of man he is when I don't know *anything*? I don't know what he does, or how he paid for this house, or why he wanted me, or anything!"

Her last word is barely shy of a wail. Deborah nods, slowly.

"I can tell you he doesn't like it when people fuss or yell or carry on," she says. "You won't be doing yourself any favors if you lose your composure. I know you're only a child. I know you should be focused on childish things. But that isn't how things happen here, and if you want to do well in your uncle's household, you'll need to adapt quickly."

Floretta composes herself, sniffling as she wipes her nose with the back of her hand. "Tell me about him," she says, almost a command.

"He's a stern master, and he keeps his household with a firm hand; Miss Cottingsly is his eyes and ears belowstairs, and you can't say anything around her that you don't want getting back to your uncle. She allows no secrets to linger in her domain."

Floretta says nothing, waiting for more.

"As to his profession, he's a scientist of sorts. He doesn't like it when others interfere with his business. He'll tell you more when he thinks you're ready to hear it."

"But I'm here *now*."

"So you are, young miss," agrees Deborah. "And as presentable as we've given you the tools to make yourself. Come, have a seat at your dressing table, and I'll brush out your hair for you. You have such lovely hair, it seems a shame to let it tangle and snarl as you have. Let me take care of it."

Floretta is tired and scared and alone. She allows herself to be directed to a seat in front of a large silvered mirror, sitting pliantly while Deborah collects her brush and moves into position behind her, beginning to gently coax the knots out of her hair.

"As to why your uncle wanted you, I would lay a guess that it's because he considers you to be already his own. He has no other living relatives, and has never taken a wife. There's power in blood relation, and he wouldn't want that power loose in the world when it could be safely contained inside his walls. Consider it a compliment of sorts, that he would want to keep you close enough to keep you safe."

"He's not my father, though." The statement is also a question, and a test, sounding out the waters of her confusion for any deeper drop-offs, any hidden dangers.

"No, he's not." Deborah sounds so sure that Floretta relaxes slightly, letting her half-formed worry go. "Even if he were the sort of man who would press himself upon his own sister's child, he'd never be the sort of man who could leave his *own* child behind. When he received the letter from your village, he had no idea what it might be about. I heard him discussing the matter with Miss Cottingsly, and while your mother's name was mentioned, it was in the context of debts or inheritance, although he thought both quite unlikely. It seems that he was wrong. You are a debt and an inheritance at the same time, something to care for and comfort, which could bring either great good or great ill upon his house."

Deborah doesn't sound like she cares which of those two choices should come to pass; her voice is serene, her hands steady as she runs the brush through Floretta's hair, pressing a little deeper with every careful sweep.

Floretta lifts her eyes to the mirror, watching the woman behind her. Deborah is paler than most of the women in the village, protected from the sun as she is by the walls of Uncle John's house; no laboring in the fields for Deborah, with her soft hands and unbowed back. Her hair is ash brown, and her eyes are a deep, almost muddy blue. She's no great beauty, no temptation to a man who lives alone, and she holds herself less like a servant than she does like a traveling ambassador from some far-distant land.

It's that paradox of carriage that puts courage into Floretta's tongue. "I saw you glowing last night. Why were you glowing? How were you glowing? No one glows except for the winter women, and they never come inside houses where they might get warm enough to thaw."

A stutter as the brush catches in her hair, Deborah's hand slipping on the handle before she recovers herself and takes a deep breath. "The winter women?"

"They come out when the snows fall, sometimes. There was one for a long time. She had black hair, like broken ice, and she walked and didn't leave any footprints behind. She went away last winter, and the new winter woman is blonder than anyone else I've ever seen, so blonde it's like her hair is all the way white, and she still stumbles sometimes. She still leaves footprints behind." How Father Clemence had scolded her when she'd pulled him out into the field to see! The winter woman's feet had been substantially larger than Floretta's own, but that hadn't stopped the good father from accusing Floretta herself of running barefoot through the snow when she'd breathlessly pointed at the prints, pressed deep and crisp into the surface of the snowbanks.

"Anyway," Floretta continues blithely, not seeming to notice that Deborah has stopped brushing her hair, is standing frozen behind her. "The winter women glow, sort of silver-gold. You were glowing just silver. I thought I was imagining it, and then you came closer, and I wasn't imagining anything at all. Why do you glow? Are you a winter woman?"

"I am not a Seasonal Incarnate," says Deborah, sounding choked. "And I understand why your uncle wants you, if you can already see them. Most people can't. They fit into the places where the world bends, and they're invisible unless you're looking from the right direction. Usually, the right direction has to be taught."

"It can't need to be taught to everyone, or no one would have been able to learn so they could do the teaching," says Floretta, reasonably enough. Her reflection blinks wide, guileless eyes at Deborah. "Who taught you to look?"

Deborah swallows, hard, her throat working in the mirror before she puts the brush down and steps away from Floretta. "No one had to teach me. People like me, we just have to . . . open our eyes."

"People like you?"

"People who glow."

"Oh," says Floretta, and that seems to be the end of that. She slides from her seat, turning to face Deborah. "I'd like my breakfast now."

Deborah nods and leads her from the room, then down the stairs to the kitchen. They don't talk, but she can feel Floretta's eyes on the back of her neck, measuring and weighing her in a way she's not entirely comfortable with. There's a sharpness to the child, one that reminds her of ice in winter, frozen ponds ready to swallow the unwary whole. Floretta seems sweet and innocent, but appearances are all too frequently deceiving. There's no telling what this child will be, given a little time in her uncle's company.

Deborah only hopes that she can help to guide Floretta down a kinder path than the one she fears awaits her.

She can only hope that both of them survive the guidance.

* * *

John has been in the parlor for some time.

On any ordinary day, he would have finished his breakfast and gone downstairs to begin his work for the day, not seeing the surface again until lunchtime, assuming he didn't work straight through to dinner. He does, sometimes. He's a single man who has yet to go the Pygmalion route for finding himself a life's companion, and while he may one day weaken sufficient to become a sculptor, that day is not yet here.

Instead, he's sitting at the table waiting for his newly found niece to descend, his eggs getting cold and gummy and his coffee drunk down to the dregs, beginning to wonder whether he made a mistake in bringing her back here. Her fear and confusion had been well apparent during their drive, her eyes darting to the windows like a trapped animal, like she thought she could wiggle free and escape. And then she had been in his home, small and grubby and out of place in his parlor.

But Miss Cottingsly had seen what he saw when he sent the girl to see her in the kitchens. He spoke to the housekeeper this morning, when she brought him his breakfast, and she confirmed his suppositions. "Power, yes," she said. "Such power as I've rarely seen in a grown alchemist, much less in a child. She'll be able to remake the world when she's old enough to focus her will and understand what she's asking it to do. I don't know where she could have come from, but there's a touch of the otherworldly about her. I'm sure you noticed."

"I did," he lied. He hadn't. He'd seen the power in her small frame, the potential to change the world, but not its possible origin. He had assumed, foolishly it seems, that the power was passed down by her mother, that Elisabet had been a potential alchemist in her own right. He never met the girl, after all. She could have been virtually anything and he would never have known.

"I'll have her properly trained by summer's end," she said, confidently smug as only a woman who knew her power and position could be. Miss Cottingsly is one of his proudest creations. The mind of the women she had been before her deaths, the soul of a beast, proud and faithful and willing to die in the defense of what she considers her own. She doesn't remember what she was before she met him, what she could have been had she survived to live her petty human lives; he broke down and remade her in the image of his own needs, and she serves now, content with the only life she can imagine.

"See to it that you do," he'd replied, and gone about his business comfortable in his belief that Floretta—something had to be done about that name; it couldn't be allowed to stand longer than was absolutely necessary, would need to be replaced as soon as he understood her nature well enough to give her something better—was soon to be brought properly to heel. Her power, whatever its source, would be bent under his hand, and the world would be all the better for it.

With time, he might come to understand what Miss Cottingsly meant by "a touch of the otherworldly." It could be almost anything. Perhaps she was inclined toward a season, and risked being called at their next coronation. Perhaps she was tied to some lesser natural force. Whatever the source of the strangeness his housekeeper perceived, he would claim it, tame it, and turn it toward useful ends.

Footsteps on the stairs snap him back into the present, and he looks toward the door, waiting for the moment when his great-niece appears. She's wearing a grubby dress little different from the one she had on yesterday, but her hair has been properly brushed and pinned back: there may be hope for her yet.

She looks nervous, verging on terrified, like she can't imagine anything good will come of her sitting down to breakfast. He watches her in silence, still waiting.

She comes closer, almost tiptoeing, and stops some feet from the table to drop an unsteady curtsey. He nods in response, a slight dip of his chin, acknowledging her manners. A dog will never learn not to bite if it isn't rewarded for its good behavior, and he would prefer a well-trained dog to a biting one. It's only reasonable.

"Good morning, Uncle John," she says, and he adds her backwoods accent to the list of things he'll need to have changed about her. Really, that priest did her no favors by instilling so many things in her that he'll be forced to unmake and redo. He'll need to send someone to show the priest the error of his ways, as soon as he's certain he'll be keeping the girl. (He's already more than halfway sure. For all his flaws, he did love his niece, and he never gives up on something he's decided he owns. He owns her now. She's staying with him.)

"Do you always sleep so late into the day?" he asks.

"No, sir," she replies, with respectable politeness. "The bed was strange and very soft, and the journey yesterday was very tiring. I slept longer than I intended, and more deeply than I think I ever have before. I apologize for my tardiness."

"How can you tell that you were tardy?"

"Your eggs, sir."

He frowns, and she sees the question in that expression, because she continues:

"Their tops have hardened, and the whites are all cloudy and gunky-looking. That only happens when eggs have been sitting out for longer than they ought to be. And your coffee isn't steaming."

John blinks, glancing to his cup. "Perhaps I prefer my coffee cold."

"Perhaps," she says, in a tone that makes it clear she knows he doesn't. She looks around and, finding no serving dishes, takes a seat in front of the other place setting.

John picks up a small bell from beside his own plate, ringing it lightly. Miss Cottingsly appears in the doorway as if by magic, carrying a covered tray which she moves to place in front of Floretta before turning to go.

"Miss Cottingsly," says John.

She stops, turning back to face him. "Yes, sir?"

"I need fresh eggs and another cup of coffee. I'm afraid I was distracted, and allowed my breakfast to cool."

She sniffs, but doesn't comment on what that distraction could have been, only returns to the table and removes his plate. "Right away, sir."

"Thank you, Miss Cottingsly."

She bobs, then slips away, carrying his rejected breakfast with her.

Floretta watches this play out with enormous eyes. She's never seen anyone speak so dismissively to another adult, and she wouldn't have imagined the terrifying Miss Cottingsly taking orders so unflinchingly. She doesn't move to uncover her tray, only remains still, like she's afraid of being noticed.

"Well, eat," says her uncle, in a tone he probably considers encouraging, but which really comes across more as an order. She removes the cover from her tray, revealing eggs and toast and a slice of ham, pink as a sunrise and glistening with fat. Her mouth starts to water at once, and it's all she can do not to lunge for her silverware and begin shoveling food into her mouth.

"Eat," repeats her uncle. Agonizingly slow, she picks up knife and fork and begins carefully cutting into her meal. Every cut is a stab at her hunger, a line drawn across the ravenous need to be fulfilled.

The food tastes as good as it looked. She forces herself to chew slowly, swallowing only when she's certain she won't choke. Her uncle John watches her the whole time, measuring her motions with his eyes, taking note of her manners, and the deficiencies therein. She's midway through her plate when Miss Cottingsly returns with a fresh plate to set in front of him. She, too, takes note of Floretta, the stiffness of her motions, the care with which she chews. Meeting John's eyes, she gives a small, approving nod, then pours him a fresh cup of coffee.

"That will be all, for now," he says, and she bobs a curtsey before slipping from the room, leaving the pair of them alone.

Floretta's breakfast is almost gone. She sits back in her chair as John begins to eat, watching him cut into his food with smoothly practiced motions. It's not until he's taken the first bites that he looks to her and tilts his head to the side, frowning.

"What am I to do with you?" he asks.

"Put me back where you found me?" she replies, hopefully. And for a moment, she thinks he might: for a moment, she wonders if he might not realize his mistake and let her go. It's a long-enough moment to let the image of herself stepping out of his carriage like a queen blossom behind her eyes, her dream-self filled with the knowledge of far-off Boston, the sophistication of a girl who's seen the city. She could go home, but she would never be the same again. She has already been transformed.

"No," he says, as the pause is ending. "I don't think so. But that was a good attempt at changing my mind. You may make another tomorrow, if you'd like. No more today. I won't abide insurrection in my own home, and that means you'll limit your attempts to influence my decisions. Do we have an understanding?"

"Yes, sir," says Floretta, meekly.

"There's no need to sound as if you fear me," he says. "I can be your greatest ally, if only you'll allow it. Your mother's mother was my sister, Margaret, and no finer flower of American womanhood has ever walked the world. She chose to settle with her husband in the village where you were born, and nothing I could say would sway her. After she died, I tried to bring your mother here to live out her days in safety and comfort. She was no great beauty, you understand—whoever your father may have been, you take after him—but she was my flesh and blood, and there's a power in that. What belongs to you can be used against you, always, and I would prefer to guard my vulnerabilities."

Floretta blinks at him, mouth hanging slightly open in her bewilderment. The things he's saying may make sense to him, but to her, they're so much sound, words strung together in unnatural orders, like shining beads on a silver string.

"Close your mouth," he snaps. "You look like a cow when you gape at me like that, and I'll not have anyone saying that my household shelters a simpleton."

Floretta closes her mouth with a snap.

"Miss Cottingsly will see to your new wardrobe today. I don't want to see this dress again, or any of the others you brought with you from the woods. They'll be burned as soon as you have something less offensive to the eye to wear in their stead."

"But these are my dresses," Floretta protests. "I don't have anything else."

"You will." He pauses then, looking at her closely. "Did any of them belong to your mother? Are they sentimental in some way?"

"No," she answers, speaking to the second question rather than the first—while one of them was her mother's, she feels more sentiment toward the gifts from Father Clemence. She doesn't have the feeling her uncle would care to hear that, or that he's a man who trades much on sentiment.

"Then to the fire they go," he says, pleased. "I'll have a tutor hired for you by the end of the day. You'll learn all the lessons you should have had thus far, and we'll start your proper education as soon as I'm sure you're ready for them. Do you have any questions for me?"

"I . . ." She stops. He's already half-answered her most important question: he wanted her because she's blood of his blood, and he wants to protect himself. This was never about her at all. Who she is doesn't matter, maybe *can't* matter, in the face of his incomprehensible concerns.

"I don't think so," she says, in a small voice. "I will miss my home, and the good father, but I'll try to be a good ward for you. I'll try my best not to bring shame upon your household."

"I believe you will," he says. "Are you ready to begin?"

She can't answer. She can only nod.

* * *

The days that follow are among the hardest of Floretta's life. She sees her uncle only at meals—breakfast and dinner—where they sit alone in the great dining room, attended on by Miss Cottingsly and, more rarely, by Deborah, who comes and goes like a ghost, and doesn't glow silver again. Not in Uncle John's presence, anyway; on occasion, in the upstairs halls, she flickers and shines, placing a finger to her lips to signal Floretta to silence when she sees the girl watching her. It's their secret, small and strange and somehow kept away from the man who rules both their lives, as surely as a storybook king might rule his kingdom.

She's been there a week before her uncle raises the question of her name: "I don't like it," he says one night, over a dinner of roast chicken and vegetables. "Your mother would never have chosen a French name for her only daughter. I'm not sure who did. It makes you sound like a *Canadian*." He says the word like it's the direst of insults.

Floretta can only blink at him. "But it's my name," she protests. "It's who I am."

"You will change it," he says. "By the end of the year, either you will find a name you can prefer, or I'll choose one for you. You're young yet. When you're grown, you'll not remember Floretta Bearse in the slightest. You'll be someone else, someone better and new, and that woman will carry you into your future."

Floretta doesn't know how to answer that. She has never even considered that names could change. Oh, she knows that when she grows to adulthood and marries, she'll take her husband's name for her own, and some people have nicknames, ways to call for them more quickly, but their *names* remain the same beneath it all, fixed points around which their person can turn. If a name can change so casually, will the person who carries it even be the same beneath? Or is he speaking true when he says that she'll be someone else?

She doesn't know the answer. She isn't sure she ever wants to. She looks at him with wide, bewildered eyes, waiting to hear what he says next.

"Your new name will be something more suited to this house. It will be elegant and fine and it will mark you as my own, and you will carry it proudly. Do you understand me?"

She doesn't. "Yes, sir," she says, and it's a small lie, small enough that he either doesn't notice or doesn't count it. Instead, he nods, and rises, leaving her alone at the table with the remains of her dinner in front of her. She scrambles to rise in turn, pushing her chair back, so that she isn't seated while he stands. She's still learning the rules, but she knows even now that sitting while he stands is not allowed.

"You'll have riding lessons tomorrow," he says curtly. "See to it that you sleep well tonight."

Then he's gone, striding out of the room, leaving her behind. She stares after him in silence, and when Miss Cottingsly comes to clear the dishes, she clears Floretta as well, shooing the child upstairs to her room.

* * *

Days pass. The memories of the wood and the village and the meadows fade. Father Clemence sends word once a fortnight, and while Floretta is mostly forbidden his messages, she does manage to snatch a few of them from the postman, squirreling them away to read in private. He writes of babies she will never know, harvests brought in without her, and people thriving in her absence. The hole in his own life is apparent at first, but quickly closes and fades away, his world expanding to fill the gap she left behind when she was taken away.

Most of all, he writes of rain. It began raining when she left the village, it seems, and the fields are growing greener than they have in her lifetime. Stomachs are full, tables are laden, and their small hamlet seems set to become the paradise he has always believed that it could be. With her gone, everything is better. He doesn't say so in so many words, but she can read what's written, and she knows what's really being said. It stings and soothes in equal measure. She can't be there to see them thriving, but they will survive even if she never once returns. Like a princess in a storybook, she has been offered up as a sacrifice to something far greater than herself.

But the princess in a storybook will have a happy ending when all is said and done, and Floretta no longer believes that is a possible ending for her. She goes through her days in dry, rainless Boston, looking out the windows of her uncle's house, waiting for the hour when all will begin to turn in her direction, and nothing changes but the lessons she is offered day after dusty day. Miss Cottingsly is not her only tutor, or even her primary, although she has her share of lessons with the hard-eyed housekeeper; a man scarcely old enough to carry the title comes twice a week to teach her sums, and a woman slightly older comes as often for comportment and Latin. Why her uncle feels she needs to learn Latin is unclear, but she knows enough not to argue with him. Arguing with him only shakes the walls and reduces her dinners to dry meat and plain boiled vegetables, still eaten at the table in full view of his seasoned and gravy-moistened feasts.

No. She has been here long enough to learn the virtue of staying silent and going along with what's expected of her, and what's expected is that she attend her lessons and learn the things he sees fit to have her taught. If that means dead languages and scientific concepts not normally considered appropriate for a girl of her age—a girl of any age, really—then that's what she'll do. She will be his niece, she will be his protégée, and she will learn what she's offered.

Those days turn into weeks, until one night she sits at her dressing table brushing the tangles from her hair and sees Deborah step into her bedroom with an armload of fresh linens, glowing as silver as starlight in the mirror. It's a mellow, lambent light, and it has no business coming from a human skin. She hates it, and she covets it, and she doesn't understand how Deborah can have it when she can't. It doesn't seem fair, that some people should glow when others don't.

It doesn't seem, maybe, like those people are actually people, if they can do things that people aren't supposed to do. Envy and disdain hatch in her heart, terrible sisters that can prepare a body to do almost any terrible thing, if they're given the room to stretch and grow.

She turns to face Deborah, and the light is still there, still steady, still pouring from the older girl like honey from a beehive. She frowns. "Deborah."

"Miss?"

"You're glowing again."

Deborah blinks and straightens, and the glow dims but doesn't die. "I'm sorry, miss. It's not exactly something I can control."

"Why do you glow sometimes? My uncle says you have to answer me when I ask you things. He says I'm going to be the mistress of this house someday. That means you'll answer to me, and I want to know. Why are you glowing? You said you're not one of the winter women. What are you?"

"I'm the moon."

It's a small answer, simple on the face of it, and yet it's large enough to change the world. Floretta frowns. "How can you be the moon? The moon is in the sky, and you're in my bedroom. It doesn't work."

"I'm not *always* the moon, only sometimes. I'm a minor moon goddess, Selene. I shine in the dark places, and sometimes I open doors into the space between our world and the center of the universe, so that I can shine on the heart of reality and keep it beating properly. Olympus calls me home when there's need of me."

"Olympus is real?"

"Yes, and no. It's not a place the way Boston is a place, but it's a sort of impossible city where the forces that control everything around us can gather and keep the world turning. It's where the rules are made. It's where I belong. I just can't go there more than once a month, when my Lunar's heart is full and shining through my skin. I'll go there tonight, and I'll shine and shine and shine until it hurts me deep inside. That's why I glow. Because I'm the moon."

"I don't like it," says Floretta sharply. "People shouldn't be moons."

"I didn't have a choice," says Deborah. "I was born like you, and then one day Selene woke up and told me that I was also going to be her. Like with the winter women. You said the one near your village had changed, that the new one left footprints in the snow. That's because the old one died, and someone new had to become the winter in order for the seasons to keep turning. The world is a lot stranger and more structured than you realize."

"If you're the moon, why are you here?"

For the first time, Deborah looks truly uncomfortable. "Everyone has to be somewhere, even the moon," she says, deflecting.

Floretta is not to be dissuaded. "Yes, but why *here*?"

"Your uncle is a . . . a powerful man. He studies a branch of science known as alchemy. Do you know what that is?"

Floretta has heard the term before. She nods.

"Alchemists know a great opportunity when it's presented to them. It's why he wanted you. There's something about you, Floretta. I just don't know exactly what it is." Deborah's voice turns achingly sincere. She means what she's saying, every nonsensical syllable of it. "But something about you is born to moonlight and starlight, snowfall and sun. You're not an embodiment. You have our fingerprints about you."

"And you're here because my uncle wanted you?"

"Your uncle doesn't know about me, not in the way you mean," says Deborah. "He can't know about me. Alchemists . . . when they know about something, they want to own it. They want to take it apart and make use of it."

"So he could use you?"

"He could. And he could probably kill me in the process. You can't tell him about me."

"Then why would you tell me?"

"Because you asked. And because if I'm going to trust you—and I want to trust you—I have to start somewhere. We're watching your uncle because something great and terrible is going to begin in this house. We want to be here when it happens. If you're willing to help us, we could stop whatever it is from hurting anyone who hasn't already been hurt."

Floretta considers this a moment, then turns back to the mirror, resuming the slow detangling of her hair. "I understand," she says.

"So you'll keep my secret?"

"Will you take me to Olympus with you?"

"I can't. You wouldn't be able to survive the passage."

"Oh." Floretta continues brushing. "It's not fair to ask people for favors you aren't willing to return."

"If you tell him what I am, he might hurt me. If I take you to Olympus, I *will* hurt you. They aren't the same favor."

"I see," says Floretta. "I won't tell."

Deborah breathes a sigh of relief and returns to her business. She doesn't see the way Floretta is watching her in the mirror, the sharp focus in her eyes, the way calculation has chased away wonder.

Even the moon doesn't know everything. The world would be so much simpler if it did.

* * *

The next morning, Floretta goes to breakfast armed with questions. She waits until her uncle is seated with his own coffee in hand to offer up the first of them, looking at him with wide, innocent eyes as she asks, "Uncle John, what's an alchemist?"

He almost chokes on his coffee, stopping himself at the last second to spit and sputter, catching his breath. He stares at her as he does.

"Where did you hear that word?" he asks, finally, and there's a condemnation in those words, a complete willingness to destroy whoever may have told her what he is.

Fortunately, Floretta has an answer: "Everyone in the house says it, when they think I'm not listening. What does it mean?"

"An alchemist is like a scientist and a philosopher at the same time. It's someone who looks at the world and thinks, 'I could improve on this,' and then does it. We use science and art and philosophy and magic, and we blend it all together into a weapon and a tool and a transformation. We'll control the universe one day, when we've bent enough of it to our designs, and we're the reason reality doesn't pick itself to pieces."

"You make embodiments?"

"No. Embodiments are primitive, involuntary things, like bits of grit inside oysters turning into pearls. They're reality exuding stopgaps against the tides of chaos that would sweep everything good away." He pauses then, gaze sharpening. "What do you know about embodiments?"

"I know the winter women sometimes walk in the snow outside the village where I used to live," she says. "And the summer men, but they're harder to see. They don't walk barefoot through the snow. I know some people are also the moon, and I'm not."

He goes very still, gaze sharpening still further, until his attention is a knife ready to flense the flesh from the world. "Do you know anyone who's the moon?"

Floretta is silent for a moment, considering her reply. There's a world where she lies, where she chooses to protect Deborah at a potential risk to herself. Father Clemence's daughter would have chosen to exist in that world, would have tried so hard to be good and live up to his expectations of her that she would have put herself into harm's way to keep the housemaid safe.

Father Clemence's daughter didn't have terrible hatchlings tearing at her heart, whispering to her about how she lost everything when she was snatched away from him—*everything*—and how it's not fair that Deborah should still get to shine. That she should have what Floretta can't, and that she should be so very clearly something Uncle John *wants*, something he needs more than anything. Father Clemence's daughter was wild, but she was never jealous.

Not like Floretta.

This isn't the world where she lies. She left that world behind some time ago, and she doesn't have a path back. This is the world where an alchemist came and swept her away from everything she'd ever known, the world where she's being shaped, one carefully sculpted lesson at a time, into something she wasn't. She's always been the daughter of a storm. It's only since she's come to Boston that she's started learning how to hold back her squalls and take her time. She's learning to calculate, going from natural disaster to unnatural disaster through the slow, ambient alchemy of her uncle's house.

"I do," she says.

His brows lift. "Who?"

"I'm not sure I remember."

He scowls as he looks at her. "What do you want?"

"I want friends my own age, and I want to see them at least twice a week. And I want to play in the park. I'm tired of being locked up inside and never seeing the sky." She looks at him with calm calculation. "I think you could give me those things without changing whatever it is you're trying to do with me."

(She doesn't know it, will never know it, but this is the moment when he stops looking at her as a potentially useful tool and begins looking at her as his presumptive heir. She has it in her to be powerful, and he's seen enough over the past months to know that she's clever. Until this moment, he wasn't sure she could learn how to focus that cleverness, or that she would ever find a way to reach past biddability for the fierce self-interest he'll need her to have if she wants to thrive in the world he occupies. That she might not care about that world has never occurred to him. It certainly hasn't occurred to him that she might one day want to burn it to the ground.)

"I think those things can be arranged, for the clever niece who handed me the moon," he says.

A flicker of the girl she'd been growing up to be shows in her eyes. "You won't hurt her, will you?" she asks.

Uncle John takes a great, ponderous breath. "Of course I'm going to hurt her," he says. "If you know enough to know what I am, what I do, I can't understand why you're even asking me that question. A moon isn't really human; none of the Incarnates are. They're universal impulses walking around in human skins, like scarecrows that have torn themselves loose from their fields. They're a collection of useful parts and pieces, and I have a use for each and every one of them. I'm going to hurt her. If you're very good, and you don't have any further objections, I might even let you help."

Floretta considers this for a moment, weighs the promise of his approval against the sound of Deborah's laughter, and comes to a conclusion that was inevitable from the moment she decided to tell her uncle what she knew: "All right," she says. "I'll tell you."

He smiles, and keeps smiling as he receives the name.

He's still smiling when night falls, and he waits for Deborah in the upstairs hall, a silver rope in one hand and a sharpened razor in the other. He ties her wrists as she screams, and no one in the house comes to her rescue.

When he drags her to the room at the bottom of the stairs, the room that is always locked, the room she has never entered in her employment here, it is to find Floretta already waiting, seated primly on a stool at the very back of the room, her hands folded neatly at her knee, watching the door in wide-eyed silence.

Deborah catches her breath, and begins to beg. "Floretta, please," she says, words quick and tight with panic. "I don't know what your uncle is doing, I don't know what he thinks he's doing, but you have to help me. You have to tell him that this is wrong. Please, Mr. Baker!" And just like that she's back to begging John directly, jerking on her bonds and struggling to get away. "I won't tell anyone, I swear. This can be our little secret. I won't say *anything*."

"Of course you won't," he says, voice warm and reasonable. "You won't have anything to say."

He moves across the room to an iron ring set into the floor, forcing her down into a chair that has been set atop a piece of slick, well-oiled canvas before bending her over double, his elbow at the small of her back, his hand against the back of her neck. He releases her neck to grab the rope that binds her wrists and tie it roughly to the ring, trapping her in place.

"The moon is waning," he says, stepping away while she thrashes against her bonds. She has known she was in danger since the moment he grabbed her, has no illusions about what happens to moons who fall into the grasp of alchemists; still she fights, still she struggles to get away. "Your aspect will show more brightly as your time of divinity approaches. When you shine despite yourself, that's when I will harvest you. Until then, you'll be kept."

"That isn't how we *work*, you stupid man!" she gasps. "I won't shine for you, I won't!"

"I think we both know that isn't true," he says, almost gently. "Come, niece. We have other places to be."

Floretta rises delicately, and hardens her heart against Deborah's begging as she follows her uncle to the door. She glances back only once at the woman, bent double and not glowing at all as she sobs in her chair. She glances back, but doesn't say anything, just follows her uncle out of the room.

He closes and locks the door behind himself, smile flickering out and fading as he looks at her.

"You had best be telling the truth about her," he says. "She was a good housekeeper, and I don't want to replace her over a child's lie."

"I didn't lie," says Floretta. "She was glowing. She told me her secret name was Selene. She's a moon."

"Good," he says, and together, they walk away.

* * *

Seven weeks pass, one day following another. Abovestairs, the life of the house continues. Floretta takes her lessons, John does whatever it is he does when he isn't concerning himself with the education of his niece, and Miss Cottingsly trains her new housemaid, teaching her everything she'll need to know in order to serve in the house of a master alchemist.

A new tutor is added to the ones Floretta already has, this one teaching her classical Greek to go alongside her Latin, and the mythology of all the many Olympian gods. She learns the names of muses and heroes, and none of them mean anything to her, not even the ones who have already touched upon her life. Still, she likes the sound of them, likes the way they hang in her ears, like stars set into a clouded sky.

Every night she accompanies her uncle down to see Deborah beneath the stairs, and every night the former housemaid spits at them and swears she will not shine. Her wrists are scabbed and torn, and her skin is ripe with sweat, the ground beneath her ripe with other, even less pleasant things. Uncle John won't allow her bath or basin, won't rinse the floor with bucketed water, for, he says, once her divinity is proven, every scrap will be of value.

That's why he still feeds her, even though he could easily excuse starving her for her insolent refusal to do as he's asked. It's such a simple thing, asking the moon to shine. Why is she refusing him even now, when she knows she's been well and truly caught? It makes no sense. There can be no worse ending than the one she already faces, no worse trials than she already endures.

Then, seven weeks after her capture, John and Floretta descend and open the door on a room awash in silvered moonlight. Deborah looks at them, defiance in her sunken eyes, and John grips Floretta's shoulder in sudden triumph.

"Watch her," he says, and turns, leaving the two of them alone.

Deborah looks her dead in the eye, then thrusts her hands out as much as her bonds allow. "Let me go," she says, and it's more of a command than a plea.

"No," says Floretta.

"Surely you can see that this is wrong. I'm being held prisoner. Your uncle is a madman, a monster, and I deserve my freedom!"

"No," repeats Floretta. "You're not a person. You're a celestial body, and there's no law against stealing the moon. There would be, if anyone thought that you could do it, but we've done something impossible, my uncle and me, and so there's no one to say that we can't. He's done nothing wrong. I've done nothing wrong. He's going to be a king among the alchemists, and he'll raise me up on high beside him, and I'm not going to let you go. It's wicked of you to even ask."

"I'll show you wickedness," snarls Deborah, and throws herself against the limits of the rope that holds her, moaning as it rips roughly through the scabs circling her wrists.

Floretta watches this with almost-academic detachment. "That looks like it hurts," she says. "You should maybe not do that anymore."

"You little . . . You understand that you're condemning us both, don't you? He'll kill me, and he'll never let you go. He can't now. You've seen too much."

Floretta's smile shows all her teeth. "That's what I'm counting on," she says. "I can't go back to Father Clemence. He wouldn't have me now anyway, after everything I've seen and done in Boston. He wouldn't know what to do with me. I want my uncle to keep me here forever. You're helping me get what I want. And that means I'm not going to help you get anything *you* want. It would only hurt me."

Her uncle returns, a dark presence behind her. She turns at the sound of his breathing, and sees that he is wearing a leather apron now, carrying a bucket full of tools. He moves toward Deborah, not caring what he steps on, what squelches underfoot.

"Keep glowing," he commands. "I know your kind can move in and out of divinity at will, and I need you to stay divine."

"If I refuse?"

"If you refuse, you have no further value to me," says John, simply enough. "If you refuse, I'll start removing parts, and I'll continue until you glow again."

"You're going to remove them anyway."

"Yes," he says, almost panting with anticipation. "But I can make sure it doesn't hurt as much. I have tinctures and I have solvents, things that will ease and even dissolve the pain. Cooperate and this can be an easy release back into the sky. Refuse, and I'll make sure you understand every ache and pain the flesh can be subjected to."

Deborah stares at him, silver light dancing in her eyes. Then she sighs, and bows her head, and he gets to work.

He doesn't tell his niece to leave the room. Floretta lingers behind him, watching him as he carves up the woman she betrayed, and with every cut he makes, another part of the girl she was falls away, unnecessary in this bright new world of art and alchemy. She was happy in the forest, but now she's here: she'll be the person Boston wants her to be.

Deborah bleeds silver moonlight, and Floretta envies her that, a little. Even if bleeding silver means Deborah has to be the one tied to the chair, it's still something special and magical, and most of all, *visible*, out in the world where no one can pretend it isn't happening. Floretta would bleed silver if she could.

(And the thought has just enough time to form before it short-circuits itself, dies in a snarl of static like lightning lashing out of a clear night sky. No moonlight for her, no starlight or winter winds. She was made for something more important than any of those things.

She was made for Olympus.)

Deborah screams in the beginning, screams with every stroke and cut, her flesh opening like a storybook behind the motion of the knife, her silver blood washing everything irrelevant away. Before long, she isn't screaming anymore. Before long, she's just sagging in her chair, head dangling, motionless, and her blood continues to glow where it pools on the fouled canvas beneath her. There is no drain in this room. Floretta had wondered about that at first: when the farmers back in her village had butchered calves or suckling pigs, they'd done it in places where the blood could drain away. Here, though, her uncle is trying to gather every scrap of silver.

Blood that glows is probably easier to clean up than the other kind, since you can see every last bit you've missed as long as you keep the lights down low. She's not allowed to hold the knives, but he gives her little sponges and vials and she dutifully gathers as much of the glowing silver from the floor around her as she can, pressing it out of the edge of the rug with her fingertips, sponging it off her shoes.

It's the most amazing thing she's ever done, and it stays amazing as her uncle moves from slicing and slashing to actual dissection, cracking open the impossible geode of Deborah's body and carefully levering her organs free. He holds each of them up like the rarest of prizes before he slides them into the cold chest he had prepared for this moment.

It takes forever. It doesn't take any time at all. It is a moment and an eternity, and when he turns to Floretta, there is a smudge of silver glowing on his cheek, like a streak of impossible starlight. He smiles, approving in a way he has never been before.

"Thank you," he says. "I was concerned you wouldn't understand what we do here, but you've proven yourself beyond my wildest dreams."

"What are you going to tell the rest of the staff?"

"Miss Cottingsly understands my work. She won't need to be told anything, and she'll see to informing the others. You like your new housemaid?"

There's something almost perverse about having this conversation over Deborah's body, but Floretta doesn't dwell on it; not dwelling will become a hallmark of the woman she's going to be when she grows up, never looking back, never slowing down. "Not as much as I liked Deborah."

"Well, whose fault is that?"

She giggles, just a little. "Mine, I suppose. She'll do. I can teach her to be tolerable, and she doesn't glow, so the work won't be wasted. We're not going to need to worry about taking her apart."

"That's for the best." John starts to turn away.

Floretta seizes her opportunity. "I think I know the name I want now."

"Oh?"

"Yes." With the moment upon her, she feels suddenly shy, like she's doing something wrong by speaking what she's been dreaming out into the world. "I want to be called Asphodel."

John blinks, then frowns. "Why?"

"It's a flower, so I'll still have the name I had in the beginning. That feels important, like putting the whole road on the map when you sit down to draw it. And it's Greek. I like my Greek lessons a lot." She almost squirms under the weight of his attention. "It feels right."

"It's not a name."

"It is a name, it's just not usually a name for a person. I've met people named 'Rose' and 'Lilac.' Why can't I have a different flower for my name?"

"A fair argument. Will that be all?"

"No. I want her name too." She indicates the unmoving shape of what was once Deborah.

"Asphodel Deborah Baker?" asks John, confirming.

She nods once, firmly.

"Very well," he says, and once again, the future is set. There is only one path forward from here, one inevitable, implausible road between this moment and the future, terrible and glorious as it is. She will be remembered, even as he will not.

That is, perhaps, the most fitting punishment either of them could possibly endure.

Because that is the thing about endings, my dears, the thing you must all remember, and keep close and secret next to your own hearts, which have not been replaced with black-winged birds, but still beat strong and true: that is the thing you must hold to as the improbable road bends toward the burning Kingdom of the Queen of Wands, which has smoldered endlessly in the absence of its Queen, and would burn eternally waiting for her. Endings are where we suffer the deepest losses, where we look with critical eyes upon the toys with which we play and cast some of them aside forevermore, no longer to be pieces in our games.

Endings are where we can afford to let them go. Keep this close and foremost in your mind, and when the moment arrives, remember that I warned you: remember that I told you from the very start that this would be so.

We have walked with Avery and Zib since the beginning. We have seen them tested and tried, seen them succeed and seen them fail, and soon, we may see one of them fall. There are many ways into the Up-and-Under. There are almost as many ways out again, and not all of them run in both directions. I will tell you this much now, to set your jangled nerves at ease: they came via the same path, and they traveled the divided, elemental lands via the same road. When they leave, however, they will each of them go alone.

Will knowing this now change how you see the story?

Will it shift a part of you into the future, into the time when you have been here before and cannot see this all with fresh and open eyes? I do not know. That, my dears, is up to you.

But here and now, we have traveled past the borderless beginning and through the murky middle. We must now approach the inescapable ending, which has always been coming for us, which has always been here. We will go as Avery and Zib did, side by side and hand in hand, and I will not let you go. Unlike the children we accompany, we will return by the same road, you and I, and I will bid you a fond farewell before you turn toward other stories, other storytellers, and leave me consigned to the kingdom of the past, where I may rest a little while.

Only know that I will always have been here, and you will always have been here, and although time divides us in all other ways, we will have been here together. Hold that knowledge fast, and trust in me now, and let me lead you onward toward the final counting of our quarters. Now is where we join them, five children walking on a soap bubble passage stretched across the sky, moving closer and closer to the burning land below.

And the children walked on. . . .

—From *Under the Smokestrewn Sky*,
by A. Deborah Baker

BOOK II

Lead

Do I dare
Disturb the universe?
In a minute there is time
For decisions and revisions which a minute will reverse.
—T. S. Eliot, "The Love Song of J. Alfred Prufrock"

I am the candle in your kitchen
I am the rain upon your face
I am the very best of reasons
For any man to fall from grace.
—Talis Kimberley, "The Finding of the Feather"

Cleansing

TIMELINE: AUGUST 21, 2018.

The air tastes like fall and the future, a glorious blend of possibility, promise, and—Lilianne pauses in her giddy inhale to cough into her hand, shifting her books to her other arm to avoid dropping them—leaf mold. Definitely leaf mold. Attending school on a campus with multiple creeks running through it and plenty of overhanging trees was not going to be kind on her allergies. She coughs again, then digs her inhaler out of her pocket and takes a throat-clearing puff, letting the vapor sting her sinuses before she tucks it away again and continues on her way.

She's not the only new graduate student being welcomed by the mold off of Strawberry Creek: she sees at least two others taking hits off their own inhalers, their motions very different from the furtive care taken by the people who think they can stealth-vape after an hour spent without their drugs of choice. She's not going to tell on them, but she still takes note of their faces. These are the people she'll need to avoid in the future, lest their addictions become her asthma's problem.

It's not that she has an issue with smoking, per se. Back home in Alabama, more than half the kids she'd known through the school GSA had been smokers, and having too much of a problem with it would have cut her out of her only available social circle. Better to clutch her inhaler a little closer and have people she could talk to who would understand at least a little of what she was going through. Better not to burn any bridges she might need later.

She hugs her books a little closer, the shade of the overhanging trees suddenly much colder than it was only a moment before. She's not that person anymore. She never has to be that person again. She's a graduate student now, and she's going to publish her thesis relating to her official major—American history—while she focuses properly on her true major, and she's going to transform herself in every way that matters.

Squaring her shoulders, she walks briskly onward, shaking off the chill.

She's so focused on walking briskly onward, on projecting the idea that she's utterly untouchable and not at all disoriented by her new surroundings, that she doesn't pay proper attention to those same surroundings. In a moment straight out of a college movie, she walks straight into an attractive-looking Indian woman roughly her own age but—and this is important to the physics of the moment—easily eight inches shorter, sending the stranger sprawling.

The woman hits the brick surface of the quad with a bone-rattling thump, her own books spraying in all directions. Lilianne gapes at her, momentarily unable to process what's just happened. Part of her brain is reminding her that she was hoping to run into a pretty girl at school, another part is howling that knocking people over is not the best method of making friends, and a third is advocating loudly for sinking into the pavement, never to be seen again.

She decides—as much as she's currently capable of deciding anything—to split the difference, and begins rapidly apologizing. "I am *so* sorry! I was about a million miles away, and I guess I just didn't see you there—I mean, obviously I didn't see you there, I don't go around running into people on purpose—but I'm so sorry and are you all right?"

By the time she stops babbling out her half-coherent apology, the woman looks more amused than irritated. She still doesn't move, resting her weight on the heels of her hands and just watching Lilianne, like she's waiting for her to finish.

When she does, she lifts one hand, holding it up like an invitation to offer aid, and says, "You must be new around here. There's always traffic on this part of the quad, even in the middle of the night. We have a terrible infestation of LARPers. They like to play vampires between the hours of ten and four. Can I get a hand?"

"Oh. Oh! Oh, I'm so sorry." Lilianne scrambles to get her books firmly under one arm while she extends her offside hand to take the woman's own.

Tugging the stranger to her feet takes what feels like no effort at all. Cheeks burning bright and hot enough to be actively uncomfortable, she lets the other woman go, taking half a step back at the same time. She's tall enough that it can be upsetting, sometimes. She's been told that she looms. Looming isn't a great way to make friends, especially not with perfectly put-together women whose eyeliner looks like it could be used to stab God. She's not sure the stranger is wearing any mascara; her eyelashes look like they may just *be* like that, thick and lush and charcoal-dark.

Some people get all the genetic luck. Lilianne realizes that she may not be looming, but she's definitely staring. She forces her eyes away, the burning sensation in her cheeks getting even stronger as her ears join in the fun. She must be red as a fire truck by this point, so red she's visible from space.

"I think your face is about to catch fire," says the stranger, as she bends to start collecting her own books from where they've fallen, scattered all around her in a surprisingly elegant arc. Which only makes sense, really. Lilianne can't imagine this woman ever doing anything inelegant.

"I'm so sorry," she manages to say without stammering, and that shouldn't feel like such a major accomplishment, but right now, it's what she has, and she'll take it. "Can I make it up to you somehow?"

"Smooth," says the stranger, flashing her a smile like a searchlight. It's almost too bright to look at directly, and somehow, it takes some of the sting out of Lilianne's cheeks and ears, dulling the burn to an almost-tolerable level. "Is this always how you meet girls?"

No chance of answering that one without stammering. "I—ah— I mean— I didn't—"

"Relax! I was just kidding." She's laughing now, and still laughing as she offers Lilianne her hand, this time to shake, not pull her off the ground. "I'm Smita. It's nice to meet you . . . ?"

"Lilianne," says Lilianne hurriedly, and she's never been so glad to have chosen something easy to pronounce, something that rolls trippingly off the tongue, as Shakespeare put it. She knows too many girls with multisyllabic names they stole from anime that had been meaningful to them before their eggs cracked, and she can't imagine getting one of those names out with stumbling over it right now. (She knows even more girls named "Crystal," which is basically the "Taylor" of the trans set. Fortunately, it never called to her. She always knew she was going to be a flower, just like Asphodel. Just like the woman who showed her the way.)

"Lilianne," says Smita, smiling.

Lilianne swears on the spot that she will never change her name, never accept a nickname (apart from "Lily," which was the whole reason she chose the name to begin with) from anyone else. It's poetry on Smita's lips. It's a prayer. And the god that's being prayed to must love her very much, or she wouldn't be here to hear the prayer as it's spoken.

Smita doesn't say anything after that, just raises an eyebrow, clearly waiting, and Lilianne realizes she needs to speak. That's how conversations work, isn't it? Both parties have to participate, or there's not really a conversation going on, just a handful of words that will fade all too soon to silence.

"I, uh, sorry," says Lilianne. "I'm new here—which you knew. I'm from Alabama, originally. My parents are still there. I'm here to get my PhD in American history, with a focus on early American children's literature. It was the best way to thread the needle between English and history, and I felt like I needed both of them if I was going to be anything like happy. I, uh. Are you a student here?"

She can't possibly be so lucky. This living goddess must be a professor, or a visitor, or something else that means Lilianne is never going to see her again after this moment inevitably ends. She's fallen in love at first sight before—a natural risk for a queer girl in small-town Alabama, where her options were limited even before she started registering them, where it was safer to keep her head down and her heart tucked away from prying eyes. She's never fallen in love like this, where it's so solid that it feels like she's breathing around a rock, like it's weighing her down and choking her at the same time. She can't breathe for all this love. She can't breathe, and she can't spit it out, no matter how much she wants to—and she doesn't really want to.

She is in love with Smita, and she wants to be in love forever, and she knows she won't be able to hold on to this feeling for much longer, so she's going to do whatever she can to make it last while she can.

Smita is smiling and nodding like Lilianne just asked a perfectly reasonable question, rather than vomiting words all over her. "I am. Still," she says. "I've been here awhile now, and I'm in biogenetics. I'm trying to identify a variety of biological markers that may serve as warning signs for various genetic conditions and lineages. It's all very complicated—I won't blame you if you don't understand it. Sometimes I'm not sure that *I* understand it."

Lilianne blinks. "You must be really, *really* smart," she says.

Smita laughs. "I don't know that I'd describe it like that," she says. "So what brings you to Berkeley?"

The real answer isn't something she can expect anyone halfway reasonable to believe, and the backup answer isn't one she's willing to give to this goddess made flesh. For right now, she wants to exist in a world where Smita is perfect, and not a world where she's had the chance to show herself as flawed as any other human.

"I got accepted for the research year," she says. "I was studying at the University of Alabama before, and that was a great school, very solid. I just needed to get out of the South for a little while, you know?"

"I do," agrees Smita. "Sometimes the only thing you need more than a hug and a hot beverage is a change of scene. I guess coastal California is about as far from the South as you can get, hey?"

"This isn't coastal."

"Not in the technical sense, but we can be standing on the shore of the Pacific in just a few hours. Take the BART to San Francisco, catch a cable car or rent a bike, and there you are, looking at the waves rolling in. It's a really nice day trip. You should take it some time."

"Are you not from California?"

"Nope," says Smita. "I grew up in Seattle, even closer to the ocean than we are here. I was at the beach every other weekend."

"Why only every other?"

"I was at the library the rest of the time." Smita's eyes widen fractionally as she finishes speaking, and she leans around Lilianne to wave to someone she's just spotted. "Erin! Over here!"

Lilianne turns to see who Smita's waving at, and watches as another ridiculously attractive woman half-jogs over to join them. She's curved and muscular where Smita is lithe and soft, with strawberry-blonde hair and a peaches-and-cream complexion that any Hollywood star would kill their stylist for. A dusting of freckles covers the bridge of her nose, and her eyes are an impossible shade of blue that Lilianne immediately dismisses as colored contacts.

She's too pretty. Smita's prettiness is earnest and honest. This woman's prettiness feels more like a lure, like the shiny light an anglerfish dangles in front of its prey before it swallows them whole. Lilianne clutches her books a little tighter, ready to turn and run if the moment demands it.

"Are you all right?" asked the newcomer—asks Erin—as she slows to a stop next to Smita. She doesn't appear to have noticed Lilianne yet. There's still time to run.

"Just chatting with my new friend Lilianne," says Smita.

Time's up. Erin swivels to look at Lilianne with those blue, blue eyes, and it's all Lilianne can do not to squirm like a moth pinned to a specimen board. If she had wings, they'd be beating frantically to signal her escape right about now, she knows that much without the need to think about it.

"Hello," says Erin, with surprising caution. She's standing so that her body is positioned between Lilianne and Smita, a perfect wall of flesh and bone and sinew. There's nothing coastal about her voice. She sounds like the Midwest made flesh, like the cornfields of Ohio and the rolling Kansas wheat, all of it somehow pressed flat and given flesh, here in the form of a wary blonde college student. "I'm Erin. It's nice to meet you."

It makes sense that Erin should be cautious. If Lilianne had a girlfriend who looked like Smita, she'd be cautious all the time.

For a day that started with such absolute conviction, it certainly has devolved into a series of ifs, hasn't it? The thought is amusing enough that Lilianne is able to summon up a smile as she extends her hand toward Erin. "A pleasure," she agrees.

"Lilianne's studying American history," says Smita.

"What do you study?" Lilianne asked.

A flicker of something more sour than cautious crosses Erin's face, there and gone in an instant. "I used to study theology," she says, reclaiming her hand. “I finished a while back. I just stuck around town to deal with some unfinished business. And because my housemates would never remember that normal people run the dishwasher if they didn’t have me around to remind them.”

“Hey,” protests Smita. “You make us sound like we’re a bunch of slobs. We’re not slobs. We’re just . . .”

“Academics?”

“Yes. Academics.” Smita turns a pleading look on Lilianne. “You’ve gotten distracted by research and forgotten about the clothes in the washing machine, haven’t you?”

“I think just about everyone has.”

“Ugh,” says Erin. “I don’t understand how you people have managed to live long enough to reach adulthood.”

“Luck, skill, and a phenomenal bodyguard,” says Smita. “It was lovely to meet you, Lilianne. I hope I’ll see you around the campus?”

“I hope so too,” says Lilianne, managing, somehow, not to say that she’ll arrange it if she has to bribe the office to give her a copy of Smita’s schedule. People tend to view that sort of thing as creepy, and the last thing she wants to do is upset her new friend.

Or friends. Erin is still looking at her steadily, and her smile has faded; she’s just a predator now, studying the new gazelle at the watering hole.

“Yes,” she says. “I’m sure we’ll see you around. Smita, come on. We’re going to be late.”

“And I know how much you hate lateness,” Smita agrees. She hooks her arm through Erin’s, and the two of them walk off, leaving Lilianne behind.

She watches them go until the crowd closes up behind them, and they’re officially gone. Then she glances around, making sure that no one else is watching her, and takes off for the comforting chaos of Telegraph Avenue.

Telegraph had been one of the only tangible things she'd been able to explain to her parents when they'd asked her why she wanted to go to graduate school so far away from home. Half thoroughfare, half carnival midway, it's a chaotic expanse of specialty stores and street vendors, the sound of voices and buskers playing all manner of stringed instruments drifting sweetly through the air. Due to city ordinances about street food, there's just one semi-illicit tamale cart and another selling roast nuts; beyond that it's all pizza, donuts, and noodles from the storefronts, served hot and steaming in Styrofoam containers.

She fell in love with Berkeley the moment she saw Telegraph Avenue, the vendors in chainmail and leather and layered skirts like something from a medieval market, the college kids wandering by, the parents of college kids clutching their purses and looking around themselves with wide, terrified eyes, like the tall man with the bushy red beard was going to mug them in broad daylight. There's a booth selling wound-wire insects with two glass jars labeled GIVE ME YOUR NAME and GIVE ME YOUR GENDER. Both are half-full of slips of paper like wishes thrown into a sacred well.

She doesn't stand out on Telegraph, no matter how tall she is, no matter how awkwardly she sometimes moves, or how obvious it is that she's still getting used to the intimate embrace of her bra, wrapped around her ribcage like a lover's arms. (Not that she's had many lovers, or wanted many lovers; this is the only one she intends to take with her to the grave.) Everyone here is brand-new, even if they've been walking these tangled urban miles for years on years. Everyone here belongs.

About half the vendors know her already. They flash quick smiles or bob their heads as she passes them, even the busker with the electric fiddle and the leather bustier. Half the Avenue is in love with their fiddle-playing angel, and the first time she remembered Lilianne's name, it was like the heavens opened up and shouted their approval from on high. The campus is a beautiful dream. Telegraph Avenue is well on its way to becoming a beautiful reality.

She walks two blocks down from the campus, then turns left, heading for a small food court, where she unlocks a near-hidden door set into the wall just past the ramen shop, revealing a narrow staircase up into the darkness. She climbs quickly, not looking back. Like Orpheus before her, she has long since learned the dangers of looking back.

Not that she has a true love to lose to the depths of the Underworld. Not that she ever expects to be called to katabasis. That isn't the sort of thing that happens to or for or around girls like her. She's fine with that, honestly. Extravagant childhood dreams aside, no one who wants to live dreams of life recast in Greek mythology. She'll be content with what she has.

The stairs are just steep enough that even after weeks of climbing them, there's a pleasant burning in her calves by the time she reaches the top. One of her roommates says that they're lucky to live in a place that guarantees them a daily workout without needing to pay for a gym membership. Lilianne isn't so sure about that. But she *is* sure that they're lucky to have found off-campus housing for less than the cost of a kidney a month. The Bay Area real estate market isn't just horrifying: to a girl from small-town Alabama, it's literally unbelievable. The prices here are some fairyland shit, and her father looked like he was going to have an aneurism when she asked for help with her deposit.

But he helped her. Her parents have always been willing to step up and help her, first when she was a child, then when she was a terrified teen standing in front of them with her heart in her hands, informing them that they had never actually had a son, only a daughter who was finally feeling brave enough to let them see her properly. She credits them with everything she is today, with setting her feet on the path she's walking now into adulthood, with showing her that anything could be possible if she was just willing to put in the effort.

(They also taught her that linear time is a mug's game, especially when the world around you has been looping over and over again for the better part of half a million years. Why can't two people meet in college and have a college-aged daughter twelve years later, with all the dense and delicious years of childhood sandwiched in-between? Why can't that same daughter finish her first trip through the halls of academia and walk away with her desired degrees, then go back to start all over again with a different name, a different major, a different way of looking at the world? Time is an irregular quantity, happening at different speeds depending on the situation. Why shouldn't someone with the proper tutors learn how to bend that variability to her own ends? It's not much of an advantage in this world; every day still had to be paid for in its own way, with aging or with other currencies, and she'll never be the age she should be in this moment ever again. But she gets to be the age she is, and she gets to press forward, into the sweet, wide expanse of the future. She gets to follow this road wherever it leads her.)

The door at the top of the stairs is closed and locked against the world. That doesn't mean anything: this is Berkeley, and even though it's a college town, it's still a fairly large city, with a fair amount of crime. Leaving a door unlocked is unthinkable here, just like needing two doors locked between her and the world would be unthinkable back home. She undoes the deadbolt and lets herself inside, into the dim, cool, marijuana-scented air of the living room.

"David!" she half-yells as she closes the door behind herself. "I thought we had an agreement about smoking inside!"

"I'm gonna do it anyway, so you'll be cool about it, even though you're an uptight weirdo?" suggests the voice of her roommate, coming from the kitchen rather than the couch. She turns toward the sound like a sunflower toward the light, and watches as he emerges, a Hostess cherry pie in one hand. He's shirtless, wearing a pair of dark blue sweatpants, and the geometric tattoos across his chest and upper arms are fully revealed, black ink on dark skin. They're old enough to have healed and settled, permanent parts of his body, and still fresh enough that the lines are crisp and unblurred.

He makes an impressive sight, even in the gloomy clutter of their apartment, with blankets tacked up over the windows to hold the sun at bay and the natural clutter of four college students more interested in extracurriculars than in housekeeping. The garbage goes out on time thanks to Raven, who can't handle the smell of anything that's been out for more than a day, and none of them have time for pets. Their rather laid-back approach to cleanliness makes Lilianne grateful for the covered windows; as long as she doesn't have to look at it, it can't bother her.

Raven found this place first, and when people look at her and Lilianne like they expect the two girls to take care of the housework, she laughs her odd little rising-and-falling laugh and says that her parents never taught her how to clean. "My mother spent her whole life being groomed to be some man's perfect trophy wife, and she didn't want that for me, so she made sure I wouldn't have the skills for the position if he showed up and wanted to give it a go," she'd said, the first time she was asked. The second time, she'd given in, and everyone had regretted it, as the kitchen was almost worse after she was done than it had been before she started.

She still had to do her share of the chores, but discussions of shifting the lion's share onto her shoulders had died with dirty silverware put away alongside the clean and old spaghetti sauce dried onto the plates in the cupboards.

Lilianne's excuse is similar, but was delivered more quietly.

She's more competent with a sponge and bucket than Raven is; if nothing else, she'd started out as an agriculture major, and despite the amount of mud and animal manure agriculture involved, it required clean workspaces whenever possible. She worked for years to keep her chickens and goats healthy, to understand their relationships to their surroundings, and when she'd decided to pivot to something less organic, she'd retained the ability to do her own damn laundry.

Still, David and Snake are smart enough to understand that while pushing the work off on their two female roommates is shitty and patriarchal, they might be able to get away with it, but doing it to just one of their roommates makes them look like assholes. Do it to the cis girl and you're saying the trans girl isn't enough of a girl to be your maid; do it to the trans girl and you're saying that she deserves less respect than the cis girl. It's a lose-lose act of patriarchy, and the men she lives with backed down as soon as they fully understood that.

They're a weird lot, the football star, the local girl, and the two professional students. Technically David's a professional student too, playing for the Golden Bears and spending most of his days down at the school training center, but Lilianne and Snake are the ones who really dedicate their lives to their studies. Snake is an entomologist by training. He'd argue that he doesn't get the title until he gets the degree, but anyone who coos to house centipedes like they were kittens and breeds his own cockroaches deserves to be called by the name of his profession. His dedication to the exoskeletal borders on the unreal.

David has a major apart from football, but he's not a grad student yet, and so she can't be bothered to remember it for more than a few minutes at a time. Which is probably shitty of her, but hey, she gets a few less-than-perfect personality traits. Everyone does. If she wants to be a little arrogant, she's allowed.

And then there's Raven. Unlike Snake, who begged them all

not to look when he filled out his rental paperwork, her parents actually gave her that name, actually looked at their red-faced little potential of a person and thought, "She looks like someone who's going to need a manifest connection to a trickster god." She was born in one of the nearby suburbs, and has lived in or around Berkeley for her entire life, which is somewhere nebulously between twenty-five and forty: young enough to still have a sense of adventure that drives her to take more risks than is probably good for her, old enough that she's no longer willing to sit or sleep on the floor. It's because of Raven that their shared living room is dominated by large, soft couches, three of them crammed in at odd angles, all rescued from curbs and sidewalks.

But the apartment has four bedrooms, a kitchen, and a living room. It's almost embarrassingly large when compared to the student housing. Raven was the one who found it and posted flyers looking for people to share it with her. The rules are simple: no smoking, no sex in public spaces, no pets, although there's no guarantee the house will be pet-hair-free: several of Raven's friends have service dogs of one type or another, and Rachel's seizure-alert dog sheds like that's his actual job.

Snake's insects aren't pets. The landlord doesn't consider anything with an exoskeleton a "pet," and as long as they don't tell him about the roaches, he doesn't care much about the rest of them. Not telling him about the roaches is one of the household rules. He's a pretty calm guy, but there are limits.

David quirks an eyebrow and takes a bite of his Hostess pie, and Lilianne realizes she's been standing silently in the doorway too long for normal social behavior. She winces, just a little, and starts across the living room with the forced nonchalance of someone trying desperately to seem normal.

"How was your day?" she asks.

"First day of classes, so no practice," he says easily, dropping back onto the couch with the grace he brings to everything he does. Sometimes Lilianne considers hating him for that. He moves like a predator, like someone who understands every inch of his body and what it can do. And then she dismisses the idea of hatred as illogical, because he *earned* that awareness. He's at the gym more often than he's anywhere else, even the football field, and his weird friends and bizarre diet don't seem to hamper his goal of being the most well-conditioned man in Berkeley.

"I had classes," she says. None of which had involved actual learning, for her: she's acting as a TA for the head of her department, and her day has been spent showing undergrads around, helping them understand the concepts behind the syllabuses they were supposed to read week ago, and directing them to the student store for the books they just forgot to buy. It's been a lot, and even though it brought her nothing new, she feels like her brain is so full that it might explode at any moment.

Academia will do that to you.

"Good for you." David yawns, teeth flashing white against the dark of his skin. "Oh, wanted to let you know: I'll be out late tonight. Don't wait up."

"Don't wake me," she counters.

"No promises," he says, and smirks.

David has a small flock of rotating girlfriends, women he disappears with for entire nights, coming back in the morning shockingly refreshed and ready to face the day. She's never seen him miss a workout due to a date, and she's seen him go on plenty of dates. So whatever's keeping him away, it won't be a problem.

Lilianne rolls her eyes, more because she knows it's the expected reaction than out of any actual distaste. "Whatever," she says, and keeps walking.

"Don't you have a doctor's appointment tonight?"

She stops. "What?"

"You wrote it on the house calendar."

"Ah. Yes. It's virtual. I'll be in my room. Please keep Snake and

Raven from bothering me, at least if they get home before you leave. I'll see you tomorrow."

"But—"

"Goodnight, David." And on she goes, heading for the hall, heading for her room, heading for the point where she'll be safe from questions and expectations and everything else the world has got to offer. She'll call her endocrinologist in a few hours. For right now, she just wants to lie on her bed and disassociate so hard she feels like she's dissolving, breaking down into motes of dust and floating away with the languid movement of the indoor air.

She's been in this apartment for almost two months, and yet her room is still a wonderland of cardboard boxes piled high not only against the walls, but in freestanding towers throughout the rest of her carefully apportioned space. When she packed and took her things away from Alabama, she'd been so sure that she was limiting herself to the essentials, that she was keeping herself lean and light and ready to pivot on a moment's notice. Now, crammed in with absolutely everything she owns, it feels like she's on the verge of becoming a hoarder.

(How do her parents handle having an entire house to fill with the leftovers of their lives? It seems irrational to stay in one place for that long, to put down roots so deep and strong that pulling them up becomes virtually unthinkable. But it is, for them. She's tried to bring up the idea of moving out to the coast, of leaving Alabama behind. They'll certainly see her more if they move to California. The political climate is shifting. Some of her classmates want to say that transphobia is over, that the world is changing, but she can see the writing on the walls. History likes to repeat itself. She'd rather not be standing in the refrain, and she wants to see her parents again before she dies.)

Lilianne drops onto the bed, books still clutched to her chest, eyes on the spiderweb network of cracks in the ceiling. There was a massive earthquake in Berkeley a few years back, and it's harder to find a building that hasn't sustained some light structural damage than one that has. She's the newest arrival to this city; all three of her roommates wave off the possibility of a collapse like it's nothing, like only a fool would be concerned about the ceiling coming down in the middle of the night. They're not worried, and so she shouldn't be, either.

She's not worried. She knows why the earth shook here in Berkeley, and what that motion signified. It's the reason she's here. It always has been. The UC Berkeley History department is good enough, but it's not world-famous; there were better places she could have gone to study if all she wanted was an impressive name on her resume.

No. Berkeley matters for other reasons.

With a sigh, she rolls onto her side and stacks the books on the floor next to her bed, then rolls back into her original position. She'll meet them soon enough, Reed's cuckoos. They're both in Berkeley, according to the information she's been able to find, the son of Ethos and the daughter of Kairos, the two halves of the Doctrine of Ethos made manifest and walking the world like the people they're pretending to be. Their existence is the proof of all Asphodel Baker's theories, the ones too wild and too ambitious for the American Alchemical Congress. The ones that left Baker effectively ostracized for the latter part of her life, that drove her to create James Reed to continue her work.

The theories that, in a very real, causally traceable way, killed her are alive and well and making their lives here in Berkeley, and Lilianne hates them for that, even as she yearns to know them, to position herself close enough to see into their nest and understand what fuels them, first and finally. She has more experience with incarnations than most young alchemists, self-trained or no: her mother and father have been serving the autumn and spring since much longer than she's been alive.

It's their service to the seasons that has allowed her to live her own life at the asynchronous tempo she prefers, skipping over the bad parts, stretching out the good ones like a tape played in slow motion. Time has a generous relationship with its most loyal servants. But she wasn't tapped for that same service. There's nothing of the summer or winter in her, no seeds of spring or acorns of the fall. She is as human as they come—blood and bone from side to side—and any mysterious transformations she undergoes must come from the outside. She can do part of it on her own. If she can catch Asphodel's cuckoos, learn the last secrets of their creation, and apply them inward, she can achieve the rest. The cuckoos were vessels made to contain the uncontained, to hold what the universe hadn't seen fit to embody on its own.

If she modifies her own vessel in the right directions, she may be able to catch her own embodiment.

They're somewhere in this city. She doesn't know their faces and she doesn't know their names, but she knows the Alchemical Congress abandoned this place after their losses reached a certain unforgivable volume, after they had to decommission and desert a hard-won urban lab location. She'll find the lab first, locate the door, and work her way down to where the Congress spun their secrets like spiders crouching in a darkened corner. They must have left something behind in their rush to flee the city. They must have given her something.

This would be so much easier if she had anyone she could talk to, but she's entirely self-taught. She learned about alchemy from her parents, who dismissed it as people playing party tricks with power, the efforts of the unhappily natural to become something more than what they were. Oh, her parents hated alchemy, had so many stories of unsuspecting seasonals and their attendants being swept up and taken apart to use in tests and tinctures. They said it was cheap, said it was cruel, said it was beneath her.

They might as well have signed her up for classes.

She found all the basic texts she could, found enough to learn that Asphodel Baker had encoded all her secrets in the Up-and-Under books, and then threw herself down the rabbit hole of children's literature, dead alchemists, and the battle between Baker and Baum. There was so much to learn, in the beginning. There still is, but she no longer has the novice's wide-eyed awe, the ability to be so amazed that the world drops away and leaves her swimming in her studies, drifting miles from the shore.

Now she learns page by agonizing page, honing her studies in secret, conducting her first clumsy experiments based on what she can decode from the writings of alchemists past. That is the one thing her mother has always seemed to at least halfway admire about the alchemists, the one part that makes her think she might be forgiven when the veil slips and her parents eventually, inevitably learn what she's become.

The secrets are here, in Berkeley. She knows it. Everything she's ever wanted is here. She just needs to find it.

She's still thinking about her next steps when sleep slides in and steals her away, down into the deep places where all secrets are kept for as long as the world endures.

Death

TIMELINE: AUGUST 21, 2018.

David waits until his strange housemate has removed herself to her room and shut the door. Even after he hears it click firmly home, he stays where he is for a count of twenty, giving her the opportunity to come out again if she feels the need. She doesn't reappear. He exhales as he swallows the last bite of his convenience-store pie, creating a momentary paradox where his body can't decide whether or not it's choking, then wipes his hands on his sweatpants and starts toward the couch with great strides of his long legs.

She's an alchemist. He's more certain of that with every time he sees her. And if she's an alchemist, he needs to tell Judy, because she'll want to know. (She'll also want to know how he wound up living with an alchemist, to which he'll say he wasn't home when Raven interviewed their new housemates, and he had only been on the lease for about two weeks when she signed: he hadn't had any sort of seniority-based veto power at that point. He still doesn't. Going to his strictly natural house organizer and saying "Hey, Raven, don't mean to stress you out or anything, but I'm pretty sure the lady down the hall would slit both our throats in the night if she thought she could trade our cooling hearts for power" isn't going to get her evicted, but it might make him homeless. And besides, if there's an unaffiliated alchemist in town, isn't it better for them to keep her where they can see her, where they can know what she's doing? He's making excuses and he knows it, but this is above his pay grade. Judy will know what to do next. Judy always knows what to do.)

(Well, that isn't entirely true. Judy didn't know what to do when it turned out that their area senior, the Lunar who was supposed to keep them all safe and shining, had secretly sold them out to the American Alchemical Congress. Judy had been caught as flat-footed by that one as all the rest of them, and had barely been able to keep herself alive long enough to help everyone else. But Diana is dead and gone, impaled by a peach tree in the everything, and her body has never been found. When all is said and done, David is happy to put his faith in Judy. People who don't have a tendency to wind up dead.)

He walks to the couch and digs through the pillows until he finds the shirt he was wearing earlier, white ribbed cotton with no sleeves, and pulls it on over his head. He prefers to let his tattoos show when he can. His divine aspect is Máni, Norse god of the moon, and his tattoos are his way of honoring that side of himself. The skinhead punks who sometimes lurk around the bars on Shattuck don't like having a Black man who could clearly break them walking around with symbols they've decided belong to them tattooed on his arms. Is it petty? Sure. Is it fun? Absolutely. David is a literal god. He refuses to be intimidated by a bunch of jumped-up little men who think the speed with which they sunburn makes them better than him.

Snake is still at school, and Raven is asleep in her room, where she'll stay until shortly before sunset, emerging only when she absolutely has to. She likes it when she knows where her people are, and since they're all technically subletting from her, it's easier to let her have her way. David pauses to grab a Post-it from the stack on the coffee table, scrawling a quick note that says he'll be out late with some friends from the team and sticking it to the fridge.

Then he makes his exit, the lie still tingling in his fingertips.

David doesn't really have many friends from the team. Oh, the guys like him well enough—he's a good player, and he almost never misses a practice, heals fast enough that he almost never misses a game, either—but he hasn't gone out of his way to cultivate them. The friends he left back home when he came to school would be baffled. He'd always been the first to the party and the last to leave, the one laughing loudest with a lager in his hand and his arm curved around the waist of some sweet young cheerleader whose name he might not remember the next day. He hadn't had friends, he'd had legions, scores of high school heroes ready to go to war on his command.

And he still likes to party now that he's in college. Judy used to get on him about it, the way he seemed to think beer was a human right and women were a renewable resource. She wasn't wrong to ride him about it back then: he'd had less respect for the work than he should have, and had fairly regularly neglected his duties to the other Lunars and to the Impossible City. That changed when Aske died. She'd been the Sámi goddess of the moon, and she'd been a freshman girl from Minnesota named Eliza, and she'd been his friend. He hadn't been entirely in love with her, but he'd been on his way, and he'd been able to see clearly just how infatuated he was going to become. He hadn't minded one bit. She was the sort of girl who deserved to have someone fall in love with her over and over again.

Sometimes he thinks he's still falling in love with her over and over again, even though her part in the pantheon is over and done. Even though she's gone.

Anyway, after Eliza, he hadn't been able to see his endless collegiate party in the same light, and he still can't. It all seems shallow and a little pointless, if it can't save the most innocent of goddesses.

He thunders down the stairs to the food court, waving to a few familiar faces among the gathered patrons as he locks the door, then heads for the street. He won't be seeing his nonexistent team friends today; he'll be seeing his fellow Lunars, and hopefully not getting mobbed when he tells them about a suspected alchemist in their midst.

He'd like to be wrong about Lilianne. She's a nice girl, as gawky, awkward girls from the middle of nowhere go. She pays her share of the rent on time, and doesn't judge him much for being more interested in the gridiron than the grind. She doesn't seem to know enough about football to have realized that his chances of a professional career are dwindling with every semester he spends on the collegiate field; he's very close to becoming one of those men who peaked early and now haunt the site of their old glories, frustrating the newer players and antagonizing their former coaches.

That's not going to be him. Being a Lunar means he heals faster, recovers from little complications with more grace: he'll never tear an ACL or have to deal with a head injury that puts him on the bench for the back half of a season. He's not invincible, but he's hard to harm, and he ages more slowly than someone without his ties to the divine. He has the time to spare, and when he's ready to move on from his college days, the recruiters will be shocked by how much stamina he has left in him. All he has to do is wait it out.

But Lilianne . . . she's from Alabama, and they take their football seriously there. She should know enough to see that he's spinning his wheels, and her casual acceptance of the situation tells him she has no idea. It's strange. One more oddity to put in a column that's increasingly tilted toward "alchemist" without containing anything conclusive. Oh, he wishes she'd do something blatantly alchemical, melt a frog or turn milk into beer or something else that violates the laws of nature but will tell him clearly that he's doing the right thing by telling Judy about her.

And then she doesn't do anything obvious, but all the little bits and pieces of her reality add up a little more, and all he can do is admit the truth.

It's late afternoon, the golden hours of sunlight and warmth and leisure, all the college kids freed from their classes and most of the nine-to-five workers finally released from their offices and desks. The sidewalks are crowded, not so tightly that he can't talk, but sufficiently to slow him down as he heads down Telegraph away from the campus. He's heading for the secret suburban Berkeley, the residential neighborhoods tucked away where most people will never look or see.

He didn't know about them himself when he first came to study here, not really. Oh, he'd known that the people who worked in the city would have to live at least semi-locally if they wanted to be able to afford their own professions, but he'd never really stopped to think about where exactly that would put them. The college tours had had less reason to focus on the spreading blanket of apartment buildings and private homes than they did to wander the aisles of the local supermarket, pointing out brands of jam.

He passes the Whole Foods Market, parking lot packed with people who don't know about the much-superior nearby Berkeley Bowl. Sure, it can be hard to park at the Bowl, but their produce is fresher, and they keep their own flock of chickens. Knowing that much makes David feel a little smug, like he belongs here while those uninformed tourists don't. He's a resident of Berkeley now. No one gets to make him leave.

Especially not some Alabama alchemist, no matter how nice she is when she's not conspiring to chop poor, innocent Lunars up and add them to her alchemical nightmares.

With a snort, he turns down the next street on his journey and keeps on walking.

* * *

A long, long time ago, longer than anyone can really say for sure, certain aspects of the natural universe got a taste for experiencing the rest of the universe through human perceptions. They wanted to see with human eyes, to feel with human hands. They wanted to walk in the world they had shaped and borne, and they wanted to be mortal and immortal at the same time.

"Possible" and "impossible" are two sides of the same coin, and it's a coin spent only by humanity. A rainstorm doesn't know that it's impossible for it to put on a Sunday skin and go dancing down at the church social, and so nothing stops it from doing exactly that. A mountain doesn't know it's impossible to fall in love. And in the beginning, the people didn't know it was impossible for the moon to be a person too, to want and wish and wonder, to come down to the world below it and feel all the things there were to feel. They dreamt the moon into human skin, and so the moon put it on, and it joined the great, surprisingly possible dance of everything there was.

But even as the universe was learning how to want more widely and deeply, even as it was reaching out and selecting skins to slide itself inside and live through, there were aspects of creation that never came together in quite so simplistic a way. They were too vast or too primal, Titans set against a backdrop of gods and monsters, and there was not room for them in the world as it was. Some ideas were too big to wear a single skin.

Enter the human alchemists, in their arrogance and eagerness—and their tiny, terrible spark of the divine, for they, like the forces of creation, seemed determined to redefine what it meant to be "impossible." They spun shells of skin and bone for those concepts, luring them out of the ether where they had been so content to linger, winnowing them down and refining them until they could be slipped into their own human hearts.

All incarnates were a little odd, a little inclined to rewrite the laws of reality around themselves. That was only to be expected when you were talking about people who were also abstract concepts too large and difficult to be easily contained. The incarnates who had been forced into existence by the hope and hubris of alchemists were . . .

Well, they were probably not supposed to exist in the first place, so it was only understandable that they would take their oddity to new heights. David turns a corner and stops for a moment, struck as always by the house midway down the block.

It's a riot of color, like a rainbow refracted through an even greater prism, then wrapped tight around a simple two-story Berkeley home. The front garden is filled with flowers and fruiting bushes, the branches of the peach tree near the fence bent low with the weight of the fruit they struggle to hold. There's a fence around the yard, but it's barely necessary: no one else is so much as glancing at the house, not even the people driving by who should be seeing it for the first time. David feels Máni stir under his skin, the god waking and stretching toward the sun in response to the sight of the house, which is practically a beacon for the preternatural. Nothing that bright can exist in this reality without some sort of help.

And help it has. The people passing as if it was nothing remarkable literally can't see what they're missing: it's screened from them, tucked between the seconds on the clock, tick-tock tick-tock. David knows the reason, knows the illusion is only possible because the human incarnation of time itself is living inside those garishly painted walls. Still, it's as impressive as it is terrifying.

Not as terrifying as the fact that he's walking toward it of his own accord, heading for the gate in the wrought iron fence. He shouldn't be here. He knows it, and Máni knows it, surging forward and briefly trying to seize control.

David pushes him gently aside, and although Máni is a god, he goes, willing to yield to the human owner of their shared body. It's always like that for the healthy relationships between the mortal and the divine: the gods know that they move into already-occupied bodies, immortal hermit crabs seeking shells to settle in, and they try to respect the fact that the humans were there first. It doesn't work like that for all the incarnates, David knows; the seasons are born beating in the hearts of their human hosts, and because of that, the humans grow up entangled and inseparable from what they might one day become. As far as he's aware, it's the same for the Horae and for the day and night. Mortal measures of time living out their lives while so tangled with the universe that they become one and the same.

Sometimes he looks at the minor incarnations and wonders whether there are any truly human humans left. But of course there are.

There are the alchemists.

He closes the gate behind himself as he steps into the garden, following the winding brick path up to the porch steps. Each board is painted a different color, all of them eye-searingly bright, none of them blending with one another. He puts his hand on the porch rail and for a moment he can't remember why he's here, what could possibly have been important enough to justify bothering the people who live here. They're important people. They must be, to have a house that's painted in so many colors. He's not important. He's no one, he has no right to take up their time, to interfere—

No. He takes his hand off the rail and gives it a look, half-amused, half-annoyed. "Upgrading the security system again, eh?" he asks, as if the air itself might see fit to respond. "It's a cute trick. I'd appreciate it a lot more if I weren't here to see my superior. You know, the lady who's banging your brother?"

It's a wild guess which one of them would have modified the house alarms in quite this manner, but he's confident he's right even before the house puts out a pulse of what feels like pure disgust and the front door swings open. Which would be all very eerie and unsettling in a haunted-attraction sort of way, if not for the redhaired woman standing just inside, her hand still on the doorknob.

There's a streak of white running from the crown of her head down through her long, shaggy bangs. It makes her look a little bit like an anthropomorphic personification of a candy cane. He's never been able to get an explanation for what did that to her hair, but her brother has the same streak, and neither of them are bleaching anything. Somewhere in the past, they were both traumatized enough to turn a strip of their hair an inch and a half wide white as bone, and given how traumatizing the pair of them are, he doesn't like to think about that more than he actually has to.

David trots up the stairs, nodding casually to the woman in the doorway, like this is no big deal, like *she's* no big deal, like he's not terrified halfway out of his mind every time he has to remind her that he exists.

"'S'up, Dodge?" he offers.

She steps aside to let him in, rolling her eyes (pale gray, like fog over the San Francisco Bay, like moonlight on the mist, and nothing living should have eyes like that: they're horror-movie eyes, the eyes of the walking dead, and her pupils are black spots in a sea of nothingness, stripping him down, seeing all the way to the bones of him in ways he never agreed to) as she does. "The usual. I've got a fresh new batch of proofs to review, and a team of Australian mathematicians who think they're about to revolutionize the field."

"Are they?"

She smiles like a slashed throat. "Like hell they are. Their work is sloppy, and they have so much hinging on a proof that I disproved when I was eleven that it would be funny if they weren't wasting my time."

"Sounds cool."

It does, actually. Dodger Cheswich is the living embodiment of mathematics, one half of the Doctrine of Ethos, and when she talks about math, it's so far beyond him that it might as well be poetry, elevated and alien and beautiful all the same. He doesn't like to talk to normal mathematicians, the ones who might expect him to understand them, but Dodger? He can listen to Dodger talk all day long.

She barks a laugh. "Don't humor me, moon-boy. Judy and my brother are up in the library. And they're both decent, so you don't need to worry about walking in on them."

David makes a sour face. "Once was more than enough."

Judy's an attractive-enough woman, all soft curves and long black hair, but finding her entangled with Dodger's male equivalent, both of them naked and her glowing a soft, lambent peach color as her divinity rose to the surface, had been more than any man should be forced to see. Unless joining in was an option, which it had most critically not been in that instance. Judy is his superior in the hierarchy of the local Lunars, and Roger is . . .

Roger is not quite as terrifying as his sister, but that's only because he spends more time remembering how to be human. Dodger treats her humanity as a limitation, something that's keeping her from truly understanding the underpinning mathematics of creation. Roger embraces his. Humanity means hot coffee and baseball games, good books and better lovers. And, at the end of everything, his sister.

David has been around them enough to know some of what they went through to find each other and, once they had been found, to stay together. They reset time itself, thousands of times, looping the world through a doomed series of attempts to be something more than alchemical puppets sculpted by a man who had no right to the forces of creation. They fought and they killed and they died, over and over again, for the chance to stay together. For Dodger, that seems to mean that they're finished with the hard part; now they get to sit back and define existence however they desire. And for Roger, it seems to mean this is their chance to be humans, *really* be humans, before things have to change again.

Both of their perspectives make sense, in their own ways. It's just that Dodger still seems so lonely sometimes. She's the living, beating heart of the mathematical underpinnings of the universe, Kairos made flesh, and she's lonely. That can't be good for creation.

David's pretty sure she's not asexual, but he thinks she might be aromantic. That would make sense. Erin's told him that the embodied Doctrine is designed to protect itself, that the Math child will always dedicate their entire life to the protection and preservation of the Language child. Falling in love with anyone else would only interfere.

"What's so important that you can't wait for Miss Peachy-pants to finish flirting with my brother and go meet you on the moon?" asks Dodger, snapping him out of his brief contemplation of the inner workings of the universe.

"We're not supposed to meet up until next week, and I've got some information I'm pretty sure she's going to want before then," says David. "I'd tell you, but I don't want to start problems before I'm absolutely sure."

"What, and you're afraid I'm going to go off half-cocked and blow a bunch of shit up? Not my style, moon-boy."

"Just let me tell Judy first."

She rolls her eyes again, gesturing toward the stairs. "Be my guest."

David smiles encouragingly, then takes off, loping up the stairs two at a time while Dodger shakes her head and goes back to the front room and whatever ridiculous thing she was doing before he disturbed her.

The house from the outside is no bigger or smaller than any of the houses around it; there's nothing remarkable about it, once you discount the paint job, something that's almost impossible to do. Still, paint can't change architecture, and even someone dazzled by the captive rainbow that is the exterior would be hard pressed not to see that there's something wrong with the internal geometry of the place.

The house isn't, shouldn't be, *can't* be this big. He climbs stairs until he passes the second-floor landing, then keeps going to a third floor that is absolutely not reflected from the outside, where the stairs end in an airy U-shaped hall, the ceiling brightened by periodic skylights. (Like the windows downstairs, they're filled with carnival glass that paints everything they shine on in still more rainbows. Their patterns are mathematical and abstract, twisting and shifting when he looks at them too closely.) The windows are their own impossibility, because he knows there's an attic above this floor, a dusty, cedar-scented space where all the unwanted objects the household generates get put.

He doesn't dwell on that. He's learned that the key to walking in impossible spaces is to forget that they're impossible, to push that fact aside and let it go. "Possible" and "impossible" are just words, after all.

The door at the top of the U creaks open as he approaches, and the narrow, bespectacled face of a man with shaggy brown hair and unsettlingly gray eyes pokes out, scanning the hall. Roger brightens when he spots David, smiling the earnest smile of everyone's favorite college professor and waving David forward, beckoning for him to come closer.

"There you are," he says, like he's been waiting for hours for David to arrive. "Dodger told me you were on the way up. You have any issues with the second floor? It's just that Kim and Tim have been experimenting with moebius strips and it can get sort of dicey sometimes."

"If they bent reality somehow, Dodger shut it down before she sent me up," says David.

"Good, good." Roger looks over his shoulder at the room behind him. His smile is different when he turns back to David, less placating, more sincere. "Judy's ready for you."

"Great." David heads for the door, and Roger pulls it wider when he gets there, letting him inside.

(Kim and Tim are also the incarnate Doctrine, or would be, if the Doctrine could manifest as more than two people at a time. It can't, not yet, and so they're effectively human teenagers trying to navigate a world in which their only purpose has been snatched away from them by the adults who now have to act as their caretakers and responsible parties. They're not okay. If they're making successful moebius strips on the stairs, it's because Dodger is enabling it somehow to help them feel better. But it's just as likely that there was never a moebius strip at all, and Roger was just buying Judy time to get her shirt back on.)

David steps through the door and into a library that wouldn't be out of place in a house ten times this size, with shelves that stretch well beyond the supposed roofline, and walls that make a lie of any remaining scrap of logic to the floorplan. This room belongs in a university, not a suburban home. And the *books*. The walls are lined with built-in bookshelves made of some dark, polished wood; some of them have glass fronts, like the volumes they're holding are in need of constant protection. Every shelf is packed to bursting with books, cloth-bound and leather-bound, spines etched in gold or silver or strange mercury lettering. This is a bibliophile's wet dream brought to life.

David's never been much of one for reading when he doesn't absolutely have to, but even he's awestruck by this cathedral to the written word. It's impractical and probably not real when Roger doesn't remember that he wants it to be, but it's still breathtaking for all of that. Sometimes you need to just let beautiful things exist.

Judy is seated in an overstuffed leather armchair, big enough that she takes up less than half of it, her cheeks reddened and her lips slightly swollen in that thoroughly kissed sort of a way. David almost smirks at the sight of her. If they weren't both members of the same rigid social hierarchy, he's quite sure they would have tumbled into each other in one of the off-campus bars long since; Judy has a reputation remarkably similar to his own, no insult intended. But much as he slowed down his extracurricular activities since Eliza died and broke his heart in ways he's still trying to understand, she slowed and apparently stopped hers when she finally met Roger Middleton.

If Dodger is Math, Roger is Language: the concept of it, the execution of it, the yearning for it. And Judy, when she's not the Chinese goddess of the moon, is a linguist. David can't decide whether her relationship with Roger is equitable due her divinity balancing out his . . . whatever it is you're supposed to call the Doctrine, or whether it's an extremely advanced form of monsterfucking. Either way, they're both happy, and Roger swears he's not mind-controlling her, so if two consenting adults want to get their freak on, he doesn't get to judge.

Judy's smart and she's pretty, which isn't essential, but is nice. Half-Chinese, half-Scottish, with long black hair streaked in early silver, like shafts of moonlight across the skin. It's easy to tell the difference between Judy the person and Chang'e the goddess: Judy has yellowish hazel eyes, while Chang'e has eyes the color of ripe peaches, to match the lambent peach glow that rises from her skin.

Roger doesn't change, because Roger isn't two people in a single skin. He's always Roger Middleton, professor of linguistic theory, and he's always the living Doctrine of Ethos. And right now, he's looking at David with the mild disapproval of someone whose afternoon make-out situation has just been disrupted for no apparent reason.

Forcing his attention to stay locked on Judy, no matter how

uncomfortable it is to stare at his superior when she's clearly just been thoroughly kissed (and he would have the same problem if it were anyone else he had to talk to in a serious and professional manner, he wouldn't be able to talk to Raven or Snake if they looked at him with excitement still lingering in their cheeks and the last glints of lust fading from their eyes, this isn't about Judy, it's not), David says, "Chang'e, I need to speak with you."

Judy lifts an eyebrow and steps up into her divinity, the spark of lust receding as her eyes turn peach-colored and her skin begins to glow. It takes less than a second before the woman looking at him is older and calmer than Judy has ever been, shrouded in an unshakeable conviction of her own place in the universe. It's as impressive as it is terrifying. Every time.

"I never get tired of that," says Roger.

For an instant, David finds himself wondering if they have sex while Judy's consigned to the back of her own mind and her body is in the sole custody of Chang'e. Does consent count when the body's owner leaves the premises in the middle? This whole situation is raising a lot of questions his own more-mundane love life has never required him to answer. It's with a strong feeling of relief that he lets go of his own mortality, allowing the god Máni to step up to the front of their shared existence, allowing himself to fade into the background.

(Consent must transfer over, when the mortal and the god are in agreement, he decides as he goes. The use of the mortal body is a form of consent, and one that can be revoked, even if it almost never is. Content that Máni knows why they came here, David sinks deeper and allows himself to slide into a meditative state, the world fading to sounds and colors, like a film projected on a distant wall.)

"Máni," says Chang'e. "Why are you here?"

"David wanted us to tell you what he's been observing. We have a new roommate in the apartment."

"You're still over the food court? Living with the woman named after a bird?"

"Raven, yes. She offered rooms to a man named after a snake who keeps cockroaches in our bathroom, and to a woman named after a flower who moved here from Alabama. It's the woman named after the flower that we wanted to talk to you about."

"What about her?"

"We think she's an alchemist."

Chang'e leans forward, gaze sharpening as it fixes more firmly on Máni's face. "Tell me why."

"She keeps odd hours, even for a college student; she constantly smells of astringent herbs and unusual chemical components. I think—"

"You? Not David?"

Máni nods. "In this case, yes. I think I smelled alkahest on her two days ago, when she came back from a lab tour with a guilty look on her face and blood under her fingernails. She's doing *something*."

"We drove the Alchemical Congress out of Berkeley after we disrupted their plan to embody the secondary Lunar incarnations," says Roger. He pauses, making a face like he's just bitten directly into an invisible lemon. "I hate my life for being the sort where that sentence made actual sense. That sentence should *not* make actual sense. That sentence should not *be*."

"True enough," agrees Máni. "But it is, and it does make sense, and this is the life you have. I haven't met the woman we're talking about. If she really *is* an alchemist, it's not safe for me to step up in her vicinity."

Roger and Chang'e both nod understanding, Chang'e's expression tinted with understanding. Lunars are among the most common incarnates, thanks to the incredible cultural range of moon gods the humans have invented and subsequently embodied, and their service to the Impossible City requiring them to live in proximity to one another. They're social incarnates, and that makes them easy to find, if the person looking is determined enough. The alchemists have had the time and motivation to find plenty of uses for Lunars, blood and bone and other fluids. They even figured out how to use their remains to recreate Roman concrete. Treating it with godsblood made it almost impossible to destroy. Even their precious alkahest couldn't do the job.

With a known alchemist around, the gods were limited, because the gods were already limited by the nature of reality. Maybe in the days of lightning bolts and global floods, a human with a knife wouldn't have been so frightening, but far too few incarnate gods had that sort of control over their domains. Máni can shine bright enough to temporarily blind when he has to, and when children are in danger, he can temporarily change the phase of the moon. Impressive beyond measure, from a physics and astronomy standpoint, probably not going to stop him from getting cut open and harvested like a field.

Chang'e is a little better protected. As the goddess responsible for maintaining the peaches of immortality, she can grow a peach tree from a pit to fruiting maturity in seconds. Máni may never be able to forget how brilliantly offensive that ability can be. In the natural world, bamboo grows fast enough that it can be used as a torture device by strapping people down on top of cleared ground where young bamboo canes are trying to break through. Chang'e doesn't need straps or clear ground. She just needs to get a peach pit into position and let the carnage unfold from there.

He's seen it happen once. He'll be entirely content with his life if he never has to see—or hear—it happen ever again.

"May I speak to David, then?" asks Chang'e, politely. She could order him to step down and return David to the surface, could press the issue. That she doesn't is a sign of both respect and weakness, and it makes Máni worry for her even as he stands straighter and nods.

"You may," he says. "May I make one last observation before I go?"

"You may," she says, an echo of his own answer.

He glances to Roger, who is at least keeping quiet and mostly pretending not to listen in, but whose presence is an inescapable complication to this conversation. "I would feel more comfortable speaking if we were alone."

"And I would feel more comfortable if I were still dropped down and watching my mortal host perform human mating rituals, but here we both are." Chang'e sounds like she's losing patience with the situation. "You can speak in front of the Doctrine. He and I have agreed to keep one another's secrets, and his numeric half doesn't listen when he's with my host."

"Wonderful," says Máni. "Very well, then. I worry—we worry—that your entanglement with the Doctrine takes away from your focus on your station. We are still lessened by the losses we suffered when there where alchemists here before, and now the alchemists may be returning, sliding their terrible hooks into the fabric of our city. What will you do to protect us? When your attention is split between your duty and your desire, how can you be properly devoted to either?"

Chang'e goes very still, and the glow around her intensifies, becoming bright enough to wash away the silver of Máni's own. The various Lunar gods draw their strength from the number of believers they have left among the more ordinary world, and he has just enough time to remember that Chang'e still has a massive base of extremely active, extremely devoted followers (they named the Chinese lunar exploration program after her) before the weight of her divinity slams into him and forces him down to his knees.

She stands, moving slowly, deliberately toward him, and he hasn't felt this small, or this mortal, since he first found the path to his ascension. He feels human, breakable . . . and trapped. A small god in the face of a larger one might as well be a gnat, ready to be swatted aside.

"Mercy," he says, throat dry, voice growing thick with an accent that has never been David's, that belongs to another part of the world, another life entirely. "I meant no offense. Please."

"Be quiet, little god," says Chang'e. She leans forward, caressing his cheek with one radiance-enveloped hand, the glow of her presence so bright that he can see it even when he closes his eyes. He smells peaches, in all their stages, from the smallest budding flower to the fermenting fruit, well on its way to becoming wine.

She takes her hand away, and it's all he can do not to cry. "I should have alleviated your fears long before this, and for my silence, I apologize," she says. "My Judy is . . . unaccustomed to the mantle of leadership. We both supposed, when Diana fell, that Artemis would insist upon claiming her position. She is far older than we are, far more suited to the role. When she refused it, we were confused, and did the best we could."

Artemis is an ancient Lunar, possibly the oldest Máni has ever heard of—definitely the oldest he's ever encountered. Most Lunars live a few decades longer than they would have without their symbiotic relationship to divinity, extending their youths with the peaches grown by the various incarnations of Chang'e, whittling new shapes out of their mortal lives, but still in symbiosis, still sharing, still aging day by day. This specific incarnation of Artemis is . . . different.

Alchemists again. It's always alchemists when things go wrong, when they break from the patterns they've found for themselves across the centuries and run rampant into new territories, uncharted and unpredictable. She had been a girl named Annabelle Austin who, when she started to hear the Moon whispering to her, had been too slow to conceal the voices that followed her and haunted her dreams, and her father had learned of her condition. That had been a different time, a world where any sign of deviance from the norm had been taken for a severe and incurable ailment, and her father had been utterly distraught.

Seeking to cure his heir and only daughter, he'd turned to a so-called doctor named James Reed, paying him to restore the girl. Instead, Reed had shown a rare degree of restraint for an alchemist, and had only manipulated her, rather than taking her apart. He'd turned her into a prisoner in her own mind, forcing her down into the deep dark and leaving Artemis eternally ascendant.

It's still unclear what he was hoping to accomplish by locking one of the more powerful aspects of the Moon into a permanent ascension, rather than just killing her when he was done with his research. Maybe he'd been planning to use her like a hunting hound, a way to flush lesser Lunars out into the open for the harvest. Or maybe he'd been following the plans Asphodel left behind, obscure and unknowable, moving toward the cosmic conquest that had been his goal since his own creation. It had something to do with access to the everything, the all-space no-space channels that the Lunars use to reach the Impossible City.

Whatever it was done for, it's left them with an Artemis who's far older and more powerful than she should have been, who's only really controllable by her incarnate Hind, a sheltered former lab experiment who'd believed herself to be an alchemist transformed by careless research. The thought that Artemis might take over the Berkeley-area Lunars after Diana's death had been more optimistic than logical, and even then, the optimism had been severely tempered by the knowledge that letting her run things might be uncomfortably close to handing power over to the Alchemical Congress.

And none of this matters now, because Artemis is gone, haunting the wilds where she belongs, her Hind beside her, and she has ceded this territory to Chang'e. Chang'e, who is now taking her hand away from Máni's face and stepping backward, leaving him suddenly cold, suddenly alone in the world.

His eyes don't want to open. The thing they most recently beheld was divinity in the purest form he may ever experience, and they're still savoring the sight. He manages, with an extreme effort, to convince them to obey his commands, and he sees that Chang'e is still there, a few feet away now, but still gleaming like the Moon itself. She has never been this beautiful.

"I'm sorry," he whispers.

"I know," she replies. "And I understand. Your concerns are not unreasonable, not after Diana, not after everything. We live in complicated times, and that leads to complicated fears. But no. I am not compromised because my mortal half-loves a man."

Roger jerks like he's been stuck with a pin, abandoning all pretense that he's not listening to their conversation as he slowly turns to stare at Chang'e. There is a clatter from somewhere far below, drifting through the half-real material of the house.

Chang'e looks unbothered by all of this, her eyes remaining fixed on Máni, her skin remaining bright with beaming divinity. "Everything I do, I do for the betterment of our community. Judy's feelings are her own. I haven't caused or shaped them in any way. But I have, perhaps, encouraged her to act on those feelings when her natural inclination might be to suppress them in favor of focusing on her position."

"Why?"

"Because there is no virtue in self-denial, whatever the world may try to say to us, and because you speak of benefiting the Lunars as if we should have no other purpose in this world. Well, tell me, Máni, which benefits the Lunar community more: an intimate relationship with the embodied Doctrine, or a suppressed attraction leading to frustration and tension between us? Judy has influence that she would not otherwise have."

"Hey, now," says Roger, sounding mildly affronted.

Chang'e barely glances in his direction. "I say again, I have done nothing to force or direct Judy's affections. She loves you because you speak more languages than she does, and because she finds you funny and sweet and protective in a very attractive way. You could release the Doctrine tomorrow and I believe she would still love you, and I would still allow it. I don't control her heart."

Roger frowns. "She's never said she loves me. This feels like a conversation I should be having with her."

"Oops," says Chang'e blandly, with no real hint of apology. "Now, Máni. I said I wanted to talk to David. I have answered your concerns, and hopefully alleviated them. Let him come forward."

"Yes," he says, and sinks back, dropping down into the dark that waits when he is not ascendant. David responds by rising, and for one dizzying moment they have equal control of their shared body. Then Máni releases the reins, and David is in command once more, leaving Máni to only observe.

He immediately whirls on Roger, hands raised in supplication. "I'm so sorry, man," he says. "I had no idea he was going to do that, we didn't discuss it, he didn't warn me. That was fundamentally uncool, and he was way, way out of line."

"Yeah, kinda," says Roger. He rakes one hand backward through his hair, momentarily looking like a disheveled cockatoo. "I don't show up at your place and start interrogating the women you're dating."

"Not currently dating anyone."

"That's not the point. Please tell Máni that Judy's friends will always be welcome in my home, but if he talks to her like that again, I won't consider him a friend."

David grimaces. "He can hear you, and he understands."

"You people and your sublinguistics," mutters Roger. "I will never understand how you don't all lose your minds."

"Divinity carves new channels for our thoughts to follow, even as ascension makes it possible for you to hold your singular self and all the words of the world in the same mind at the same time," says Chang'e, surprisingly serene. "We are all as we were made to be, and we do what we must to survive."

Roger meets her eyes, seemingly untroubled by the glow. "I need to talk to Judy when you're done interrogating David," he says.

"I understand," says Chang'e. "I would expect nothing less."

"Great. Now I'm going to go and make sure my sister doesn't come charging up the stairs to break some noses. If you'll excuse me?"

Roger turns and leaves the library, which doesn't collapse into a haze of improbability as soon as he walks through the door, but for a moment feels like it might. David tenses, waiting for the moment when the floor pops beneath him like a soap bubble. Chang'e sees, and sighs.

"The equations that expand the space inside the house are completely stable, and not dependent on human presence beyond the fact that they need the embodied Doctrine to be alive to maintain them," she says. "They hinge on Dodger more than Roger, at his request. He didn't want to get so deeply sunk in a book that he forgot to keep bending space around himself. We're safe here."

"If you say so," he grumbles, still uneasy.

"I do. Now. You wanted tell me about a possible alchemist? Why do you think there's an alchemist?"

"Máni told you about the alkahest—"

"Alkahest is just a form of acid. He could have been smelling something else."

"*I* smelled it too, and it wasn't just any acid. Alkahest is acid mixed with ozone and mercury. It smells like atoms coming apart. It smells like dying. This was something that shouldn't have been in my apartment, and I know it didn't come from Raven or Snake. It was Lilianne."

"I see."

"You don't, or you wouldn't be sounding so calm about the whole situation," he half-snaps. "She's furtive. She slinks around corners, and she approaches socialization like she's following a script. I know she has a thesis to finish, an advisor to answer to, but her classes are less coherent than mine are. She's not here for an education. I've seen the books she brings back to the apartment, and they're . . . eclectic to say the least."

"Wouldn't an alchemist be better about concealing themselves?" asks Chang'e.

"Not necessarily. A lot of them are self-taught. The Congress has taken serious losses in the last few decades, and they were very focused before that on undoing Baker's alchemical mapping of North America, trying to prevent Reed's creations from claiming the Impossible City."

"All they needed to do to keep those two out of the Impossible City was make sure they had access to the internet and too many hobbies to let them go and take over the control room of the universe," says Chang'e. "The alchemists never stopped to ask themselves what kind of person the Doctrine was likely to become."

Privately, David isn't sure *anyone* could have predicted Roger and Dodger, least of all the twins themselves. They are the product of the world and their endless looping journeys through it as much as they are of Reed's lab and Asphodel's original research. Nurture and nature both were involved, and in the final battle between the two, neither came out definitively the winner.

"No, and even if they had, I don't think they could have changed anything," says David. "Still. She's showing all the indicators that we're supposed to look for in alchemists, and even more than that, there's just this *feeling* that I get when she's nearby, like there's something she's not telling me." Belatedly, he realizes how that might sound and hastens to add, "It's not that she's trans. She told us all when she moved in, and it's not a big deal. This has nothing to do with that. Máni has been embodied as a woman before, he understands what it is to have a divide between your body and your mind. He was a little surprised when he woke up in me and realized we were Black. It's not who she is, it's *how* she is that makes me feel like she's an alchemist."

"Watch her for proof," says Chang'e, serenely. "When you know for sure, come to us, and we'll listen. We'll find a way to stop whatever it is she's intending to do to the people of this city, and we'll keep our pantheon from harm."

"Thank you," says David, shoulders drooping slightly.

"It's my job." The air around her brightens for a moment, then darkens as the light pouring from her skin fades away and it's just Judy standing in front of him, Judy looking at him with her usual expression of mild disappointment, like she knows he's capable of so much more than he's been showing her. "I am going to kick your ass," she says, and her tone is pure New Jersey, an accent that only comes forth when she's genuinely angry or annoyed. Most of the time she speaks with the bland non-accent of a Hollywood star, the received pronunciation of America. "You get that, right? I am going to kick your ass so hard you'll hit pelvis when you try to pick your nose."

"I don't . . . I don't think that works, anatomically speaking."

"Ever taken a human physiology course? Because I don't believe you have. If I say I can kick your ass all the way up into your sinuses, it's in your best interests to believe me. Out of self-preservation if nothing else."

Judy's more than a foot shorter than he is, and built like an out-of-shape linguist, not a walking wall. The odds of her successfully kicking his ass are incredibly slim. He still takes a step back, putting his hands up defensively.

"Hey, now, I'm sorry I interrupted your date! But I've been thinking about this for a while, and as soon as my suspicions hit near-certainty, I was pretty sure I was required to tell you!"

"You were right about that part," snaps Judy. She sighs then, shaking her head. "You really don't know what you did, do you?"

"No," says David.

"I suppose that's fair, since *you* didn't do it, Máni did. Did he *have* to start asking Chang'e about my relationship with Roger? Was it absolutely necessary for him to push her into a position where she felt like she needed to tell Roger I was in love with him?"

"What do you— Oh, fuck." David winces. "I should have picked up on that faster. I'm sorry. Chang'e was stepped way, way up for most of that conversation, so I was sunk way, way down to keep from getting scalded by someone else's divinity. Yeah, fuck. If you hadn't told him yet, you must have had a reason, and it was uncool as hell for Máni to get you outed like that."

"Guys don't *like* it when you seem to get serious faster than they do." Judy shakes her head. "I've been dumped for that before. I really don't want Roger to dump me. I'm really into him."

"His whole weird deal doesn't bother you?"

"We have our own weird deals, *David*, or did you forget about the part where we're composite entities who timeshare with ancient personifications of the literal moon?"

Stung, he shakes his head. "I didn't forget. That's not the sort of thing you just forget." And his timeshare was the one to drag him here, interrupting Judy during her day off, forcing this whole situation to unfurl.

"Good." She shakes her head again. "No, Roger's weird deal doesn't bother me. If anything, it's part of the appeal. He's like a language in the process of learning itself. The Doctrine isn't like the Moon. It's never been human before, and until it finishes figuring out all its tenses and grammatical rules, it's going to be a little soft in the middle. A little squishy. I'm helping him find his limits—and he *does* have limits. He and Dodger only look like literal gods from the outside."

"I have seen her turn off the gravity in a room because she was trying to make a point," says David, torn between patience and laughing hysterically. "The point was 'When I call you for dinner, you come to dinner.' She turned off gravity because Kim and Tim were *late to dinner*. If that's not the behavior of a literal god, I don't know what is."

"Okay, yeah, she can get a little show-off-y sometimes. It's mostly an insecurity response. Roger's abilities are a lot more consistent and difficult to turn off. I can promise you that right now he's downstairs having a little panic attack at her, and going back over every conversation we've ever had, looking for a moment where he said something like 'and that's why you love me.' Because if he said that, I *would* love him, whether I wanted to or not. I wouldn't have a choice. That's how it works for Roger. He speaks truth into the universe. Not all truths—he can't say 'All quartz is actually ice cream' and totally rework the Earth's crust on a whim or anything. But if he said 'This specific piece of quartz is actually cake,' he might be able to eat it after. Reality wants to listen to him, on a molecular level. It makes relationships with people who aren't his sister really, really hard for him."

"He can't influence her like that?"

"He can. He just knows that if he does, she'll turn off the gravity to make him regret it. They have their own system for keeping things on an even keel. I sort of screwed all that up."

"How?"

Judy shrugs. "I showed up. I was human enough to be interesting, and divine enough to be semi-safe when that wasn't something he'd been able to say about anyone other than his sister in a very long time. His last real relationship before me was with Erin."

David jerks like he's been stabbed with a needle. "Erin? Creepy-blonde-lady-who-lives-downstairs Erin? The incarnate force of order?"

"That's the one."

David's face contorts as he tries to picture this, working his way mentally through several possible configurations before finally landing on a desperate "*How?*"

"He didn't know what she was at the time. He didn't know what *he* was at the time. Something about the way her incarnation works makes her more resistant to the Wonder Twins than the rest of us tend to be—she can actually resist him, at least enough that she was able to sleep with him in order to keep an eye on him for a lot longer than any normal person would be able to manage. But finding out that she'd been pretending to be in love with him so she could spy on him for the alchemists kind of did a number on his heart. He's terrified of hurting me. I've tried and tried to make him understand that Chang'e would tell me if he was manipulating us, but he just says no one stopped the alchemists from hurting Artemis like that's some sort of gotcha. Like one of the most powerful Lunars in our pantheon dealing with a man who's actively trying *not* to hurt her is the same thing as a terrified teenager and a human monster." Judy pauses. "Are we sure James Reed was human?"

"No?" says David. "I don't actually know who that is."

Judy blinks. "Sometimes I forget how recently you manifested. I'll do the 'famous alchemists and why we hate them' slideshow next time we have a get-together that's *not* in my boyfriend's library, okay?"

"Okay," says David. "I really am sorry."

"No, you're not," says Judy. She smiles, thin as a razor. "But you will be." She walks past him to the door, clearly heading downstairs.

After a momentary hesitation, he follows.

Divination

TIMELINE: AUGUST 21, 2018.

They reach the bottom of the stairs to find the house awake all around them. The smell of curry wafts from the kitchen, and the sound of teenage voices arguing loudly about something that sounds like *Mario Kart* drifts out of the living room. Erin, the aforementioned creepy blonde, is waiting by the front door. She's leaning against it, actually, blocking it from use, her arms folded over her chest and her unsettlingly blue eyes fixed on the ceiling, like she's performing an oracular reading of the swirls in the plaster.

David slows, until he reaches the floor an easy eight feet behind Judy, who's walking up to Erin like there's nothing wrong with approaching the scariest woman in the world. (Dodger can manipulate the laws of physics like a champ, but Erin? Erin will just stab you. Over and over again. And then she'll wash the blood out from under her fingernails. Worst of all, she'll never stop smiling, not even when the police show up to cart your corpse away—and somehow, no matter how much blood winds up on her clothing, she'll never get caught.)

Erin's disinterested gaze flicks from the ceiling down to Judy as she approaches. "So you finally came downstairs."

"I had to finish talking to my colleague before I could exactly walk away," says Judy, voice calm and level. "Hello, Erin. You're looking less homicidal than usual today."

"Thus proving that looks can deceive, because I'm feeling more homicidal than usual," says Erin. "Isn't it funny how things sometimes work out that way? I wanted to have a word with you before you left."

"I thought you might."

"Roger's . . ." Erin's eyes flick to the kitchen doorway, then back to Judy. "He's a special boy."

"I knew that."

"No, see, after today, I'm not so sure you did. Roger isn't one of your little Lunars, who's going to be all honored by you deciding to pay attention to him. He's a basic function of the universe. We still don't know what happens if you break half the Doctrine."

"Good thing I wasn't planning on breaking him."

Erin lifts an eyebrow. "Really," she says, voice becoming a flat drawl. It isn't a question. It isn't quite a statement, either. It's a grammatical oddity, sarcasm made audible and painfully heavy.

"Really," says Judy, with absolute conviction.

"Maybe you should tell *Roger* that," says Erin. "He's in his office right now, sulking like the enormous twit he's occasionally determined to be. You two staying for dinner?"

"Depends on who's cooking," says Judy. She looks around. "I know where Roger is, and I can hear the kids. That just leaves—"

"Smita is cooking," says Erin. "None of us want toast and botulism for dinner."

Judy nods.

David has only experienced Dodger's cooking once; usually when there's company she just sets up assembly lines of sandwich fixings and lets people get on with things on their own. He doesn't really remember the time she made dinner for them. He's either blotted it out intentionally or one of the Doctrine helpfully edited his memories to make eating easier for him. Either way, he's happy to join Judy in nodding his agreement with Erin's statement.

"You two play nice," says Judy, looking between the pair before she turns and walks down the short hall to Roger's office. A quick knock later and she's slipping through the door, out of sight.

David turns his attention back to Erin, smiling uneasily. "Hey," he says.

"Hey," she replies, sounding utterly disinterested. "Does this mean you're staying for dinner?"

"It smells good, so yeah, if I'm invited, I'm down to stick around."

She rolls her eyes. "I didn't say you were *invited*, I just asked if you were staying."

"In most houses, that would be the same thing."

"Would it, really? Or do you just take it that way, and count on people being too polite to contradict you?"

David's still trying to figure out his answer when the shouting from the front room reaches a fever pitch and Erin points to the open doorway, a dour look on her face. "You, go," she says. "You were their age fifteen minutes ago, whatever that age actually *is*. Maybe you can keep them from killing each other."

David laughs, and Máni laughs with him, stirring in the darkness of David's hidden heart to remind him that he was once followed across the sky by a pair of children whose mythological significance has been so diluted and forgotten that they no longer manifest. He misses them, Hjúki and Bil, and if he has any regrets about becoming David, it's only that David has no children or younger siblings of his own, leaving Máni with no one to take care of.

You'll make a great dad someday, thinks David, and he means it. He does want kids, and it's hard to think of Máni as being anything other than a fantastic father when he gets the chance.

He's a little surprised when the only reply he receives is a feeling of overwhelming sorrow, weighted heavily down by regret. He doesn't have time to press further, because he's already stepping into the living room, where the teenagers on the battered brown canvas couch freeze at the sight of him, the boy's hand still pressed flat against the girl's cheek where he was shoving her away. They're both clutching video game controllers, the wired kind, connecting them to the console under the television.

The living room is another of the house's many oddities. It has at least four different, mutually exclusive appearances, which it rotates through depending on the needs of the household. There's the one with the leather furniture and all the bookcases, which has been seen less and less frequently since the library was finished; there's the one with the whiteboards and the bare walls covered with careful equations written in erasable marker; there's the one with the big central table, and there's the one that currently exists, with the comfy-looking couch that could have been stolen from the early seventies, the statistically normal number of bookcases containing a slightly statistically abnormal number of books (some things can't be helped) about things like popular culture, local history, and the flora of California, and the massive entertainment center currently being used by the two resident teens to take out their bloodthirsty impulses without actually needing to clean the rugs.

"In my day, we just skipped straight to *Mortal Kombat*," says David, strolling over to squish himself onto the couch with the pair. "Less chaos, but plenty of opportunities to decapitate each other."

"We're not supposed to play violent video games," says the boy, dark brown hair flopping down to half-cover his pale, whiskey-brown eyes. They're as unnerving as Roger and Dodger's eyes, in their own special way.

Designer people. Sometimes David wishes he could meet the

man who built half this household, just for a brief conversation. But Roger and Dodger got there a long time before he came into the picture, and from the stories he told, they didn't leave much of the man for him to have a conversation with.

Pity.

The two teens are definitely twins: coloring aside, they have almost-identical faces, and they're still the same height, despite the vagrancies of puberty working its will on them. The girl's hair is white with a distinct undertone of cornsilk green. If she were paying to have it dyed that color, her stylist would be a genius. Since she's not, and since her hair refuses to take dye of any kind, her genetics are cruel. She'll always stand out in a crowd, much like Dodger does; she'll always be a target. The people created to embody the Math side of the Doctrine are supposed to draw fire away from their Language counterparts, and they didn't get a say in the matter.

Their names are Kimberley and Timothy, but everyone calls them Kim and Tim, the rhymes rolling easily off their tongues. It's only since the alchemists were basically driven out of Berkeley that the two have relaxed enough to begin fighting like normal siblings, arguing in the halls and slaughtering each other in pixelated dream worlds. David's not sure he understands the appeal of video games for the pair. The world they live in day by day is brighter and more fantastic in a lot of days—although they're still attending normal high school with normal human students, so they probably have a lot of stress to work through.

"We only have two controllers," says Tim, taking his hand off Kim's face and leaning away from her on the couch.

"That's cool." David shrugs. "I'll play loser."

"Isn't it normally 'I'll play winner'?" asks Kim.

"Yeah, but that just means the winner gets to keep playing, while the loser has to sit around feeling bad about losing. If I play loser, maybe they can win, and things keep changing up. It's not more fair—someone's still sitting out every round—but I think it's more fun."

The twins exchange a complex look before returning their attention to him. "You're weird," says Kim.

David shrugs again. "I'm a Moon. We're supposed to be a little weird. This world was built for humans, and we're just shining on it."

And that, right there, is the real appeal of this weird house and the weird people it contains: nowhere else in the world can he look at a pair of non-Lunar teens and bluntly state what he is without being called delusional, or worse. There's a freedom in being able to be truly open about his identity with people who aren't already poised to shine down over the Impossible City, in being *believed*. There's an almost drunken joy in the absence of cynicism.

"Judy's a Moon," says Tim. "She's dating Roger."

"Are you here because you're going to start dating Dodger?" asks Kim. "Or because you think you're going to start dating Dodger? Because you may want to reconsider that. Dodger doesn't date."

"Totally aware, don't date women who are scarier than I am, but thanks for looking out for me," says David easily. Their video-game avatars are moving again, racing faster and faster in their tireless pursuit of the finish line. "I am happily single, and enjoying the swinging life of a college football hero. It's not the worst position to be in, trust me." He pauses, coughs into his hand. "I mean, er. Study and get good grades and then when you get to college you can study more and get more good grades, and go into academia like your . . . I still don't know what to call them in relation to you."

"We like 'guardians,'" says Tim. "Legally, that's what they are. Biologically, they're our closest living relatives, so there's that, but they're closer to siblings than aunt and uncle, and there's no room in their lives for any more brothers or sisters. So go with 'guardians.' You're right about the academia, though. I don't think I could be happy anywhere else."

"Me, either," says Kim grimly.

"You don't sound like you believe that," says David.

She shrugs. On the screen, her little cartoon car is knocked off the rails by one of the computer-controlled racers. It falls, hitting the ground below with a sickeningly metallic crunch, then bursts into pixelated flames.

David is pretty sure it's not supposed to do that. If he listens closely, he can even hear her character avatar screaming. Kim puts her controller primly on her knee, eyes remaining fixed on the screen as she watches her brother circle the track. Her character doesn't respawn.

With only one active player left, the game is over quickly, confetti cannons erupting as cheery balloon words spell out *TIM WINS!* across the bottom of the screen. He dutifully hands David his controller, then gets off the couch.

"I'm going to go see when dinner will be ready," he says, and exits the living room with more speed than is strictly necessary—but then, he's a teenage boy. He may not be a particularly athletic one, but David remembers his own teenage years, which aren't so far behind him as to have become anything other than crystal clear. There were days when it felt like his legs didn't know *how* to walk, like there was a lever somewhere deep inside the machinery of his body that had been permanently jammed in the "run" position.

He almost misses those days, now that his body is figuring out how to slow down. He's young and strong and has all the stamina he could ask for, but learning how to walk when he could be running still feels like the first step toward learning how to get old.

He waits for the sound of Tim's footsteps to fade before lifting the controller and pressing the start button to launch the next round. "Everything okay with you two?" he asks.

"Yes," says Kim, automatically. Then she sighs, and amends, "No. I don't know anymore. We know where we came from, right?"

"Same lab as built Roger and Dodger, right?"

"Same researchers, same research, different lab," corrects Kim. "As if that part matters anymore. No one has our records. No one holds our patents."

"And that's probably for the best," says David. He's trying to cheer her up without intentionally deciding that's what needs to happen: he can hear it in his own voice, which means she can probably hear it too, hear the soft desperation to keep her from crawling any deeper into the hole she's tearing open in her own heart. "My mom used to say the world was wonderful with one of me, but one was exactly the right number. Two would be too many: none would be too few."

"There's *already* two of me," says Kim, with audible frustration. "No matter how you want to divide things, there's two of me. Tim and I are genetically identical, Dodger and I are both mortal manifestations of Math, even if she's the only one who gets to do the *job.* I have never been a singular person in my entire life."

"That has to be hard."

She gives him a withering look. Every teenage girl he's ever known has been capable of looking at him like he's the slime beneath their shoes, but she's perfected the art; he wants to slink away to think about what he's done somewhere that she can't see. Actually . . . the strength of that impulse makes him pause and look at her more keenly.

Her withering look morphs into a frown. "What?" she asks.

"You're pretty much baseline normal human these days, right? Since Dodger seized your half of the Doctrine?"

Kim looks momentarily uncomfortable. "We should really be more focused on the game."

"No, we shouldn't." He pauses the race, his own cartoon avatar freezing mid-lap, and twists on the couch to face her. “We should be focused on whatever it is you’re worried about.”

Kim sags back into the couch cushions, eyes locked on the screen. “You’re an incarnate god, right?”

“We call ourselves Lunars, or Moons when we’re being informal, but yeah.”

“Why? It sounds just as silly.”

David shrugs. “I don’t know. It’s what we sort of collectively settled on, at least this century, and it works for us. I am one current mortal incarnation of the Norse god of the moon. I’m not the only one. Máni isn’t confined to just me. He’s everywhere, like the moonlight or the wind.” At least five other places that David knows of for sure. There’s no divine hivemind between people who share the same divinity, no group chat or anything of the like, but the local pantheons talk to one another, and he’s heard of Mánis in other regions. Judy says they’re all obnoxious blockheads. He’s starting to take that to mean she likes him. She’s not nice to anyone.

Except for Roger, he assumes, and he’s seen the two of them verbally ripping strips off of each other whenever they get the chance. He can’t follow it more than half the time, because they don’t restrict themselves to English, but it has to mean *something*.

“And being an incarnate god means you have somebody else in your head with you, like, all the time?”

“Yes,” he says hesitantly. He’s really not sure where she’s going with this, or what she’s going to do when she finally gets there. It feels like he’s walking into a trap of some sort. He just can’t see the mechanism well enough to see it closing around him.

Kim’s smile is sudden and terrible, the rictus of a cornered, feral animal. “It used to be like that for me and Tim. From the time we were born, we were inside each other’s heads. Sometimes I only knew for sure that I was Kim because he’d go to sleep and I’d be able to feel the limits of my own skin until he woke up. We were barely two people. We were *never* alone. And then Roger and Dodger took their mantle. Took *our* mantle. Imagine that there could only ever be one Máni at a time, and as soon as someone else became Máni, you wouldn't be anymore."

David shudders. "That sounds like a very targeted horror movie."

"Doesn't it?" She shrugs, keeping her eyes on the screen, even though their cheery cartoon avatars aren't moving, aren't racing, aren't doing anything worth watching. She doesn't seem to care. "One moment everything's normal, and then the next everything's ripped away from you, you're alone in your head when you've never ever been alone ever before, not even for a second, not even when you might have wanted to be. The silence is so loud that it's the same thing as screaming." Her voice is dispassionate, not shifting tones or registers even as she continues. "And there's no putting things back the way they're supposed to be. You can't tell Máni you're sorry or make him come back, and even if you could, you'd be a monster for doing it. Because the person he is now needs him even more than you do. Doesn't know how to be a person without him. There's no way for you to put yourself back together. You just have to learn how to live with being broken, and if you can't, that's just too bad, because the person who's responsible for keeping you alive takes his job very, very seriously."

David hesitates before he asks his next question. It feels like tossing a live grenade into the middle of a book club, like setting an explosive charge he doesn't want to see going off. "Kim, did you try to hurt yourself?"

"No." Her laughter is a brittle, terrifying thing. "I can't."

"What do you mean?"

"I mean I can't hurt myself on purpose. I can't even stay up too late, or my eyes start closing on their own. I can use a knife to cut my dinner, but if I think about using it on myself, I can't move my arms. I can't drink alcohol or even take an ibuprofen if I'm getting too close to the overdose line. I can't hurt myself. Neither can Tim. Roger won't let us."

That sounds . . . David frowns. He can't decide how it sounds. Keeping a pair of depressed, distressed teenagers from hurting themselves sounds like a good thing, but it also sounds like mind control, and he's pretty sure that mind control is always a bad thing. People should be able to make their own decisions, and taking that away from them puts you in the same box as all the other villains.

He doesn't like to think that Roger might be a villain. Judy's sort of his boss, in a sideways kind of way, and she loves Roger, or Chang'e wouldn't have said she did. Judy shouldn't love a villain. They're supposed to be the good guys.

"I'm sorry he did that to you," he finally says, awkwardly. "I'll talk to him. Or, well. I'll talk to Judy, and *she'll* talk to him. Maybe she can get Roger to stop controlling what you can and can't do."

"She can't," says Kim. "Dodger hurt herself once, really badly. It was before we were even born—her hurting herself is part of what made Mr. Reed decide that Tim and I were needed. They've gone back and tried their own pasts a whole bunch of times since they manifested, trying to get it right and make things as close to perfect as they possibly can. But not everything can *be* perfect. If you're going to need calluses because you have to walk on sharp rocks in order to save yourself, you're going to need to build them up."

"Meaning . . . ?"

"Meaning they have to leave some of the bad things in their history alone. They can't make it so that they never get split up, or so Roger doesn't have a bad breakup with his first girlfriend—or so Dodger never hurts herself." Kim finally turns and looks at David, eyes bright with anger and defiance. "She *has* to hurt herself, or they never grow up to be the people they have to be in order to take the Doctrine away from the alchemists, even if that means taking it away from us, too. And because she *has* to hurt herself, Roger gets to always be afraid one of us is *going* to hurt ourselves, even if we don't want to. Even if we never would. Her past informs my future. Forever."

"I'm sorry," says David. It's not enough. It's what he has.

"Whatever," says Kim. She drops her controller onto the couch and rises, leaving the room just as Erin comes in, watching the girl go with a flat, disinterested expression.

She turns to David. "Dinner's ready," she says.

"Thank you," he replies, not sure what else he's supposed to say. He puts his own controller down and rises.

Time to eat.

* * *

The kitchen table isn't large enough for eight people. David knows that. It seats them all, all the same, with room for their plates and drinks—milk for most of them, iced tea for Judy and Smita, coffee for Roger.

The curry is beautiful, a deep red shot through with veins of golden ghee, chunks of chicken and onion breaking the surface like gemstones breaking through lava. There's naan, hot and soft and rich with garlic and cilantro, and heaping bowls of rice, one for each half of the table. Smita sets each of the dishes on its own individual hot pad, protecting the wood and cushioning the food at the same time, and no one moves to serve themselves until she's settled and spooning rice onto her own plate. Only then do they begin passing the basket of naan around the table, taking their pieces with approving noises.

Judy beams at Smita. "This is all lovely. And it smells amazing."

"You only say that because you can't cook," says Smita, amused.

"Not true. I can make Pop-Tarts. And I made an omelet last week that didn't come with a side order of setting the kitchen on fire."

Everyone fills their plates. David sits back and watches as the people around him eat and bicker and interact. Roger keeps "accidentally" bumping Judy with his elbow, which causes her to stop chewing and shoot him frankly besotted looks which Dodger ostentatiously ignores. Kim and Tim steal bits off one another's plates, while Erin manages to get the exact right ratio of curry and rice in every single spoonful. Not a single drop of sauce falls on her clothing, each one landing obediently back in the middle of her plate. It's companionable and homely and surreally normal, which shouldn't be possible, since everyone at this table has been touched by the preternatural in one way or another.

(Even Smita, who is perfectly normal on the surface, has had her encounters with the alchemical world. It killed her. Dozens and dozens and hundreds of times. In every timeline David has heard of, she discovered that Roger and Dodger were genetically identical, twins in every way but gender, something that shouldn't have been possible, and in every timeline except for this one, she died for that knowledge. Erin would receive orders from her masters, go to Smita's lab, and kill her. But Erin is the only one who could remember the loops without outside intervention. She's the natural force of Order, forced into a human skin and made to walk the world. Her very soul resisted the disorderly way they were rewriting the universe. And when Roger and Dodger became strong enough to resist their own masters, Erin was able to twist her orders hard enough to let her spare Smita. Her best friend. Her penance.)

When dinner's over, he lingers to help Erin clean up the kitchen while the others scatter through the house and out into the garden. He doesn't want to think about what Judy and Roger might be doing out there in the dark. It's not that he's jealous—he's not—it's just that he doesn't like to consider his superior's sex life, especially not when it might involve the porch swing he sometimes sits on. So he gathers the dishes and carries them to the sink, watching Erin portion the leftovers into sealed plastic containers and tuck them away in the fridge.

He waits until she turns back in his direction before he asks, "Hey, Erin, do you know anything about Roger, um . . ."

"Manipulating the twins to prevent them from doing anything that can't be undone without resetting reality again?" she asks, cool as an evening in October. She walks over to the sink, bumping him out of the way with her hip before turning on the water. "You know he wouldn't give an actual *order* without good reason to think that he needs to."

"I know, but forcing someone to do—or not do—something is sort of shitty, and feels like the kind of thing the other side does, not us. We're supposed to be better than this."

"Are we?" asks Erin, looking at him with one eyebrow raised. "Who says?"

David doesn't really have an answer for that. He sighs and fetches another stack of plates, setting them on the sink next to her. Then he pauses, her words finally fully sinking in.

"Wait," he says. "Again?"

Erin nods, adding soap to her half-filled sink and beginning to add the dishes. "Again. You don't think Roger went straight for the nuclear option, do you? No, don't answer that, of course you do. To you, he's just this terrifying figure who isn't technically supposed to exist—artificial incarnations are scary when you've been around as long as Máni has. I mean, hell. I *am* an artificial incarnation, and sometimes those two manage to scare *me*. I think I know more about what they're capable of than they do, and not all of it is awesome. But let me tell you a little bit about Roger Middleton. I've known him since we were both grad students, I'm pretty sure I'm qualified."

David doesn't say anything. This is a rare opportunity to learn more about the man his senior is involved with, *without* needing to ask her directly. He's not going to do anything that might make her change her mind.

"He's a nerd. They're both nerds, but for Dodger, 'nerd' was defined by being almost totally alone, all the time, forever. She didn't do friends when she was younger. She didn't do socialization. She did . . . math. It was different for Roger. He joined pub quizzes and went to baseball games and attended literary conventions and library conferences. He met other nerds, and he built relationships with them. He's still maintaining some of those friendships, even when Dodger would rather he didn't. She was alone for so long that she's selfish with the people she cares about. He wasn't. He's protective of them, because he's scared *for* them. He needs to know that they're all right."

"That makes sense," says David, thinking of the things Kim told him, of the pale scars he's seen on Dodger's arms when she relaxed enough to forget to be self-conscious about them. "I can't imagine Dodger would take losing them any better than he would."

Erin actually laughs, the sound thin and flat, like it's been pressed until it lost all joy. "She didn't. She wouldn't. So they have to keep surviving, even if they don't want to, because no one wants to see what happens when she melts all the way down."

David hesitates before asking the only question he has left: "How many times?"

"Can't be sure, I don't remember everything unless it actually concerns me, but at least five," says Erin, dunking another plate in the sink. "It varies which one of them it is, and we're going to have to find a solution sooner or later, because the silence is eating them alive. But as long as they *are* alive, the silence can have a full belly, and the world will keep on turning."

Sometimes David forgets how fragile reality really is.

And sometimes he remembers.

* * *

In a laboratory that's almost more like a bunker, made of concrete infused with godsblood and the ashes of the dead, only silence stirs.

This place has been sealed away for a year, left to be forgotten after the alchemists who had been working in Berkeley fled the city, chased away by their own creations and by an entire pantheon of angry Lunar deities. Leaving may have been the smartest thing they ever did, as it meant some of them were able to get out while they were still breathing.

(The ones who didn't were collected and repurposed by the ones who did. There is no retirement in the alchemical world. Only recycling, into smaller and smaller versions of the self, carved up and portioned out by the survivors.)

The long corridors stand empty, the rooms echo with silence, shadows gathering on every flat surface. And yet there are no cobwebs in the corners, no dust on the abandoned equipment, no small scuttling things with dozens upon dozens of legs scurrying through the shadows. Water drips from a cracked pipe in one of the main lab areas, collecting drop by drop. It has already filled the room to a level of almost two feet, but there is no mold, no fungus, and nothing seeks to claim the artificial pool as its new kingdom. There are very few true dead zones in the world, few places where no forms of life can find a foothold. This has become one of them.

Once, people lived here. Worked here. Even thrived here. Once, this was a center for learning and terrible innovations. Everything ended in an hour, and is still over, still settling into the grave of its own ambitions.

The sound of metal scraping against stone is almost offensive as it cuts through the stillness, too loud and unforgivable to be permitted. In the deepest dark at the back of the largest lab, something stirs.

It does not live. It does not dream. But it awakens.

Bit by bit, it uncurls its spindly limbs. Bit by bit, it unmakes its own mausoleum. It is neither ghost nor ghast, is something undefinable and impossible, and the fruition of a plan put in place so very long ago that there is no accounting for the changes between here and now.

It turns, slowly, to consider its dead and frozen kingdom. It will find no restoration here.

Silent, it slides into the water without a ripple. Now is the time to rest and recover. Whatever will come will come. The future can still be changed, and the past . . . the past will remain a foundation on which to build every thing that follows.

Imperfection

TIMELINE: DECEMBER 3, 1881.

It has been nine years since John Baker swept down on a small village in the forested wilds of Massachusetts and snatched up the niece he barely knew like a diving kestrel snatches a mouse from the grass, clutching her tightly in his talons and sweeping her away from everything she'd ever known. Nine years of lessons and lies, nine years of the strangest drought ever to take hold of Boston. The servants complain about it constantly, with no small amount of smugness in their tones; his property has always included a luxuriously large greenhouse, the walls made of thick-paneled glass that amplifies and focuses the sun.

More importantly, because the greenhouse is enclosed, inside, he's able to control the weather. The air is always hot and moist, and herbs and simples thrive in the near-tropical conditions he creates. If only half of them are for use in the kitchen, no one has to know that but his staff, who would never dream of commenting. They have rosemary and basil for their table while the houses around them go without, no matter how wealthy their masters might be, and if they also have foxglove and nettles and dead man's trumpets, well, those are easy enough not to harvest for the stew.

Asphodel—she has been Asphodel now for longer than she was Floretta, and on the rare occasions she has to remember the name she once went by, she regards it with curiosity and some small measure of disdain, like a snake might regard its shed and rotting former skin—walks the greenhouse most mornings, preferring the humid warmth of the world inside the glass to the punishing sun of the world outside. She is a hothouse flower in her own manner these days, rarely seen outside without a parasol to cover her head and keep the sun away.

(Even in times of drought there must be rain. It thundered last summer, just before her fifteenth birthday, and she spent the full duration of the storm in the backyard, dancing in the rain like she had no idea when she was ever going to see it again. She's always seemed most alive during storms. John has watched her when he's had the chance, when he wasn't struggling to harness the storm to his own ends. She's always lovely, his strange orphan niece, but when the rain comes down and the heavens split wide, he thinks she might be beautiful. He thinks her beauty might be the kind that destroys the world.)

Nine years in his keeping has trained a wild woodland nymph into a respectable Boston socialite, sixteen years old and set to make her debut into society in just two years more. Her hair is still copper, tamed into thick curls that cascade over her shoulders and down her back; her eyes are still layered blue like river water running over stones. If her tongue is also sharp enough to flense skin from flesh, and her clever hands more suited to scalpels than embroidery needles, those things don't show in her face, and she's well-trained enough to keep her mouth shut and smiling when she has to.

Asphodel will never be an alchemist in her own right—her femininity is too indelible, and cannot be stripped out of her through any means he's been able to discover, even when she's begged him, voice raw and aching in the air. But she'll make a fabulous alchemist's wife once he's had the chance to break her to the idea.

There have been no Moons since Deborah, although the little room has been far from unused; his art requires a certain amount of blood and bone, and a winsome teenage girl is a fabulous lure for a hunter. They've dismantled several unlucky souls in that same space, portioning them into canopic jars and white glass vials, and Asphodel has always been eager in her work, always cunning-handed and more than willing to bloody her pretty, slender hands.

Now, morning has broken on a dry, frozen December day. Lines of ice slash across the grounds, but there is no snow. Snow, which is only frozen water in the end, has been in short supply these last few years. The trees are suffering.

At the request of his groundskeeper, John has consulted with the local rainmaker, a toothless old alchemist who used to live in farm country, where he made his fortune calling rain out of empty clouds. The man is famous in certain circles, for his ability to control the weather. He wasn't able to summon up so much as a drizzle.

"Something's taken a dislike to Boston," he said, almost leering. "Something doesn't think we deserve the rain. Can't say what it was, or who, but something has it out for us, and won't let me through. There's powers greater than alchemy in this world." His eyes turned canny then, focusing on John. "This all started about when you brought that girl of yours home. Could be a virgin sacrifice would break through the wall."

"We're men of science, not superstition," John snapped in return. "Asphodel is a good girl with a good head on her shoulders. She's going to make a fine alchemist's wife one day, and whoever wins her hand is likely to climb to the height of our field solely on the basis of her support. We're not . . . slitting her throat to bring back the storms. The notion is absurd."

"There's something connecting her to the strangeness in the weather. If we snap that connection, things may return to normal."

"I came here to request rain, not discuss the sacrifice of my ward. This conversation is over."

He'd stood then, leaving his brandy behind as he turned and stormed out of the old alchemist's office, leaving him and his outdated old ways behind.

That was almost two months ago. The old man's house burned down a week after their meeting, the rainmaker still inside. It was the sort of accident that makes the papers for days after, a true tragedy, especially since all the homes surrounding his were left untouched by the flames, which had been intense enough to devour the structure whole.

The idea of arson was never suggested. No one had been seen going into or coming out of the old rainmaker's house all day, and that sort of fire would have been impossible to orchestrate without someone on-site. Miss Cottingsly had smelt of lamp oil and smoke for days afterward, and had been required to stay in the kitchen when the constabulary came to inform John of his colleague's death, out of the path of anyone who might have had their suspicions raised.

It perhaps says something about John's character that he thought murder was a perfectly measured response to the mere suggestion that Asphodel might be part of the force keeping Boston drier than a bone, and could serve them best by being removed. She is *his*, his property from stem to stern, and until he hands her to another man for safekeeping, he won't tolerate even the impression of a threat against her.

He can't.

But this is December, and Asphodel walks the back garden alone, slipping out of the kitchen door with her shawl pulled tight around her shoulders, heading for the greenhouse. John watches her from the dining room window until she vanishes around the glass corner of her destination. Only then does he look away. He won't be able to see her once she's inside. He never can.

And so he doesn't see when, upon getting out of sight of the house, she shrugs her shawl off and hangs it on the skeletal structure of a nearby bush, turning toward the fence. Dried-out ivy clings to it, some of the leaves still a dark, waxy green, all of them laced with frost. Even in the absence of snow, the cold comes.

There is an old gate in the fence, half-covered by the ivy, long since locked by the groundskeeper and given over to the tangled, matted vines. She's not sure her uncle has ever known the gate was there; it existed before he bought this house, and it opens onto a narrow stretch of green between their property and the next, a boxed-off remnant of an older arcade that must have been among the first structures in Boston before it was forgotten and left to fall to ruin. She discovered the gate through discovering the arcade, following the shapes of broken arches from the sidewalk to the back of the block, taking note of the shape they made between the houses.

She can escape from the property whenever she wants to, and only the fact that her uncle provides her with everything she could ever wish for keeps her from running. When she was Floretta, she would have run without hesitation, fleeing back to the forest and the doddering old priest who'd had the custody of her early childhood. Now, the gate serves another purpose.

As she watches, it inches slowly open, and a man—a boy—no, a man is revealed. His hair is black as midnight, spangled with specks of ice like tiny, shining stars, and his eyes are the color of the frost on the ivory, white layered over green. He's wearing a summer suit, not at all appropriate for this weather, and his smile when he sees Asphodel is as warm as the summer sun.

"Hello, pretty sparrow," he says, voice rich with the developing accent spoken in the bright young state of Maine, a region still finding its identity in the snowy lands below the Canadian border. It's French and New England and a little bit of broad Appalachia. She thinks he sounds incredible. She could listen to him speak forever if she had the chance.

She's not going to have the chance. She knows that, and she accepts it. For right now, she smiles and drops one shoulder, tilting her chin toward the other, the gesture practiced and coy and designed to show the long pale sweep of her neck, graceful and lethal as a swan's.

"Hello, Charles," she replies, smiling at him, and oh, it's wonderful to stand out here in the crisp cold air and look at a boy—a man—a boy her own age, one with a broad chest and strong hands, who smiles at her like she's a miracle he doesn't deserve and never could. Her uncle wouldn't approve if he knew, she's certain of that: in his eyes she's still seven years old and newly arrived in Boston, helpless and naïve and vulnerable to every danger the city has to throw at her.

Charles is no danger. He's the son of a fur trader from the high border, raised in snow and timber, and the snow follows in his wake. He's not the Winter King, not the king of anything, but he might have been in another lifetime, were the position not being so jealously guarded by the man who currently holds it. He's handsome and he's brave and he's mostly human, and he recognized her as his equal the moment that he saw her.

Neither of them has any fear of a coronation, not in their lifetimes, and without a crown or a labyrinth to walk, he's just a man. And there's nothing of the supernatural about her, nothing of the alchemical, even if she sometimes feels the storm fronts passing overhead in the marrow of her bones, even if her skin sings when the lightning flashes. They're perfect together.

Charles Booker is her first love. His name is thunder on her tongue, his hands are storms against her skin, and when she hurries to him in the shelter of the greenhouse, and he puts those hands around her waist, he holds her like she's the most fragile, most delicate thing the world has ever known. He holds her like she's precious.

She's not used to that sort of treatment. She's been a trinket to be traded and a pupil to be taught, but she's never been a prize to be held on to. It's intoxicating, thinking that she might have some value that's intrinsic to *her*, that can't be taken away. That this princeling, this scion of Winter, might be able to see what no one's ever seen before.

Asphodel reaches up to trace her fingers along the soft skin of his cheek. He shaved before coming to see her—he always shaves before coming to see her, he has for the last six months, and she's sure he'd keep doing it forever if he thought it would make her smile.

"Did you find what I asked you for?" she asks, barely managing to mask her eagerness.

Charles's perfect lips draw downward in a frown. "I asked everyone who might know, all the Jennies, all the Jacks, and none of them could tell me anything about why the rain avoids Boston," he says. "I even tracked down an incarnation of Artemis, running wild through the woods near my family's home, but she couldn't tell me anything worth hearing. She said the sky over Boston was forbidden to everything but the Moon until the storm settled. But the trouble is that there's no storm. I have no idea what's going on."

Asphodel sighs. It couldn't have been this easy. She'd known that from the beginning, but still, she'd allowed herself to hope, if only for a moment. If he could solve the storms, end the drought, then he would be useful enough as he is. As a man. As the man she loves. He's young and he's strong and he's earnest and she wants to spend her life with him, and she knows she can't possibly do that, that it was never an option, because she needs him for other things.

"Oh, Charles." She slides her other hand up to join the first, so that her palms cup his cheeks, her fingers spread out like she's trying to hold his entire face at the same time. "You promised you would find the answers I was looking for."

"And I tried, sweet love, I tried," he says, grasping her wrists and pulling her closer to him. "I asked everyone I could think of, without alerting the alchemists."

Asphodel grimaces. She wanted to do this the easy way. Uncle John says that's her greatest weakness, aside from her sex: she always wants to do things the easy way when she can, like hard work is some sort of danger to be avoided as often as possible. Having Charles find the reasons behind this unholy drought would have been easy.

If he can't . . . she loves him. She loves him with the bright, fierce passion of a girl who has never loved anyone like this before. She loves her uncle in a distant, almost clinical way: she loves Miss Cottingsly the way a person might love a dangerous animal, a dog inclined to biting or a wolf brought in from the wilds. But Charles she loves as a woman loves a man, and it's such a new experience that she wants to savor it forever. She wants to keep him.

She can't keep him.

She draws him down for a kiss, their first, her lips pressed soft and warm to his. He tastes like maple-sugar candy made in the first snows of winter, and he pulls her closer still, holding her tight. As he does, she moves her foot, heel coming down on the small stick she placed there earlier this morning. The sound it makes is terribly loud in the cool, still air, and he jerks away, eyes searching the garden around them for some sign of an observer, some hint they're not alone.

"Asphodel?" he whispers.

She keeps her chin raised and her eyes on his face. His sweet, perfect face. "Yes, Charles?" she asks.

"Your uncle . . . he doesn't suspect us, does he?"

"No," she says, and she speaks with absolute honesty—her uncle has nothing to suspect. Her uncle knows about Charles, knows about the potential Winter she's been courting under his nose, knows she would never have told him had she not been convinced he was going to fail in his quest to bring back the rain. They have an agreement, she and her uncle. If Charles came back with answers, he would be spared.

Sadly, he did not. Sadly, she will have to bid her sweet love farewell.

"Good." He exhales, offering her a wavering smile. "I do not like to speak ill of your family, for I know you care for him, as he cares for you, but . . . alchemists are dangerous creatures, my darling girl. They think themselves lords of reality on the basis of a few lines of text written in their books, inkpot gods who would control or unmake us all upon their whim."

"Inkpot gods, are they?" she asks, and she can't keep the frost from her own voice at that question. He hears it—apparently even sons of Winter can be chilled, under the right circumstances—and reels back, looking at her with wide, bewildered eyes. How like a calf he looks, when he stares at her like that. She was a village girl once. She knows what it is to live with barnyard animals.

She can't imagine loving one.

"Petty tyrants railing at reality's laws, I suppose?" She lowers her hands from his face, jabbing a finger at his chest. "You are speaking of my uncle, good sir. If you truly wished to marry me, as you have said you do, you would have to gain his blessing. And with the way you speak of him, I wouldn't dare to bring you before him to request it."

"Sweetest, I—"

"I am not an alchemist, but only because their precious Congress has no room for women. It's not my fault I was born a daughter when I could have been a son. Would that I were a man. I would dip my quill so deeply into the inkwell that there would be no other gods before me, and woe betide the man who rose to challenge me! But no, I must be a woman, and so they forbid me the art of alchemy, and I am reduced to lesser arts. I am reduced to *you*."

She steps back then, and if his absence is a blow to her senses, hers is a knife to his throat. He gasps as if suddenly deprived of air, his hands opening and closing on nothingness.

"Sweetest?" he halfway whispers.

"I love you, Charles," and it thrills her to say it so baldly, to offer the truth so boldly to the universe. "I have loved you since first you smiled at me, and this winter has been the sweetest I've known in all my sixteen years. But I played at flirtation because I needed to know why it will not rain, and you are inhuman enough that it seemed you might bring home the answer. You did not, and so it seems I must be quit of you."

He gasps again, his mouth remaining open in a silent scream. Asphodel looks at him impassively, watching as a bright red flower unfurls its spreading petals on the breast of his summer suit. He follows her gaze to his chest, and for a moment, he can only look bewildered. She's not even sure he knows that he's bleeding.

Then Miss Cottingsly pushes him forward, off the blade of her knife, and he crumples to the ground like so much discarded washing, a heavy bag of meat and bones and stillness. The diamonds in his hair begin to melt as soon as he falls, reacting to the lingering heat of his body.

Asphodel sighs.

"Take heart, sparrow, he was never the one for you," says Miss Cottingsly. The old housekeeper's voice has warmed considerably from the days after Asphodel's arrival; she speaks now like she actually cares about the girl, like she would be unhappy if something were to harm her.

That's the only thing about her that's changed. While Asphodel has gone from child to blossoming young woman, and her uncle has begun to gray at the temples, Miss Cottingsly remains precisely, stubbornly the same. Asphodel suspects she knows why. She's seen the stitches at the housekeeper's wrists and running down the back of her neck, seen the places where the skin has been patched so smoothly that there is no scar.

"He was so nice, though," she says plaintively.

"The frozen boys always are," says Miss Cottingsly. She rolls Charles's body over onto his back, then bends to hook her arm around his chest and hoist him up onto her shoulders, holding him as easily as a sack of flour. She either doesn't notice or doesn't care that he's leaking blood onto her shirt. "Did he find what you were looking for?"

"No," says Asphodel mulishly. "He said no one had the answers we needed."

"Chin up, Delly. It was a clean kill. He didn't suffer, and now your uncle will have something to keep him occupied until the thaw."

Asphodel sighs again as she turns away from the sight of her suitor slung across the housekeeper's shoulders. She feels so full of sighing that she might as well be the winter wind incarnate, even though she knows there's no such easy path for her. Even though she understands her own humanity. "And it's always best to buy his patience when it's available for sale."

"Clever girl," says Miss Cottingsly appropriately. She starts across the yard.

Asphodel follows after, hurrying until she's walking ahead of the other woman, as befits the lady of the house. Manners, after all, must be observed.

* * *

If John Baker is surprised by the speed with which Asphodel returns from her morning walk, he manages to conceal it quickly. He's less successful at concealing his shock when Miss Cottingsly appears with a dead man slung across her shoulders, barely two feet behind the remarkably calm teenage girl. He rises with unseemly haste, pursuing them down the hall.

He reaches the kitchen door just as Asphodel pulls it open, her head half-turned toward her shoulder as she continues saying something to the housekeeper. "—and find him. Please wait here until I do. I want to explain."

"Explain what, my dearest darling niece?" asks John, and is gratified when she jumps, letting out a small, squeaky shout of surprise. He looks at her calmly, waiting for her to compose herself.

Miss Cottingsly bustles inside, the dead man he saw through the window still across her shoulders. He's wearing an unseasonal dove-gray suit, and there's a spreading bloodstain on the back, making it more than obvious how he died. John frowns, sharply, eyes darting over the body and dismissing it as irrelevant to the situation.

Which seems slightly ridiculous, because the entire situation is about the corpse right now.

"Uncle, I—" begins Asphodel.

He shakes his head. "No," he says. "I'll ask the questions and you'll answer them, do you understand? Nod if you understand."

Asphodel nods.

"Who was this man?"

"The potential Winter I told you about. His name is Charles Booker," she says, trying not to wince at the past tense buried in her uncle's question. "He's the son of a fur trader from Maine. Relatively well off, enough so that his parents intended he should enter society to seek a wife, but not so wealthy as to be quickly or easily missed. He has a tendency to wander off when he's supposed to be looking after his father's interests. Anyone who expected to see him today will take his absence as a sign of distraction, rather than foul play."

"How do you know him?"

"I met him at Grace's garden party at the end of the summer. You were there."

"Yes, I was." John frowns, casting his mind back to that day. As always, he spent most of the gathering watching Asphodel closely, keeping track of the people she spoke to as well as the ones who seemed to take too close of an interest in her. Their family relationship means he doesn't have Father Clemence's social issues: it's right and reasonable for a man to take in his own niece, and there's nothing salacious about it. But it does mean that protecting her virtue is one of his primary concerns at almost all times.

Slowly, he says, "You spoke to the usual array of young ladies, and a few newer ones who've only recently joined the social set. But I don't recall any young gentlemen catching your attention. Was the boy working as one of the servers?"

"Perish the thought." Asphodel wrinkles her nose. "He was in the rolling chair parked near the fence. He was a charming conversationalist. His parents had sent him to the city to stay with a business partner of his father's while he recovered from a summer illness. It had left him weakened and all but comatose until the weather began to turn."

John's eyes widen minutely as he realizes what she's alluding to. "Is that how you knew he was a candidate for the Winter throne?"

"Indeed," she says. "The current King shows no signs of stepping aside, but still the season prepares its scions. Charles had the potential to serve the Winter. He was closely tied enough that he sickened when the weather warmed, and was only restored when it cooled again."

"Asphodel . . ."

"He was a handsome young man." She watches as Miss Cottingsly carries him over to the kitchen table and dumps him there. His blood will soak into the wood, but he's far from the first corpse to be deposited there. "He said sweet things and admired my hair. You never admire my hair."

"You're my niece. As long as you're presentable, I have no cause to admire your hair."

"He charmed me. I was charmed. I appreciated the opportunity to be charmed. It happens so rarely." She finally turns back to her uncle. "He was tied to Winter. Winter is a season, and seasons come with their own weather patterns. I set him to the question of why it never rains in Boston. I told him the truth: that you would give him your blessing to court me in the open if he could find that truth for me. He tried his best, but it seems a scion of Winter is not up to the question. When he failed, as I had known he must, Miss Cottingsly secured him for your use. His parts won't be as powerful as the Winter King's would have been, but they should still have their properties. Perhaps he can help us with the question after all."

"Perhaps," says John, voice turning thoughtful. "He didn't test your virtue or dishonor you?"

"I'm not compromised if that's what you're asking," snaps Asphodel. "My virginity is intact, and the only kiss he gave me, he offered as he died. I'll bottle it before lunch. A maiden girl's first kiss, with a son of the seasons, must be a powerful trinket for your collection, no?"

"Not powerful enough to forgive you meeting with him without telling me."

Asphodel's expression melts into dewy-eyed dismay. She clasps her hands under her chin as she stares at her uncle. "I only wanted to make you happy," she says. "He was willing to do what I asked because he liked me. He didn't know you, and what he did know—that you were a powerful alchemist, associated with the American Congress—frightened him. I give you the body of the man I was falling in love with, I offer you my first kiss, and you'd be angry with me for not telling you my plan when your presence would have ruined it? Uncle, I don't understand. You say I can't be an alchemist because I'm a woman. Now you don't want me to be a woman either! What *can* I be?"

"You can be serious for a moment," he says. "We both know you're not actually upset right now."

She drops her hands and her expression at the same time, returning to the cool, assessing look that has become her default. She's not his daughter, but sometimes he thinks she might as well have been. Sometimes he's so proud of her that he could burst.

"Better," he says. "I don't disapprove of your plan, or of its results. I do disapprove of you going behind my back and involving my staff with something that could easily have become dangerous. Do we know if he told anyone about you? If someone will come here looking for him now that he's gone missing?"

"Yes, we know, no, he didn't, and no, no one should come looking for him here."

"You sound very sure of yourself."

"I am."

"Very well, then. Clean yourself up and meet us down in the basement. It seems we have a Winter scion to dismantle. It's best done while the blood's still fresh."

Asphodel actually bounces onto her toes at that, delighted beyond suppressing her response, and rushes over to kiss him on the cheek before she spins and runs for the hall.

John waits until he's alone with Miss Cottingsly and the corpse, then turns to his housekeeper. "Well?"

"I watched her the whole time," says Miss Cottingsly. "She was as careful as she says she was. The girl has a deft hand with deceptions. I might consider putting bars on the windows if I were you. She knows what waits her in two years' time, when she's old enough to enter society and thus the market. You won't let her be an alchemist, but you've left her suited to very little else. She'll be trying to find a way to change the future, lest she wind up an alchemist's wife when she'd rather be the hand that holds the wand."

"Alchemy is not wizardry," he scoffs. "What we do isn't magic. It's science. Magic cannot raise the dead, nor make a person from the pieces those same dead leave behind. If I were a wizard, you wouldn't be here."

"How gingerly you sidestep my point," says Miss Cottingsly. "Yes, you made me, and a clever job you did of it. I can't remember the women I was, not even in my dreams. But I know you got the idea of me from that Shelley woman's book. How can you be so sure women have no gift for alchemy when you made one from another woman's blueprint?"

"Shelley was no alchemist," says John. "She wrote what her husband ordered her to write."

"She outlived him by thirty years. Don't you think that if he had been the alchemist, he would have been able to stop himself from drowning? You see what you want to see, much as this poor boy did." She gestures toward the body of Charles Booker. "It may serve you just as well if you're not careful."

"That's enough out of you," he says sharply. "Do your job. Get the corpse to the basement. And never tell me how to raise my niece again."

"Yes, sir," she says, and bobs a quick curtsey before she moves to retrieve the body. John Baker rolls up his sleeves and follows her down to the basement, where the work can properly begin. The dissection will serve him best if the body is yet warm when it begins.

There is so much work to be done.

The improbable road reached the base of the mountain and began to snake gently upward, following the curves and dips of a natural pathway worn into the stone. The group continued to walk along it, allowing the road to lure them up and away from the ground. They had gone perhaps twenty feet up the side of the mountain when Soleil made a small sound of discontent.

Jack turned to look at her. "What is it?" he asked.

Wordlessly, she pointed to the ground beneath their feet. Jack looked down.

The path they walked along was glittering black stone. The improbable road, fickle as ever, was gone, and they walked now without its iridescent guide to see that they reached the right destination.

Unlike Soleil, who remembered so little of the world that she might as well have been a stranger like Avery or Zib, or Niamh, who came from a place so deeply drowned that she had never had purposeful need of the improbable road, Jack had been raised to respect and revere the road, which was the only true connection between the Kingdoms that could be accessed by those too common to carry a crown. The Kings and Queens could go where they liked, as could their Pages and consorts; the Great Owls were all but a law unto themselves. For everyone else, there was the road and only the road, and all else might as well have been stories and lies.

To see the road desert them now sent a shiver of cold

slithering down his spine to wrap around his stomach, tight and constrictive as a hungry serpent. Jack swallowed and kept walking. Zib was not yet heavy in his arms, and the Palace of the Queen of Wands was as yet up ahead, still unseen. If the road had left them, either it disagreed with their destination, or it felt that they no longer needed its guidance.

Jack had no way of knowing one thing from the other, and so he continued onward, trusting the road not to have left them walking into danger. The improbable road had no true loyalties save to the Impossible City, which was its source and destination. They sought a place to care for Zib, yes, but they also sought the missing Queen of Wands at the request of the Great Owls themselves, and a way to access the Impossible City. Without the Queen, the City would fall to war, and the road would suffer as much as anyone else. He had to trust the road.

They all did.

—From *Under the Smokestrewn Sky*,
by A. Deborah Baker

BOOK III

Iron

All the earth and air
  With thy voice is loud,
As when night is bare,
  From one lonely cloud
The moon rains out her beams, and heaven is overflow'd.
—Percy Bysshe Shelley, "To a Skylark"

Underpass Mary's not long been a god.
She was once only salt stains and rust,
But faith can work wonders and now that's her job
Ever patient, she does what she must.
Daily they bring her their candles and prayers—
The skeptic, the hopeful, the proud, with
Strong faith or weak faith or no faith at all
And she does what she can for the crowd,
And she gives them what comfort's allowed.
—Talis Kimberley, "Underpass Mary"

Growth

TIMELINE: AUGUST 22, 2018.

It's not until the clock strikes midnight, a gentle chiming from her phone as the alarm goes off to notify her, that Lilianne rolls out of bed, smoothing her hair back with one hand, and reaches for her shoes. She didn't entirely mean to nap for as long as she has, sinking in and out of a variable doze like a glass orb floating in the ocean, now on the surface, now four feet below, but still buoyant the entire time.

Most nights are like that for her. No matter how tired she is, her brain never slows down enough for her to truly *sleep*. Other people talk about long hours of unconsciousness, about deep dreams that seem to entirely replace the waking world, lives lived in the stillness of slumber. She's never experienced that. Even as a child, she would be partially aware of herself as she spent her mandated hours with her eyes closed, letting them rest in a way her mind never did. Sleep is a companion, not a friend. Never once have they truly embraced each other.

The apartment is silent as she creeps to the door, hesitating long enough to listen. Raven is primarily nocturnal, but she'll usually be out between the hours of ten and three; Snake sleeps nights so he can make his morning classes without endangering himself. The animals he works with aren't malicious, but they can't be handled safely unless the handlers are fully aware and alert. One slip on his part and someone's getting bitten or stung—or worse, one of his precious specimens is getting stomped to death.

She doesn't know where David is. Some nights, he's in bed by nine, like the good little athlete he is. Others, he's gone until the sun comes up, and him coming in is what wakes her. She's sure she'll spot the pattern in his schedule eventually, but until then, she needs to move quietly. He could be passed out on the couch again, or he could be somewhere else entirely. There's just no way to know.

Letting herself out of the room, she creeps down the hall to the living room, where she's relieved to see no David by the dim city glow coming through the windows. She really is alone for now, and she holds that solitude like a cloak as she creeps onward to the front door, unlocking it and slipping out onto the landing.

She doesn't exhale until the door is shut and locked again behind her. Her roommates aren't her keepers; they probably wouldn't have said anything if they'd been there to see her go, just waved and dismissed her nocturnal activities as her own damn business. And yet, the fear of discovery has never needed to be rational. It's enough that it exists, coiled at the bottom of her belly like a snake prepared to strike.

The food court is silent when she reaches the bottom of the stairs, the individual storefronts closed, the oil cooled for the night. They'll wake up in the morning, some earlier than others, putting out breakfast offerings of hot donuts and fried-egg sandwiches. A few of the local homeless sleep on the tables and benches of the central eating area, and Lilianne looks at them with sympathy as she passes, careful not to disturb them. California is an expensive place to live. According to Raven, it gets more expensive every year. Add that to the remarkably forgiving weather and it isn't such a surprise that when people lose their homes, they often choose to stay in the places they know, where they're not dealing with readjustment to their environments on top of everything else.

Better to suffer where the rain tastes right, that's what her mother always said, and she's not one to argue with her mother. She clutches her satchel close as she steps out of the food court and onto the street beyond. Someday the rain here will taste right, she knows. Someday this place will be her home. But not yet. Not tonight.

The night is far from silent, despite the stillness of the street around her. No bars this close to campus, although they thrive only a few blocks away: they're still open, music blasting and neon flashing as they offer their temporary escape to the people who come seeking it. The bouncers are large enough to make even David seem small, and the air around them always smells of a mix of stale beer, sweat, and soft desperation, running down the walls like sap running down the side of a maple tree. No, those are not her destination.

Instead, she turns away from the downtown nightlife, fixing her eyes on the secret, half-hidden part of Berkeley, where normal people live normal lives, and abnormal people hide themselves in plain sight.

Every city she's ever seen has been like this, dividing itself into separate chambers, like they're unknowingly seeking the seashell heart of their existence, pursuing the Golden Mean above all else. There's always overlap—her own apartment is proof of that, a little oasis of residence in the middle of a sea of commerce. In the other direction, there's the home daycare, the living-room salon, or the corner bodega. Nothing is ever entirely one thing or another. Alchemy pursues purification, but humanity thrives in the blended spaces. That's how it's always been, and how it will always be, and the reason not every human is an alchemist, which is for the best.

One day—one day very soon—they'll be able to enter the Impossible City, and whoever claims it first will be as untouchable as the sun itself. On that day, for the chosen, the purification can begin, and whatever form it takes will be the right and righteous one. All of humanity can be as god-touched and glorious as the Lunars, as the Doctrine, as her parents. And all she has to do is get there.

The thought carries her through the silence of the streets, onto labyrinthine lanes lined in grass-fronted houses, the smell of dew and slightly metallic recycled water hanging heavy in the air. Their gardens are California impossibilities of bright flowers and ripening fruit. Many of them have lemon or orange trees, adding their citrus-sharp smells to the air. It's so far from Alabama that it aches, serving only to remind her that she's left home behind.

It was a surprise to her parents when she abruptly changed her aim from her lifelong dreams of Boston to far-off Berkeley, but she couldn't explain to them exactly why, couldn't tell them that the most exciting developments in modern alchemy are happening in Berkeley—a city, paradoxically, that no longer hosts any alchemists of its own. They're all gone, scattered to other places after the rise of Reed's cuckoos and the destruction of their main lab. But everyone she's spoken to has confirmed that reality is thin here, malleable in a way it wouldn't be without the weight of the various greater incarnations distorting it. A tincture that can heal scars somewhere else might be able to regrow an entire skin here. Pastes to cure baldness that wouldn't work anywhere else might grow whole new heads of hair, provided they were made in Berkeley.

Hormones brewed and blended to change endocrine systems can potentially rewire them to a level otherwise seen only in utero, making mass physical changes to soft tissue and reproductive systems. She didn't become an alchemist for the sake of easing her transition, but if she can make use of the natural properties of the space, why shouldn't she?

Once the sounds of campus have fully fallen behind her, she reaches into her coat and withdraws a rhyolite pendulum. It's nothing special to look at, light gray and faintly speckled, knapped down to a point with obsidian tools. She bought it from a metaphysical shop downtown, surrounded by the scent of incense and patchouli. (The owners lack the powers they advertise so freely. They're just normal humans with a decent grasp of what it takes to run a business. In this case, that's a good thing: the pendulum wouldn't work as well for her if it was already imbued with someone else's essence.)

Holding the pendulum out at arm's length, Lilianne focuses on it, slightly narrowing her eyes as it begins to sway gently back and forth. She holds her hand as steady as she can, watching as the pendulum's steady rocking gradually evolves into a slow spiral, moving independently of anything else. (It's not truly independent, keyed into the motion of the universe unfolding all around it, but for someone standing on the surface of the Earth, it might as well be.)

The spiral grows larger and larger, winding out and then winding back in, until the pendulum develops a strong list to one side. Lilianne nods and turns to face in that direction, letting the swinging stone guide her wanderings. Onward she goes.

Through the night, down populated streets, past darkened windows like eyes into the worlds and lives beyond, the sleeping people she will never know. Step by step she extends the distance between herself and her room, all her possessions, the person she pretends to be. Here, in the dark, she isn't Lilianne the student, Lilianne the transplant, Lilianne the trans woman. She's only Lilianne the alchemist, and she's going to remake the world.

There is a vacant lot up ahead, incongruous among the rows and rows of tidy houses, and she barely notices the woman stepping out of it onto the sidewalk, barely sees her in the haze of searching and discovery. The woman pauses to pull something out of her purse, and for the second time in a single day, Lilianne collides with a stranger, knocking her to the ground.

Wait: no. Not a stranger. As she automatically grabs for the falling woman's arm, Lilianne realizes she *knows* her. She knows very few people in Berkeley so far, but she knows this one, with her beautiful face and her thick black hair. She can no more stop knowing her than she can unring the crystal bell of her own heart, and so she just freezes, pendulum still spinning in her unoccupied hand, to stare at Smita.

Smita recovers her composure before Lilianne does, using the firm anchor of the taller woman's grasp to pull herself to her feet, shaking her head until her hair falls in a black ink river down her back. She's wearing a tan jacket, something like a short, stylish trench coat, and carrying a large leather purse. And she's still the most beautiful woman Lilianne has ever seen, so beautiful that it almost hurts to look directly at her. It's like staring into the sun.

"We keep running into each other," Smita quips, half-dryly, and it's such a dad joke that it breaks through her beauty for just a moment, allows Lilianne to recover her composure and risk a dry, shallow laugh.

Smita gives her an assessing look. "What brings you this far from campus?" she asks. "Forgive me if I'm making assumptions here, but when we met earlier, you didn't strike me as a local. I don't normally find out-of-state students wandering around the residential neighborhoods, especially not after midnight."

Because it *is* after midnight now, well after midnight, sliding into the deep slow hours of the morning. These are the best hours for alchemy, which is a form of debate as much as it's a science, even if half the alchemists Lilianne has known would never admit it; through alchemy, they can negotiate with the universe, argue with the rules it chooses to follow on a daily basis, and sometimes win in ridiculous ways, rewriting everything to suit themselves. The fewer waking minds there are nearby, the easier it becomes to win those arguments, because there's no one available to offer contradiction.

"I, uh . . ." she says. "I just wanted to go for a walk, you know?

And I guess I moved away from all the noise and fuss coming off the campus just sort of automatically. I didn't want to run into anybody."

"I can go," says Smita.

"No, that's all right," says Lilianne hurriedly. Maybe too hurriedly: Smita looks momentarily amused, as Lilianne's cheeks burn. Still, she soldiers on: "I don't mind a little company. You're not a stinking drunk frat boy telling me how tall I am like he thinks I somehow never noticed, or a sorority girlie looking at me like I'm some sort of a threat."

"Well, you know, they might be right about the threat." Lilianne's heart sinks, only to rebound back into her throat as Smita continues: "You do keep walking into people."

Lilianne smiles. "Only you."

"Oh, so I'm special? Well, I'm flattered. Every girl wants to be special. I just feel like I could be special without hitting the ground quite so many times, you know?"

"Picky, picky. And what are *you* doing out here? Is there something interesting in that vacant lot? *How* is there a vacant lot in the middle of the block? I thought the local real estate market was so tight that any open ground would have been snapped up and overbuilt by now." She takes a step toward the point where the sidewalk ends and the rough, rocky ground of the lot begins. For some reason, for just a moment, she smells peaches.

Then Smita is in front of her, hands raised and a disarming smile on her face. It's like she can't decide whether she's distressed or not. "Remember the earthquake we had a few years back? The house that used to be here had a bad-enough gas leak that the whole thing burned to the ground. It was a nasty piece of work. Anyway, the owners still own the plot, and they're planning to rebuild eventually, they just haven't gotten around to it yet."

"And the something interesting?"

"I was visiting a friend who lives over there." Smita gestures vaguely. It's hard to tell which of the neighboring houses she's trying to indicate; it could be any of the three on the far side of the lot. "Cutting through is faster than trying to find my way through the maze of little streets between here and there. I don't know what I'll do when they rebuild the house that's supposed to be here. Learn to go the long way around, I guess."

"Huh," says Lilianne, and takes another step toward the lot. She keeps smelling peaches, and she can't figure out why . . .

But Smita doesn't move, and if Lilianne keeps going, she's going to knock the other woman down again. She stops where she is, bewildered.

Smita smiles. "I'm out on the street because my friend needed to go to bed," she says. "You met her earlier—Erin? And anyway, if we're not going to visit her, there's really nothing there but a bunch of rocks and old, broken glass. You can get hurt wandering around in the dirt if you don't know where it's safe to step. You want some company?"

Lilianne can keep arguing, keep trying to get into the vacant lot, but why? There's nothing there, and the strange smell of peaches could be coming from almost anywhere. A nearby tree or Smita's shampoo. The world is filled with tiny mysteries that were never intended to be solved. She can leave this one safely alone.

So instead she turns her body halfway back toward the pendulum she's been ignoring for these last few minutes. It isn't swinging anymore. Instead it's spinning in small, tight spirals, each one pulling toward the same unseen destination.

"What's that?"

Smita's voice is, for once, an intrusion. Lilianne flinches away, eyes flicking between her pendulum and the other woman, trying to decide her response. If she tells the truth, Smita will think she's strange—assuming Smita doesn't think that already after everything that's happened so far. Smita thinking she's strange would really be the least of her problems, a blip in the cosmic weight of the universe. But still, it's something to consider. Lilianne has always been awkward around women, and yet, even for her, developing a crush and grinding it into the dust in a single day's time would be an impressive new record. She'd rather be able to dream about Smita for a little longer, even if it can never be forever.

The trouble is, she can't think of a single lie that makes her look any less strange. "I was taking my pet rock for a walk" is the sort of statement that gets mental health professionals involved, even here in Berkeley, where some people truly believe that Snake's cockroach colony is also an emotional support animal.

When the truth and the lie are both ridiculous, it's easier to keep track of the truth. So Lilianne sighs and says a silent farewell to the sweet dream of Smita before she explains, "It's a dowsing pendulum. They're more accurate than the rods, at least for me. Never had much luck with rods."

"A . . . dowsing . . . pendulum?"

"Mm-hmm. It's made of rhyolite. There's lots of it around here. You want to use a mineral that's found where you're searching. Back home in Alabama, I'd be using hematite or blue star quartz, just to be sure my intent is in harmony with the land around me." That's a lie. Back home in Alabama she'd be using a pendulum of baked red clay with some hay mixed in for structure and solidity. Back home in Alabama she understands what the land *wants*, not just what the land *knows*, and she can tailor her choices better for the understanding.

Smita gives her a half-frustrated look. "That's what it's made of, not what it is."

"It's a stone dowsing pendulum. You use it to find things."

"What are you trying to find?"

In for a penny, in for a pound, as the sages say. "Have you ever heard of alchemy?"

There's a beat as Smita's eyes widen, and it looks almost like she's going to step away, back over the boundary into the rocky vacant lot. But she holds her ground and composes her expression, eyebrows relaxing, and in a neutral voice says, "That was a Greek thing, wasn't it? Philosopher kings and wizard scholars and that sort of stuff?"

"All the inkpot gods," says Lilianne, with audible relief. "It's not magic, it's scientifically applied force of will, and some of it's deeply silly, but some of it really isn't. Some of it works, if you know how to do it properly."

Smita nods. "I've heard a bit."

"Really? Oh, that's amazing! So many people have no idea about alchemy, or they think it's all just fairy tales and positive thinking, like you can good-vibrations reality into doing what you want. A lot of it's just about finding the sympathies and harmonies that exist in the world, and then twisting them around until they take the shapes you want them to have." It's a miracle, but Smita is still watching her, still looking like she understands and can accept what Lilianne is saying.

The most beautiful woman in the world *and* she's responsive to the idea of alchemy? If she didn't already know the gods were real, this would be enough to convince her. This feels like the opening verse to everything she's ever wanted in her life.

"Are you an alchemist, then?" asks Smita.

Lilianne snaps back into the present, leaving her wondering thoughts of alchemical fulfillment behind. "I'm trying to be," she says. "I'm self-taught. The . . . the American Alchemical Congress has been a little broken up recently, and even if they weren't, they're pretty sexist. A lot of them still don't think women are suited to alchemical studies, like our brains will run out of our ears and try to escape if we have to contemplate the process of purifying base minerals or transforming one flesh into another."

"That sounds very shortsighted of them," says Smita, semicautiously. But she does move a step closer, and it's hard not to see that as a good sign.

"Oh, it is. Some of the most talented alchemists the world has ever known have been women, and shutting them out just keeps America behind the curve."

"You make it sound like there's some sort of weird alchemical arms race going on," says Smita, laughing lightly to show how absurd she finds the very notion.

Lilianne nods. "That's exactly what's happening, actually. There are Alchemical Congresses all over the world, and they're all trying to be the first ones to unlock certain essential functions of the universe. There was an outpost here in Berkeley until very recently."

"Really? In Berkeley?"

"Yes. They built a permanent lab and everything." Lilianne looks at her pendulum. "They sealed it off due to staffing issues, and I'm trying to find it, in case they left anything useful behind. The Congress has access to all sorts of things that a self-taught alchemist isn't going to be able to acquire. I'd like to see what I can learn."

And then Smita's hand is on her arm, Smita is *touching her*, fingers resting lightly on the curve of her elbow. Her skin is warm, and Lilianne never wants her to take her hand away, not now, not ever. "Why?"

"Why what?"

"Why do you want to know?"

It's a simple question. It's an impossible answer. Smita just learned that alchemy exists, may not even believe in it—not when it's just a swaying rock and a strange midnight story. Explaining incarnations and the transformative potential of a place like Berkeley may be several steps too far, taking her fragile acceptance out of the realm of fact and sending her spiraling down into disbelief.

"I've always been interested in what it takes to transform one thing into another," says Lilianne carefully. "I like to understand what the universe is made of, because you can't really change what you can't comprehend. People should be able to control their destinies. We should get to choose what we're going to be, even if other people don't agree with us. It's your body and your life; why shouldn't you be the one making all the decisions?"

"How does that explain the quest for knowledge?"

"Like I said, I like to understand," says Lilianne. "If I don't know what all the options are, how am I supposed to decide which one I want? Haven't you ever wished that something about your life could be different?"

Smita chuckles, bleakly. "You have no idea."

There's a story in that answer, heavy and strange and simultaneously unconnected and perfectly in harmony with the rest of their conversation. Lilianne looks at it and decides that she doesn't have the time to pull that reply apart and study what it's made of: she needs to move along before the hour gets too late and it's no longer safe for her to follow the unceasing pull of her pendulum.

"Anyway, you asked what I was trying to find. I'm looking for the lab."

"Why would you want to find *that*?"

"Why would I want to find the permanent lab the alchemists built here in Berkeley before they abandoned it? Because it's still out there somewhere, sealed off and waiting for an enterprising young alchemist to find it and claim it as her own. Who knows what they left behind when they fled? I could find all sorts of things that will help me with my research, and some of them probably shouldn't just be left lying around for people to stumble over."

"So they'd be safer with you. These terrible secrets."

"Well, yes. I know I'm trustworthy." Lilianne pauses, realizing how that sounds. ". . . and I guess that's exactly what someone who shouldn't be trusted with impossible secrets would say, huh?"

"Probably," says Smita. She smiles, lips closed so that the expression pushes her cheeks upward, forming a dimple that Lilianne can't help but think of kissing. It's right there, so close and so perfect. "I guess that just means I'll need to go with you and see this 'lab,' in case there's something dangerous in there. It's not safe for you to go alone."

"If you want," says Lilianne, forcing her voice to stay light. She starts walking again, and wonder of wonders, Smita walks alongside her! Smita is *actually coming* as she looks for the lab! Her skin feels too tight and her heart is beating too fast, and she doesn't know what to do with any of this.

"So . . ." she says, rather than focusing on her own feelings of radiant distress. "You're from Seattle, right? Doesn't it rain there all the time?"

"That's just what we tell the tourists, so they don't get funny ideas about moving there," says Smita. "I always expected I'd graduate and go back, get a job at one of the big biotech firms. I miss the mountains so much it aches some mornings. They have mountains here in California, but it's not the same. Just like both places have evergreens, but we have fir and hemlock and pine, not redwoods. It's hard to be transplanted."

"So why stay?"

"A lot of reasons, really. You met Erin earlier—she's my roommate. We've been living together since just after college, and she *hates* rain. I can't leave her, and she has absolutely no desire to live in Seattle, no matter how much I reassure her that we exaggerate the amount of rain for comedic effect. My work is here. I really thought I'd be able to bounce from firm to firm and keep studying the same cell lines and genetic markers, but private scientific research turns out to be a twisty little maze of NDAs, all of them almost exactly alike. I'd have to start over from the beginning." She sighs heavily. "Maybe someday. A girl can dream, right?"

"Right," agrees Lilianne, as she feels the foundations of the sandcastle future she's been dreaming of with Smita start to crumble and fall away. She knew it wasn't going to happen from the start—beautiful, polished, presumably straight scientists don't date unfashionable, unkempt trans historians from Alabama—but after running into the other woman twice in one day, it had been starting to feel a little bit like fate. She's a big believer in fate. Hard not to be, when your mother is literally the incarnate fall and your father is the incarnate spring and they keep building a big semi-Euclidian labyrinth behind the house to test the new monarchs of the Summer and Winter. Fate might as well be a regular dinner guest from the way she understands the world.

"And what does Erin do?" she asks, and is proud of herself for how light her voice manages to sound.

"She's a chaplain at one of the big hospitals in San Francisco. I know that sounds ridiculous when you've just met her, but she has a theology degree, and a lot of experience dealing with stressed-out people who have big personalities and no real interest in eating, sleeping, or taking their vitamins. She does a lot of good. Not as much as she maybe feels like she should, but a lot all the same."

"Theology and biotech are pretty separate disciplines. Did you meet through school, or just while you were both enrolled?"

"Actually, yes," says Smita, with a little laugh that feels like an electrical jolt running the length of Lilianne's spine. "One of my other roommates, Dodger, was living with her off-campus. Her, and a woman named Candace who died in the earthquake. Dodger and I were much closer to being peers than Erin and I ever could have been, and we became friends, inasmuch as Dodger ever really *did* friends back then. Erin sort of came along as a package deal. Then, after everything, Dodger needed someone to come and help her with the rent, and Erin just showed up one day, put her stuff down, and said she lived with us now."

The story feels rehearsed and incomplete at the same time, like Smita's leaving out pieces she doesn't think need to be shared. Lilianne gives her a sidelong look. The names of Reed's successful embodiment have never been published outside the Congress, but she knows they were in Berkeley, and she knows that the female member of the pair had some ridiculous literary reference of a name to allow her to rhyme with her counterpart . . . but that would be too much of a coincidence. She can't have met the most beautiful woman in Berkeley, only for that woman to be living with Reed's cuckoos. That would be impossible.

"How many people do you live with?" she asks.

"There's six of us in the house, all told, but we have plenty of space for everyone to have their own room, which is honestly the only way I could live with those weirdos," says Smita. "If I had to share a room with one of them, I'd be on the first commuter flight back to Seattle, and just leave my stuff behind. Stuff isn't worth *that*."

No way she's living with the Doctrine. No matter how big the house is, Reed's greatest creation would never be lowered to sharing with that many people.

Lilianne glances down at her pendulum. It's still swinging and pulling, but less vigorously now; they're almost on top of whatever it is they're looking for. She looks up again, scanning the nearby streets, and doesn't see anything.

"We should be almost there . . ." she says, giving the area around them another look.

"Over here," says Smita. Lilianne turns, and the other woman is standing next to a storm drain, the grate rich with rust and trapped leaf litter, slowly becoming mulch as the autumn weather wears it down. Even in California, there is rain, and it falls on Berkeley as often as it does anywhere else. The sewer below is probably disgusting.

"What about the drain?" Lilianne trots over to join Smita, looking down into the darkness through the slats of the grate. Her pendulum stops swaying and points, straight as an arrow, down into the dark.

"I think this is what we're looking for."

"Why would you think—"

But Smita is crouching, closer to the grate, close enough that she can reach down and push some of the fallen leaves aside, revealing a tetractys scratched into the metal. "Isn't this a sign of Pythagoras?" she asks, wide-eyed and so innocent that Lilianne feels instantly bad about her rising suspicion.

"What do you know about Pythagoras?" she asks, not so besotted that she's forgotten everything she knows about being careful.

"Scholar, philosopher, mathematician—I'm a scientist, there's no way I got through grad school without learning more about all the dead Greeks than anyone really needs to know. But this is one of the symbols he designed, isn't it?"

"It is," says Lilianne, and glances again at her motionless pendulum, excitement starting to spark behind her breastbone. Her hand isn't perfectly still, but the pendulum is. It dangles without swaying at all, pointing straight down into the drain.

She's found it. The sealed lab. She's found it, and now that she knows where it is, it's hers to claim.

Smita is a problem, though. She looks up, focusing on the other woman for a moment. Smita has a stick in one hand and is using it to peel back the layers of fallen leaves, peeling them away from the grate like the skin off of an orange. It doesn't seem to be about keeping her hands clean; she pulls leaves off of her stick when necessary, tossing them carelessly aside. It's just a matter of having something to do with her hands.

Lilianne recognizes that simmering anxiety, that need to stay busy all the time, forever, no matter what else might be going on. No matter how inconvenient it might be. There are no further symbols etched into the grate: only the tetractys, the four-leveled pyramid, with four dots at the base and a single dot at the pinnacle. It's such a simple design that it seems strange to credit anyone with having "invented" it, and yet it hadn't been so much as conceived of before Pythagoras made it one of his secret symbols.

The grate is still filthy, even with most of the dead leaves removed. It also looks like it hasn't been secured quite right. Shoving her pendulum into her pocket, she bends down and hooks her fingers through the bars, tugging on the metal.

"This is a tetanus shot waiting to happen," she mutters.

The grate shifts. It doesn't quite come loose in her hands, but her pulling is enough to move it. Raising her head, she looks wide-eyed at Smita, who grins. It's an almost-feral expression, absolutely delighted by everything that's happening.

"Need help?" she asks, and without waiting for a response she leans forward, so close that Lilianne can smell her shampoo, to hook her own fingers through the bars on the other side of the grate. Pulling together, they're able to lift it free, revealing a water-choked passage on the other side, a ladder descending down into the dark.

"I never liked these shoes anyway," says Smita, and rises from her crouch, gesturing grandly to the hole. "Ladies first."

Lilianne straightens more slowly. "You're coming down with me?"

"Well, yeah. I've come this far; I want to see how this all plays out." Smita shrugs. "Your magic rock led us to a secret passageway. How can I say no to something that exciting? If I go home, all I have to look forward to is doing the dishes."

Maybe it's the sincerity in her tone, and maybe it's just that Lilianne *wants* to believe her, but she nods either way, turning to sit on the edge of the exposed hole in the street, grasping the rough concrete sides before she lowers herself down, feet scrabbling a bit for purchase on the rusty ladder. Shifting her grip from the opening to the ladder, she begins her descent into the dark.

Smita waits until Lilianne has gone far enough to open a little distance between them before lowering herself into the dark and beginning her own descent, hands clutching the rails so tightly that bits of rust bite into her palms. Step by step they make their way below the city, until, with a splash, Lilianne's questing feet find the water.

It's colder than she would have imagined possible, so cold that it momentarily takes her breath away, soaking through her clothing with a speed that feels almost malicious. She continues going down until her feet find the ground below the ladder, water coming nearly to her waist. Digging her phone out of her the pocket of her sweater, she moves it to her bra where it has more of a shot at staying dry, then pulls her pendulum back out, only realizing after she does that it's pitch-black down here: she won't be able to see what, if anything, it indicates.

"Lily? You still there?" asks Smita. The tunnel around them catches her voice and amplifies it, bouncing it back and forth off the walls until it seems to fill the entire world.

It would be so easy to abandon her in this moment. It wouldn't even take an effort. All Lilianne would need to do is move away, letting the sound of the water cover her retreat, and Smita would lose her forever.

But Smita is the most beautiful woman she's ever seen, and she's brave and wild enough to go on an alchemical adventure with a near-stranger, risking everything to unravel a mystery. That's the sort of thing that Lilianne finds almost impossible to resist.

"I'm over here," she says.

A second later, the flashlight on Smita's phone comes on, casting a pale white light throughout the area. Lilianne blinks, squinting as she waits for her eyes to adjust to the brightness.

"You okay?" she asks, blinking rapidly until the ghost images stop dancing behind her eyelids and she can see Smita clearly. The shorter woman is almost up to the bottom of her ribcage in the water. She must be freezing. Cold spreads more quickly when it hits the body's core.

"Just a little damp," says Smita. "But I'm not sure how long I can stay in this water before I start freaking out. Do you know which way we're supposed to go?"

"Got the pendulum." Lilianne holds it up, then gives it a light tap to start it swinging again. Immediately it starts tilting toward something at the far end of the corridor, moving in sharp arcs far too wide to be explained by her initial push. "This way," she says.

"You lead, I'll follow," says Smita, and the two of them start off into the dark, leaving the ladder and the watery midnight light from the storm drain behind them.

* * *

The water doesn't get any warmer as they wade through it. But it also doesn't smell like anything, doesn't leave a greasy film on their hands, and there's an impossible lack of bobbing artifacts to bump against them: no sticks, no leaves, no unpleasant biological remains. Lilianne keeps wading forward, letting the pendulum be her guide, softly reassured by the light from Smita's phone and the sound of the other woman's breath.

It's starting to get shaky: she's freezing. Lilianne looks back at her, concerned. The light's too thin for her to see whether the other woman's lips are turning blue, but Smita's shivering hard enough that it's visible, and she can barely force a smile when she meets Lilianne's eyes.

"Don't worry about me," she says. "It's not so bad."

"We need to get you out of here."

"There's no way we're making it back to the ladder at this point," says Smita. "We just need to keep pushing forward, and we'll find our way out of here. If we don't, we don't, and Erin will kick my ass tomorrow."

She sounds distressingly certain of that, like she can't imagine a reality where she isn't alive for Erin to kick her ass. Lilianne briefly considers the alternatives, and decides to subscribe to Smita's version of the world. It's kinder than the one her own mind keeps trending grimly toward, the one that remembers how many people die of hypothermia when the ice breaks every spring. She turns back around and keeps walking.

"I think you'll like her once you get to know her," says Smita, clearly talking just for the sake of hearing herself, for the sake of having *something* to hang on to in this seemingly endless dark. "Erin can be a little prickly at first, but she warms up fast once she realizes you're not planning to hurt any of her people."

"Protective?"

"I think they defined the word so they'd be able to describe her someday. It's not her fault. Her brother died when she was young, and she wasn't able to save him. So she tries her best to save everybody else. She's never forgiven herself for not being there when he needed her."

This feels too personal for Lilianne to know about someone she's only met once, and then essentially in passing. She frowns into the darkness, feeling her stomach twist like she's swallowed something bad.

"I'm so sorry," she says.

"It is what it is. But we all try to forgive Erin when she gets a little overly intense, because she doesn't know any other way to be. She didn't have the upbringing for it."

The water is getting shallower, or else Lilianne is getting so cold that she can't feel it anymore. She reaches down with her free hand, and while her thighs are still wet, the denim clinging to them like it's never going to come off again, the water level is considerably below where she expects it to be. Hope sparks through the sourness of her stomach, chasing it away.

They might survive this.

Onward they walk, following the pendulum ever deeper into the dark.

Protection

TIMELINE: AUGUST 23, 2018.

The water keeps getting shallower until they're not wading at all, they're stepping up onto a concrete platform. The tunnel is otherwise unchanged, but just being out of direct contact with the water makes it feel warmer . . . for now. Lilianne knows that won't last for long. Their bodies will realize that they're still wrapped in wet cocoons, still buffeted by cold air, and the freezing will resume, if it ever actually stopped to begin with.

But Smita isn't shivering as hard, and the motion of the pendulum is getting more and more focused, not swinging at all any longer, only pointing toward whatever lies ahead. She shakes it, trying to see if she can change the direction of its focus, and nothing she does will make it shift or swing: it only points.

They're almost there.

It's almost anticlimactic when the light hits a rough concrete wall, free of waterlines or graffiti. In the center is a door, plain wood painted white, like something you might find in the back halls of a hospital. It's unimpressive enough to loop back around to becoming impressive in a unique, half-terrible way.

"Is it locked?" asks Smita.

"I don't know, but my pendulum wants us to go there," says Lilianne. She steps forward, Smita's reassuring light at her back, and reaches for the knob.

"The light will guide me home," she murmurs just before her fingers close around it, mantra and plea and prayer all at the same time, so jumbled up together that they can't be picked apart.

She grasps the knob. She turns it.

The door swings inward under her hand.

She pushes it about a foot open, revealing a narrow strip of darkness that manages to be even deeper than the darkness in the tunnel. A faint smell escapes, like formaldehyde and some kind of cleaning fluid, lemon-bright and utterly impossible.

"Is this it?" asks Smita.

Lilianne almost wants to snap at her, to remind her that they're both here for the first time, that she has no more way of knowing what's going on than Smita does. But even more than that, she wants to squeal and throw her arms around the other woman, dancing with delight over the fact that it's here, it's really here, they *found* it.

The lost lab is hers. All she has to do is step inside and claim her destiny.

"I think so," she says. "I *hope* so. And I hope that it has a working dryer, whether it is or not." She grasps what little bravery she has left and steps forward, pushing the door the rest of the way inward. Smita follows her, phone raised to cast as much light as possible.

They're in a kitchen, large and industrial, with chrome shelving and countertops. It looks like the sort of thing you'd expect to find at a summer camp or school, someplace where the staff is expected to feed enormous numbers of people very quickly and out of industrial vats. It's hard to imagine so many alchemists in one place that this sort of setup would be necessary, but here it is, and it's even harder to imagine another situation that would put this many *people* in a windowless underground kitchen and force them to eat whatever the cafeteria could produce.

The walls are concrete. The floor is tile. The ceiling is high, and yet the room doesn't echo as they step inside, or as the door swings shut behind them. Lilianne shifts to stand closer to Smita, like she thinks the warmth off her body could help the smaller woman without the need to touch her.

"There must still be power down here," says Smita.

"Why would you say that?"

"We can still breathe."

It's a simple statement, and yet. There are no windows: the door, when closed, forms an almost perfect seal. There's no way air is getting down this deep without some sort of ventilation system, and there's no way it would be this fresh if the vents weren't actively doing their jobs. Lilianne blinks, then turns to start scanning the nearby walls.

"What are you looking for?" asks Smita.

"The light switch," says Lilianne, and then: "Ah-ha!" She moves toward the wall, then flicks the switch she spotted there.

The fluorescents overhead sputter and groan as they flicker into life, filling the kitchen with a lambent white light that makes the flashlight immediately unnecessary. Smita grunts approval as she flicks it off, then moves to stuff the phone into her pocket. She freezes before she can finish the gesture.

"Try your bra," says Lilianne. "That's what I did. It should still be dry enough to be safe."

Smita shoots her a grateful look, then tucks the phone into her bra, safely away from her sodden clothing. She turns, looking at everything around them with wide-eyed curiosity.

"The alchemists built all this?" she asks.

"I think so," says Lilianne. "If I'm right and we are where I hope we are, they definitely did."

"How? This must be right under at least one major intersection! There's no way they could build this much without someone catching them!"

"Have you ever heard of Roman concrete?"

"What?" Smita blinks at her, clearly thrown by the sudden change of subject. "Concrete?"

"Yeah. It was this famous Roman discovery. A concrete that could move with its environment, meaning it had incredible tensile strength and didn't buckle in earthquakes. It could even heal itself under the right conditions, or follow lines drawn by the people who used it, constructing whole rooms without the need for an architect. But then Rome fell, and the secret of the concrete was lost."

"That sounds a little close to magic for me," says Smita dubiously.

"Not magic. Alchemy. It was pure human innovation and science being bent toward fulfilling the needs of the alchemists who made it. There was nothing magical about it."

"And that has what to do with this lab?"

"This whole place was built using Roman concrete, following lines of resonance implanted in the soil." Lilianne tries to make her answer sound as matter-of-fact as possible, like this is the sort of thing Smita should expect. "Modern alchemists working for the Alchemical Congress rediscovered the secret a few years ago, and they were able to use it to build labs all over the country."

Oh, she'd been so excited on the day the news of the discovery leaked into the independent alchemists' community, when the whispered rumors became openly spoken facts. One of the cockier alchemists she knew, a boy from Decatur, Georgia, who had been refining gold out of sand since his eighth birthday, had even managed to acquire a brick-sized sample of the stuff, which had looked entirely unassuming until it was hit by a hammer. Watching it put itself back together with the methodical silence of a healing muscle had been sobering in the extreme.

"It's the real deal," she says, more sedately. "It works, and it should stand up for centuries, even in earthquake country. It just recovers from whatever people throw at it."

"That should be the sort of thing that changes the world," says Smita.

"It was, and it did, and then the world forgot about it, and now the world doesn't deserve it anymore," says Lilianne. "Lost knowledge belongs to the people who rediscover it."

"But you said it was the Alchemical Congress who rediscovered it. Why are you talking like you should have any say in what happens to the information? You just said that it doesn't belong to you."

There's an unexpected sharpness in that question, and for a moment, Lilianne isn't sure what she's supposed to do. The moment passes. "If it belongs to one alchemist, it belongs to all alchemists. We're equipped to understand it, and that's the most direct form of ownership there is. This place is Roman concrete. No steel to rust, no wires to corrode. Just solid, self-healing stone shot through with vents and wiring. It'll still be here long after the city of Berkeley is forgotten. It may even have grown by then, depending on the blueprint they used. If they told the lab how to expand itself over time, then that's exactly what it's going to do, year after year, until the entire underground is just rooms and chambers."

"All empty," says Smita. "The alchemists are gone."

"For now." Lilianne takes another look around. "The place isn't even dusty. The self-cleaning processes are still working."

"Is that part of the not-magic magic concrete?"

"No. But there are ways to program air scrubbers, modified fungus and the like. We prefer to work with the natural world whenever possible, because alchemy is the oldest of the natural sciences. It doesn't require anything falsified."

"Huh," says Smita.

Lilianne leads her to the door, testing it to see if it, like the door into the sewer passage, has been left unlocked. When the knob turns, she grins, giddy as a schoolgirl, and says, "I bet we can find some towels in one of the main labs."

Smita doesn't have time to object before Lilianne's through the door and she's alone in the empty, echoing kitchen. Her soaking-wet clothes are sticking to her body, pressing her core temperature further and further down: she needs those towels or she's going to freeze.

But she stays where she is, and does not follow, and is finally free to think about what she's done for the first time since she decided she was going to do it.

* * *

Smita looks around the abandoned kitchen, no longer making any effort to disguise her curiosity, and shudders. Lilianne may or may not know the secret to the Roman concrete, but Smita does. She's known it since Artemis and Kelpie came for dinner a month or so after the eclipse, when the two Lunars were still adjusting to their freedom and their new partnership, the ancient goddess of the hunt in the stolen body of a rich man's daughter—no partnership theirs, despite the way it usually works for Lunars, thanks to the actions of her host's father and one Mr. James Reed—and an orange-skinned lab experiment still getting used to the way the world worked. They're an odd pair, but they're never more than a shout away from one another, keeping close even when they don't realize what they're doing.

It was Kelpie who told her, in a slow, shaking voice, that the alchemists had rediscovered Roman concrete, and that the miracle substance was made possible by infusing it with the blood of minor Lunars, picked off from around the edges of their respective pantheons. Artemis had made a terrible choking noise when Kelpie said that, and actually left the table for several minutes to calm herself, pacing along the fence line with her head hanging low and her hands clenched into fists.

Artemis herself never voluntarily worked for the alchemists. But it was her careless interaction with her host that had seen them both delivered into the hands of James Reed, giving him the opportunity to learn and document more than he had any business knowing about the Lunar psyche, the ways the embodied divine interacted with their mortal dwelling places. With that knowledge, he'd been able to write the studies all the alchemists after him had used to exploit the Lunars.

Without her, they would never have figured out that godsblood was the missing component of the fabled concrete. They would never have started forcing their own Lunar incarnations. Dozens of minor Moon gods had died because Artemis was careless with her incarnation. She had received her Hind, the other half of her personification, missing for centuries, for the same reason. It was a hard contradiction for anyone to live with.

They're walking in the halls of the dead. It's not quite a haunted house, not quite a tomb, but something worse, something that belongs in one of the horror movies that Kim and Tim sometimes watch in the living room, two bodies huddled under one blanket, screaming and jumping when the monsters show their faces. Smita doesn't like those movies, doesn't need those movies; if she wants to be terrified, all she needs to do is close her eyes and remember the dozens of times she's died at Erin's hand, the knife sliding between her ribs, the flames from the Hand of Glory licking at her flesh. It's hard to be a normal person surrounded by the fruits of misapplied alchemy.

Maybe that's why she followed Lilianne, why she's here now, in wet clothes with no cellphone service, what feels like miles below the surface of the city; she's the only normal human in her usual social circle, the only person not built in a lab, and sometimes she wants to step away and pretend, for even a few minutes, that normalcy is still possible. Not that this is normal. But Lilianne is an aspiring alchemist, and that means keeping an eye on her is the normal thing to do.

Smita craves normalcy. Some days she mourns the life she thought she was going to live, the one with a solid job and a good marriage and two or three adopted, beloved children running around the big yard of her suburban house, filled with genetically modified grasses that don't grow above a certain height and thus never need to be mowed down. It's a fairy-tale postcard of a possible future that would never have come to pass even if her life hadn't been so thoroughly derailed.

She shivers and finally moves toward the door, passing through it to the empty halls beyond. Lilianne has managed to find the lights here as well: the hallway, which is plain, undecorated concrete, the walls not even painted, the floor not softened by even the most industrial of carpets, is lit by a soft white light from above, unflickering and static. It adds an odd unreality to the place, which is unreal enough to begin with.

Doors lead off the corridor on both sides, spaced about fifteen feet apart, as far as Smita can see. She doesn't know where Lilianne has gone. She has no way of following. She looks back over her shoulder at the kitchen. She could go back to the swamp, try to wade her way back to the ladder—their journey here was direct, if long, and there are no turns to take or miss. But the water was almost cold enough to kill her the first time, and she's already half-frozen. If she tries to wade back to the ladder, she'll die.

She's died before. But those times, it had been at Erin's hand, and Roger and Dodger had known to look when they irresponsibly rewound time and tried for a better ending. While she's certain Erin will eventually find her body, will notice the disruption created by her absence, she's not nearly as certain that the twins would be willing to go through the complexity and strain of a new time loop just to bring her back.

(And one thing she's learned from her repeated deaths, even if they were undone by almost-human hands: dead is still dead. She's died every time she was killed, and it never got more pleasant. This isn't a video game where there are no consequences for falling off a cliff or missing a button press. This is real life, and it never lets you go without making you pay for it.)

Smita stops where she is, cups her hands around her mouth, and calls, "Lily? You here?"

There's a clatter from somewhere up ahead, sudden enough that for a moment it feels like her heart has stopped beating. Smita freezes, not even shivering, and waits to see what she's just called down on herself.

The door swings open, and Lilianne's head appears around the edge, the other woman beaming as brightly as a kid on Christmas morning. "There you are!" she virtually chirps. "I figured you'd follow soon enough. Come on, I found one of the locker rooms."

"They have locker rooms?" asks Smita, and hurries down the hall to slip into the room.

As promised, it's a locker room, even if it looks more like the sort of thing you'd find at a fancy spa than in a sports complex or gymnasium. The lockers are made of red cedar slats, all of them polished until splinters become an unthinkable horror for a different age. Benches of the same wood stand a few feet away, bolted to the floor. There are even showers, and a long row of sinks with accompanying mirrors and power outlets, perfect for personal grooming.

Lilianne is holding a fluffy white towel in one arm, which she thrusts at Smita. "You need to get dry," she says. "You're short enough that you were a lot more submerged than I was, and I don't like what that means for your core temperature. Most of the lockers have robes in them if you want to take a shower."

She sounds so earnest that Smita almost laughs in her face, even as she takes the towel and wraps it around herself, shivering again now that warmth has become a possibility rather than a distant dream.

"I don't really want to be naked and wet in the creepy abandoned underground lab," she says.

"So you'll just be wet, then?" Lilianne shrugs. "Suit yourself. I was going to suggest that you get clean and warm and put a robe on, and then we can go looking for the laundry facilities. I won't stay in here while you shower. There's a lab next door. It's abandoned for the moment, but I can explore it until you're ready for me to come back. I don't want you to be uncomfortable, but I also don't want you to get hypothermia."

Smita glances over her shoulder at the shower stalls, curtained off and more tempting than words can easily express. "Are you sure the water works?"

"Yes, and the temperature is adjustable. Whatever systems they set up down here, they're self-contained and still operational. There's shampoo and conditioner in the lockers if you need to wash your hair, and soap already in the stalls." Lilianne looks at her, earnest and pleading. "Please just . . . get warm? And out of those wet clothes? I'll see if I can find something else for you to wear if the robe isn't enough to make you comfortable, but anything would be better than running around in wet denim."

"*You're* running around in wet denim."

"I'm not shivering the way you are. And I'm going to look for sweatpants whether you shower or not. I just need to explore more than I need to boil myself."

Smita doesn't want to be the kind of person who needs to stop for a shower in the middle of a dangerous adventure. She wants to be the kind of person who barrels merrily onward, a wrecking ball striking the problem with a resounding ferocity. She takes another look around the locker room, sags, and sighs.

"I'll shower," she says.

"Thank you," responds Lilianne, with a fervor that makes Smita realize her lips must be as blue as a child's after jumping into a lake. "I won't go more than two rooms away, and I won't come back in unless it's to put dry clothes on the bench, promise."

"All right," says Smita. "Thank you. I'll be right out."

Lilianne puts the towel down on the nearest bench, flashing her an awkward smile, and moves toward the nearest curtained-off shower stall.

The nearest locker contains shampoo and conditioner, as promised, and with the layout of the shower heads, there's no reasonable way to be sure she's not going to get her hair wet: she grabs both bottles, taking them with her into the stall, where she sets them on the shallow shelf provided for just this purpose and begins peeling off her soaking-wet clothing.

Lilianne was right: she feels better almost instantly, even as the cool air of the locker room hits her skin and reminds her just how close to freezing she really is. She tosses the clothes out of the stall and onto the locker-room floor, sending a silent prayer to whatever gods might be listening (rather than incarnate and dating her housemate) that there will be a dryer that can be used to make her underwear something she can wear again. The thought of wading back to that ladder in wet underwear is a step too far after the past few hours. She'll stay here before she allows it to become a reality.

Blessedly, when she turns the taps, the water works as well and heats up as quickly as she could have hoped, cascading down over her in a glorious, cleansing tide. She just stands there for several minutes, letting it warm her from the outside in. First the shivering stops. Then she begins to feel like she could actually survive the trek back to the surface. Then, as the last of the ice in her belly lets go, she begins to truly appreciate the enormity of what they've discovered.

Roger and Dodger told her about the secret alchemical lab hidden in the very heart of Berkeley. They don't keep secrets in their household. They used to keep secrets, too many of them to truly count, and all that got them was separated, murdered, and put through endlessly repeating loops of the same short years, preventing them from moving forward into a better or brighter future. No. Secrets are too dangerous to allow past the front door.

They told her about it, and of course she listened, of course she nodded and asked all the right questions, learned as much as she could about their discovery . . . and then forgot virtually all of it, because it didn't matter, did it? The alchemists were gone, and after the way they'd been driven out, the Congress wasn't going to send anyone else to take their place. Berkeley was free, and the lab was just an artifact of a worse time, one that wasn't coming back.

But all their stories hadn't been able to convey the enormity of the place, the fact that it had hallways long enough to echo, or an internal support structure that seemed designed to care for dozens of people all at the same time.

And none of what they'd done or explained to her had been enough to keep independent alchemists out of the city, which was the truly dangerous part of the whole situation. She couldn't explain the people she lived with to Lilianne—secrets were dangerous, but some secrets weren't hers to share. She couldn't change the other woman's mind about alchemy, couldn't convince her to leave it alone and live a normal life, one beyond the reach of the Alchemical Congress.

Why does she care so much, anyway? She lathers shampoo into her hair, scrubs with frustrated ferocity, and rinses the suds away before reaching for the conditioner. She only *met* Lilianne today: she's basically a stranger. The number of things Smita can say with conviction that she knows about Lilianne can be counted on her fingers. She's from Alabama; she's studying American history, and cares enough about American children's literature to have made it her focus—although the fact that she's an alchemist means she's probably only doing that so she can study the Up-and-Under books in an endless loop, searching every period and paragraph for Asphodel Baker's secrets. She's an aspiring alchemist, advanced enough in her studies to have made a dowsing pendulum and be able to learn certain secrets from her peers, not so advanced that she can pass up the call to adventure. She's tall, and has thick, dark brown hair that needs to be styled better, but is still beautiful.

There's not much else. When someone she knows that shallowly wants to risk her life exploring an abandoned alchemist's lab, why shouldn't she just *let* them? Why did she have to invite herself along?

The sound of a door opening and closing again makes her tense, goosebumps breaking out on her arms and the back of her neck despite the heat of the water. "Hello?" she calls, pitching her voice loud enough to be heard over the shower. "I'm still in here."

The door closes a second time, which means it must have been opened a second time . . . but no one answers her. Lilianne, if that was her, must have realized her mistake and left as quietly as she could.

Despite the knowledge that she's alone again, Smita finishes her shower as quickly as she can, and when she turns off the water she freezes for several seconds, listening for any signs that someone else might be in the room. There aren't any. Finally, cautiously, she pulls the curtain open to reach for the towel.

A pair of sweatpants is folded on the nearest bench, along with a soft-looking long-sleeved shirt of some kind and a loose white coat that would be better suited to a researcher of some sort. Smita blinks, several times, before beginning to dry herself off.

She'll get dressed in a moment.

* * *

Lilianne feels like a child somehow magically granted access to Santa's workshop. The real one, at the North Pole that only exists in movies, where elves make the toys and it's basically Christmas all year long. The place where miracles can happen.

This lab is a miracle. A terrible one if she stops to think about it for too long: the Lunars are a class of incarnate, just like her parents, and just like her parents, they didn't have any choice in what they manifested. Someone died to make this place. Maybe more than one someone. And since the minor manifestations the alchemists are able to catch are almost always young, they may have been teenagers or even children. It's a horrible thought.

But their deaths are in the past. They can't be unmade or undone, no matter how much she may wish they could be. And this place, this glorious, wonderful, impossible place . . . well, it's still here, and that makes it the most important thing in the world.

Keeping her word to Smita has proven more difficult than she expected it to be. True, two rooms in each direction, including across the hall, leaves her with eight new places to explore, but there's so much to see, and she just wants to run along the halls, cackling with delight at her own cleverness and incredible good fortune. Cleverness because she was able to craft a pendulum accurate enough to get her here in the first place; good fortune because no one else has been here at all. There would be signs if they had been, things out of place on the lab tables, the more valuable tinctures and components missing from the shelves. But no, no. It's all here.

Everything she could ever want or need, from mercury and purified copper all the way to vials of godsblood and a few precious flasks of alkahest, and it's all hers for the taking. She'll be able to push her studies forward by *years*—and that doesn't even take the books into account.

The room to the right of the locker room is storage, napkins and extra towels and refills for the soap dispensers, flasks and vials and spare stoppers. It's like a glorious cross between a janitor's closet and the cabinets at the back of her high school chemistry class, and she could spend hours in there alone.

Next to it, however, is the first of the actual labs. It's small, and was clearly being used for botany at one point: some of the bonsai trees are still alive, their roots dry as dust but their branches straining toward the grow lights on the ceiling, which were already on when she stepped into the room. The younger plants are dead, all of them, wilted and collapsed in their pots, and without some sort of guide to the experiments that were being performed here, Lilianne knows she'll never be able to understand them. No one can study every discipline, and even within alchemy, there is specialization.

Going in the other direction from the locker room brings Lilianne to a second lab, almost identical to the first, but with empty cages in place of dead plants, a dissection table, and several texts on anatomy. The tools are stainless steel, clean and beautiful, and Lilianne can't bring herself to touch them. These were working alchemists from the Congress, and they were willing to build their foundations on the blood of a non-consenting Lunar. There's no telling what those tools may have been used against.

She's always known that alchemy is built on a bed of bones. She would have known it from the first time her parents recoiled from the word, looking at her with a horror and revulsion that she hasn't seen on their faces since, and had never seen before. But until this moment, she's never really had to face the full reality of it. What alchemy costs, what it demands . . . that price is built into the very stone around her, and for a moment she can feel the weight of it pressing down, too heavy to be borne.

The room beyond *that* is a library, large enough to be enthralling, small enough to make her think that similar rooms must be strewn throughout the structure, tucked away behind unassuming doors and filled with books relevant to the work going on in the closest labs. She picks up a book on incarnate animals and is almost instantly lost, sinking into the pages detailing all the ways in which the standard incarnations can occasionally manifest in horses, or dogs, or other creatures close enough to humanity to have picked up some of their simpler attributes. Skimming through it raises questions about domestication, and whether humans might not be considered domesticated by the divine.

It's an unsettling thought. She puts the book back down, reluctantly turning toward the door. She has more rooms to explore, and Smita won't be in the shower forever. She's managed to stay within the range she promised, and she feels like she should get some sort of reward for that.

The feeling is ridiculous enough to stop her in her tracks for a moment. She has this whole lab to pillage at her leisure, with no one to stop or slow her. She already has all the reward she'll ever need.

Pleased with her own revelation, she leaves the library and turns back toward the locker room. Once Smita is clean and dry, they can find another way out of here, some elevator or hidden stairwell that doesn't require wading through a sewer to access. She'll get Smita to street level without endangering her again, and then maybe they can exchange numbers, give her a way to contact the most beautiful woman in the world when she's done looting the abandoned toys the Congress left behind.

Maybe they can be friends. She's fine with that, as an outcome; she doesn't need Smita to return any interest she might have, miraculous as that would be. Friendship is in some ways a greater reward than romance, which never seems to last as long. Given a choice between having Smita in her life for a long time or a good time, she'll take the length.

The locker room door is still closed. She raps her knuckles against the wood, echoes rolling down the hall, and leans closer as she calls, "You all right in there? Sorry, but I didn't find any sweatpants in the rooms right next door. I'm sure there's a laundry room somewhere, but you may be in that robe for a little while."

"What are you talking about?"

The question comes from behind her, not behind the door. Lilianne turns. Smita is standing in the hall, dressed in sweatpants, a soft sweatshirt, and a lab coat that stands out crisp as new-fallen snow against her deep brown skin. Lilianne decides in an instant that Smita should always wear white. It somehow makes her even lovelier, which shouldn't be possible.

Smita is looking at her with confusion, brows furrowed and lips drawn down in a small, bewildered frown.

Lilianne blinks, looking back to the locker room, then to Smita again. "You found clothes," she says, awkwardly.

"You *brought* me clothes," corrects Smita. "I wish you hadn't come inside without asking, but at least I'm dry now. Let's go."

She turns and starts down the hall, not pausing to see whether Lilianne is following her.

Uneasy, Lilianne does.

* * *

Smita towels herself dry, moving as quickly as she can manage before hanging the towel on a nearby rack. Her limbs are weary, exhausted beyond what makes sense for how much exercise she's had tonight. Cold will do that, she supposes. It has a way of sapping the strength from everything.

Thinking about the cold reminds her of the pale woman who'd collapsed in their front garden last year, dropping like a stone as soon as she crossed the border into Dodger's captive artificial summer. Melanie, her name had been, and she was the living soul of Winter, the season and the concept in one. Her traveling companion and boyfriend, Harry, had been beside himself after seeing Melanie go down, and getting the two of them awake and on their way had been most of the work of an afternoon.

She hasn't seen either of them since, but she's heard Melanie laughing from Dodger's phone when it was set to speaker, and she knows they won their race to claim the crowns of their seasons, becoming something more than human, something less than gods. It's all so complicated, and some days she feels like she's the only real human left in the entire world, the only person not somehow tied into a universal concept instead of ordinary human days. The cold never sapped Melanie's strength away, because the cold was her burden and her birthright.

Smita's only birthright is a clever mind and dexterous hands, and some days she thinks she has more in common with the alchemists her friends revile so much than she does with her friends themselves. One day they'll realize that she's too human to belong, and then she'll find herself cast out, alone in a world that no longer entirely makes sense after everything she's seen.

The clothes Lilianne found for her are surprisingly well-fitting. She pulls them on, feeling safer and more secure with a layer of fabric between her and the rest of the lab. This shower room could fit into any luxury spa in San Francisco, but she's still punishingly aware of the weight of the city high above her, the tons of earth just waiting to come plummeting down and make this place her tomb.

The white coat that was stacked with her new clothes is definitely a lab coat, the sort of thing alchemists wear when they're doing their experiments. The sort of thing Smita herself used to wear when she worked in active genetics labs. She looks at it for a moment, expression grave, before shrugging it on and rolling her shoulders to make it hang correctly down the line of her body. Like everything else, it fits precisely.

"If she doesn't make it as an alchemist, Lily has a career as a personal shopper ahead of her," she says, as much to hear the sound of her own voice as to break the silence. She gathers her wet clothes from the floor, wrapping them in the towel, and turns to the door.

The hall is empty, and she doesn't hear Lilianne moving around anywhere nearby, which is odd, since she'd seemed utterly sincere about not going more than two doors in any direction. Feeling suddenly uneasy, Smita hurries to check the rooms that would fall under Lilianne's promise. She doesn't find her, not in any of them. She's truly alone.

Panic gripping her heart like a dead man's frozen fingers, Smita whirls and runs back to the kitchen where they initially entered. At least if she can see the door back to the sewer, she'll know she has a way out of here, should she need it. She hasn't put her wet shoes back on yet. She can't quite bear the thought of shoving her dry feet back into the cold confines of dripping nylon and rubber. But she *could*, if she needed to, and if she moves fast, she might be able to make it out of the sewer before she freezes—

And it's a moot point anyway, because when she opens the door that should lead to the kitchen, she finds an office on the other side, complete with hefty oak desk and wall lined in matching shelves, each one heavy with books. She freezes in the doorway, hand still on the knob, before pulling the door shut again and backing away, looking up and down the hall. This was the right door, she knows it was. And yet . . .

Rooms don't just rearrange themselves like that, not in the real word, not outside the sometimes-unreal confines of her own home. She must have just counted wrong. She turns toward the next door, trying again.

A supply closet.

The next two doors are a small lab and a shockingly sterile sitting room. There's no sign of the kitchen, or of Lilianne. She's been abandoned, deserted in a place that no one else knows how to find. She's trapped.

Smita has been through more than any woman in her position should be asked to endure. She's died, dozens of times, due to the orders of alchemists, at the hands of an alchemical creation. (She doesn't always think of Erin in terms of her origins, anymore, but she still knows what the person who's become her best friend really is. Has known long enough that she no longer thinks of her as anything else, no matter what happens around them.) The panic grasping her heart is no longer icy cold: it's a burning plume of terror, igniting her from the inside out.

There must be a way out of here. There *has* to be. Smita turns and runs, fleeing down the hall. The sound of her bare feet slapping against the tile is the only thing she leaves behind.

* * *

Lilianne walks down the hall at a measured pace, Smita beside her, moving with an eerie silence. She glances down at Smita's feet. They're bare, and she would expect to hear at least a little sound when they strike the ground. But there's nothing, only the sound of her own steps echoing along the empty hall.

Something is very wrong. With the entire situation—and, terribly, with Smita. She looks precisely as she did when they first met on the quad, save for her clothing, but didn't her hair seem like it would be softer, before? Less like the polished carapace of some infinitely complex insect? And weren't her eyes kinder?

The light is harsh here in the lab, endlessly bright and unvarying. Maybe that's what saps the kindness from Smita's eyes, what squares the corners of her mouth. Maybe it's all the situation, and there's nothing wrong at all.

Lilianne turns a corner, and there before her is a lab with an indented floor, easily three feet below the level of the hall from what she can tell. The angles are warped by the water that has filled the space, dripping from a crack in the ceiling. Cracks shouldn't be possible, not here, in this shell of godsblood and alchemy, but this one has opened wide enough to let a leak break through, water falling inexorably to drown the lab.

The light casts strange ripples across the near-motionless surface. Lilianne takes a moment to stop and gape at the scene in front of her, one more impossibility added to a day filled with them, one more obstacle to overcome.

Her first thought when she feels Smita's hands press against her back is joy, like she's become a source of comfort for this woman she's only just met, like her seedling crush may have the chance to bloom.

Then Smita is shoving her, hard, and she's tumbling into the freezing water that fills the lab, mixed with who-knows-what chemicals from the desks and workstations it covers. She gasps, flailing frantically to get her head above the surface, then turns, straightening, to stare at Smita.

But it isn't Smita anymore. It was never Smita to begin with. The figure standing at the water's edge is easily seven feet tall, neck elongated and swan-like, hands dangling by digitigrade ankles. The clothes that fit so well a moment ago are now almost a mockery of human attire, clinging to a body that's more insectile than mammalian.

Not-Smita grins, showing jagged, needlelike teeth that would look more at home in the mouth of a viperfish than a . . . whatever this is.

Then, with an inhuman ease, the creature is sliding into the water, disappearing immediately below the surface, and Lilianne doesn't know where it is, and she doesn't know what it's going to do, and this—all of this, this entire journey into the unknown—has been a mistake.

Aggression

TIMELINE: AUGUST 23, 2018.

Smita runs and keeps on running until she hits her first dead end. It's a featureless white wall, identical to all the other walls she's seen, except that this one has no doors or corridors attached. It's like a maze down here, everything so close to the same that she can get turned around while she's standing still, or as good as: she wishes now that she'd thought to mark her trail as she fled, to leave *something* behind for her to follow.

But maybe even that wouldn't have helped. She's been carrying her wet clothes this whole time, and they're still dripping, despite the towel she's wrapped around them. There should be drops of water on the floor to mark where she's been, and there aren't. It's like the tile has been drinking everything she offers it.

It's like the lab doesn't want her to know where she is, or how to go back in the right direction.

Smita stops and just stares at the wall for a moment, trying to understand how this can be happening. Then she turns.

"I am a woman of *science*," she mutters. "I am fully capable of getting myself out of here without any help or guidance. If anyone can get out of here, it's me." She begins marching back the way she came, letting the fingertips of her free hand trail against the nearest wall.

She's no Ariadne, to weave a ball of thread capable of unraveling a labyrinth, no Theseus fated to defeat the minotaur, but she's clever and determined and she's survived worse than this. She's survived the Erin she still sees in her dreams, with the burning hand of a murdered man in one hand and a naked knife in the other. She's survived the end of time itself. She can do this.

So she walks briskly. She doesn't run, she doesn't hesitate, and she doesn't look back. Looking back is how it ends for so many of the girls in movies that look far too much like her current situation. She's not going to be one of them. She's going to make it out of here.

She walks until her feet hurt, until the cold of the tile has chased away the last of the warmth the shower left in her toes, until she wants to scream from the unending monotony of it all. She walks until there's nothing left in the world but walking, and when she stumbles, toes numb from the distance they've consumed, she catches herself against the wall and looks to the nearest door.

About half the rooms she's seen so far had some sort of seating inside, and right now, that's what she needs more than almost anything. Something to drink would also be nice, but she doesn't trust anything she might find down here.

Pushing herself away from the wall, she takes an unsteady step toward the door, then another, until it's right there in front of her, until the knob is in her hand and she's turning it to the right, the door swinging open as she pushes it inward, revealing another small, private lab. There's a large armchair, upholstered in plush brown leather, and a large desk. Flicking the lights on, she steps fully inside and moves to sit, not really looking at anything beyond the chair. Nothing matters yet, nothing but that.

Sinking down into the soft embrace of buttery leather, Smita sighs, then turns her attention to the nearest bookshelf. It's covered in volumes she's never seen before, and she spares a fleeting thought for Roger's library at home. He'd be thrilled if she could bring these all back for him, and she probably wouldn't see him for a week or more.

"Judy would be *furious*," she says, chuckling dryly, and reaches for the first book whose title is written in English. It's a biography of Asphodel Baker, one of the only times she's seen the woman's name written out in full. Normally she's credited as "A. Deborah Baker," the name she used when she wrote the Up-and-Under books. That's the version of the old alchemist the world remembers.

That's not the one Smita finds as she opens the book and begins flipping idly through its contents, only skimming at first, then reading more and more closely. It's a biography, yes, but it's a biography of Asphodel as alchemist, not Asphodel as author. This is the woman that only the Alchemical Congress knew—and even they, not particularly well, given the number of times she's credited with a discovery on one page, only to have that same discovery minimized and downplayed on the next, like nothing she's ever done could truly matter enough to be worth remembering for longer than a footnote.

The book is thick. There's no way she can stay awake long enough to read it all, even if it was safe to try. Lilianne has abandoned her: at this point, there's no other conclusion she can reach. She's been wandering through this massive underground complex long enough that she should have run into the alchemist by now, if she were still here. This was all a trap.

It feels paranoid to think that way, but why else would Lilianne have "just happened" to wander by their house as Smita was stepping out of the yard? She couldn't possibly have predicted when Smita was going to go for milk. She must have been watching, which meant she must have known where the house was. No one knows where the house is unless they've been invited—and Lilianne has never been invited.

No, this was all too easy, right up until it became impossibly hard. She closes the book, then tucks it into her purse before withdrawing her phone and checking the time. It's almost four o'clock in the morning. Erin will notice that she's gone soon enough, and once Erin notices, this will all be over. The living incarnation of Order will track her down more quickly than anyone else in the world could hope to manage, and all Smita has to do is stay alive until then.

She's tempted to stay exactly where she is, to relax into the leather chair and keep reading about the atrocities Asphodel committed and participated in in the name of her beloved alchemy: according to the book, she revealed her personal maid as a Lunar to an older alchemist before she turned ten, allowing the girl to be cut up for parts. And she was in her teens when she lured a potential incarnate Winter to her yard and sacrificed him in the same way.

The book's author presents these events like they were positive things, like any young alchemist should be proud to emulate her by doing the same. Like once someone was an incarnate of the universe, they didn't get the rights afforded to a human anymore . . . not even the right to stay alive. Smita's known for years that her beloved childhood author was an alchemist before she was anything else, but this is the first time she's really had to face the things Asphodel did in her pursuit of power. She was a monster.

All alchemists are monsters. She was a fool to think that Lilianne might be different just because she's funny and awkward and kind. None of those things would stop her from cutting the people Smita loved into pieces if she thought that it could advance her art.

She probably hadn't been hoping for Smita when she started watching the house. She'd probably been hoping for a piece of the Doctrine, either incarnate or potential. Smita spares a moment to consider how *that* would have gone for a self-taught alchemist without anyone to back her up, then lets the image go. It isn't going to help her now.

With regret, she levers herself out of the chair and slings her purse back over her shoulder, turning toward the door. Erin will come for her, but that doesn't mean she can sit around like some damsel in distress. Who knows what secrets and horrors the alchemists may have hidden here? She needs to learn what she can while she has the opportunity.

The halls seem, if possible, even longer and emptier than before, and the tile is even colder, almost freezing under her bare feet. Smita shivers and fights the urge to go back into the safe little room with its nice leather chair and carpeted floor. She can do this.

She can. She starts walking, not heading anywhere in particular, and only screams a little when Lilianne steps around a corner and into view. Pressing a hand to her chest to keep her hammering heart inside, she catches herself against the wall and wheezes.

"Don't *do* that," she says.

"Do that," echoes Lilianne, and . . . is something wrong with her voice? It's only two syllables, but something about them is discordant enough to send a shiver along her spine. Lilianne's Alabama accent is gone, replaced by a harsh, almost-metallic scrape.

"Lily . . . ?" She doesn't have to force her fear. It just comes out, whether she wants it to or not.

And Lilianne smiles.

And that is definitely *not* Lilianne, because the smile keeps going, extending out and out and out until it reaches just behind her ears. Her lips part, and her mouth is a forest of teeth, sharp as razors and serrated like a shark's, clean and white and terrible.

She takes a step forward and Smita takes a step back, away from her.

"Naughty little thief," says the non-Lilianne. "Taking things that aren't yours. Might have let you go if you hadn't done that—only no, wait, wouldn't have, because you already stole our water, used our soap. Covered your scent for long enough to make it less fun to follow you through our halls. Shouldn't have done that, either. You've made so many terrible choices, little thief. Make one more. Choose not to run."

Smita doesn't need to be told twice. She spins on her heel and bolts down the hall, running as fast as she can to put some distance between herself and the imposter.

Her mind races as she runs, moving even faster than her body. Lilianne can't be the enemy. If she were, the lab's defenses, whatever they are, wouldn't be emulating her to get Smita close enough to attack. Or maybe she is, and the lab just doesn't realize that Smita's had the time to put the pieces together. Or . . .

She could hang the rest of her life on "or." If it distracts her too badly, if it slows her down, she could die on "or." She shunts those thoughts to the side as fiercely as she can and keeps running, heart pounding hard, feet pounding harder. She has no idea what the thing behind her is, whether she can outrun it, or whether she can hide. She should have paid more attention when Kim burbled about the secrets of alchemy, when Dodger interrogated Kelpie about the horrors she'd been accessory to. She wouldn't be in this situation if she'd paid more attention.

Splashing drifts down the hall from up ahead. Smita finds it in herself to run even faster, practically sprinting toward the first sound she's heard since getting out of the shower. The creature commented on her hiding her scent by bathing; maybe if there's standing water and she wets herself down, she'll be able to do it again. This could all be over if she can reach the water.

Then she rounds a corner and finds herself facing a half-submerged lab, the floor sunken in comparison to everything else around it. There's no good reason for that design choice, but it doesn't matter. Pulling her purse off her shoulder, she throws it, complete with its precious cargo of biography and phone, into the dry part of the lab. She doesn't slow down, and less than a second after she makes her throw, she's splashing into the water.

Lifting her arms out in front of herself, Smita takes a deep breath, and dives.

The water is cold enough to feel like a slap across her face when she hits the surface. She manages not to inhale, barely, and forces herself to stay submerged, waiting for the moment when something else will splash into the pool.

It doesn't. Slowly, cautiously, she rises, until just the top half of her head is exposed. She turns back toward the dry portion of the lab, opening her eyes. The water clinging to her lashes casts the room in diamond glints, light bouncing off the water and making it difficult to see. The creature is still there. It no longer looks remotely like Lilianne. It barely looks bipedal. It's bent near-double, sniffing at her purse with the focus of a hunting hound.

It starts to raise its head and look back toward the water, scanning for her. Smita hastily ducks back under. The water stings her eyes. She has no idea what it might be mixed with, and right now, she genuinely doesn't care. She can take as many showers as it takes to feel like she's clean again. And if whatever's making her eyes burn melts her skin, well, she'll deal with that when the time comes. Anything short of death can be dealt with, here in the dark below the ground.

Something is moving in the water with her. She feels the ripples created by its passage as they bounce against her, and all concern about the thing that chased her here vanishes, replaced by concern about being grabbed by a creature she can't see. Her heart is beating hard enough to hurt, and the water is cold enough that she's already starting to freeze again. She can feel it sinking into her tissues, insulating fat rapidly becoming a layer of coolant wrapped around her organs.

She surfaces again, scanning the water's surface frantically for signs of where the motion might be coming from. The light from overhead is still glaringly bright, but somehow only penetrates a few inches into the water, leaving the depths unfathomable and far darker than they should be.

As she's scanning, she finds Lilianne. The *real* Lilianne, she presumes, unless the lab has devoted the resources to making multiple decoys; this one is soaking wet, crouching atop a desk shoved against the far wall, only the top inch or so of it visible above the water. Her hair hangs in her face in ropey coils, and her mascara has run down her cheeks like inky tears. It would make sense for her to be crying; her left shoulder has been flayed open, muscle and tendons exposed. And it looks like some of those cuts may go all the way down to the bone. She's holding herself so perfectly still that it makes sense Smita didn't spot her before. She must be freezing, and possibly going into shock from the blood loss, but she's not moving.

Smita rises a little farther out of the water, straightening so she can take a step toward Lilianne. Lilianne's eyes widen in sudden fear, and she sits back on her heels, waving frantically for Smita to stay where she is. Smita blinks.

The creature behind her is showing no signs of getting into the water, more interested in sniffing at Smita's purse than in pursuing its prey. It begins to occur to her that this might not be a good thing. Based on Lilianne's shoulder, whatever she's in the water with is nasty enough that the creature may just not feel like fighting over her body. Lilianne is still gesturing frantically.

They're about ten feet apart. There's a monster she can see behind her and one she can't see somewhere in the water. When in doubt, better to choose the danger that might not be as dangerous as your mind is making it out to be. She sinks back down into the water and pushes off against the floor, swimming as slowly as she can toward the other woman, restricting herself to a breaststroke that will disturb the water as little as possible.

She feels the ripples pass again, so close that it's like having a massive fish pass by barely outside of arm's reach. She shudders and keeps swimming, moving slow, expecting to feel a clawed hand close around her throat or ankle at any moment.

The anticipated attack doesn't come. She surfaces to breathe and sees the desk only a few feet away. The water is deep enough for swimming, but shallow enough that she can stand up, and so she does, wading the rest of the way to her destination. Lilianne watches her with wide eyes, clearly terrified, and when Smita begins to hoist herself up onto the desk's top, Lilianne reaches out as if she's going to push her away.

"No," whispers Smita, more harshly than she intends to. She winces at the sound of her own voice.

On the other side of the lab—the other side of the water—the not-Lily's head whips around, attention caught by the sudden noise.

Smita tenses, moving again to boost herself onto the desk. This time, Lilianne doesn't move, just huddles where she is, as far away as the limited space allows.

It's not until both her feet are out of the water and she's able to cross her legs, settling into the dubious safety of the dry world, that she turns to Lilianne. The other woman is still watching her with terror in her eyes.

"I'm really me," whispers Smita, making her voice as small as she possibly can. It still carries in the near-silence of the room, causing the thing that chased her here to look over again, lips pulling back from its lips as it hisses. "What *is* that thing?"

Lilianne worries her lip between her teeth. "There are schools of alchemy," she whispers back. "Some of them focus more on creating life than they do on creating gold or medicines. We call it takwin—literally 'creation.' If someone was brewing homunculi down here, they could have been left behind when the alchemists fled. I've never heard of homunculi that could change shapes, but

I'm not that advanced, not compared to someone who might be doing their work in a place like this."

The creature on the other side of the lab straightens, becoming more immediately bipedal as it does, and leans against a shelf as it shakes one long, spindly finger at the pair of them. "Ah-ah-ah," it says, and its voice remains a twisted parody of Lilianne's. "I let you get away from me, little thief, but I didn't give you permission to hand someone else your homework. If you want to know what I am, come over here and let me whisper in your ear." It runs a horribly elongated tongue along its serrated teeth, leering.

Smita catches her breath and shakes her head. "No, I don't think so," she says, in a perfectly normal tone of voice. The creature isn't making any effort to be quiet, so why should she? Anything that might be attracted by the sound of voices is already going to be attracted at this rate. "I have *some* slivers of self-preservation remaining."

"Little thief," croons the creature. "Little liar. Little snack. I'll swallow you whole."

"Which is precisely why I'm remaining where I am."

"I can enter the water if I want to."

"Can you?" She cocks her head politely to the side. "I think I would like to see that."

The creature begins pacing back and forth at the top of the steps leading down into the pool. "I think you wouldn't. I would have your entrails for my own enrichment if you saw that."

"And yet you're not doing it. Why not?"

"*Smita*," hisses Lilianne, grabbing her wrist to emphasize her point. "Maybe we don't taunt the horrifying alchemical creation?"

Because there's nothing else this can be. There are wonders in the world, natural miracles, incarnations of ideas that were never meant to walk in flesh, but even those things follow their own forms of natural law. The universe makes only what it needs. It doesn't need this creature, with its overly jointed arms and its mouth full of teeth stolen from some other species, some other phylum. Someone *made* this. A person, acting with clear, if misguided, intent.

"And maybe we do," says Smita. She turns to face Lilianne, the real one. "Why are you on this desk? What was in the water with me? Why can't we just swim away, looking for another way out of this fucked-up situation?"

"You were," says Lilianne, voice dropping back down to a whisper as she shoots an uneasy glance at the surface of the water. "It was you. You . . . you found me in the hall. But you weren't you anymore. You were something terrible. You pushed me into the water."

"I didn't," says Smita, with calm certainty. "I would never. Pushing another woman into even clean water when she hasn't requested it is offensive. Depending on the circumstances, it could even qualify as assault."

Lilianne blinks, several times, before wiping her eyes with the back of one hand and shrinking further in on herself, trying to become as small as possible.

"Whatever chased you here, it wasn't me," says Smita. "Any more than what chased me here was you."

The creature watching them from the other side of the water snarls again, frustration becoming audible. "Come back *over* here," it demands. "I promise to make it quick if you come here of your own free will."

"I'm not sure your promises have much weight anymore," says Smita. "I've been gone for some time now. Erin's going to come looking for me."

The creature takes a step back, fear flashing across its face.

"Oh, good," says Smita. "I thought you might know who I was talking about. She'll find me, you know. She *always* finds me. I am her cross to bear, and she's mine, and that means she always, always finds me. Will she find you at the same time?"

"Smita?" asks Lilianne. "What are you talking about?"

Smita glances over at her, grimacing apologetically. "I'm afraid I lied by staying silent while you explained the basic principles of alchemy to me. I know the basics, and more than the basics, and more than enough beyond that to have spoken up. I didn't because . . . I was enjoying listening to you talk, and I wanted to know what *you* knew. How you would explain all the things we were walking into, what you would think was important enough to mention, what you wouldn't."

Lilianne gives her a horrified look. "You're an alchemist?"

"No," says Smita. "I'm not an alchemist, and I'm not a product of alchemy either. I'm a victim. I've died for your great art, hundreds of times, and now that I'm alive and aware of what's happening around me, I never intend to be caught off guard by alchemy again. Which is why"—she raises her voice, looking pointedly back toward the creature—"I am not a fan of being cornered by manmade monsters who refuse to explain themselves to me. I find it quite rude, actually."

The creature on the other side of the water shows its teeth again. Smita scoffs.

"You're very frightening, when you're chasing someone half your size through a place they don't know," she says, scornfully. "Terrifying. But you're not so scary when you're just standing there, and clearly afraid to *get in the water.* You can go now. The adults are talking."

Lilianne gives her a bewildered, disbelieving look. Smita smiles at her, clearly trying to be reassuring, and just as clearly failing.

"I understand some of the allure of alchemy," she says. "I've considered it, a time or two. I even joined one of those ineffective suburban covens for a little while, all about raising energy and giving it back to the earth. Making our intent into a tool and focusing it at the universe. It was fun. Healing, even, because it reminded me that not everyone who's trying to change the world is doing it out of a desire to control everything around them. I learned plenty from my time with the coven."

"Then what happened?"

Smita looks at the water, at the ripples without a visible source, made by whatever lurks below the surface. "Alchemists happened," she says darkly. "The ones who built this lab. They were trying to find a friend of mine who they had decided was their property, and they found the place where we met instead. They killed one of our members. They widowed another. Using monstrous things they called 'aufs,' made out of dead people and bad designs. And they kept coming and coming and coming, until some more friends of mine convinced them that Berkeley wasn't their kind of town after all."

Lilianne stares at her, open-mouthed and even more confused than she was before Smita started her explanation. "But . . . this was a proper stronghold of the American Alchemical Congress. There's no way some random friends of yours could have convinced its keepers to abandon it just like that. That isn't how the Congress *works*."

"Lily," says Smita. "My friends aren't random. They can convince just about anyone to do just about anything if they have good-enough reason to try."

"They won't come for you, you know," says a voice, eerily like and yet unlike Smita's own.

She closes her eyes and lets her head hang forward, half-dry hair forming a curtain around her face. "I suppose you're the thing in the water?" she asks.

"I am," says the voice. "I was. I could be again. I am an etiäinen, and I was made to mirror whoever trespassed here."

"So you steal my face and expect me to be impressed by the audacity? You hurt my friend and expect me to welcome you despite the blood on your hands? Go back to the water, beast. If Erin doesn't see you, she may not unmake you for what you've done."

Smita manages to keep her voice level, but she's worried, truly. Worried about the amount of blood Lilianne is losing, the amount she's already lost; the damage to her shoulder is deep and looks like something out of a medical textbook, not the kind of injury she wants to see a friend, even a newly made one, carry.

She's worried about a lot of things. This is the sort of place one goes to worry.

The voice draws closer, although there isn't any splashing, and nothing to indicate that the speaker has climbed up onto the desk to make itself more clearly heard. "They won't come for you," it repeats. "I can smell the sympathy of your skin. You're nothing's incarnate, and you're no shaper of realities. You're just a human being. Weak, frail, not worth saving."

"You say that, but she's saved me so many times it defies description," says Smita. "She'll come for me."

"And when she doesn't, when you have to go into the water, I'll have your pretty little inkpot god-in-waiting for a snack to fill my belly, and make the hours go quicker," says the voice. "I'll have her, and my cousin will have you, and we'll both be fed as we slink back into the shadows to wait for the next little lunches to come wandering down."

"That's why you didn't attack me." Smita turns abruptly, opening her eyes, and finds herself face-to-face with a parody of herself. It still wears something that is recognizably her face, but rotted and ripped away, with no nose, and with eyes sunk so deep into their sockets that looking at them is like trying to see something deep below the ground, shrouded and shaded and hidden away. Its hair is lush and black, and that alone looks healthy, like all the resources it has left have gone into that hair.

Smita looks at its nearly lipless mouth, its bristling rows of needled viperfish teeth, and smiles with her own soft lips, showing square white teeth designed for nothing more than chewing, not ripping or rending flesh from bone.

"You can't touch me, can you?" she asks. "Whatever an etiäinen is, you can't hurt the one whose face you wear."

"You'll never get her to dry land, and if you try, my cousin will have you for a prize," snarls the creature. "I can't hurt you, but I can hurt her, and my cousin can do what I can't. You'll never leave here alive."

"Maybe that's so, but you'll forgive me if I don't take your word for it."

The creature draws back from her. Then, to her dismay, it starts to laugh, a sound like gas bubbling up from chambers deep in the earth.

"No need, no need!" it says triumphantly.

It's not looking at her anymore. Smita's eyes widen as she realizes that it's looking past her, to Lilianne. She whips around, grabbing the other woman by the arm just before her slow lean to the side would have sent her tumbling into the water. She yanks, and Lilianne flops over on top of her, blood still leaking from the wound in her shoulder.

Her eyes are closed.

* * *

Smita usually tries not to think too hard about the first time she remembers dying. It's a dark, terrible thing to remember, and more, the human mind is not designed to retain memories of its own death: her thoughts shy away from the reality of what she knows she's been through, refusing to dwell on the details. But the details are there, buried deep under justifications of careful self-delusions, and she can confront them when she has to.

It was confronting them that led her to take several classes on first aid, on basic paramedic skills. She won't be ready to serve on an ambulance any time soon, and she's not planning to go to nursing school, but she can apply a tourniquet and bandage a wound. She knows what to do.

She hasn't been looking closely at Lilianne's injuries while she argued with the etiäinen in the water. Now, however, she hasn't got a choice, and so she looks.

The gashes are as deep as they seemed from a distance, slicing through muscle and fat like they offered no resistance. Somehow, the creature managed to miss the brachial artery, although it's entirely possible that was on purpose: this is an alchemical creation, after all. It may know enough about human anatomy to play with its food, keeping Lilianne alive as long as possible for the sake of having more time to enjoy toying with her. Smita peels off her sopping-wet lab coat, then looks to the etiäinen. Almost primly, she grabs the cuff of one sleeve and stretches it out as far as it will go.

"Can you cut this off at the shoulder?" she asks. "I don't have any scissors with me."

The etiäinen blinks at her. "You want me to *help* you?"

"If she dies while I'm on this desk with her, I'll do everything in my power to keep her from falling into the water where you can get her, and if you could take her away from me, you would have done it already," says Smita calmly. "If you cut the sleeve off like I'm asking, I can bandage her shoulder, and she'll stay alive. That means you get another chance at hunting her down."

"You think like an alchemist," says the etiäinen, and there's a note of delight in its voice that wasn't there before. It extends its hand, wiggling its fingers with their surplus of joints, then slashes its claws down and through the sleeve.

The sleeve comes off in Smita's hand. She looks at it, nods, and says, "Thank you. This will do nicely."

She turns her attention back to Lilianne, wrapping the cut-off sleeve around her shoulder and tying it tight.

Lilianne screams as soon as the fabric tightens, grinding against the damage that's been done to her shoulder. Her eyes snap open, and she struggles to sit upright, Smita pushing enough to help her, then grabbing her arm to keep her from toppling off the edge.

"Hey, Lily," she says, trying to sound soothing. "Hey, you're okay, you're okay, you're—well, you're not okay, you've been ripped open and you've lost a whole lot of blood, but you're as close to okay as you're going to get until someone comes down here to get us out."

"No one's coming," moans Lilianne. "No one can find this place."

"We have at least two people who don't need to find it, because they've been here before, plenty," says Smita. "I'm pretty sure my roommates have been here before. I wasn't with them, because they try not to lead me into life-threatening situations if there's any other choice. They still think of me as being innocent and easily frightened. I don't blame them much. That's exactly what I was, for the longest time you can imagine. They'll be here. They'll come. Whenever I'm in danger, they come."

Lilianne blinks at her, then slumps against her, not making any real effort to stay upright. "I screwed it all up," she says, dolefully. "I didn't find the lost lab. I found the people who'd already found the lost lab, and I let you think I was stupid, just babbling on at you about things you already knew."

"I never thought you were stupid, Lily. And I wasn't being fair. I was letting you think all this was new to me, because, well. We've had some issues with alchemists in my household. They're not always very nice people." She gestures to the etiäinen, the one in the water and the one out of the water. "They make things that aren't very nice either. It can be a little terrifying sometimes, and we don't enjoy it. So I didn't let on that I knew most of what you were saying. And I did learn new things. I learned about you."

"Me?"

"You. All the alchemy in the world couldn't have prepared me for you. It's just words and recipes. You're a person, and you're lovely. Fun and funny and so passionate about the things you care about! Even if those things are alchemical. And you weren't wrong about this place. There's a lot you can learn here."

"If I die here, I guess I'll learn what it's like to be eaten by an etiäinen," says Lilianne.

"Don't even think like that," says Smita firmly. "You're not going to die here."

"That's what you think."

Footsteps in the distance, hard soles against tile floors. Not the sound of someone who's removed waterlogged shoes after a slog through the sewer; not the sound of another etiäinen, either. Smita brightens, sitting up straighter.

"You're *not* going to die here," she repeats, more firmly. Then she raises her voice and calls, "This way. I'm over here, this way!"

The sound of footsteps becomes the sound of running, and a moment later, two figures swing around the corner of the hall. Erin, strawberry hair skinned back into a ponytail, and Artemis, holding a moon-dark bow with an arrow already notched, the whole thing glittering faintly in her hands.

Smita smiles. "Took you long enough," she says.

The two etiäinen hiss, and the one on the dry side of the lab whirls, lunging for the pair. Artemis releases her arrow, which flies straight and clean to embed itself in the etiäinen's throat, sticking out like an exclamation point. The etiäinen makes a choked gurgling sound, then falls sideways, landing in the water with a splash. A dark cloud begins to spread out from the point of impact, staining the water black as pitch.

Smita turns to the remaining etiäinen. "Run," she suggests politely. "Run, and don't look back. You helped me, so I can try to keep them from chasing, but you have to run, or they'll kill you where you stand."

The etiäinen blinks at her. Its eyelids move side to side, not up and down, and Smita spares half a second's thought for the reasons behind that: what could have encouraged the alchemists to design their creation in such a way? Then it shakes its head.

"You have no reason to be kind or trust me," it says. "I've had a taste of your companion. I'll take another, if I can. This is a promise."

"You won't have the opportunity," says Smita. Erin and Artemis are moving toward the edge of the water, Erin pausing to kick the fallen etiäinen's hip and confirm to her satisfaction that it's dead.

"Go," says Smita. The etiäinen looks unsure. "You can attack Lilianne later, if you have the chance, and we'll stop you, and you'll die. Or you can run, and live peacefully here in this lab for as long as you're able. You won't leave, I'm sure of that. The world outside won't be able to sustain you."

"Yes, run," calls Artemis, drawing her bow again.

The etiäinen hisses, then ducks under the water, vanishing without a ripple. Smita sags.

"Shouldn't have done that," says Lilianne. She's almost slurring her words, exhaustion and blood loss catching up with her and stealing the hard edges from her already-sugared diction. "Can't trust them. Not the life we make in labs."

Erin laughs, a hard, bitter little laugh, and steps into the water. "You should listen to your new friend, Smita. She's saying all the right things."

"Quiet, you," says Smita. "What took you so long?"

"It took me a while to realize that you were actually gone-gone, not just hung up at the store. After that, I had to follow you all the way to the storm drain, find the tetractys, and realize where you must have gone. That's when I called Artemis. The people who built this lab were sneaky assholes, and I didn't trust them not to have activated some sort of security precautions before they left. I wanted backup."

The thought of Erin, terrifying Erin, feeling the need for backup is almost as frightening as the situation. Smita shudders, watching Erin wade toward them. If the etiäinen is just lurking for another attack, this is when it will come.

But nothing happens. Erin reaches the desk and holds her hands out for Smita to take, easing her down into the water. "That was really stupid of you, just so you know," she says. "You shouldn't go running off with strange alchemists, no matter what the circumstances. You could have been seriously hurt!" She pauses. "You weren't seriously hurt, were you?"

"I'm not hurt, just really, really cold," says Smita. "I think I may have the beginnings of hypothermia."

"Dumbass," says Erin fondly. She looks past Smita to Lilianne, expression hardening. "I remember her from campus earlier. She was awfully interested in you before. Is it just because she was trying to lure you off somewhere alone?"

"No. We ran into each other when I was going out to get milk after dinner. She's hurt, Erin. Can you be chill until we know she's not going to bleed to death?"

Artemis is still pacing at the top of the stairs, arrow notched and aimed at the water. If anything moves, she's ready to shoot it. Erin glances back over her shoulder at the Lunar.

"Afraid to get your feet wet?" she asks, snidely.

"Afraid of whatever nightmares the alchemists may have decided to pour into the pool," says Artemis.

"You're a goddess of healing, aren't you?"

"A patron," Artemis corrects. She stops pacing. "I can't actually heal people by laying on hands, but I can understand what's wrong with somebody if I get close enough to have a good look. I am not close enough, and I'm not getting in the water if I have any way to avoid it."

"Wimp." Erin sounds almost fond. She turns back to Lilianne, huddled on the desk. "Hey. Alchemist. Come over here."

"No," mumbles Lilianne. "You're a scary lady."

The blood loss is clearly getting to her. She's barely holding herself upright without Smita there to lean on. Smita shoots Erin a half-panicked look. Erin, for her part, only sighs.

"Yes," she says. "I'm definitely a scary lady. I've worked hard to cultivate my reputation as absolutely terrifying, and I don't like you. You lured my friend into a dangerous place, underground, and I found her huddling in a situation straight out of a horror movie. So I very much want to be scary at you. But Smita wants us to help you, and that means I need you to come down from that desk. She's already cold. I want to get her out of this water as fast as I can, before something happens and she goes down. I can't carry you both out of here."

"Please, Lily," pleads Smita.

Lilianne slowly uncurls from her huddle, scooting down the desk until her feet are dangling in the water. Some of the blood that's managed to soak into her jeans spreads out around her ankles in an expanding ring of red, and Smita tenses, waiting for the surviving etiäinen to appear and yank her under.

Nothing happens. Erin reaches out, grasping the sides of Lilianne's chest, and lifts her down into the water as gently as she can. Lilianne grunts, the motion probably putting pressure on her injured shoulder, but she doesn't struggle or try to pull away, and under the circumstances, that's the best Smita can hope for.

Together, the three of them wade to the stairs, where Artemis is waiting to help them back up onto dry land. She looks at Lilianne's injured shoulder and wrinkles her nose in clear disgust, then looks around the lab. "They must have a first aid kit in here somewhere," she says, and it's so ordinary, so predictable a reaction to the situation around them that all Smita can do is laugh until she cries.

She keeps crying when the laughter stops. In the moment, it feels like the right thing to do.

Courage

TIMELINE: MAY 11, 1891.

Asphodel lounges on the settee in her uncle's parlor, waiting for him to come home and rage at her for spoiling another potential match. Eight years of trying to get her married off to one of his alchemist peers, to settle her like a cuckoo in someone else's nest, and all he has to show for it is a string of broken contracts and an increasingly aged and insouciant niece who insists on calling herself his apprentice to anyone who slows down enough to listen. It doesn't matter how many times he tells her that women can't be alchemists. She points to her experiments, to her research, and asks him why not, over and over again, like her stubborn refusal to accept reality can in the end remake the universe.

But then, isn't that what alchemy is? It's an effort to remake the universe, to tame it, to turn its own systems of belief tame and grasp them with a human hand. The incarnates are errors, aberrations. Through the act of intentional creation, they can be purified and brought properly to heel, with the guiding hands of the alchemist to keep them moving in the right directions. Asphodel's refusal to be directed toward some less weighty future is a sign of the alchemy in her veins, the science in her soul.

If only she weren't a woman. She's often considered the portions of the Great Work that would allow her to make herself over as a man, to slide into the ranks of the worthy as one of their acknowledged own, but she's never been able to bring herself to act in that direction. For one thing, while she's met souls whose final form did not suit the body they were born to, she isn't among them: she is a woman born and a woman bound to be, with a woman's heart and a woman's yearnings. She would make a miserable man, no matter how much she worked to play the part.

No, that happy resolution is not for her. She'll be a woman and an alchemist both if it kills her. She'll change the world on her own terms, and let anyone who says she can't be damned.

The front door slams as her uncle makes his entrance, and she sinks a little deeper into the settee, savoring her last moments of peace before he thunders through and tears everything asunder. His heavy footsteps draw his path along the hall.

Asphodel waits until he draws almost level with the parlor before she calls, sweetly, "Is all well, Uncle?"

"You know full well it isn't," he snarls, shifting his trajectory to storm into the room, where he stops and glares at her, eyes dark with irritation. "The Congress is debating what's to be done with Boston. It hasn't rained in more than a year."

The rains, which had come sporadically when they came at all, dried up entirely following Asphodel's nineteenth birthday. For seven years, Boston has been dryer than a desert, watered only by the winter snows, which fall more thinly than they once did, and by the occasional, incredibly dear downpour. And now it seems that even those have stopped.

"What do you mean, what's to be done?" asks Asphodel. "It's a city. Thousands of people live here. We have water from the rivers, which still flow as they ever have, down to the sea. There's nothing to be *done* with Boston! Even if we didn't have the rivers, we'd have the harbor. Saltwater can be purified with very little effort. Tell the Congress that if something must be *done* with Boston, they should set themselves to the challenge of removing the salt from the harbor. We'll have enough to drink for a century's time, and the seas will be none the less for the exchange."

"Oh, I see," says John, coldly. "And the farmers? The people whose gardens are too far from the river to haul the water to their thirsty roots? The firetrucks and the farriers? We need more water than the rivers can provide."

"Find a better rainmaker."

"There are none left willing to tend to Boston. We've exhausted our supply." His hands flex at his sides, opening and closing and finally balling into fists. "Perhaps I should have been listening to them long since."

Asphodel, with the hard-won ear of a prey animal for a predator's approach, sits up straight, shoulders locked into a precise line. She vibrates like a finely tuned harp string, caught in the moment, stiff and unyielding. "What do you mean, Uncle?"

"I mean that since the first, they've been mentioning that the strangeness in the weather has some connection to you, *niece*. That you have a tie to the missing rains. There have been suggestions, in the past. I could send you back to the village where I found you—"

"You wouldn't," protests Asphodel, horror audible in her voice. She begins to rise, hands raised in supplication. "I wouldn't know how to survive in such a place, in such a wilderness. You've domesticated me, Uncle. You can't be cruel enough to throw me back to the pigpen you pulled me from. If that was your intention, you should have left me from the beginning, let me grow into a woman who could survive in such a place, not taken me as a toy to be discarded when you tired of me."

"I'm not tired of you," he says, wearily. "I'm attempting to save my city, regardless of whether it's worthy of being saved. I could send you back, or I could offer you up as a virgin sacrifice to the skies, slit your belly to read the answers in your entrails, and let death void whatever hold you have over the missing rains... What's so funny?"

Because she's no longer holding her hands up to ward him off; she's holding them over her mouth, like she can't contain her mirth through any other measure. Dropping her hands, she shoots him a look made of equal parts amusement and exasperation.

"Uncle, I'm twenty-six years old, and you've been throwing me at every eligible alchemist on the Eastern Seaboard since I made my entry into society. Do you truly think I would still qualify as a *virgin* sacrifice?"

He scowls. "I think you're a good girl with a proper upbringing who would never shame this house by dallying with a suitor while unmarried."

"Then you should have told the suitors as much," she says, smoothing down her jacket with her hands. "While I won't disabuse you of your beliefs, I suggest you not fall back on the idea of virgin sacrifice as your solution if you want it to do anything other than leave you with bloodied hands and one less niece. You could follow the example of Miss Cottingsly and make an auf of me, but I doubt you'd appreciate the results. Everyone would notice, and an auf can't be trusted in polite society the way I'm expected to be."

"Reckless girl," he says, sounding almost amazed. "Did you spoil yourself on purpose?"

"I am not a piece of fruit, to be so easily made rotten," she says, tartly. "And no, I didn't lay with the men you found for me to spite you, or to damage them. I did it because I wished to, and they wished me to, and between us we found a place where wishes were made true. I have no regrets, but no, Uncle, I didn't look to the future and ask myself how best I could be protected from you deciding to murder me in order to bring back the rain. I've lived my entire life without much rain. I see no reason to die for it now."

"Asphodel . . ." He rubs his face with one hand, shoulders suddenly slumping. He looks very old in that moment, very old and very defeated. "Child. I have done my best to do right by you, but you make it very difficult at times."

"Doing right by me would mean allowing me to study alchemy, as has always been my purpose and destiny," says Asphodel hotly. "Only allow me the use of your lab, and of Miss Cottingsly, and I'll prove to you that I have discoveries to add into the Great Work. Allow me to show you to the light—"

"What light?"

"The light of true enlightenment, which shines within us all."

"You are a woman, Asphodel. It's time you admitted how that limits you, and where it will restrict you from your mad aspirations."

"It doesn't have to!" she very nearly shouts.

He flinches back, startled. She takes several deep breaths, calming herself by what appears to be sheer force of will, then looks back to his face.

"I would be far from the first," she says. "Hypatia, Pandrosion, even Circe. They were all women, and they made great contributions to the alchemical world. In England, Mary Wollstonecraft Shelley. Her discoveries in the school of takwin have changed everything. Her books are enlightening and invigorating at the same time, like lightning striking the mind. Only America refuses to see the contributions of the female of the species. But American alchemists are perfectly happy to build upon the discoveries of women. They stand, as we all do, upon the shoulders of giants, and they refuse to admit that some of the giants might be different than themselves."

John takes a deep breath, and then another, finally looking up at the ceiling for a long moment before looking back to her. "You've been practicing that speech for some time, I think."

"Several years," she admits.

"And you're not, I must admit, entirely wrong. America is

somewhat backward in certain areas when compared to the remainder of the world. Can you blame us? We're a young nation. We need our women dedicated to the bearing of infants and the education of the children, lest the fragile identity we're building for ourselves come to pieces in our hands."

"I have never been the mothering type," says Asphodel, somewhat stiffly. "That deep inadequacy in my character has been the end of several courtships, and yet it remains, as insolvable as the secrets of alkahest. I will never play the part you would assign to me. Allow me to do what I was made for."

"The Congress will never admit you," he says. "Even if you sway me to your delusions, they'll refuse you admission."

"But you could train me."

He scoffs. "Fine, then, niece. I'll give you a sennight, and a challenge, as used to be customary when considering the taking on of an apprentice. It wouldn't do to allow any nobleman's son to buy his way into an unsuitable service, after all. The aspirants were expected to prove themselves with some great act of alchemy before they could be trained to even-greater heights."

"What do you want me to do?" asks Asphodel, although she already knows: this is a formality, an opportunity for him to offer her some less-impossible task.

But there was never going to be another task. Her whole life has been moving toward this moment, like a comet spinning along its preordained path. She is unsurprised and not at all disappointed when he looks at her, hands clenching even tighter, and says the only thing he could possibly have said:

"Bring back the rain."

* * *

A week's time is barely enough to purify lead or turn flowers into glass. It certainly isn't enough time to remake the weather, especially not when this is the only way she's ever known it to behave: her own beliefs are working against her, telling her that there's nothing wrong. Alchemy is often the art of wishing for impossible things, but always limited by the imagination of the alchemist.

So she tries to think of rain, of times when she's seen it fall, felt it striking on her skin. She tries to think of a world where rain comes commonly, and not less than once a season, or not at all. She tries and tries, and all she finds is the drought that has been her entire life.

"Why did it have to be *rain*?" she demands, turning on Miss Cottingsly. The old auf has been locked in her uncle's basement lab with her for the better part of the week, patiently doing whatever has been asked of her, fetching and carrying, bringing Asphodel book after book from her uncle's library. She has no opinions of her own, no aspirations, and no skill for alchemy. She is the living, breathing equivalent of a block of lead: inert, stable, and thus ideal for assisting someone else.

Auf are normally used as guards and hunters, weapons to be turned against the world. Watching Miss Cottingsly in the lab, it's difficult not to wonder how many of them would serve better as laboratory assistants. Asphodel is already mentally sketching new processes for their construction, new ways of refining them into something more stable and less terrible, capable of serving as an alchemist's right hand—perhaps even capable of becoming alchemists in their own right.

But all that will have to wait, until she's proven that she has the right to make such plans, that she's allowed to *learn*.

"Rain is an important part of the world, miss," says Miss Cottingsly, unfailingly polite. It's difficult to remember a time when she resented Asphodel's presence in her household. "We need it so things can grow. Plants, children, animals. Without it, we're just holding ground until we all fade away."

"How can he think *I* have any connection to the missing

rains? I've never done any workings that should have affected the weather, and I don't remember it raining even when I was a little girl in the forest."

"That's exactly why he thinks so, miss. There was rain in Boston, before you came. I believe the alchemists are starting to think there would be rain again, if only you would go."

"So it's something in my flesh?" Asphodel looks down at herself, immodestly dressed in one of her uncle's shirts under a heavy canvas apron. Her skirt is long enough to be decent, but stained and tattered at the hem. "Not only am I a woman, but I'm, what? A storm-repellent?"

"You're natural-born, if that's what concerns you," says Miss Cottingsly. "I remember when he tested your blood for the first time, and for the fiftieth. Everything about you is of this world, and not of any other. No seasons coming courting or gods descending on moonbeams."

"But something in me stops the rain."

"That is what your uncle supposes to be true."

"And you?"

Miss Cottingsly shakes her head. "I suppose nothing, miss. I'm here to serve your uncle, and when it suits him, to serve you in his stead. It's not my place to have opinions."

"The moon manifests itself in the world, as physical people. Like Deborah."

"Yes," says Miss Cottingsly, giving no indication that she has any resentment over the way Deborah left their household. "Many gods manifest in that manner."

"Is there a god of rain?"

"Yes, several."

"Who?"

"Zeus would be the most obvious. Alchemically speaking, the Greek gods are the easiest to work with: the Great Work was conceived in sight of their temples, and they still remember its founders fondly, or as fondly as gods remember anything. Zeus would also be a grave mistake. He's the king of his pantheon, and prone to fits of temper, and to forcing himself upon unwilling women. His power is such that he can get any woman with child, however young or old or"—she gestures to herself—"dead she happens to be. You are lovely and unmarried, and calling upon him would be a risk not worth the taking."

"No," says Asphodel, wrinkling her nose. "I would rather not tempt the king of the gods."

"But there are other Greek powers who might be more amenable to assisting us. The Hyades, for example."

"Those being?"

"A sisterhood of nymphs. It's their job to bring the rain when Zeus is occupied elsewhere, and they're minor-enough divinities that they manifest just like the other incarnates do. They walk in storms."

Asphodel just looks at her for a long moment. Miss Cottingsly doesn't squirm. She no longer has the animal instincts that would motivate such a reaction.

Finally, Asphodel asks, "And why, if these Hyades are out there, haven't the alchemists called on them already?"

"They're all women, and the American Alchemical Congress has always been unwilling to see certain truths, no matter how clearly they might be presented."

The thought that Boston might have endured a decade-long drought due to sexism is almost funny in its offensiveness. Asphodel shakes her head. "What information do we have on these Hyades?"

"I'll bring you the literature," says Miss Cottingsly politely, and slips out of the basement, leaving Asphodel alone.

Asphodel sighs, leaning back against the counter and resting her weight on her hands. This is what she's always wanted, what she's been demanding for years, but it suddenly seems so terribly petty, working in the shadow of men who will never see her as their equal. If even the Hyades, powers if not full gods, can be discounted due to their sex, what hope does she have?

She has the hope of stubbornness, and the sheer determination to force them to see her as clearly as she sees herself. She is Asphodel Baker, she stole her name from the fields of the dead and from the moon itself, and she will not be stopped by the prejudices of foolish old men. She'll be the best of them one day, and when she is, they'll all bow down before her.

And in the meantime, there's work to be done. She turns back to the book open on the table at the center of the room. People have used ceremonies to summon rain throughout recorded history. Ptolemy recorded many of them in his works, and while he lived and died so many centuries ago that there's almost certainly information missing from what he had recorded, newer discoveries that had yet to be added in annotation, he provided a solid starting point.

There are no specific records of Greek rainmaking rituals, perhaps because Zeus was enough of an ever-present threat that they saw no reason to invoke him. The Romans are a bit better documented, but their main ritual, the aquaelicium, requires a special stone. The documentation is murky and somewhat unclear, but after several minutes of study, she concludes that the lapis manalis, the water-flowing stone, is not a *type* of rock, but rather a *specific* rock, one which is presumably still somewhere in Greece. Given long enough to work, she might be able to isolate and re-create its properties, creating her own rainmaking stone, but she doesn't have the time or resources for that right now. She needs a solution before her week runs out.

There are other rainmaking rites, some of which might be more achievable. The Romanian practice of Caloian is tempting; there's a document variant designed for the banishment of droughts, and it has requirements she might be able to fulfill without any assistance. But that simplicity makes her wary. If it's that simple, surely the Congress would have tried it by now, wouldn't they? The only reason she can see that they wouldn't have is that the drought-banishing ritual focuses on a young woman, and they don't have a surplus of those. It's still suspect enough that she doesn't move it to the head of her list.

No. Whatever she does, it will involve calling on the Hyades, and the hope they'll have some cause to answer.

"Not over-fond of alchemists, these girls," says Miss Cottingsly, coming back into the basement with a cloth-bound book in her arms. Asphodel moves to take it from her. The title, *They Fall As Rain*, is picked out in gilt gold against the wine-red cover.

"Why not?" she asks, looking from the book back to Miss Cottingsly.

"They're lesser even than the Lunars. I'd wager the only powers less, well, powerful would be the Horae, who only really have their full strength for an hour out of the day. Useless little things. The universe should really stop wasting the effort it takes to make them manifest."

"How does that explain them disliking alchemists, then?" asks Asphodel. "I'd think being weak would make them unappealing. People like my uncle would never waste time hunting down something you'd call lesser than a Lunar when there are Summers and Winters to be had. Or even Lunars. They have their uses."

Wistfully, she recalls the days when they had plenty of the materials they'd taken from Deborah close to hand. She'd been barely better than a child then, and hadn't realized the power she could have clutched for, instead allowing her uncle to squander and barter it away. Well, she understands power now. She understands its uses and applications, and the next time they stumble across the living Moon, she'll be ready to claim her fair share.

"They're still Greek gods, miss. They still have their pride, and they don't care to be dismissed. And while your uncle would never waste time hunting for a Hyade, if he found one, he would take her, and she'd have no real defenses. They lose a fair number of their company to ill-timed encounters with the alchemical world."

"Has the Congress attempted to consult with the Hyades about the lack of rain, in any form?"

Asphodel catches her breath as she waits for the reply. Miss Cottingsly has already said the Congress discounts the Hyades for being women, but it's possible that they've at least been asked, even if they haven't been properly summoned. It's a relief when Miss Cottingsly shakes her head. This may work.

"You can go for now," says Asphodel crisply. "I'll see what I can find in the literature."

"Yes, miss," says Miss Cottingsly. She turns toward the basement stairs, walking away with no indication of being bothered by the dismissal. The old auf knows what she was made for.

Asphodel caresses the cover one more time before moving closer to the light, opening the book, and beginning to read.

An hour later, she's more confused than ever. There are conflicting accounts of how many Hyades there are: is it three, or is it fifteen? They can be attracted or they can be summoned, but they aren't found where droughts linger: their mortal embodiments like to live near water, and can almost always be found in sight of either a river or the sea. She slams the book, frustrated. There's been a drought in Boston for most of her life. She won't find any Hyades here.

But if she can find one elsewhere, this may still be a solvable problem. She takes a deep breath, calming herself, and opens the book again.

The Hyades are associated with Dionysus, the Greek god of wine, and can sometimes be attracted with the same offerings that would be used for him. She makes a silent note to ask her uncle exactly when the Congress marks the beginning of the drought, and get a bottle of wine from that year. Almost as an afterthought, she decides to also request a bottle from the year she was born. If the rainmakers are right and she's somehow tied to the absence of the rain, that year might have more sympathy with the situation.

Were it not for Miss Cottingsly's unprompted reminder that she's entirely mortal in her making, Asphodel might begin to wonder if she were one of these Hyades, if maybe her manifestation had gone wrong and started repelling what she was intended to attract. But no: the auf who serves her uncle's household is fully capable of lying, but not to her. Not to anyone with Baker blood in their veins. It's a small failsafe, bound into the work of her construction, making her a safe right hand and confidant for her uncle's unending labors.

She closes the book, clutching it to her chest, and leaves the basement. Time to tell her uncle what she's learned, what she knows, and what she suspects.

Time to begin.

* * *

"—so you see, by refusing to acknowledge that women might be the solution to the problem, the Congress has extended the drought far beyond the necessary; this could all have been resolved some time ago, had they only been willing to act as men, not huddle in their private clubhouse like boys."

She keeps her chin high and her voice level as she speaks to her uncle, watching doubt and dismay crawl across his face like worms into a grave. Finally, he scowls.

"You'd blame the Congress? They're great men, Asphodel. Better men than I, and better men than you could ever be, sex entirely aside. They move toward the platonic ideals of our philosophy, and they'll remake the world."

"In your lifetime?" she asks tartly. "Because I doubt that, but it might be so, if they were willing to open their minds and their doors and actually *look* at the world outside their textbooks. More than half the Lunars are women. All the Hyades, all the Horae. They shut themselves off from power by refusing to entertain that which betrays their philosophy."

"What do you need, niece?"

Once he abandons her name, she knows there's no point in continuing her argument: it is, in its own way, a statement of surrender. So she smiles, and stands a little straighter, and says, "A carriage to New Haven, the loan of Miss Cottingsly for the journey there and back, two bottles of wine, some incense, a silver knife, and a bronze bowl. I'll come back successful or not at all."

"I've put too much effort into your raising to wish to lose you to shame."

"You misunderstand me, Uncle. If I fail, I'll likely be dead."

He blinks, raising his eyebrows. "Is that so?"

"There are no clear rites for summoning the Hyades. They dislike the company of alchemists, and their power is limited enough that most people never bother. Dionysus, on the other hand, loves them dearly, and is more commonly called upon via alchemical ritual. If I call on him, and have the connection to the absent rains you claim I do, perhaps one of them will come instead."

"You gamble with dangerous stakes, Asphodel."

"I have no choice." She lifts her chin again, looking at him sternly along the length of her nose. She'll never be as tall as he is, but she's enough taller than she was when first she came here that he seems small when looked at in this manner. How could she be afraid of someone so small? "I was born to be an alchemist. You saved me when you found me and brought me to Boston, and you damned me when you said I could never be your apprentice. If I die calling upon a god who has no interest in my company, let me die, and know that at least I fell with a book in my hand and a secret on my lips. If I succeed and survive, the Congress will allow me to be trained. That's the only life that matters to me. Give me what I've asked for, and give me my future."

"Foolish, wayward girl," he says, almost wonderingly.

Her uncle has never been the physically affectionate sort, has never been inclined to touching her when such was not required, but he closes the distance between them and pulls her into his embrace, large hands splayed against her back, rough fabric of his coat rubbing at her cheek. For a moment, Asphodel is too shocked to do anything but lift her arms and hug him in return.

Their embrace lasts for only a handful of seconds. Then he's pulling away, releasing her, and she's stepping back, still unsettled by his actions.

"You'll have everything you need," he says. "And I know I'll see you again, when you've finished what you've started."

Asphodel smiles.

* * *

The Congress, through her uncle, gave her a week to bring back the rain. Three days have passed before Asphodel arrives in New Haven, borne to her destination by the finest carriage her uncle could hire. Miss Cottingsly sits across from her, face betraying nothing of her thoughts as she holds her carpetbag in her lap and watches the countryside slide by outside the windows.

Asphodel is doing a far worse job of concealing her emotions. She worries one fingernail between her teeth, stripping tiny pieces of skin away and swallowing them whole—never leave any piece of yourself where someone else might find it, even if another alchemist scavenging flecks of skin from the roadside is punishingly unlikely—until she comes near to drawing blood.

She pulls her finger reluctantly from her mouth, shaking it to ease the sting, and looks out the window again. They're almost to their destination, a place called Morse Beach. There's a house there, owned by a local alchemist who's promised her privacy for the duration of her working, even as he laughed at the very idea of a woman calling down one of the powers entirely on her own.

What would he think if he knew that she was working from a ritual originally designed to call on Dionysus, but modified for a smaller prize? Most alchemists don't bother with gods anymore, unless they're like the Lunars, filled with useful parts and easily dismantled. God-working is difficult and dangerous, and the rewards are rarely worth the risks.

Asphodel thinks this is because of the changes in attitude between the modern alchemists and the alchemists of antiquity. In Hypatia's age, the gods were stronger. They were more of a threat. And because of this, they were approached respectfully, when they were approached at all. No one in those days would have dreamt of summoning one of the Hyades with the intent to do her harm. All the incarnates, even those who weren't considered strictly divine, were approached with a degree of care that she's never seen from the Congress.

She'll kill the Hyade if that's what it takes to bring back the rain, but she'll do it gently if she can. She doesn't want to be a god-worker, thankfully, and after this, she doubts she'd be able to if she tried: no god is going to approach her willingly after she sacrifices one of their own.

And it's worth it. For a life of alchemy, it's worth it.

The carriage rattles to a stop. Asphodel looks out the window, takes note of the large house in the distance and the otherwise-empty beach, and nods to herself. It's a pleasant afternoon in May: the absence of beachgoers is its own testament to the man who agreed to help her with her task today. He must have done something to discourage them, to leave her with the space to do her work.

Opening the door, she uncurls herself from her seat and steps out into the open air, bringing her basket of tools with her. Miss Cottingsly follows, her own bag hanging loosely in her hands.

(It had to be Miss Cottingsly, and not her uncle or one of his allies. Auf are neither alive nor dead, but a strange and impossible third thing, making them difficult for many incarnates to see clearly. She'll need Miss Cottingsly before this day is done, if she's estimated her next steps correctly.)

They walk until they reach a flat stretch of high, rocky ground, with the beach spread out beneath them, waves beating ceaselessly against the shore. It's beautiful. Asphodel can appreciate that. She opens her basket, removes the jar of iron shavings, salt, and dried rosemary, and carefully casts her compass 'round, drawing a perfect circle more than six feet in diameter. It uses up every speck of the material she prepared, exactly as it was intended to do.

The wind blowing off the sea doesn't disturb so much as a single grain of salt. Once her careful blend of summoning agents falls, it stays precisely where she put it, as if she had buried a ring of magnets under the top layer of the soil. The circle cast, she sets up her candles, eight in total, and lights them all from a burning bundle of dried, rolled grape leaves.

When the last candle is lit, she drops the burning leaves into her bowl of bronze, picking up the bottle of wine that dates to the beginning of Boston's drought. "Great Dionysus, god of epiphanies, father of wine, he who comes, I entreat you to join me here."

She tips a measure of the wine into a silver cup, and an equal measure into the bowl, extinguishing the last of the flames with a hiss.

"I am but a humble mortal soul, and I come to beg you for your wisdom and your insights, to solve the puzzle which now plagues my kind. Answer me, if my offerings seem sweet, and let me drink deep of your brilliance."

She waits, expectant, and the world teeters on a razor's edge, silence broken only by the crashing of the surf. The moment passes. The flames still burn, but the air remains the same, the sky is unchanged. She looks to Miss Cottingsly, silently pleading.

The auf shrugs. "Suppose he didn't like what you were offering. You have two vintages left to hand; see if he might prefer drinking one of those."

Because Miss Cottingsly exists in the strange hinterland between the living and the dead, she can speak during the summoning ritual. Asphodel can't, unless it's to entreat, to cajole, to continue what she's already begun. Until the gods answer her, or don't, she's trapped in the text of a play she didn't write, whose lines she's only half-memorized.

Hand shaking, she puts down the bottle of wine and picks up its twin, an older, dearer vintage. Not *too* dear—she's only twenty-six—but dear enough that her uncle frowned when he realized she would need it, and that he wasn't likely to get any measure of it back again. It had taken some quick talking to convince him that it would be an offense to the god she was trying to summon if she brought a decanter when the whole bottle had been available.

The cork comes loose easily enough, and she waves the bottle to let its scent pass into the air before adding a solid measure of wine to both the bowl and goblet.

"Gentle Dionysus, lord of revels, I stand beside the sea and call you for reasons both sacred and mundane. The rain has stopped in the city of Boston. Our flowers die, our fruits wither on the vine. I need your aid, you who knew the gentle Hyades, you who danced beside them in the rains they called, to bring back what we have somehow lost."

The pause is longer this time, a drop of silence spreading slowly from the center of her circle like a ripple through standing water. Asphodel holds her breath until it, too, breaks and fades away, and she stands alone.

"One vintage left," says Miss Cottingsly, and her voice is almost mocking, cold in a way Asphodel has never heard before.

"I have offered you wine both sweet and aged," says Asphodel, voice somehow remaining steady as she sets the second bottle beside the first and pulls the knife from inside her vest. Its edge is very sharp indeed, and looking at it makes bile rise in the back of her throat, sharp and burning and terrible. "I have but one bottle left to open, and it is the bottle only I can pour."

She lays the edge of the blade against the smooth plane of her forearm and presses down, hard enough to split the skin, drawing a line of brilliant, gleaming red from elbow to wrist. The pain is almost secondary to the shock of the moment: she has cut herself, sliced into her own body like a butcher might cut into a lamb, and like the lamb, she bleeds.

She can't bandage the wound until the ritual is over. She just has to hope the answer comes quickly, before she passes out from blood loss. Miss Cottingsly has assured her that she can patch any injury "like new," and that there's no way Asphodel will die from something as simple as a slashed forearm, but it's hard to believe that when she's bleeding *everywhere* how is there so much blood? How is this happening so quickly?

But she is her uncle's niece, and she's been training for this moment for as long as she can remember, even if neither of them truly understood that was what she was doing. She tilts her arm so the blood drips down into the bowl of ash and wine, then shifts the goblet to her other hand, dropping the knife in the process, and bleeds into it as well. The wine swallows her blood without a trace, red meeting red, unchanged.

This time when the bell of silence rings, it spreads and keeps spreading, swallowing the world. Everything seems to slow, even the waves growing still. Asphodel's head spins from the blood loss, and she feels drunk despite not having tasted a drop of wine.

Someone comes walking down the beach below.

It's a woman, wearing a long, diaphanous gown that whips around her like seafoam, tangling around her legs as she begins climbing the shallow hill toward Asphodel's circle. As she draws closer, Asphodel can see that her hair is dark and her skin is pale, unfashionably so; she must have never seen the sun. Her dress is as white as the foam that it so resembles, and does her no favors in either cut or color; she is a washed-out ghost, a drowned girl gone walking.

(In later years, when her days are consumed by the Up-and-Under, Asphodel will look at her own descriptions of the Drowned Girl, Niamh, and see this moment again. It will not make her heart any softer . . . but she will write a kinder ending for her Drowned Girl, and she will be glad of it.)

Asphodel-now, Asphodel-bleeding, Asphodel holds her breath and watches the woman come, unwilling to be the one to break the silence.

The stranger does it for her. "Well met, alchemist," she calls, as she approaches. "You called?"

"My lord?"

The stranger's laughter is a bell ringing in the darkness. "No," she says, once her amusement has passed. "I am not my student-nephew, who brings the wine, who brings the brightness of true thought. I am nothing half so great as he. But you called him on our behalf, and I am come, as you requested, to see what you desire."

Asphodel's entire body feels light, the blood dripping from her arm taking all her weight with it. "You are one of the Hyades?"

"My name is Phaesyle," says the woman. "We all have names. We're not just the living embodiment of rain, you know. They name the Horae, but we're lucky to get a number, much less the personal touch of our own—"

"Thank you for answering me," says Asphodel. She isn't sure how long she can stay upright, but she's sure that once she collapses, whatever she's done here will be undone. "Do you know why it doesn't rain in Boston?"

"You mean you don't?" Phaesyle's astonishment is entirely unfeigned. She gestures toward the goblet in Asphodel's hand. "That's for me, isn't it? Give it here. I need a drink if I'm going to deal with this."

Asphodel holds the goblet out in offering. "Come and take it," she says.

"Come into your circle, you mean? Little alchemist, how foolish do you think we are?" Phaesyle gives her an indulgent look. "But then, you're bleeding more than you intended, I think, and you're no real threat to me now. And I want a drink."

She steps into the circle, hand outstretched for the goblet. Asphodel passes it to her, and watches as the Hyade drinks it dry in one long swallow, not pausing to savor or to breathe.

"Better," says Phaesyle, dropping the goblet to the ground. She eyes Asphodel. "I find it hard to believe that you don't know. Have you never asked yourself where flowers come from?"

"My lady?"

"They follow the rain," says Phaesyle. "They come after the storm. You came after the storm, little flower, when he lay down with your mother and claimed her as his own. We're distant cousins, you and I—very distant, because you were born in mortal flesh and embody nothing but yourself, while I have lived for centuries in one skin after another, moving between embodiments as the need arises."

"I don't understand. What are you . . . ?"

"Rain is not always born of storms. He summons some of my sisters with him when he travels, but the rest of us stay clear of his presence, because he's not a faithful man. He may have loved your mother, once. That won't keep him from our beds if he finds us walking too close to what he calls his own. You bar the rain, little alchemist, because there's too much of lightning in your blood. You keep the storm away, until your father comes to face you."

"But . . . I'm mortal-born! I've been told so many times."

"And none of that matters where *he* is concerned. The only storm that can sow fully human flowers. You aren't divine, but you're of his garden, all the same."

"How can I bring the rain back to Boston?"

"Leave? Die?" Phaesyle shrugs. "It's all the same to me. Nothing will break the barrier of your blood but blood itself."

"That was what I was afraid you'd say," says Asphodel. She straightens. "Thank you for coming. I appreciate your attendance more than you can know."

"I'm a goddess, if only a minor one. I know precisely how well my presence is appreciated, and I appreciate the wine. I am pleased to have seen you so closely, daughter of the storm." She begins walking backward, the silver goblet still held loosely in her hand.

The sound she makes when Miss Cottingsly's knife slides between her ribs is small and tight, more surprise than pain. Her eyes go wide, face tilting upward just enough to let her gaze lock with Asphodel's, and the silver goblet slips from her hand to clatter on the ground. It's already empty: there's nothing left to spill.

She doesn't say anything, doesn't offer any portentous last words, only drops to her knees and collapses face-first over the border into Asphodel's circle, Miss Cottingsly's knife still protruding from her back.

"That was more efficient than I expected," says Asphodel, trying to sound like she's not disturbed, like she sees women stabbed in front of her every day.

"Been doing my job for a long time now," says Miss Cottingsly. "I'd be a poor housekeeper if I didn't know how to kill someone on the first hit, and keep them down once I've decided to. Will we deal with her here, miss?"

"No, that's not the plan," says Asphodel. The beach is still empty below them, the house of her uncle's associate still dark, with no signs of motion in the windows, but that could change at any moment. The alchemical world protects its own, as much as it can manage. That's not going to help her if the authorities get involved. "We'll take her back to the house, and deal with her there."

"Yes, miss," says Miss Cottingsly mildly.

Together, they're able to carry the things they brought to cast the circle and the body of Phaesyle back to their carriage. The driver watches impassively as they hoist the dead woman inside. He doesn't offer to help them, but he doesn't react as if they're doing anything strange, either, and under the circumstances, Asphodel is just as happy with his apparent disinterest as she'd be with anything else.

The bronze bowl of blood and wine is tipped out onto the sand, a final offering and almost-apology to Dionysus, who probably wasn't anticipating the loss of one of his teachers when he chose to refuse the summons.

The last thing Asphodel does is break the circle, dragging her foot through the line and scattering it. As soon as the individual grains have been disturbed, they begin to shudder in the wind, shifting and blowing away. She watches for several seconds, reassuring herself that in a few hours, nothing will be left behind. Then she turns and walks back to the carriage, joining Miss Cottingsly and the corpse inside. Her uncle's associate would be glad to help her dismantle Phaesyle, and even gladder to claim her as salvage, claim her as his own. Asphodel is only a woman. She will find no salvation here.

They have to go.

The journey back to Boston takes forever and no time at all simultaneously. The sun is low by the time they arrive, half-hidden by clouds which have chased them here from the seashore, following until they seemed determined to cast down an early night over the world. She and Miss Cottingsly sling Phaesyle's arms over their shoulders and carry her like a drunken or exhausted friend into the house, moving quickly so as to minimize their time on the street with a corpse.

Together, they drag the dead Hyade down to the basement, where they lay her out on the table and Asphodel washes her hands in the sink, steadying herself for the dissection.

When she turns around, Miss Cottingsly is there, holding the bone saw in one hand. "Ready when you are, miss," she says.

Asphodel takes the saw, trying to push down the feeling that she's about to be rather dramatically unwell. "Thank you, Miss Cottingsly," she says. "That will be all."

The auf nods, and turns to ascend the stairs.

Asphodel and Phaesyle are alone.

"I really am sorry," she says, and approaches the body. "It's not your fault. But we need the rain, and I promised my uncle I would find a way to bring it back. You understand. I'm sure you understand. Or you would, if you were alive. Dead people don't understand much."

Incarnates, when they die, leave their borrowed human bodies behind and move on to be reborn in a new skin, a new story. When Deborah died, she bled silver only for as long as her tissues remained warm. When Charles died, his body froze, but only for as long as natural ice might last. It thawed quickly, and he was just meat after that, as frail and fallible as any human to have ever lived.

Phaesyle has been dead for hours, and Asphodel isn't sure what will happen when she cuts into the other woman's flesh. Still, she positions her basins to catch anything that drips from the table, and she makes her first cuts with hope singing high in her heart.

A gush of watery blood, so dilute that it runs almost clear, cascades out as she slices into Phaesyle's shoulder, the force of the gout sending it pouring over the table's edge and into the waiting basin. Asphodel smiles in her relief, and keeps on cutting.

The Hyade's body is a miracle of impossibilities. Her tissues, like her blood, are virtually clear, as if her entire body had been made of rainwater; her heart is a ghost nestled in her chest, more white than red. Asphodel plucks it reverently from its nest of arteries and connective tissues, and she knows, down to the very bones of her, that this is the answer they've been looking for.

Charles said the rains would stay away until the storm settled. Standing here, holding the heart of a goddess of rain, Asphodel feels the storm she has always been distantly aware of calm. A decision has been made, somewhere far away and out of sight, and now they are free to continue on.

Heart in her hands, she climbs the basement stairs and walks toward her uncle's study. The door is open. He looks up when she steps into the doorway, looking unsurprised to find her standing there with a bone-white heart in her hands. She smiles as he meets her eyes.

"I'm going to bring the rain back now, if you'd like to come and see," she says.

He blinks, rising. "You're so sure?"

"I'm positive." The heart is still, dead, but still she feels the power in it thrumming through her hands. The rain is ready.

"I'd like to see."

"You're the one who taught me about sympathy," she says, as she leads him through the house. "How a whisker is also a cat, and a fingernail is also a man. A piece of the thing is the whole of the thing, if you hold it at the right angle, if you see it in the right light. This heart belonged to a woman who was the rain, once. She walked the world as a rainstorm in a human skin, and her heart is still the rain, still falling. All I need to do is bring it to the sky."

Her uncle frowns, looking uncertain, but he doesn't object, only follows her to the back door, out under a sky gone charcoal-gray with clouds. How long has it been since Boston's skies have been so blackened?

Asphodel digs her fingers into the heat of the heart, nails piercing through the tough external layers with an audible pop, and then, straining to complete the gesture, she rends the organ in two. It tears like paper, muscle pulling apart from itself, and she holds the two halves up to the sky.

"Whoever has stopped the rain over Boston, return it now," she says. "I know your name, and I will not speak it, and I reject your storm. I want no part of what you've done."

And the rain begins to fall.

Slowly at first, a few fat drops tumbling to the bone-dry ground, and then faster and harder, until a wall of water is slamming down on top of them. Asphodel stays where she is, eyes fixed on the sky as the rain runs over her. Her uncle takes a step back.

She turns to face him, and her eyes are bright as lightning, her voice, when she speaks, made rich by thunder. "You figure out how to stop it," she says. "I've done my part. I'll expect my training to begin tomorrow."

She drops the two broken halves of Phaesyle's heart to the ground and walks away, back into the house, away from the rain that falls unceasing on the city behind her.

Wondering what he's done, her uncle watches her go.

When they came to the end of the path, it was not to find themselves on the mountain's peak, or perhaps it was only that their definition of "peak" was incorrect, for they were at the top of the mountain, standing on a lip of stone no wider across than Soleil was tall, with the sheer fall back to the plains on one side, and a second, even more terrifying drop into a cauldron filled with bubbling lava on the other. A strut of stone jutted from the center of the roiling volcano, and atop it stood the Palace.

Unlike everything else they had seen in this place, it was neither charred nor ashen. It gleamed like a spire of rainbow crystal in the light that filtered through the clouds, at once transparent and every color the world had to offer. It had been carved into the rough shape of something Avery could recognize as a castle, but it was still rough and jagged around the edges, looking more grown than made, like it had simply chosen to take on a form they could identify with a seat of power.

A narrow bridge led across the lava to the palace doors. Avery and Niamh both eyed it with worry, for their own, if similar, reasons. Jack, however, stepped onto it without hesitation, walking straight toward the doors with Zib still dangling in his arms. Soleil followed close behind him, stepping lightly, seemingly unbothered by the potential fall into the volcano. The Page flitted back and forth between the two groups, still leaving sparks in her wake.

"The path you followed up the mountainside was narrower, and you didn't fall," she said, flipping upside down again as she addressed Avery. "Why do you fear falling here?"

"Because that's lava," said Avery. The Page looked politely puzzled. Avery frowned. "People from America die if we fall into lava."

"Then you go to the Impossible City via the graveyard path," said the Page. "Someone always does. Your drowned girl did, once."

Avery glanced to Niamh, who nodded.

"I told you I had been to the City, before I became too possible to tolerate," she said. "The graveyard path is always open to the dead, when we make our first journey. It's impossible for a dead person to make a trip on their own, until they find the graveyard path. That makes it possible for them, and the contradiction will get them past the gates. Once. Only once."

"That's not fair," protested Avery.

Niamh looked at him with tired, level eyes. "Child, when did anyone tell you that the Up-and-Under would be *fair*? Water doesn't care for fair or unfair when it drowns you. It only desires to drown. . . ."

—From *Under the Smokestrewn Sky*,
by A. Deborah Baker

BOOK IV

Gold

Go and catch a falling star,
  Get with child a mandrake root,
Tell me where all past years are,
  Or who cleft the devil's foot,
Teach me to hear mermaids singing,
Or to keep off envy's stinging,
    And find
    What wind
Serves to advance an honest mind.

—John Donne, "Song"

Truth can take us so far, beyond that we go by trust
Are you as scared as I am at what's happening to us
It's hard on you, but sometimes I just have to run and hide
But it's your arms I'll run back to, and your face I wear
  inside.

—Talis Kimberley, "The Face Within"

Authority

TIMELINE: AUGUST 23, 2018.

Lilianne groans as consciousness comes seeping back around the edges of her mind, pulling her out of the deep, healing darkness of sleep. She's stretched out on something soft, and while her shoulder still aches, it doesn't *throb*, doesn't pound with every beat of her heart. It feels like the blood inside her body is staying there, like she might be a closed system, capable of survival.

She just doesn't know where she is. The air is cool, and smells faintly of oiled leather and old paper. It's a library smell, a familiar, comfortable smell. It's the smell of her father's office back in Alabama.

It's not the smell of the underground lab, or of her current off-campus home. The apartment smells like the ghosts of old marijuana cigarettes and the soft, almost-sweet scent of Snake's cockroach colony, which fills the bathroom like a strange sort of incense. None of those smells are present here. Only books and stillness.

With an effort almost exhausting enough to send her spiraling back down into the silent dark, Lilianne forces her eyes to open. She's looking up at an unfamiliar ceiling, plain wood stained dark to balance the amount of light coming in from the windows. What she can see of the walls without turning her head is mostly books and shelving, dark oak without a sign of dust. She blinks, several times, trying to find the strength to move and look anywhere else.

A dry voice to her left says, "The alchemist's awake."

Lilianne blinks again and tries to ask who the speaker is. Her lips refuse to move. The effort shows her how dry her tongue is, how stuck to the top of her mouth. She's entirely defenseless.

"Are you sure?" This voice belongs to Smita. There's an edge of anxiety to the question, terror, concern, and relief all mixed together.

"I think I can tell the difference between someone who's awake and someone who's asleep," says the first voice. It's female, Californian by accent, with a vague disaffection that Lilianne's used to hearing in teens who would rather chew their own arms off than spend time with their families. She dealt with a lot of them during her years volunteering as a receptionist at her father's pediatric practice.

Just the thought of the practice is enough to summon a pleasant hallucination of the old, familiar place, its polished floors, its clean, primary-colored walls. She's halfway back down the slide into unconsciousness before she realizes what's happening and tries to catch herself, digging her heels into the waking world and refusing to tumble any further. The stop is jarring, from the soles of her feet all the way to her still-aching shoulder.

Wait. Why does her shoulder only ache, like something she injured weeks ago and is well on the way to recovering from? She remembers the etiäinen shedding the illusion of Smita's face and lunging for her, the way its claws caught and tore at the meat of her shoulder, the hot feeling of the damage spreading through her body. She remembers the blood running down her arm to feed the water, and the etiäinen lurking just barely out of reach, strangely unwilling to come up onto the desk where she was huddled. She's sure there was a reason for that. She just needs to figure out what it was, in case this ever comes up again.

Because I'm definitely going to be wandering around a lab originally staffed by high-level alchemists who didn't have time to defuse their tricks and traps before they fled again in the future, she thinks, words caustic and biting in the silence of her own mind, and the loathing in the thought is enough to snap her eyes open again. It's the same ceiling as before, which makes it feel more likely to be real.

Whatever's going on, it's actually happening, and that means she's going to have to deal with it.

Someone nudges her left arm. That gesture should send an explosion of pain through her shoulder. That it doesn't makes her suspect that while this is really happening, it may be happening to her after she's already dead. If the afterlife is some sort of strange private library, she'll . . . well, she'll be pretty much okay with that.

It's just a pity that she got Smita killed, too.

"I'm sorry," she manages to rasp. Getting her jaw to move takes everything she has, and she's suddenly, deeply relieved to already be lying down. She sighs, closing her eyes again. Sight or sound. If she has to choose between them, right now, she needs sound more. "Didn't mean to . . . kill you."

"No one's dead here, Lily," says Smita urgently. Cool fingers wrap around her own, twining through them and tugging, like their owner believes they can fix everything if Lily will just sit up. "This isn't the afterlife."

"If it were, I'm sure someone else would do the laundry," says the dry voice from before.

Smita scoffs. "As if you've done a load of laundry since we moved in here? I keep telling you, there aren't any little fairies who come in at night and take care of everyone's washing up."

"But somehow I never run out of clean underwear," says the other voice. "Check and mate, Smita. Give up and admit the laundry fairies are real."

"I will not. Now stop distracting me." Smita tugs on Lilianne's hands again. "You're not dead, you didn't die in the lab, you're in my house—"

"Your house?" asks the dry voice.

"—and I just need you to wake up so I can be sure that you're okay," says Smita doggedly. "Come on, Lily. I just met you. You don't get to go and die on me yet."

"Plus I really don't feel like dealing with a corpse tonight," says the first speaker. "We're not alchemists here. Body disposal is not our strong suit, and if you make me try to contend with yours, I'm going to put it someplace really embarrassing, just to make you feel bad about dying in my house."

Lilianne opens her eyes again. The rest of her body still feels like an immovable object, something so far outside her control that it might as well be back in that lab, disconnected from the rest of her, but at least she can open her eyes.

"Good job." The owner of the dry voice finally leans into view. It's a woman, pale, with unsettlingly gray eyes and hair that *must* be the product of a ridiculously talented stylist given utterly trite directions. Why else would they have dyed it to look like she's a candy cane? Shocking red and equally shocking white combined is not a good look on anyone outside of Santa's village, but this woman doesn't seem to realize how ridiculous it is, only eyes Lilianne with detached curiosity.

"Thanks for not being dead," she says. "Smita would have been utterly impossible to live with if you'd been dead."

Lilianne stares up at her, silent and motionless.

The woman sighs. "I'm Dodger, by the way. Dodger Cheswich. This is my house, if you care, and it was my kitchen floor you were bleeding all over earlier. You're welcome, by the way. My usual response to people bleeding on my floor is expulsion, not medical care."

"She's not serious," says Smita. "Dodger, tell her you're not serious."

"Oh, I am entirely serious," says Dodger, deadpan. "My parents should *not* have been allowed to name their own children. But they were, and so my name is my unrealistic cross to bear."

"I meant about throwing people out when they're injured."

"Oh, no, I was serious about that, too. I don't like blood. Too many bad memories. Lucky for your alchemist here, my brother is a soft touch who never met a stray he didn't want to save." Dodger shrugs. "So, you're welcome. And now that you're awake, you should figure out how your arms and legs work and come downstairs for something to eat. You need to replace all that blood you've lost." She steps away, quickly vanishing from Lilianne's field of view.

Smita tugs on her hands, trying to pull her into a sitting position. "You get used to Dodger, I promise," she says. "She's brusque, but she cares more than she tries to let on. I think you might like her, if you gave her a chance."

Lilianne snaps her attention back to Smita. She's wearing a fresh shirt, something clean, and her hair has clearly been washed and brushed out since the lab. She's still the most beautiful woman Lilianne has ever seen. It's hard to think of anything that would change that.

Really, it's hard to think right now, and so Lilianne gives up trying and focuses instead on her body, which is weak and sore but not actually injured in this moment. It should listen to her when she tells it what she wants. Even if it doesn't want to, she's strong enough to make it listen. She's been overcoming worse obstacles than a little blood loss her whole life. She's been forcing her way through locked doors since the day she became aware of what locks were, and she can beat this.

She can beat this. She can.

She takes a deep breath, rolling slightly to the side without letting go of Smita's hands, and tightens the muscles of her core until they lift her off whatever she's on top of, raising her inch by agonizing inch into a sitting position. Smita never lets go of her hands, not even when her grip becomes too tight, not even when she almost pulls the smaller woman down on top of herself. Finally, she's sitting up, and can see that what she's sitting on is a reading couch, one of the ones that looks halfway to being a really strangely designed bed, and she's definitely in a library, although not one she's ever seen before.

Which makes sense, since that Dodger woman said this was her house. Lilianne's never met her before; she obviously wouldn't have been in her house if she hasn't met her. She slumps against the back of the couch, finally releasing Smita's hands, and waits for the world to stop spinning around her.

It feels like it might be quite a wait.

Smita sits down next to her, nudging her legs until she swings them around to put her feet on the ground. "I was worried about you," she says, earnestly. "You passed out before we got up to the street. Erin and Artemis had to carry you back here."

That name . . . Lilianne's eyes widen fractionally. "The woman with the bow and arrow," she says. "You called her—but she can't be."

"A Lunar?" asks Smita. She smirks a little, like a kid with a secret too good to keep for long. "Yes. She's one of the current incarnations of the Roman goddess of the moon. There was a period where we had her *and* an incarnation of Diana in town. That got messy."

"How did it end?"

"Diana died." There's a calm to that reply that Lilianne doesn't like. They were just wandering around a lab made possible by the sacrifice of one of the Lunars, and yet she doubts even its architects were that unbothered by the idea of ending a life.

Smita holds up her hands, apparently reading the direction of Lilianne's thoughts in her expression. "Oh, no, none of us killed her. It was a Lunar thing. We just weren't horribly upset when we found out about it, especially given what she'd done."

"What did she do?"

"She was selling other Lunars out to the alchemists. It turns out that incarnate moon gods don't like it very much when you treat them like exploitable resources, and they hit back as soon as they saw an opportunity. The alchemists left Berkeley for a reason, Lily. And Berkeley isn't in any hurry to have them back again."

Lilianne is speechless. She leans back into the couch and just stares at Smita.

Smita sighs, head drooping. "I'm sorry I lied to you. I really didn't feel as if I had any choice, not when you were talking about finding things that we'd decided were best left lost. If it helps at all, I felt bad leading you on. I should have said something right from the start."

Lilianne tries but can't quite conceal her wince. If Smita had openly admitted to everything she knew about the alchemical world right from the start, she would have asked her to stay behind, to go away and let Lilianne search on her own. The pendulum had worked; Lilianne would have managed to find the lab with or without Smita. And if she'd found it on her own, she has every faith that she would have died down there. Their escape had been partially luck, but mostly Smita's friends caring enough to come looking for her—caring, and having the particular set of skills that had made finding her possible.

"It's okay," she croaks, throat dry and words reluctant. "I wish you hadn't lied, but I can't be mad that we're both still alive."

"Good," says Smita, relief obvious. "I would hate to have you mad at me because we didn't die. I won't lie to you again if I have any choice in the matter."

"Good." A wave of weariness washes over Lilianne. She closes her eyes, sinking deeper into the softness of the couch.

Then Smita's hands are on her shoulders—and both those things are miracles, Smita touching her and the absence of pain when she does; both of those things are sweet dreams she would have been perfectly content to leave unrealized, being practical enough not to wish for the truly impossible—and she's being pulled back into a proper sitting position. "Hey," says Smita. "No sleeping. It's time for staying awake. We need to get you downstairs so we can feed you properly, and you can meet everyone else."

"How many people are *in* this house?" asks Lilianne sourly, opening her eyes unwillingly. "I didn't sign up for some sort of Addams Family reunion."

"We're not the Addams Family," says Smita. "We're not all related, although some of us are *very* related. Some of us are more related than is technically biologically possible."

Lilianne tries to puzzle through that statement, then abandons the attempt as her head begins to throb again. She's too tired for this. She's lost too much blood.

Although she supposes it's not lost. She knows exactly where she left it. It's just that the greatest alchemist in the world wouldn't be able to extract it from solution and return it to something that could fill her veins. The blood she left behind in the lab is gone forever, no longer hers, never to belong to her again.

"I don't want to go down stairs," she says instead, a weak defense against a frightening situation.

"I'll be right there to make sure you don't fall." Smita slides to her feet, still holding Lilianne's shoulders, then slides her hands down the other woman's arms until she's gripping Lilianne's wrists, pulling as hard as she can without hurting her.

Lilianne groans. She's bigger than Smita; she could stop this just by pulling briskly away, and might even get a lapful of Smita for her troubles. But Smita looks so earnest, so hopeful, and she really *does* want to understand how they were able to heal her shoulder so quickly; she should be looking at months of recovery, not wishing for a little arnica to ease the ache away. So she stands, allowing herself to be pulled, and tries to repress the flash of delight she gets when Smita beams at her, bright as a floodlight.

Smita is not her friend. Smita lied to her. Smita has taken her to a house full of people who apparently know more than normal people are meant to know about the alchemical world. Smita can't be trusted. She needs to remember that, no matter how pretty Smita is when she smiles.

She *has* to remember.

Smita releases her right hand but keeps hold of her left, pulling her through the sun-soaked library to the door on the far end. "The house is a little weird, architecturally speaking, but it's not dangerous," she says. "Just keep your eyes on me, and don't pay attention to anything that doesn't make sense."

Then she's opening the door and pulling Lilianne into a U-shaped hallway illuminated by carnival-glass skylights. It's like walking through a rainbow, or into a cartoon, something from the eighties, when technology had just discovered a way to display every color the eye was capable of perceiving and animators decided to throw them all into the same scene as often as they possibly could. The walls are lined with more shelves, and many of those are lined with books, but they seem almost incidental after the book-choked confines of the library.

There is, as promised, a staircase leading down. Smita goes first and Lilianne follows, taking each step one foot at a time, like someone recovering from a long illness: she steps down, waits to be sure she has her balance, then adds her second foot to the same tread, pausing before she retreats the process. It's slow, and makes her feel terribly fragile.

Smita doesn't say a word, only keeps guiding her down, to a dimmer second floor that looks like it's mostly used for residential purposes, individual doors closed against the public spaces. There's another staircase there, and Lilianne barely has time to catch her breath before Smita's guiding her down this one as well, into another sun-soaked hall, this one clearly on the ground floor: there's a door with several inset glass panels (more carnival glass; was this house built by circus performers) that must lead to the outside, and rather than stretching out in front of the stairs, the hall flows around them and leads deeper into the house, creating a central corridor that only makes sense on the ground.

The front door is at the far end of a small, box-like entry foyer, large enough for two more doors, one to the left and one to the right: the lefthand door is closed, but Lilianne can hear voices from behind it, deep in some incomprehensible conversation. Smita starts tugging her in that direction. Lilianne digs her heels into the floor, refusing to be moved.

"Do I have to?" she asks.

Smita turns to give her a half-frustrated look. "You do, actually," she says. "You'd be dead now if Artemis and Erin hadn't come to find us, and if Isabella hadn't been willing to come and help Roger talk your veins back together. They were shredded, just like everything around them. Your survival was a group project, and it's polite to thank the people who did all the work. Which doesn't include me. I'm good at drawing blood and tying off a few stitches, not at complicated semi-alchemical surgery."

"Semi-alchemical . . . ?"

"The things that chased us down there are called 'etiäinen.' They're alchemical creations, sort of like the auf, except unlike auf, they don't start as living things that get taken apart by alchemists who don't care about other people's right to exist. They start as inert materials, and they're brought to life from there. Alchemists seem to create in three categories, as far as I've been able to determine: auf when they have a corpse they don't want to waste, etiäinen when they *want* a few corpses, and cuckoos when they're creating life that's meant to have a more-complicated purpose."

Lilianne is struck silent by the ease with which Smita reveals things that she herself hadn't been able to discover until she'd been studying alchemy in secret for more than a decade. What has she stumbled into?

Falling into immediate giddy infatuation with beautiful women shouldn't be this complicated. She makes a silent vow to never do it again.

(She'll keep that vow, but only because she'll never see another woman as instantly beautiful to her idea of the world as Smita. Smita is perfectly suited to her desires, and she's stuck.)

Smita tugs her again. "Come on," she says. "I'm forgiven for bringing an alchemist home, given the state you were in when I got you here, but that degree of forgiveness isn't going to extend to you being openly rude to my housemates."

Lilianne's feet feel like lead. But she's an alchemist; purifying lead is one of the first tricks she learned. She wills them back to flesh and bone, and once again allows herself to be pulled onward, whether or not she wants to go—and she doesn't want to go, she *doesn't*, there just isn't any way this can be avoided, not in truth, not for long—to the kitchen door, which Smita pushes open like it's nothing remotely important. Like this is just another day.

* * *

The kitchen is large and comfortable, if built in an architectural style more common to parts of the Midwest than it is to California; they could be stepping into an Indiana farmhouse, into the sort of space that's been used for generations of Thanksgiving dinners and hundreds of family birthday parties. The floor is scuffed blue linoleum, the walls are white, and the appliances are a dizzying array of colors, some of which Lilianne is fairly sure haven't been manufactured since the seventies.

It's a good thing the kitchen is so large; if it weren't, it would never be able to hold this many people. There's the human candy cane Lilianne saw in the library when she first woke up, and there's a tall brunet man with a matching white streak in his hair. It looks even sillier on him than it does on her, which increases her quiet conviction that it must be natural: no one would look that goofy on purpose, not even in Berkeley, which sometimes seems to be trying harder than is healthy to stand out from the crowd. The pair of them are leaning against one of the counters, the man cupping a large mug in his long-fingered hands, the woman with her arms folded over her chest.

The woman from the lab is seated in the breakfast nook, next to another woman, this one with bright orange skin, horns, and sideways-slit pupils, like a goat's. Lilianne has never seen a person so blatantly artificial. She's crammed in next to Artemis, their shoulders touching, and it's shocking seeing a cuckoo—because she has to be a cuckoo, she *has* to be, everything about her is engineered and deliberate—that close to a Lunar with neither of them seeming alarmed by the proximity.

A dark-haired woman who looks like she's half-Chinese perches on the counter to the other side of the brunet man, sipping from a bottle of orange-pink liquid. Her shirt is covered in dense writing, and from what Lilianne can see, it doesn't stay the same language for more than two words, telling some complicated, incomprehensible joke.

Erin is near the stove, stirring something that smells sweet and bland at the same time. Probably oatmeal.

And then there is David. Her housemate David, standing a few feet away from the Chinese woman, arms folded and face set into a scowl. Lilianne jumps a little when she sees him, feeling an odd mix of relief and panic, like she ought to turn and run before he notices her. Which is silly, because there's no way he doesn't know she's here. Not if he's been here the whole time.

Before she can even finish asking herself why he's here, he meets her eyes and says, curtly, "Lilianne."

"David." Her mouth isn't as dry as it was when she woke up, but it still hurts to talk, and so she doesn't try for more than that single-word acknowledgment that she recognizes him, that she's not going to try pretending that she doesn't.

"I was on my way home after dinner and a lot of therapeutic video games when Erin here"—he hooks a finger toward the woman in question, who looks up from her pot and nods, once—"came running in and told us all that Smita had gone and cracked open some rotten egg of an alchemist's lab, and needed help. Artemis is the best of us for actual physical dangers, but they still didn't want anyone else leaving before they got Smita back. You were an unexpected bonus."

There's something in his eyes that tells her he's not necessarily her ally here. They share an apartment, but they aren't *friends*. She's not the person he thinks of when he has news to share, whether good or bad or deeply strange.

He's not going to defend her against these people if things go badly.

"Do you need to sit down?" asks the brunet man, looking directly at her. His eyes are the same pale gray as Dodger's; that, and the similarity in their facial features, makes her think they're some of the extremely related people Smita mentioned before. Still, his voice is warm and kind, and the question seems entirely sincere. "We can get you a chair if you need to sit down."

"Do we really want to make the alchemist more comfortable?" asks the Chinese woman, setting her bottle aside. She produces a peach pit from a pocket and begins flipping it between her fingers like a streetcorner magician with a trick coin. "I'm all for a little discomfort."

"She's a guest here, just like you are," says Erin. "That means we follow the rules of hospitality, even if we don't necessarily want to. Even if we're not completely happy having certain people in our home. The rules are what keep us from collapsing into chaos. You don't want us collapsing into chaos, do you, Judith?"

"Full name, you're in trouble now," says Artemis, almost snickering.

"That's not my full name, just my full American first name," snaps Judith. "You couldn't pronounce my full name."

The brunet man puts a hand on her arm. "Let's try not to fight until we're done figuring out what's actually going on, okay?" he says.

Lilianne feels suddenly much more inclined to try to get along with these strange people. This man should be an inspirational speaker or something. One of those folks who get paid to stand up in front of crowds and tell them how they're supposed to live their lives to maximize their synergies and experience their experiences. He just has one of those voices.

Smita nudges her with an elbow. "Hey," she says. "Don't drift off into some pretty fantasy about world peace, okay? It can be hard to focus your thoughts the first time Roger talks to you. But don't worry, you'll get better. As long as he's not actually *trying*, you can generally shrug him off."

Lilianne blinks at her, then at the brunet man—Roger.

His name rhymes with his sister's. That's funny. Most parents of twins try to avoid that sort of symmetry. It's too cutesy, and it denies their children the right to forge their own identities, outside of the sometimes-confining structure of twinship. Rhyming names are a form of sympathetic connection; some alchemists, like the late James Reed, have been known to use that sort of thing to forge bonds between—

Between—

Lilianne's eyes widen. Washed-out eyes, paler than anything she's ever seen in nature. Matching white streaks, like they both somehow experienced the same injury, bleaching the hair follicles in a specific stretch of the scalp. Even the languidly predatory way they both move, like neither one of them can imagine a world where they're not the most dangerous things in the room. There's at least one Lunar and a girl who looks like some sort of weird sexy demon Oompa Loompa, and yet they still think of themselves as the apex predators of this space.

"You're Reed's cuckoos," she blurts, everything she knows snapping together to make a single, indisputable picture.

"Told you she'd get it on her own," says Dodger. She turns to face her brother. "Pay up."

"Dodge, you bet me a week's dishes. How am I supposed to pay up *right now*?" Roger sounds tired. Lilianne's only known them for a few minutes, and she can already tell that having Dodger for a sister must be absolutely exhausting.

"That's your problem," says Dodger, shrugging off his concern.

Lilianne feels like she's going to lose the breakfast she hasn't had yet all over their kitchen floor. James Reed died because he managed to embody the Doctrine of Ethos. Everyone knows he succeeded, just like everyone knows he was behind the bombing that killed much of the American Congress. There's no proof, no one is ever going to be able to provide an actual timeline of events that paints him guilty in the eyes of the unconvinced, but still, everyone knows.

As to the Doctrine, Lilianne knows he succeeded with them because her own parents told her so, right before they went back to building the next iteration of their labyrinth. All the incarnate forces knew when he harnessed the Doctrine and sealed it in human skin. That big a disturbance in the nature of reality wasn't exactly subtle, wasn't precisely the sort of thing that could be overlooked so easily.

She's been dealing with incarnate forces since she was conceived; her mother was already sworn to serve the autumn when

Lilianne was gestating in her womb, and there's never been a time when she knew her parents as anything other than slightly otherworldly. And that doesn't make this any easier. The Doctrine is huge, a god-level power—true gods, the ones who stopped incarnating long ago, because they no longer fit within the confines of the world. The various lunar and oceanic gods may manifest, but Zeus doesn't. The ones who can remake reality in their own image don't appear anymore.

She can't be here. She can't be in a room with these people, who barely understand how to *be* people, who are more like concepts thinly wrapped in sinew and skin. She has to go.

Lilianne begins to turn away, pulling her hand out of Smita's in the process.

She doesn't even have time to take a step toward the door before Erin is asking, tone mild, "Going somewhere, alchemist? But you haven't had your breakfast yet. And you haven't explained what the *fuck* you're doing in our city. You want to come sit down and take care of things before you go?"

"No," says Lilianne. "I want to go. I can't— I shouldn't— This is not a safe place for me to be."

"Why not? Did you have bad intentions toward the occupants of this house? Should we be making sure you *can't* leave, no matter how much you might want to? Come and sit down. Eat your breakfast. Answer our questions." Erin's voice remains level throughout, the kind of perfect calm one hears from people on the absolute edge of losing their tempers. "You're already here, Lilianne. You can't get out of here without us letting you, and we're not ready to let you yet. This doesn't have to be unpleasant. You have a choice in how this is going to go."

Lilianne casts a desperate glance at Smita, then sags. "I'll eat," she says.

"Good."

Lilianne turns back toward the table—as promised, another

chair has been produced, pushed up against the one empty space like an invitation she isn't allowed to refuse. She walks over, slowly, and pulls out the chair even more slowly. Its legs scrape against the tile, loud and unforgiving, and she swallows as she sits, all too aware of the eyes on her.

"Maybe we should all introduce ourselves," says Smita, "so we can stop *terrifying* my houseguest?"

"Is it really a guest when you dig it out of the basement of a sealed alchemical lab and let it bleed all over the living room floor?" asks Erin. There's a thin line of malice in her voice that wasn't there before. She walks up behind Smita, dropping a bowl of oatmeal onto the table in front of her, not quite hard enough to spill, but definitely high enough that Lilianne jumps. "Eat," she instructs, and walks away again.

"Thank you?" says Lilianne, twisting to watch her walk away. "I really don't mean to be a bother—"

"But you are, and sometimes we just need to come to terms with that," says Erin, returning to the stove.

This is already going well. Lilianne turns back to the table, where the Lunar she met before meets her eyes and gestures extravagantly to herself.

"I'm Artemis," she says. "Goddess of the moon and the hunt."

"Most Lunars don't introduce themselves as their divinity," says Lilianne, off-kilter from the oddness of that introduction.

"Most Lunars aren't as old as I am," says Artemis. "My mortal host is named Anna, and she's not really with us anymore, thanks to an alchemist named James Reed who got hold of her while she was in a bad mental place. He put her in a worse one. Really, I think you'll find that a lot of the problems in this house come from alchemists in general, and that man in specific. I introduce myself by my divinity because I never step down anymore. I'm always awake, and I'm always Artemis.".

"A lot of the problems, most of the people," says the orange woman. "My name is Kelpie, and I used to think I was an alchemist, until the Congress sent an inspector to shut down our lab and reallocate our resources. That's when I found out I was actually an alchemical creation. I'm technically a cuckoo, since I'm a manufactured embodiment, but since I'm an embodiment of something that used to happen naturally, it's a little hard to pin me down with a specific label like that. I'm Artemis's Hind. I run before the Moon when it shines down on the Impossible City."

"I am neither a consequence of nor a practitioner of alchemy," says Judith, with a lazy wave. "I'm one of many current incarnations of Chang'e, goddess of the moon and keeper of the peaches of immortality. I keep the pantheon young for as long as it needs to be. And I had a hand in healing that shoulder of yours. You're welcome, and call me 'Judy.' This 'Judith' bitch sounds stodgy as hell."

"You— How?" asks Lilianne. "You're not a god of healing. How did you—"

"You can't be immortal if you're dead," says Judy. "Peach pulp from my trees can be used to patch up almost any wound, when absolutely necessary. Slapped a bunch of that stuff on your screwed-up shoulder, and we were able to get you a long way toward living. But it was a group effort, and I can neither claim nor desire all the credit."

Lilianne's eyes flick to David, and she tenses, waiting to hear what he'll say.

He looks directly at her, arms still folded, and says, "We've met."

"You've mentioned," says Judy. "I didn't expect this to come to a head quite so quickly when you told us that you thought one of your roommates was an alchemist. Have you considered taking another look at the other two?"

"They're not alchemists," says Lilianne. "I'd know by now if they were. They're just normal people who had the bad luck to move in with me."

"Unlike me," says David.

"I swear, I had no idea you were anything other than a football player who'd answered the ad Raven posted about looking for roommates," says Lilianne, half-desperately. "I was just relieved that you weren't transphobic. I didn't know you were . . . whatever it is you are. I swear, I wasn't trying to hurt you or complicate your life. I needed an apartment. That's all."

"I *am* a football player," says David. "It's just that I'm also Máni, the Norse god of the moon. And I'm part of this little debrief because I was here already, telling everyone about the alchemist in my house, and how concerned I was that you might do something if we didn't find a way to prevent it. Looks like I was running slightly later than I needed to be on that one, huh?"

After Artemis and Kelpie, Lilianne can't exactly bring herself to ask what these people have against alchemists. Mouth dry, she can only nod, and say quietly, "I wasn't planning on doing anything bad to anyone. I wasn't planning on doing anything to anyone at all."

"Yet," says Erin.

Lilianne's head snaps around, eyes going wide and bewildered.

The other woman shrugs. "You weren't planning on doing anything to anyone. Alchemy, it has a way of . . . escalating, shall we say. You start out and it's just vials of mercury and moonlight, but it doesn't take long before you start thinking how the blood of a living Lunar would probably combine the properties of those two things without the need for any messy compounding. You start to think that if you go and catch a falling star, you might be entitled to more than just a few idly granted wishes. And finally, you start to think other people are just preservation systems for lab supplies. It's a slippery slope, and I've never known an alchemist who didn't slide down it to one degree or another. You can't devote yourself to learning things man was not meant to know and then be surprised when knowing those things impacts who you are as a person."

"Have you known many alchemists?" asks Lilianne. "Maybe you just knew rotten ones. Ones who were always going to go bad. Ones who didn't have the privilege of being raised by my mama. She'd slap the evil inclinations out of anybody."

Erin looks, briefly, amused. "I've known a lot of alchemists in my day, yes," she says. "They made me, after all. And I lived in their custody until my owner decided I needed to be socialized like a real girl and sent me off to live with some of the 'less important' alchemists. The ones who worked independently, the way you do. I didn't really see much difference, beyond resource levels. So yes, we took David seriously when he came to us saying there was an alchemist in his house and he was getting worried about what that alchemist might do. I admit, nothing we've seen so far makes me think that he was wrong."

Lilianne blinks, sitting up a little straighter. "They *made* you?"

"Yes."

"But—Roger and Dodger are Reed's cuckoos. The Doctrine is only two parts."

"The Doctrine should have been four," says Erin. "But that's neither here nor there, and it's a philosophical argument as much as an alchemical one. No, I'm not part of the Doctrine, and thank the stars for that, because if I had these assholes in my head all the time, I think I'd blow it off."

"I don't understand."

"Erin was built to embody Order," says Dodger, tone implying that she's trying to be helpful. "She is the living spirit of keeping things organized and functional."

"And my penance is being trapped in a house with all these chaotic freaks," says Erin.

"But what about—" Lilianne begins.

Seeing the expression which sweeps over Erin's face, she stops, clamping her lips shut and feeling suddenly as if the best thing she could do would be to disappear, to sink into the earth and never be seen again.

"My brother's name was Darren," says Erin stiffly. "He embodied Chaos, and the alchemists—the ones you idolize enough to emulate—killed him. Now, since Order and Chaos never learned to incarnate on their own, and I'm still here, no new Chaos has appeared. The first test of the artificial embodiments has come down firmly on the side of 'not gonna happen.'"

"Don't say that too loudly," says Roger.

"Oh, we're pretty sure it's going to happen for *them*," says Erin. "Your successors are primed and waiting. When you die, they'll flytrap that Doctrine right down their gullets, same way you did. But Darren and I were constructed, refined, and didn't have any understudies waiting in the wings. Someone would have to build a new Chaos if I was going to be balanced out again." She cuts her attention sharply over to Lilianne. "Don't offer. That isn't the way to endear yourself to me."

"Erin," says Smita, chidingly.

"Well, it's not," says Erin. "We were never meant to exist. I'm glad I do: I feel like I've paid the universe back for the violence of my creation. But that doesn't change the fact that I'm part of an invasive species, something that wasn't meant to be here in the first place. I'm an irritant in reality's skin. The scar tissue I form may be protective for the flesh beneath me, but that doesn't make it a good girl."

"We'd be dead without you," says Roger.

"I know, and that's half of why I say I've paid the universe back. The other half is Smita." Erin shrugs. "We find our victories where we can."

Lilianne feels like she's drowning, washed away in a tide of contradictions and complications, all so complex that she wants some sort of guidebook or explainer for these people, who they are to each other, who they intend to be to *her.*

Roger turns his attention back on her, and the drowning feeling gets worse. The weight of his attention is heavier than anything she's ever felt before. It could crush her if she let it, smashing her flat under the pressure of it all.

"And you've already guessed who we are," he says. "Reed's cuckoos. His masterpiece. Lucky us." He lifts his coffee mug to his mouth, taking a long drink.

"Lucky everyone," says Dodger. "It could have been a lot worse than us."

"Could have been a lot better, too, but this is what we have to work with," says Erin. She glares at Lilianne. "Eat your oatmeal, alchemist."

Lilianne finally picks up the spoon, taking her first bites of beige goop. It's . . . surprisingly good, flavored with maple syrup and what taste like fresh peaches given a quick simmer in some sort of butter-and-brown-sugar mixture. She keeps eating, trying to make the somewhat terrifying embodiment of Order happy. To make all of them happy, really. Somehow her search for the lost lab has turned into breakfast with the scariest assortment of people she can possibly imagine.

"As I was saying," says Roger. "I'm Roger Middleton, and I'm the Chair of the Linguistics Department at UC Berkeley. I understand you're a student there. You'll probably see me on and around campus—I like it there, so I tend to spend a reasonable amount of time in my office. I am also, thanks to the man who made me, the living embodiment of Language. I can speak anything if you give me a few minutes to listen and adapt to it. I can read anything if you give me just a little bit longer than that. And reality follows my instructions."

"Meaning . . . ?" asks Lilianne.

"Meaning I try very hard to suggest and ask, rather than instruct, which is a funny position for a teacher to take, but there we are. If I tell you to do something, you'll do it. You won't have a choice. I told your shoulder to stop bleeding, and it stopped, long enough for Judy to get her layer of peach pulp over the wound. Putting you back together was very much a group effort."

A group effort Lilianne doesn't fully understand, given the way Erin is looking at her, like she'd far rather rip her apart than help to keep her in one piece. She doesn't say anything. She's learning, quickly, that these people will keep talking as long as they're not interrupted: she can learn more by letting them ramble on than she can by trying to guide them. For now, anyway.

"Yes, yes, we're all very special and clever," says Dodger. "I'm Roger's twin sister, Dodger Cheswich—and yes, we have different last names. Reed made us, but he wasn't exactly the child-rearing type. He had us adopted by families on opposite sides of the country, as far apart as he could get us without sending us to different continents."

"He would have done that if he hadn't been so determined to make you in the shadow of the American Alchemical Congress," says Erin. "This is where Asphodel Baker was thwarted, and where she once defined the field of play. He had to thumb his nose at them in his own creator's domain."

She slants a glance at Lilianne, like she's waiting to see how the young alchemist will react to what might be two large revelations: that James Reed was also an alchemical construction, the first known cuckoo, or that he'd been made by Asphodel Baker, best known as an author of children's literature.

Lilianne is trying not to antagonize these frankly terrifying people, but all she can do upon receiving that look is shrug. "Yes, and?"

She knows about Asphodel Baker. She chose her *name* because of Asphodel Baker (and because her mother's mother was named

Lily, and if she was going to trade the name they gave her in for a newer model, it seemed kind to keep some connection to the family that has been so supportive and loving during her transition). And she's an alchemist! Every female alchemist knows about Asphodel Baker. It's one of the first things they learn when they start their studies: the alchemical world exists, the American Congress is mired so deep in sexism and tradition that it barely acknowledges women can *read*, and Asphodel Baker was the best alchemist North America ever produced.

She was a rare talent, a prodigy, one of those storybook savants who arise once a generation, if that. Asphodel definitely fell on the "if that" side of the equation, because it's been five generations since her birth and no one's seen another alchemist like her. There may never be anyone like her ever again.

James Reed was an influential-enough figure that he features in basically every alchemical text written over the last hundred and fifty years, but he always appears as a fully grown individual, no family, no history, no past. Just James Reed, apprentice to Asphodel Baker—first and last apprentice she ever claimed in the public forum. He was her legacy. The reports disagree on whether he was only her student or also her son, also her lover, also her creation.

Lilianne came down on the side of "lover and creation" a long time ago, seeing James Reed as possibly the only person Asphodel could ever have allowed herself to love: a man of her own manufacture, who knew what she wanted him to know and started from a place she understood, even if all self-aware creations must one day move beyond their beginnings. He was his own man, but he was also hers, and knowing what she knows about Asphodel Baker, that must make him the only man she could ever truly love.

Everyone is staring at her now. Lilianne wilts a little, trying not to squirm in her seat. "I'm sorry," she says. "I thought everybody knew about Asphodel Baker. She's sort of, well. She's something of a hero to women in alchemy. She was a trailblazer."

"Hear that?" asks Erin of Roger and Dodger, tone snide. "She blazed trails."

"Is that what the kids are calling it these days," mutters Roger, without the upturned lilt at the end of his sentence to indicate a question. His "is" was apparently rhetorical. He focuses on Lilianne. "We don't get to tell you how to think or what to do with your life. We could. *I* could. We all know that, and we're too ethical to go 'blazing trails' through your free will. If I told you to go home and never think about alchemy again, you'd do it. You'd do whatever I told you to, and you'd think it was your own idea if I worded it the right way—which I would absolutely do. I am very, very, *very* good at being specifically the kind of monster I was made to be, following Asphodel's blueprints. She wasn't a hero. She wasn't the Queen of Wands. She was the mother of monsters."

"When he starts breaking out the Up-and-Under, that means he's serious, and someone's going to have to rock him to sleep tonight," says Dodger, tone flat. "He's not wrong, though. Asphodel wrote those books to keep her teachings safe for future generations, and she's both the Queens we see over the course of the series, Wands *and* Swords. Both of them have parts of her to share. The Queen of Wands wants everyone to be safe inside the Impossible City, which is Asphodel wanting to lift people up, to teach them. But the Queen of Swords wants everyone to be under her control, mind, body, and soul, which is also Asphodel. She split herself in two, just like she split the Doctrine, because it was the only way to make her small and simple enough to live on in children's literature."

"That's ridiculous," says Lilianne.

"Is it?" asks Dodger. "Because I didn't finish my introduction. Everyone else got to go end to end, but not me. So this is me, reclaiming my time. I'm Dodger Cheswich. I'm Roger's twin sister, and I am the living incarnation of Mathematics, which translates way too frequently into being the living incarnation of Time. Try not to think about it too hard. I don't work on campus, unlike half these weirdoes"—she indicates everyone else with a sweep of her hand—"but I was a student there. I finished off the healing on your shoulder by pushing everything to move faster, so that the tissues had months to recover in minutes. Genetically, Asphodel Baker is my mother, and if she ever decides to crawl out of whatever shallow grave Reed dropped her in, I'll be front of the line to break her nose."

"Just her nose?" asks Erin, voice mild and curious. "I'd think you'd be a lot more creative than just a nose."

"I'm trying to be mindful," says Dodger.

Erin laughs, the sound as wild as a grackle's cry.

Lilianne squirms. "All right. Not that I don't appreciate you coming to save us—I do, I really, really do—but now that we're done being in danger, can I go?"

"Sorry, no," says Roger. "We need you to tell us everything you know about the lab you found, and the alchemists who used to work there. It's important. And we're not going to let you leave until you do."

Lilianne looks around at the motley assemblage surrounding her, and for the first time since waking up in their library, she feels truly, inescapably trapped.

Healing

TIMELINE: AUGUST 23, 2018.

Things get awkward after that. Lilianne isn't sure how to talk to people who seem intent on holding her captive, and her captors seem content to let her process the situation and explain it to them later. It's not until David pushes away from his spot at the counter and starts for the door back to the hall that Lilianne moves, twisting in her seat and holding out an arm like she thinks she could stop him. He's bigger than her in every respect, taller and broader, with biceps as big around as her thighs. There's no way she can force him to do anything.

But she doesn't have to force him. He stops and looks at her with easy curiosity, waiting to see what she's going to say.

"David, please," she begins. She falters there, not sure how she's supposed to continue. "I didn't . . . I haven't done anything wrong. Please. Just take me home."

"Do you know why I hate alchemists?" he asks, philosophically.

"What?"

"It's a pretty simple question. Do you know why?"

"Of course I don't know why. How could I possibly know why, when I just found out that you know what an alchemist *is*? I have no idea what might have happened in your past that would make you hate alchemists."

"There was a girl who went to school with us," he says. "Her name was Eliza, and when she wasn't being a beautiful, sweet, generous girl from Minnesota learning how she was going to become a woman and stay all those things at the same time, she was the Sámi goddess of the moon. I liked her a lot. She was a good friend, and I hoped we'd get to be something more than friends once she'd had a little more time to get comfortable here in California. And I guess we did get to be something more than friends. I got to be the one who found her body."

Lilianne gasps. She knew it had to have been *something* that put true loathing in his eyes when he looks at her, now that he knows what she is. Now that he understands.

"The alchemists who built that lab you like so much, they were trying to find a way to use the Lunars—to use *us*—to get to the Impossible City. Are you enough of an alchemist to know what the Impossible City is?"

"It's a fairy tale," says Lilianne. "Asphodel used it to represent the alchemical ideal, the melding of elements and the place where their purified forms could exist in material space. It's the home of the aether. It's Olympus. It's not *real*."

"It's real," says Judy, moving to stand next to David. She even puts a hand against his arm, golden-pale skin against umber dark. "The Impossible City exists. Didn't you ever wonder why there are still so many moon gods when most of the pantheons are down to one or two manifest representatives, if they even have that by this point? We should be irrelevant by now, but instead we show up by the dozen. We're the Walmart clearance sale of gods."

"Why?" asks Lilianne.

"The Impossible City," says Judy, like that should be obvious. And maybe, from context, it should be. "It's a real, solid, tangible place, it's just not a part of this layer of reality. But it's the control room of this universe, for lack of a better way of putting it. Without the Impossible City, everything falls apart. No more gods, no more monsters, no more embodiments. No more gravity, either, most likely. Take out the City, you take out *everything.* And it's connected to this universe through a place we redundantly call the everything."

"It's sort of like the improbable road if it were really a place you could go," says Smita, her interjection strange and almost out of place after the lecturing Lunars. Both David and Judy turn to give her a look, and she looks boldly back, shifting closer to Lilianne, until her hand is resting on the other woman's shoulder, protective and unmoving. "But it doesn't seem to have quite as many opinions, based on everything you've said about it."

"It has some," says Judy. "The everything connects us to the Impossible City, and every night, Lunars travel through the everything to cross the sky above the City. It keeps the place anchored to our reality. It keeps the City from slipping so far out of phase that our reality starts going with it."

"And whoever controls the City controls *everything,*" says David. "Those alchemists you're so fond of, they were really into the idea that they could be controlling *everything.* Not 'the everything,' literally everything. They came up with a plan. All they had to do was drain a few Lunars—something they were already doing to build their little labs—and they could use the blood and the open passages into the everything to get to the City. I'm not sure what they planned to do from there."

"There was a plan," says Kelpie. "It wasn't a *good* plan, but it was a plan. They were going to use the blood of the Lunar they'd killed to keep that entrance to the everything open, and lure Artemis in with me, so she could use it to get to the window over the City. Pry it open, and then the alchemists could go through and start breaking stuff. I'm not sure they understood just *how* real the City really is. It's real in a way that we don't so much have here, and all they'd have done by jumping through the window is break their ankles."

"But they didn't know that," says David, glaring at Lilianne like he thinks he can kill her with nothing but his fury. "They thought this would be easy, if they just committed a few unforgivable crimes first. And Aske . . . she was sweet and gentle and naïve and defenseless. So they smashed her skull in."

Lilianne knew something like this was coming, has felt it coming since David said he'd found Aske's body, but the bald truth of it is still enough to take her breath momentarily away.

"She was bleeding silver when I found her," he says. "All that divinity just leaking out of her like a broken promise. She was bleeding silver, and it wasn't fading, maybe because she died in the everything, maybe because she died so close to the City. Whatever the reason, it didn't stop, and we didn't have a crematorium—"

"Or know what would happen if we put her into one," adds Judy.

"—so we just had to *leave* her there. Inside her branch of the everything. It took her with it when it collapsed, and her parents think she just ran away or something, they'll never know what happened to her, they'll never know that their daughter was the goddess of the moon, or that she died because some alchemists decided to be assholes, or that she was loved, and we'll never know how amazing she was going to be. You want to know why I hate alchemists, Lilianne? That's why. Because they think they're more human, and thus more important, than all the rest of us. They think they get to matter in a way that we just don't. I'm sorry you felt so small that you needed alchemy to make you feel bigger. And I'm sorry one of us is going to be moving out by the end of the month." He swipes his hand roughly across his eyes. "Judy, I'm out. Call if you need anything."

He storms out of the kitchen then. He doesn't look back.

Lilianne hunches down in her seat, very aware of Smita's fingers on her shoulder, very aware of the hostility in the room. "I'm sorry," she says miserably. "I didn't know about the—the City or the Lunars or any of—I didn't know."

The words aren't enough. The words could never be enough.

But Artemis leans forward, putting one elbow on the table, and says, "It's all right. You didn't know, which means you didn't have a chance to do anything unforgivable. All we need to do is figure out why that lab was important enough to leave that sort of protection in place when they left it, and then we can let you go. You don't have to be responsible for any of this."

She sounds so reasonable, so rational, that Lilianne's heart jumps, hope blooming where only terror was before.

"Or you could be, if you wanted, and we could kill you before you endangered one of us," Artemis continues. The hope withers on the vine, collapsing into ash and aching. "It's all up to you."

"No pressure," adds Erin.

"What I can't figure out is why the lab's defense systems would still be active when it's been abandoned for this long," says Kelpie. The orange girl hasn't spoken much, and hearing her is enough of a novelty that Lilianne focuses on her immediately, almost relaxing.

Kelpie isn't relaxed. If anything, she's tenser than Lilianne was a minute ago, her head down and her shoulders up, leaning against Artemis like she's afraid the other woman is about to disappear and leave her here alone.

"The lab was already being shut down when everything went wrong," she says. "After the man from the Congress came in and killed Margaret, there wasn't any reason for the doors to stay open. She'd been the lead on all our biggest projects. She was . . . she was my creator, I think, but before I knew that, she was my friend. She did her best to protect me. She's the reason I got away."

That's a new name. Lilianne turns to Smita, mouthing curiously, "Margaret?"

Smita shakes her head. Either Margaret isn't important beyond being a dead alchemist, or Smita will explain later. It doesn't matter much in the moment. Lilianne returns her attention to Kelpie.

"By the time Artemis killed the man from the Congress,

everyone else was gone," she continues. "There were just a few auf left, and they should have fallen apart not long after the doors were locked. I don't know what, if anything, could have caused them to continue to operate autonomously for this long."

"Auf are simple," says Erin. "They don't perform complex functions."

"Unless they're like Miss Cottingsly," says Lilianne, desperate enough to contribute that she doesn't think before she speaks.

"What do you mean by that?" asks Erin, voice dropping toward something deeper and more dangerous.

Lilianne understands using the timbre of your words to control how people think about you. Her voice trainer likes to lecture her about it whenever she gets tired of her exercises. "*You don't have to sound any one way to be a woman*," he says. "*But if you want people to view you in a certain light, sounding the part is one of the fastest ways to get them heading in the right direction.*" Tone and pitch matter more than most people realize. She can hear Kelpie's distress and reluctance, but Erin's suspicion is even louder. She talks like she's about to open an interrogation, and it's terrible, and it's honest, and that makes it even worse.

"Miss Cottingsly was Asphodel Baker's uncle's head maid," she says, carefully. "No one knows whether he made her or bought her from another alchemist, but the records are clear: she was with him for more than twenty years, and with Asphodel after his death. We don't have anything to indicate that she was unraveled intentionally. Odds are good she just reached the end of her functional use and fell apart on her own."

Erin is still watching her with narrowed eyes. Lilianne swallows.

"Miss Cottingsly was definitely an auf," she says. "Asphodel wrote about her extensively, and she fits every qualification as we understand them today. Despite this, she was able to maintain a household and serve two different alchemists, over the course of decades. We don't know why she was decommissioned, and she was never caught by the locals. There's no way she could have done that if she hadn't been capable of complex functions."

"Was she one of Asphodel's creations?"

"No. She was already in Boston when Asphodel's uncle adopted her. We don't know who made her or what they did differently than the normal approach to making an auf. I don't think she's important. I just . . . we can't dismiss them all as incapable of complicated actions, is all."

"All right," says Judy. "That makes sense, and is good information to have. Thank you for providing it."

"Those things we encountered in the lab, the etiäinen, they're different from auf," says Smita. "Can they manage complex tasks?"

"They didn't start as living tissue, and they don't have to forget what it was like to die before they can function," says Erin. "So yeah, they're much better for complex tasks, especially if those tasks let them break things. The alchemists didn't figure out how to make non-violent minions until they cracked the secret of making cuckoos."

"What was the 'secret,' anyway?" asks Dodger. She shrugs. "People who actually understand alchemy like to go on and on about how there are all these subtle important differences between things, and they really, really matter, we can't even put a value on how much they matter, but we can't possibly explain them to you. I *am* a cuckoo. I'd like to know how we were made."

"You never asked before," says Erin.

"I was a little preoccupied with my potatoes and learning how to be a person in the world, not a theoretical concept in the ether," counters Dodger. "Everything happened so damn fast, and when it stopped happening, we were suddenly effectively gods, with a couple of teenagers to keep alive. You can forgive me for being a bit incurious while I adjusted to the new status quo. But I'm adjusted now, and I'm asking. What the fuck is a cuckoo?"

"That is a very complicated question," says Erin, slowly. "You are, and I am, and Roger and Kelpie both are. That Winter girl who came here with her boyfriend—"

"You mean the new Winter Queen," says Roger, half mumbling into his coffee cup, so that it swallows his words like stones.

"—she was, but he wasn't. Cuckoos are artificial people who can embody concepts just like a natural-born incarnate would."

"That's not complicated at all," says Dodger. "That's kinda boringly simplistic."

"I wasn't finished," says Erin. "Alchemists worked for centuries to figure out what we call cuckoos. Auf and etiäinen and a dozen other alchemical constructs that don't matter right now, so I'm not going to list them off, they were all a consequence of alchemists trying to create cuckoos. They wanted to control the laws of the universe by turning them into biddable, obedient children."

Dodger laughs, short and sharp and startled. She composes herself, then shoots a look at Roger and starts to giggle. He does the same thing, actually lowering his coffee mug in the process.

"Biddable?" asks Dodger. "They were trying for biddable?"

"Don't forget 'obedient,'" says Roger. They both break down giggling again.

Erin watches them indulgently for several seconds before she claps her hands together and says, "If we're doing this, we need to be doing it with a little more focus. Can you come back to earth and join the rest of us?"

"Sorry, sorry," says Dodger, wiping her eyes and making a flicking gesture, like she's dismissing tears of mirth. "We'll be serious, we promise."

"We'll be very, very good," affirms Roger.

Erin gives them both a skeptical look, then resumes her explanation: "No matter what materials they began with, they never managed to make a vessel that could contain the forces they were trying to control. It seemed impossible. Several alchemists, especially among the American and European Congresses, insisted that all possible forms of alchemical life had been discovered already. There wasn't any way to do what needed to be done."

"So what changed?" asks Roger.

"Asphodel Baker changed," says Kelpie, eyes on Erin. Her gaze doesn't waver as she asks, "Isn't that so?"

"Yes," says Erin. "It wasn't just incarnate forces that alchemists couldn't handle: before Asphodel, they couldn't create constructs capable of mastering alchemy in their own right. She made the first self-aware constructs, and she didn't start with Reed. Those constructs are also considered cuckoos. They're your cousins, in a way, and they manage their own affairs for the most part. When Reed destroyed the American Congress, dozens of constructs were released from their masters. They're still out there, living ordinary lives with bones made of carved ivory or organs made from purified metals. No one will ever know, unless they get autopsied by particularly open-minded doctors. Asphodel figured out the first steps. James Reed did the rest."

"What did Reed do? What did *Asphodel* do? And what does any of this have to do with that lab?" asks Artemis. "I say we just pry open the door, drop down a bunch of explosives, and blow the thing back to hell."

"Two problems with that," says Judy. "First, it's under a fairly large area of residential Berkeley. If we blow it up, a lot of innocent people are going to die when the street collapses inward. It's going to be messy and horrible, and it won't make us any better than the alchemists."

"And secondly?"

"Secondly, they built the damn thing from Roman concrete infused with the blood of the divine. The blood of my people. It's self-healing. Blow it up, kill a bunch of people, and then have to deal with the apparent local mass psychosis when it puts itself back together and they can't handle that much proximity to the alchemical world." Judy shakes her head. "Unless you have a mechanism for breaking down the base components of the lab, physical demolition isn't the answer."

"It was just a suggestion," says Artemis sullenly.

"As to what this all has to do with the lab, we know they were making cuckoos there." Erin gestures toward Kelpie. "Proof positive that they were up and running and doing what they came here to do."

"It wasn't just me," says Kelpie uncomfortably. "I was just the only survivor."

Artemis puts a hand on her arm, and she leans into the Lunar, clearly seeking comfort.

"What Asphodel did to change things was exist," says Erin. "There was something about her that was . . . strange. She wasn't an incarnate anything, but her blood had a vitality in it that didn't make sense according to the ways we usually measure such things. By using her own blood as part of the quickening process, she was able to create constructs who could *think*. Who could harness the forces of reality and bend them to their own will. Those constructs were a large part of why the Congress continued to reject her even after she began making breakthroughs in the application of then-modern science to alchemy. What did it matter if she could use electrical current rather than lightning to power her workings if you were worried about those same workings deciding that they needed to rise up and destroy you? But Asphodel never managed to embody anything beyond humanity."

"It sounds like that was more than enough," says Smita. "We're moving into breaking-the-laws-of-god-and-man territory here."

"Oh, we've been there since day one," says Erin. "After Asphodel died, James Reed inherited all her property—including her body, which the official record says he broke down into its smallest components, and used to manifest his own works. Every incarnate force to have been caught in the canopic jar of a cuckoo's heart did so because it was following the legacy of Asphodel Baker."

"Didn't we know this already?" asks Dodger. "I already said Asphodel was my biological mother, when I was trying to be all cool and terrifying for the new girl. I know I did. I was there."

Erin sighs, beleaguered, and Lilianne feels suddenly sympathetic toward her. It must be hell, trapped with the living Doctrine and forced to play the straight man to their apparent determination to take absolutely nothing seriously if they don't absolutely have to. "You're not putting the pieces together," Erin says, and turns to look at Lilianne and Smita. "Kelpie was asking why the lab's defense systems would still be active, why it would send etiäinen after you when, assuming you've both told us the truth, you didn't do anything more hostile than take a shower and drip on some floors."

"Yes, why?" asks Smita.

"I've already told you," says Erin. "They were making cuckoos. That means the lab here in Berkeley contained a certain quantity of Asphodel Baker's remains. She was the mother of monsters. Not all her children are estranged, and the ones who aren't will keep their mother safe."

Silence falls over the kitchen, heavy and awkward. Roger is the first to break it, lifting his mug and scowling as he finds it empty. "And now the doors are open," he says. "The seal on the lab's been broken."

"The door wasn't locked," says Smita. "It was technically open this whole time."

"Not if the alchemists closed the doors intentionally when they fled. On a sympathetic level, that would have sealed the whole place off, and kept whatever was walking around inside contained. But now the seal is broken. Whatever's in there can potentially get out."

"That means we have to go back in," says Artemis. The others turn to look at her. She's looking down at the kitchen table, shoulders tight. "If the etiäinen are active, and the security systems are still functional, that means Asphodel's remains are still down there. They weren't removed when the alchemists left. We can't let those get into someone else's hands."

"Someone else?" asks Lilianne, blankly.

Artemis shoots her a venomous look. "You. Some untrained, independent alchemist who doesn't have anyone to stop them from doing something deeply, deeply dangerous with one of the most powerful alchemical ingredients ever to have been discovered."

"And as long as it's down there, the other alchemists have good reason to come back to Berkeley," says Roger grimly. "You know what that means."

"It means I need to make more coffee," says Dodger.

"It means we're going back down there."

"Same difference," she says, and moves toward the coffee machine.

Smita shoots Lilianne an apologetic look. "I'm very sorry about all this, but it looks like you're going to be coming with us on a field trip. I hope you don't mind."

"Would it matter if I did?"

"No," says Smita. "But I'm sure we can find you something clean to wear. Come on, I'll show you to the guest room."

* * *

Everyone else waits until Smita leads Lilianne back out of the kitchen to the stairs. Then they all begin talking at the same time, voices overlapping until they press each other flat, like sheets of vellum stacked up on an academic's desk. They get louder and louder, their collective objections piling so high that it seems impossible for them to get any higher.

"*Quiet!*" snaps Erin.

The rest of the room falls silent, Roger blinking owlishly at her while the others just subside. No one moves.

"Yes, we're going back into the lab," says Erin. "No, I don't know exactly how you fight an etiäinen, but I know you *can* fight them, and Artemis and I did a pretty good job of knocking down the first one we saw."

"It didn't like having an arrow in its throat," says Artemis. "Maybe we can try a little more of that. I don't think we can talk them to death."

"Yeah, but etiäinen are notorious for getting back up again after they've taken a hit," says Erin. "We don't know if the one you shot actually stayed dead, or even stayed down. We have to assume we're fighting enemies that can just come for a second round."

"Gee, that's pleasant," says Roger dryly.

"Oh, it gets worse," says Erin. "There may be other protections, or areas we can't enter without triggering something way nastier than a couple of face-stealing security dogs. Which takes me to the point that Artemis is *really* not going to like, but it's non-negotiable."

"And what's that?" asks Artemis, in a dangerous tone. The air around her is beginning to sparkle with captive silver moonlight. She's always awake, thanks to the effective death of her mortal half, but she isn't always stepped all the way up into her divinity. That requires effort, and right now, effort is what she's putting forth.

"Kelpie has to come with us."

"Over someone else's dead body," says Artemis.

"They made her in that lab. No one understands it like she does. If we're trying to avoid the traps, we need her."

"No," says Artemis.

"Arty, she's not wrong," says Kelpie. "I grew up there. Nobody else who's left knows it as well as I do. If I go, maybe no one has to get hurt."

"If you go, *you* could get hurt," counters Artemis. "I can't allow that."

Kelpie takes a sharp breath, pulling slightly away. "I am my own person and I make my own decisions, even if I'm considered a minor Lunar incarnation. You don't get to tell me what you can and can't *allow*."

Artemis looks stricken. "But you could get hurt," she repeats, like that's the only argument that matters.

"Anyone can get hurt, anywhere," says Kelpie. "I hit my elbow on the kitchen counter this morning. You can't keep me out of the kitchen, and you can't stop me from going to this lab. I'm needed."

"I wish you wouldn't," says Artemis, voice going small.

"And I wish you'd trust me to take care of myself," says Kelpie. "I know this is hard, but it's what we have to do." She looks back to Erin. "I'll come. I don't know the whole lab—I was always kept on a pretty tight leash—but I may be able to help you navigate the place without setting anything off."

"I'm coming too," says Judy. "I'm the senior Lunar for this area, and I can't let my people go into potential danger without me. That would make me as bad as Diana."

They don't mention the former area senior very often, but everyone who knew her understands how hands-off she was, how willing to let her people risk themselves while she stayed safe in her office, well away from whatever happened to be going on. Roger looks over at her, then puts a hand on her shoulder, squeezing reassuringly. Judy smiles at him.

"I think we're all going, except for maybe David," says Dodger. "It's going to be a good old-fashioned field trip into absolute mortal peril. Roger, I am giving you verbal permission, in the sight of most of the people we know, to give me instructions while we're down there, if that's going to make the difference between success and failure. I won't get mad at you for telling me what to do, even if it does feel like spiders running around the inside of my skull."

Roger blinks. "You're really worried about this."

"I am," says Dodger. "We closed up that lab and just forgot

about it. We never asked ourselves what was going to happen next, or whether it could still be dangerous even if it wasn't actively being used. Whatever comes out of that place is at least partially on us. I don't know how much more collateral damage I can handle."

"I know, Dodge," he says softly.

"And it's not like we can just go back and try again at this point," she says, frustration evident. "There are too many variables now, too many things we wouldn't be able to recreate in order to get ourselves back to right here. I like it here. I like it here better than I like farmer's markets and being left alone. I like all of the people we've collected. I don't want to lose any of them because we tried for a reset and didn't remember what day we were supposed to go to Costco after you got off work."

"I know," says Roger again.

She sighs, slumping against the counter. "I just want this all to be over."

(Later, she'll look back on that statement and think it was careless for the living incarnation of half the natural forces controlling the universe to say such a thing, that she should have known there would be consequences. But here and now, in the moment, she's not thinking about consequences, and she's never been the one whose words impact reality in such a direct and immediate way. That's Roger's burden to bear. She can speak freely: it's *listening* that gets her into trouble, that destroys everything she's built in another turbulent collapse of broken time and unwanted undoing. But some things, once spoken, become inevitable, like the frost melting in the fields. Some things, upon being invoked, can't be put down again.)

"What about Kim and Tim?" asks Roger abruptly.

"We can call David," says Judy. "They're old enough not to need a babysitter, even if no one feels safe leaving them alone, and they like him. He'll eat pizza and play video games with them, and maybe they won't worry too much about everyone being out."

"Or we can get Smita to stay home and keep an eye on them," says Erin.

"Oh, so *my* girlfriend gets to walk into danger because you say she has to, but *your* girlfriend gets to have a pizza party? How is *that* fair?" asks Artemis.

"First off, Smita isn't my girlfriend," says Erin. "I am, sadly, irredeemably straight. Smita is my . . . Roger, I need a word."

"Expiation," says Roger. "Piaculum. Atonement."

"Atonement," says Erin, seizing on the first word she can actually recognize. "Smita is my atonement for everything I did, especially to her, while I was still trying to force the Doctrine to become manifest. I killed her so many times that the reality around the event started to get thin, and she started to remember what I'd done. She still has nightmares, because there's no reaching back and wringing that out of her timeline. She's not a Lunar. She's not an alchemist. She's a biologist. She's a perfectly normal human woman who became aware of the alchemical world because it killed her so many times that awareness became a survival strategy."

"I still don't like it," says Artemis.

"I still don't *care*," counters Erin. "I have been through so much bullshit for you people, and the least you can do is not threaten Smita. She's one of the only good things I've ever done, and if you want me to risk her when I know a reset isn't an option anymore, you can go fuck yourself."

"All right, all right," says Roger. "We shouldn't fight. We'll ask Smita what she wants to do, and whatever her answer is, that's what we'll go with, okay?"

Erin doesn't look happy. Neither does Artemis. Pinching the bridge of his nose, Roger turns to Judy.

"I know he just left, but can you *please* call David?" he asks, stressing the "please" so that it will remain a request, rather than becoming a commandment. "We're going to need him if this is going to work."

"All right," says Judy obligingly. "When did you want to go?"

"Tonight, if we can," he says. "I don't like the idea of leaving this thing lingering out there any longer than we already have. Once you've cracked the seal on the ancient evil, it's best to get it dealt with as quickly as you can."

"Is Asphodel really an ancient evil?" asks Judy, sounding half-amused.

Roger looks at her gravely. "I would put a stake through her heart myself if I knew where it was hidden," he says. "She's the root of everything that's happened in my lifetime, and I've repeated this life a *lot* of times. We need her to stop threatening our family."

"All right," says Judy, and heads for the back door, already pulling out her phone.

* * *

The guest room is large enough to be confusing, with two large windows looking out on the backyard and a bed big enough to get lost in. Lilianne looks around herself in bewilderment, eyebrows lifted high, before snapping her attention back to Smita. "How big *is* this house?" she asks.

"As big as Roger and Dodger need it to be," says Smita. "This whole place is sort of negotiable, in terms of its relationship to physical space. There's a house here, even if most people can't see it half the time, and I think it's two stories, maybe three bedrooms?"

"That's ridiculous," says Lilianne. "This house is *much* larger than you're describing."

"Yes, it is," agrees Smita. "We all have our own bedrooms, even Kim and Tim, and you've seen the library. Roger and Dodger have offices, too. There's no way this whole house fits inside the footprint of the house you'd see if you went outside. You get used to it, living with the manifest Doctrine. They do what pleases them, first and always, and they don't like being cramped."

Lilianne sits down on the edge of the bed. "This isn't supposed to be happening," she says.

"I know this isn't how you were expecting to spend your day, but I promise, they're not bad people. They're not malicious or vindictive. You'll be fine when this is over."

"That isn't what I meant."

Smita frowns. "So what did you mean?"

"Reed was following Asphodel's blueprint to reach the Doctrine, to call it down in human flesh and convince it to stay, because he wanted humanity to have access to its power. It wasn't supposed to be . . . to be two people hiding in their house and doing whatever the hell they wanted to do! It was supposed to be for *everyone*!"

"You mean it was supposed to be for the alchemists." Smita's voice is cold: for the first time since they got back to the house, she sounds like she and Lilianne might not be on the same side.

"Well, no . . . it was for everyone, but the alchemists would be the ones to interface directly with the Doctrine, yes. If we tried pushing the manifest Doctrine in front of the whole world, they'd rip the host apart."

"You don't think very highly of humanity, do you?"

"I—"

"Think we need to be protected from all the secret dangers that we can't quite see, that no one's bothered to tell us about."

"That isn't what—"

"Alchemists aren't better than everybody else. They're just in a different graduate program. Roger and Dodger aren't hurting anyone, and creating a cuckoo seems to me like it's very similar to creating a child. You don't own them once they're ready to leave the lab, or even before that. They don't owe you anything."

Lilianne looks up at her, visibly trying to understand. "If you're not prepared to have a queer kid, you shouldn't have children," she says, with exquisite carefulness. "That's what you're saying."

"Yes, it is," agrees Smita. "If you're not ready to have an antisocial Doctrine that just wants to take a few years to figure itself out before it tries doing anything else, don't force essential attributes of the universe to become manifest. Manifest forces are people too."

"I know that!" protests Lilianne.

Smita pauses to frown at her. "I'm not actually sure you do."

"I do, because my parents are both incarnates," says Lilianne. Normally she wouldn't tell people about them: normally saying "my father is the living spring" gets people to look at her like there's something wrong with her. "My mother is a Stingy Jack, and my father is a Jack in the Green. They met, they fell in love, they got married, and they had me. And they weren't disappointed when they learned that I wasn't an incarnate anything, even if I think my childhood included more than the standard number of weird field trips to see whether I might resonate with something they hadn't thought of yet." They hadn't been disappointed to learn that she was a girl, either, something that she was eternally grateful for: it would have been so easy for them to make her transition a terrible thing, and instead they'd looked at it as just another turn of the seasons, one thing melting into the next, as natural as sunrise.

Smita blinks at her. "So you're . . . incarnate-adjacent?"

"I guess, if you need something to call it that's more precise than just 'their kid.' But I think it's why my eyes have always been open to the alchemical world. I didn't need to be traumatized or eased into it. I grew up there."

"It's interesting," says Smita. "Even the Lunars call it 'the alchemical world.' All the incarnates I've met do. But why should they do that? Alchemists didn't invent the world. They didn't make the rules. So why do we name it after them?"

"I think because the majority of people aren't manifest anything. They aren't incarnate anything. But they have the potential to become alchemists. It's the alchemical world because the alchemists have the numbers."

"That makes sense," says Smita, voice turning thoughtful. "Are you comfortable with the idea of going back down to the lab? Because I know my housemates, and they're absolutely going to be heading back down to make sure everything is taken care of. They're probably going to want you to go with them."

"I wouldn't want to be left behind."

"It's not going to be safe. You could get seriously hurt. We don't know how this is going to play out."

"No one ever does." Lilianne gestures to the room around herself, hands spread wide. "This is all . . . this is so amazing for me. I'm in a house that's basically built from living probability. This isn't an alchemical creation, except that it is, because alchemy created the Doctrine. This whole place is the culmination of Asphodel's life's work."

"You're really fond of her, aren't you?" says Smita carefully.

"I've idolized her since I learned who she really was," says Lilianne. "Everything she did, everything she overcame, the way the Congress treated her . . . she's inspirational. She achieved so much despite all the obstacles they put in her way, and she paved the path that hundreds of female alchemists have followed since. She recreated herself in her own image. I've been trying to do the same thing for as long as I can remember. The Asphodel your friends described isn't the one I knew."

"You know her as the Queen of Wands," says Smita. "We know her as the Queen of Swords. And she was both, mother and monster-maker, benevolent guardian and cruel destroyer. We're just standing on opposite sides of her divide."

"I know people are complicated," says Lilianne. "But I chose my name because I wanted to be a flower, like her. It's not so easy to accept this version of my hero who's somehow worse than all the human monsters who have ever lived."

"You may not have a choice," says Smita. "If you're going to be around here, you're going to be around people who have very good, very real reasons for disliking Asphodel. Hating her, even."

"But they wouldn't exist without her!"

"And even they would admit that that might be better," says Smita. "Their existence is unnatural. They were *made*. This isn't IVF or fertility treatments: this is someone sitting down with a workstation and putting together a person from the cellular level on up. I love my friends. They're basically a second family to me, and I'd do almost anything for them. But I know how hard things have been for them, and I understand why they feel the way they do about Asphodel. I'm not going to ask you to change the way you think about her. I'm just going to ask that you be understanding of their feelings. They've earned them."

Lilianne squirms. She looks down at the floor, then says, "I just met you yesterday."

"I know."

"I thought you were really pretty, and maybe, if I got to know you, and you seemed like you might be okay with it, I'd ask you out for coffee or ice cream or something one of these days." Those suggestions feel unbelievably juvenile after everything that's happened in the last twenty-four hours.

"Really?" Smita sounds surprised.

"Really." Lilianne squints up at her. "You have to know that you're beautiful. I mean, you have a mirror, you see yourself every day, this can't be a shock to you."

"It's not, but—I mean. I didn't even know you were—" Her cheeks redden, visible even against the rich brown of her complexion. "How could I have known that you were into girls? I just *met* you!"

"Which is my point. We just *met*. We're supposed to be in that sort of awkward, just getting to know each other, everything is new and surprising and strange stage. Not moving straight to arguing about childhood heroes and the ethical applications of alchemy." Lilianne shakes her head. "This is all moving really fast, and not in any of the directions I had wanted it to go. Am I allowed to leave? If I wanted to go back to my apartment, could I?"

Smita looks uncomfortable. "I told you you'd need to come back to the lab with us."

"What if I promised to come straight back? I know you promised to find me some clean clothes, but I also need my medication. I need my hormones. They're not something I can just skip for a day and be okay about. They're important."

"I'm sure if you ask Dodger, she can mix up some of whatever it is you need," says Smita. "Chemistry and compounding are both math, when you boil them far enough down to their essentials. And if she can convince the universe that something is math, she can recreate it."

"I shouldn't need to recreate my medication. It's all prepared and paid for and waiting for me in my room."

"You're the alchemist. She's alchemy made flesh. Shouldn't you be more excited about that, since she's sort of your life's work?"

"But she's terrifying!"

"And that's also your life's work." Smita pauses, looking at her critically. "What was the appeal, anyway?"

"What?"

"Of alchemy. You had your parents right there, you had to know how they felt about alchemists—how alchemists interacted with incarnates, all the reasons they had to be afraid of them. What made you decide that you wanted to become something you knew your parents wouldn't be able to support?"

"I got really interested in alchemy right about when I was figuring out that I felt weird about being a boy because I wasn't one," says Lilianne uncomfortably. "Part of it was the idea that we could control our world so well that we could remake it if we wanted to—that we could remake ourselves. Transformation and transmutation and purification all seemed like pretty good ideas to a terrified teenage trans girl in Alabama. My father's a pediatrician, but he couldn't be *my* pediatrician, and I'd heard him complain about how hard it was to get some of his colleagues to understand gender-affirming care as life-saving and essential. I was scared that I'd get bad treatment or no treatment, and the idea of trying to live as a boy was . . . it was impossible. I wasn't going to do it. Either I was going to be a girl, or I wasn't going to be anything anymore. Alchemy felt like a way to survive if medicine failed me. It felt like a rope out of the hole that I was standing at the bottom of, and I didn't climb down there on purpose, but I needed help if I was going to get out."

"But it didn't do what you were hoping for . . . ?"

"It didn't need to." Lilianne shrugs. "My dad called around until he found another doctor who worked with trans teens, who was willing to listen to me and understand that until I turned eighteen, he wasn't going to be asked to do anything that couldn't be undone later, if I changed my mind. I already knew I wasn't changing my mind, and so did my parents, but he needed to hear that from somebody else before he could let himself listen."

"Sort of like my doctor keeps refusing to give me a hysterectomy, but would allow it if I had a husband to sign off on the procedure," says Smita. "Because I'm a girl, I don't get to know my own mind."

"Exactly!" says Lilianne. "I was sixteen. I knew who I was and what I wanted, and no one stopped one of the girls in my class from getting gastric bypass, or got mad when one of the boys started doing the kind of weight training that shreds your knees and leaves your muscles all weird. It was like *they* got to know what they wanted, because what they wanted fit with the majority, while I had to be wrong, because most people didn't want the same things I did."

"That must have been really hard."

"So hard." Lilianne shakes her head. "It still is."

"I didn't go through anything like that. I just got to explain to my fairly strict and traditional parents that there was never going to be a husband in the picture for them to approve of or reject, because if I got married, I was going to have a wife. I wanted kids—I still do want kids, even if Kim and Tim make me wonder why sometimes—but I was planning to adopt, probably by doing long-term foster-care placements first, not get pregnant. I had it all worked out."

"So what happened?"

"Alchemy."

Lilianne frowns. "I . . . What do you mean?"

"Dodger and I were in the same graduate class. We're not in the same discipline, at all, but we wound up sharing an orientation group, and somehow, we became friends." She pauses to chuckle. "That feels like dialog out of a bad Star Wars movie. 'Somehow, Palpatine returned.' Somehow, Dodger Cheswick, the most antisocial woman in the world, managed to make a friend when she wasn't being graded on it. She and Roger were just reconnecting after a long estrangement, and they still believed they were ordinary humans. Just people, you know? Nothing special."

"Have they *seen* their own eyes? How did they not figure out that something was going on?"

"Most people don't have the context to go 'Oh wow my eyes are a sort of weird color guess that means I was built in a lab.' Also, they had more pigment back then. Not a lot more pigment, but they were closer to gray than white. Anyway, when Dodger first introduced me to Roger, she wasn't even sure he was her brother. The first thing they asked me to do was perform a blood test to figure out whether they were related." Smita's expression takes on a dreamy, far-off cast. "The first time I looked at their results, I thought I'd cross-contaminated the samples. But the deeper I dug, the more obvious it was that nothing like that had happened.

They were just two people, phenotypically distinct, genetically almost identical. They're identical twins who just happen to be different sexes. That doesn't happen. It goes against everything we know about twin development, and it's not possible, no matter how you want to look at things."

"Huh," says Lilianne. "That sounds . . . complicated."

"So I called them back to the lab to give them the good news: they were related, they were *really* related, and I needed them to give me a lot more blood so I could make some impressive discoveries about the human genome and secure my place at the top of my field."

"I'm guessing that didn't happen."

"Gosh, you're a quick one, aren't you?" asks Smita, lightly. "No, that didn't happen. Instead, Erin, who had been watching them, notified the American Congress that someone was on the verge of discovering how absolutely impossible their genetics were, and they sent her to take care of the problem. Which meant killing me and burning all the evidence."

"But she didn't, and that's why you're such close friends now?"

"Oh, no, she did," says Smita. "Picked up a Hand of Glory and used it to get into my lab without being seen. The first time, she stabbed me and burned the place to the ground after she was done. The second time, she slit my throat. The third . . . well, I could keep doing this for quite a while, and she tells me not to dwell, because it never really happened. The Doctrine reset the timeline over and over again until they found a way to thread the needle of developing the relationship they needed to have without me needing to die in the process. It took them a long time, but fortunately, they had all the time in the world."

"If those timelines didn't happen, how can you know about them?"

"Erin is the incarnate force of Order. Disorderly things hurt her, and scarring in the timeline is disorderly, by definition. She started seeing the scars a long time ago. She carries information between resets, and without her, Roger and Dodger would never have been able to figure out how to navigate manifestation. She led them every step along the way. She was the one to insist they find a path that allowed her to save me—killing me over and over again was really bad for her, mentally speaking. But saving me required the Doctrine to focus so much energy and attention on that narrow little span that it scarred over to the point where *I* could remember it, too. That's why I can perceive the alchemical world without looking away or pretending I don't see anything strange. It killed me and then it saved me, and now part of me belongs to it, so I can perceive it just like anybody who was born to it. I've never studied alchemy. Alchemy has sure as hell studied me."

"And that's why you're still here?"

"Sadly, yes. See, they were able to find a way to fulfill the timeline's requirements that didn't need me to actually *die*. It just needed me to seem dead. So in the process of misdirecting the American Alchemical Congress, Erin 'killed' me and then hid me in a safe house she'd set up, where I stayed until the timeline caught up to the Doctrine becoming manifest. By the time they let me out, my parents had mourned and buried their daughter, and I was legally dead in every government system you can think of. They even canceled my library card. It was pretty grim."

"Are you legally alive now?"

"Not really." Smita shrugs. "We're still trying to figure out how to bring me back without setting off some cascade of paperwork that ends with my parents being informed that I've returned from the dead. My dad was already pretty old when I 'died.' I don't think his heart could handle it."

"That sounds really awful." Lilianne can't imagine being cut off from her parents like that, left with no way to go home, no matter how bad things get. She can always go home. She's so much luckier than a lot of the people she knows, because no matter what, she can go home. Her parents will always be waiting for her, always ready and willing to love her as much as she can stand to be loved. Losing that would be . . .

Well, it would be a lot like dying.

"So I don't get my picture-postcard life, and you don't get to go home until we've finished dealing with this lab, and you get to lean on the fact that we were all happy to ignore the place and pretend it wasn't there," says Smita. "In our defense, Kelpie was the only one of us who really understood enough to realize what a danger that lab was potentially going to be, and when she didn't sound the alarm, we were perfectly content to just go about our business. But that's not enough of a defense. She has trauma about that place like you would not *believe*, and it's not really a surprise that she never told us anything about it. She probably just wanted to pretend that it didn't exist and she was never going to need to go back there again. So if anyone gives you any guff—"

"Guff?" asks Lilianne, amused.

"—about being the one to find the place, just remind them that we wouldn't have seen the danger coming if it hadn't been for you," finishes Smita, before she snorts. "Yes, guff. It's a real word. I don't know the exact definition, but Roger would, if you asked him."

"I am *not* going to use the Doctrine of Ethos as a reference manual," says Lilianne.

"Why not? The rest of us do."

The thought is horrifying in an existential sort of way that would probably have been incredibly tempting when she was a teenager, but is now just distantly upsetting. Primal forces of the universe shouldn't be used like party games. It's neither right nor fair.

"Well, I'm not going to."

"Suit yourself," says Smita. "I mean it, though. If anyone tries to be too nasty about you opening the seal on the lab, you point out that we knew it existed and just *left* it there. I think the others sometimes forget they're still fallible, and start to believe they can't do anything wrong, can't make mistakes. You're an important reminder."

"Are they going to lock me in the attic forever if I make them mad?"

"No. But they might ask you to babysit."

Lilianne's eyes widen in sudden horror. "There are *children* here?"

"Worse. Teenagers. Designer teenage cuckoos, built to manifest the Doctrine and blocked when their elders did it before they got the chance. So they're surly and mean about it, and no one who values their sanity agrees to babysit." Smita smiles. "And on that note, I should go before Erin convinces Roger or Dodger that I should stay back to take care of the teens while the rest of you go into mortal danger. There are clothes in the dresser over there. See if you can't find something that fits you properly, and I'll see you when you come back out to the kitchen."

Then Smita is gone, slipping out of the room with such speed that Lilianne doesn't have time to fully realize what she's doing before it's done. Lilianne blinks, then groans and throws herself backward on the bed, staring up at the unchanging ceiling.

"Well, that sucked," she says, and the ceiling does not disagree.

Wealth

TIMELINE: AUGUST 3, 1896.

The standard term of an alchemical apprenticeship is seven years, each with its own purpose and position in the wheel that turns to mark a new alchemist's education. After five full turns of the wheel, Asphodel is exhausted, annoyed, and very ready to graduate. But the last two years are meant to represent Invention and Innovation, two of the most essential skills a new alchemist will need on undertaking their independent career. And that is why she's once again standing in the basement of her uncle's house, hands flat against the table where she's performed so many dissections over the past five and a half years. She has to come up with something. She has to create something entirely new, and more, she has to make it as perfect as she can, while understanding that her last year of apprenticeship will be spent refining it, making it ever more flawless, ever more worthy of the Congress.

She's not sure the Congress is worthy of any of the things they claim as their right, not anymore. They hoard knowledge like a squirrel hoards nuts, and while she knows other apprentices can request access to the great stores of secrets and solutions, her requests are met with blank stares and closed doors. She's her uncle's sworn apprentice, she signed the book before the Congress like any other apprentice, but too many of them still believe she'll abandon her studies the first time an attractive journeyman smiles at her, that her interests will always come second to the performance of true woman's alchemy, building a child of her own body and bringing it warmly into the world.

Asphodel has every intention of becoming a mother in her own time, but it won't be through any union with someone else's flesh. She'll craft her children through her art, the way a proper alchemist is meant to do. Her sex has nothing to do with her performance of her discipline. One day they'll see that. One day they'll understand.

And until that day, she has to find a way to *make* them understand.

Looking down her nose at the table, she says, flatly, "Again."

"Sparrow . . ." says Miss Cottingsly, catching herself short as Asphodel shoots a sharp look at her through the oily curtain of her dangling hair. "Yes, miss?"

"I need to understand how my uncle made you," says Asphodel. "Everything I have and everything I know tells me that you're an auf. Auf aren't supposed to last as long as you have, or be so damned willful. So how do you exist?"

"Oh, miss," says Miss Cottingsly. "I *am* an auf, yes. I was assembled from the bodies of dead humans."

"How did they die?"

"That doesn't matter. They were dead, and once a person dies, they no longer have any right to their bodies. The flesh becomes abandoned property. Your uncle merely took what had been left for him. He built me from the scraps they left behind. Five of them, all told."

"Why so many?"

"He wanted only the best of everything for his new helper. He chose the strongest legs, the nimblest hands, and the hardest heart, and he stitched them all together piece by piece, to make his perfect woman. Not that my womanhood matters—it was a choice solely to allow me to pass unseen in the circles he travels within. Had he built himself a manservant, people might have taken notice." Miss Cottingsly doesn't sound bothered by this essential unfairness. She's just reciting the facts of the matter as she understands them. "I'm invisible when I need to be."

"That would be an innovation," Asphodel mutters. "Invisible auf would be enough to make the Congress agree that I've fulfilled my assignment, and discovered something entirely new."

"True invisibility isn't possible."

"No, probably not, given the laws of physical reality as we understand them, but understanding can change. Changing the things we already understand about the world is half of what we do in our art."

"The other half is what, scrubbing the blood off the ceiling?" Miss Cottingsly clucks her tongue, for all the world like a nursemaid chiding an unruly child. "It's a bit disingenuous to claim that any proper alchemist handles that part for themselves. Anyone who's gone through Congressional apprenticeship will have a helper to hand to do the cleanup, and anyone who hasn't is a charlatan and a dabbler in things they don't properly understand."

"We're all inkpot gods at the end of the day," says Asphodel. She turns around to lean her hips against the table's edge, resting most of her weight on her hands. "Uncle must have done something special in the making of you. There's no other way you'd still be hanging together."

"He built me from five women," says Miss Cottingsly. For the first time, her voice slows, her words coming haltingly, as they might from a more ordinary auf. The constructs are just reanimated flesh attached to makeshift skeletons of whatever their makers have been able to steal, scrounge, or string together. They don't *last*, not like Miss Cottingsly has. She's been here since the day Asphodel arrived, and the only obvious sign of her inhuman nature is in the fact that she hasn't aged an hour, much less a day.

The dead may rot, but they don't get any older, and Miss Cottingsly is most certainly deceased.

"Does the number matter?"

"No. The sympathy is what made the difference." Miss Cottingsly paused then, meaningful in her silence.

Asphodel frowned. Most of the auf she'd encountered had been built of and modeled after men, but that couldn't be the only answer: if female auf were innately sturdier than their male counterparts, even the most sexist alchemist in the nation would have switched over to raiding women's graves. There was no difference in the tissue from a biological or functional level: all the differences would be, as Miss Cottingsly said, in the sympathy.

"Most auf are made from young bodies," she said, haltingly. "Alchemists look for strong arms and sturdy backs when they have to go shopping for components. The only auf I've met who weren't made from younger people were all former alchemists who had gifted their bodies to their children for such use . . ." And while they hadn't been able to match Miss Cottingsly for impossible vigor, they'd lasted longer than the norm, hadn't they? They'd been able to hold themselves together long after the point where most auf would have fallen apart.

Asphodel's eyes widen slightly as she focuses back on Miss Cottingsly. "Miss Cottingsly, how many of the women who were used to construct you had been parents before they died?"

"All five of them, miss," says Miss Cottingsly, sounding pleased with Asphodel for finding the answer.

"And how many of them had children who are still living today?"

"Three, miss." Miss Cottingsly's face does something complicated, like it can't figure out how to form the expression she's trying for. Then it smooths back into its normal neutrality, the bland mask she shows the world at all times.

Asphodel frowns. "Three. The other two, their children have passed?"

"Yes, miss."

"Any grandchildren?"

"No, miss. Sadly, they died quite young."

"And you know this because . . . ?"

"Your uncle was quite taken with my sturdiness. It's rare for an auf to last more than a few years, as you've noted. So he asked me to keep tabs on the surviving members of my donors' families, in case there was something in the bloodlines that was keeping me intact."

"When those children died, did you . . . ?"

"I did, miss. Your uncle requested the bodies, and I collected them for his use."

Asphodel frowns. "Did that upset you?"

"No, miss. Why would it have upset me?"

"They were your—"

"Pardon, miss, but they weren't my anything. They were the children of one of my donor bodies, and nothing more than that. They didn't have any connection to *me*. They were just meat by the time I came for them, and they were dead long before they passed into your uncle's hands. Don't make the mistake of thinking of me as a human being just because I can carry on a conversation with you. I'm something else entirely. I have been since your uncle took my base components apart and put them back together again."

"But the sympathies of those original forms remained," says Asphodel slowly. "Your components had children, and you've lived substantially longer than an auf is supposed to. Not 'lived.' You know what I meant. You've stayed functional."

"I serve my purpose."

"The other older auf I've met also held together longer than the norm. I thought it was because they'd been alchemists when they were alive, but that wasn't it, was it? They had children." And none of them had outlived their creations that she's heard of. But they, they weren't supposed to. Auf aren't built to outlast their makers. Auf are made to serve.

Right up to the end.

"Yes, miss."

"How long have you known this?"

"I don't know anything, miss. I do my job and that's enough for me."

Asphodel swallows her groan. There's no point in getting frustrated with Miss Cottingsly: she won't understand it, and it might slow things down. "Do you know any other auf whose donors had children?"

"Not outside the ones you've already mentioned."

"So it's the sympathy of the children. Of having something still living that shares your bloodline. It may be something in the nuclein, a sympathy we don't understand yet, but one that's still enough to bind." Asphodel turns back to the table, scowling down at it. Nuclein is a relatively recent discovery, a substance made inside the body and invisible to the naked eye. It might be the lost humor, the thing that brings bile and phlegm and blood all into harmony with one another. Like aether among the elements, it's the unseen something which quickens the base into the divine.

(In later years, "nuclein" will be understood as a component of DNA, one of the primary building blocks of life. Asphodel wasn't too far off with her contemplation of humors and natural balance. At the same time, she was so far off that she couldn't have reached the truth in a hundred years. She might go on to be lauded as the greatest alchemist North America had ever produced, but even she had her limitations.)

"It can't be blood," says Asphodel thoughtfully. "Not if the fathers of alchemists are also able to benefit from this sympathy. The father contributes no blood, simply a quickening—the nuclein *must* be involved in the expenditure of generative seed. It's the only thing that makes the process of conception and the father's contribution make sense. We can see that contribution in the child, once born, but he gave nothing but a moment of ejaculation."

She's wondered, often, whether her hair was a gift from her father, or whether she looks as much like her mother as her uncle has sometimes implied. She knows Elisabet was no beauty, that any loveliness she has, she must have generated on her own, or received from the storm who sired her.

His name is yet and will forever be a mystery to her. There are candidates, some more likely than others, and she suspects she knows which it was, but there's no way of being certain, not without summoning him the way she once summoned Dionysus, and she has done no god-working since the day Phaesyle bled out before her. Even if her father isn't a member of the same pantheon—and she truly believes he is, that none of this makes sense if he isn't—he's unlikely to accept her slaughter of a minor, harmless goddess without some complaint. She's almost done with her education. She doesn't have the strength or the skills to stand up against a god in the fullness of his power and deny him anything he might desire from her.

And given the god she suspects sired her, his desires could be virtually anything. He's never shied away from bedding his own children before, after all.

"Auf aren't alive," she says, speculatively. "They don't grow, don't change. And for most auf, their only sympathy is with the dead who were used to create them. They're made already linked to the grave. But an auf with children, they have sympathy among the living. They can draw on their descendants to revitalize themselves when the spark of their creation begins to fade."

Miss Cottingsly says nothing, only stands in patient silence and watches her work through the implications.

"Any living child is sufficient. It's that link to the living that matters. Using parents at the exclusion of all others would make it easier to build a workforce, to create a legion of auf who could continue to fulfill their purpose long after their creators would have reason to expect. It could save so much labor over time."

"Yes, miss," says Miss Cottingsly.

"But it's not enough," says Asphodel, voice dripping in despair. "It's not an Invention, just an expansion of something others have created and refined. It's not an Innovation, either, because you already exist; my uncle innovated when he made you, whether he understood or not. I could work and work and work, and it would change nothing of my station."

"What will you do?"

"If it's the nuclein that matters, I'll find a way to better isolate it," says Asphodel. "The aether of the body is a true innovation. It may have existed from the beginning, but if I can stabilize and understand it, I can change everything we know. I can remake the world in my own image."

"Then you understand what you need to do next?"

"I do," says Asphodel serenely. "Bring me my book. This won't take long."

* * *

Three months later, Asphodel is nearly at the end of her year of Invention, and she has as yet created nothing. She has refined some processes, found some answers that others have sought before her, but has failed to change the world. She'll be a footnote in some greater alchemist's history if she can't finish some grand invention before the year turns, another forgotten failure.

And because she's the first woman whose training has been approved by the Congress in over two decades, she'll drag all the other aspiring female alchemists down with her. The fear of exactly that is what has her in her uncle's study at almost midnight, working despite the winter storm that rages outside, lightning lashing hard against the sky. The world is so *wet* since she brought back the rain. People older than she is tell her that this is the norm, not the drought that comprised the majority of her life; it's supposed to rain and storm and empty out the heavens on a regular basis, like the sea is trying to come to land and reclaim the people who once left it so unkindly behind.

She doesn't care for it much. She has a certain fondness for the rain, since restoring it allowed her to pursue the thing she's wanted for as long as she can remember, but that doesn't mean she wants it keeping her awake, weighing down her hair, dampening her skirts, and otherwise inconveniencing her. She would gladly cast it aside again, if she could only find the Invention she needs.

But there is no Invention here. Only the flicker of her uncle's futuristic electric lights—he, along with the city's other alchemists, was among the first to have his home wired for the exciting new power, and now it flows through their walls, ready to be summoned with the flip of a switch—and the sound of rain are here to accompany her.

Electricity is much like lightning somehow captured and contained in a manmade vessel, the uncontrollable cast in glassed-in captivity. Asphodel can't look directly into the bulbs for long without ghostly afterimages dancing behind her eyelids, and so she looks off to one side, considering the light.

Lightning isn't meant to last this long. Like Miss Cottingsly, it should fizzle and fade far before it can be released from its glassine prison.

Asphodel jerks upward like she's been pricked with a needle. Perhaps that's the answer. Mary Shelley knew the path, hypothesized that lightning could be used to wake the dead. Electricity is just tamed lightning. Perhaps it can serve the same purpose.

And if she's starting with well-controlled lightning, perhaps she can control the rest of the factors as well.

Stormy nights are the best for graverobbing. Always have been.

The rain and clouds provide solid cover, while the wet conditions mean that fewer people will be out on the streets, meaning less chance of being caught. Asphodel grabs her cloak and virtually flies out of the study and down the stairs, pausing only to beckon Miss Cottingsly from the kitchen and stick her head into the parlor where her uncle is going over his papers.

"I'm off to dig up a body," she says, breathless and bright. "Don't wait up."

"I assume you're taking Miss Cottingsly?" he asks, barely looking away from the ledger in front of him.

"Of course," she says. "I have some sense remaining to me."

"Then go with my blessing." He finally glances up. "May I assume this means you've finally found your Invention?"

Asphodel takes a deep breath, steadying herself. Her uncle is her sponsor and instructor: he knows well how hard this past year has been for her, how many false starts she's been forced to abandon and how many dead ends she's pursued. He also knows how short the time remaining to her truly is.

"I believe I have," she says, finally. "But I need a body to prove my hypothesis."

"Raising the dead is no great achievement," he cautions. "You may succeed only to fail when the Congress rejects your discovery."

"If they reject me after what I'm about to do, they were never going to accept me anyway, and the Congress be damned," she says.

"That's my girl," says her uncle, returning his attention to his work.

Asphodel nods, stepping back, and heads down the hall to the door with Miss Cottingsly at her heels. Once there she slips outside, and into history.

* * *

Boston is riddled with graveyards. Officially, there may only be so many, but a fair number of people still inter their dead at home, still bury their dearly departed in backyards and under beloved trees. Only broaden your definition of the graveyard, and the city is an ossuary ripe for the plucking.

The main graveyards are too well guarded, especially on nights like this one, to make safe targets. The carriage driver follows Miss Cottingsly's directions, and Asphodel finds herself outside an old churchyard at the end of time, looking unhappily out the carriage windows.

"This is a dead boneyard," she complains, looking to Miss Cottingsly. "I need something with some meat on it, especially as I don't have the luxury of taking the time to assemble my perfect corpse. That will come later, when I improve what I've Invented."

"This is an old churchyard," corrects Miss Cottingsly. "The people who live in this part of the city are neither wealthy nor inclined toward rapid change. They still bring their dead here, when they can't afford the larger graveyards. Best of all, the city plans to relocate these dead within the next few years. If a few bodies aren't there when they do, they'll chalk it up to an error in the paperwork, not to graverobbing. This may not be a fancy place to find a corpse, but I promise you, it's a viable one."

"If you're quite certain, it's late enough that I'd prefer not to locate another cemetery. We can proceed."

The rain has been falling long and hard enough that the ground is a churned-up mess, mud and pooling water rendering footing treacherous even before they've passed the bawn that separates the street and the boneyard. Miss Cottingsly leads the way, stepping with easy confidence that Asphodel can only envy, not quite desire, as she chases the auf into the dark. They each walk with shovel and sack over their shoulders, ready for the task ahead.

"At least the rain's had time to soften the way," says Miss Cottingsly with brutal cheer. She leads Asphodel to the very back corner of the graveyard. With the earth as battered as it is, it's impossible to tell the fresh graves from the old . . . except by the headstones.

This grave is marked with the current year, and with a stone devoid of visible weathering. The letters stand out sharp and true.

"Eliza Dane," reads the name above the grave, and for a moment—only a moment, no more—a thin worm of human sympathy unwinds in Asphodel's heart. This was someone's child, someone's beloved sister or daughter. This was a *person.* What has she come here to do, that will so disturb the natural order, that deserves so much to be allowed to rest? How can she be forgiven?

She quashes the worm like she would any other parasite, smashing it flat under the force of her will. She doesn't need to be forgiven. Whatever she does here tonight, she does in the pursuit of science. She does it because she must, and because if she doesn't, someone else will.

She does it because it is her birthright, to pull life out of the storm and set it free to walk the world once more.

Her shovel bites deep into the earth on her very first strike, and she digs with all the ferocity of a seasoned graverobber. Miss Cottingsly is there to help her when she flags, and steps in to take over entirely the first time she hears Asphodel hiss in pain. "It does us no good if you tear up your hands until you can't finish the job," she says, practical and plain. "Stand aside, sparrow. This is dead woman's work."

Miss Cottingsly digs with a speed and accuracy that humbles Asphodel as she stands beside the grave, shuttered lantern held high. The storm still rages around them, pulling at their hair and drenching their clothes, but providing the cover they need to achieve their goals unseen and undisturbed. There is no sign of a night watchman, no indication that anyone cares for this place and its impoverished dead.

When Miss Cottingsly reaches the coffin, it is a plain wooden thing, unfinished, not even sanded down; nothing about this was intended to be seen. "Here we are," she says, and tosses the shovel aside before she bends to wrench the lid open.

The body inside is of a girl barely into her twenties, hair like wheat, lips still rosebud red and not yet touched by the fingers of decay. She was clearly buried in her Sunday best, and her dress, before the rain soaks it against her skin, is white lace, as virginal and pristine as anyone could ask.

Miss Cottingsly hoists the body out and over her shoulder before Asphodel can order her to do so. "That's our duty done," she says, climbing out of the hole. "If you can close the lid and toss some of the mud back into the hole, I'll be right back to help you fill it the rest of the way up. We'll be out of here soon, and the people none the wiser."

Then she's gone, vanishing off into the dark with a speed and silence that unnerve Asphodel: the old auf is more headstrong than most of her kind, both by nature and in accordance with Uncle John's orders. He wanted her to be able to care for his niece, and that meant giving her more of her freedom than would be advised for an ordinary auf. And even so, it's unusual for Miss Cottingsly to give orders or instructions, or to do anything other than do as she's told by the living masters of her household.

Asphodel uses her shovel to close the casket, and begins piling mud on top of it, one scoop at a time. She's barely six strokes in before an unfamiliar voice behind her barks out the question she least wants to hear at this hour of the night, in this storm-choked place:

"Halt! Who goes there?"

She turns. There is a man behind her, all but invisible in his black coat and hat, a brighter lantern than her own held at the level of his cheek. She should have seen the light approaching, would have, had she not taken the sudden shuddering appearance of her shadow for the lightning that still flashes overhead. She is wet, filthy, still holding the shovel, and standing in front of an open grave: the question is a formality, as her arrest will not be.

Her uncle will be able to buy her freedom, but her reputation may never recover from this night's work.

Still, she tries: "I saw this shovel on the ground, and thought some graverobber had been afoot tonight. Thank God you've found me! I can give this over to you, and you can find the culprit before they get too far away."

The guard is momentarily taken aback. Then he takes in her dark clothing, her gloved hands, and his eyes narrow. "I think I've found the only culprit I'm likely to encounter tonight, miss," he says. "You're coming with me."

"I think you're mistaken," she says, taking half a step back, very aware of her proximity to the still-open grave. If she falls in, she'll never hear the end of it. It doesn't matter that she's technically alone in this graveyard, apart from the watchman: her uncle has his ways of knowing everything that happens in the city, and he'll know. He always knows.

"Miss," says the guard. "There's no point in pretending you can run away from me here. In that dress, in this weather, I'll have you before you make it more than ten feet. Save me the work and yourself the twisted ankles and come with me willingly. We can sort this out in the warmth and dryness of the guardhouse."

Asphodel eyes him warily. He sounds sincere enough, but . . . she knows she's comely, knows some men will say almost anything to get a young woman alone with them. The sort of man who guards a graveyard is unlikely to be the sort of man who finds mud repulsive, or who would shy away from pressing his attentions on a woman discovered in his place of work. Still, she also knows he isn't wrong. If she tries to run in this weather, over this uneven ground, she's more likely to hurt herself than she is to get away.

Slowly, she straightens and adjusts the angle of her body, so that she's facing him entirely, not shying away by any real degree. "I promise you, sir, I've done nothing wrong."

"I find you in the graveyard in the dark with a shovel, and it starts to sound like nonsense when you say things like that to me," says the guard. "Come along. The guardhouse is this way."

He gestures with his lantern, and the motion casts strange shadows all around him, like the light is bouncing off of another figure, someone standing silent and motionless behind him, in the deep, unyielding darkness. Asphodel allows her shoulders to drop back to their normal level and raises her chin, smiling slightly.

The guard is smart enough to recognize the shift in her posture for the threat it is. He stiffens, his eyes going wide, then spins to look behind himself.

This casts the light from his lantern squarely on Miss Cottingsly's unpleasantly smiling face, her teeth fully exposed by lips that are pulled back in an expression akin to that of a corpse whose skin has tightened as it dried, leaving the skull unpleasantly displayed. Her eyes glitter in the light.

The guard has time for a sharp inhale, the sound building toward the start of a scream, before her hand closes over his face and tightens down. There is a horrifying crunching sound, like a walnut being smashed in a strong man's palm, and the front of his head collapses inward, obliterated by the force of Miss Cottingsly's grip. She takes her hand away, and Asphodel is treated to a brief, unpleasant glimpse of the wreckage she has made before the guard falls forward, landing heavy in the mud. He doesn't move. That's probably a mercy, considering what's been done to him.

"Was that entirely necessary?" asks Asphodel, tone mild, not accusing.

"If you didn't want to be arrested and lose the night, yes," says Miss Cottingsly. "The body is in our carriage. Shall I bring him as well?"

He's hot and fresh, covered in mud, and leaking everywhere. The mess will be incredible. And still, she pauses to consider, finally nodding and saying, "If you think you can do it without ruining the upholstery, yes. We could use the extra material."

Making an auf isn't exactly raising the dead, isn't taking a single body and using the great art to bring them back to life. It's a complicated process that involves inserting and removing and admixing a variety of components, and having a body to harvest as they work will make things all the easier.

Miss Cottingsly hoists the guard over her shoulder and vanishes once more into the rain, as Asphodel turns again to shoveling more muck into the hole. The coffin is still there; if they can get the earth they've moved replaced before the morning comes, they might be able to obscure all sign that they were here in the first place. It's an outcome to be dearly wished for.

Water trickles down the back of her coat, wetting her to the skin as she shovels. No other lights or voices appear from out of the dark, and she's well into her work before Miss Cottingsly returns again, beginning to pile muck on top of Asphodel's efforts with sure, strong strokes of her arms.

"Go back to the carriage," she suggests. "I'll have this finished in a moment's time."

Asphodel nods. "Yes, Miss Cottingsly," she says. "I appreciate everything you've done tonight."

"Only my job, miss."

"Even so."

Asphodel hesitates before she turns back toward the carriage, watching Miss Cottingsly work. Her arms are no thicker than Asphodel's own, her muscles no more pronounced, but she moves the mud with a graceful ease, making every heaping shovelful look like it weighs nothing at all. It's always like that, with the auf. They lose a certain vitality to death, but they replace it with unspeakable strength, power well beyond human limits.

Except that all auf fade and fall to pieces, given time enough. The storms of seeming life that alchemy has sealed inside their skin come to an end, and the auf follows. She's going to change that, tonight.

She finally turns and slogs through the mud back to the waiting carriage, the horses pawing at the street, the driver a dark blob in the shadows, his hat pulled low over his face to keep him from getting rain in his eyes. The anonymity it affords him is a pleasant side effect. Asphodel nods to him and steps up into the warm dry interior, immediately struck by how the smell has changed.

The air inside the carriage smells of mud, decay, and bright fresh copper, the dead guard's blood blending with and overcoming everything else. Added to the petrichor and ozone coming from outside, and it's a surprisingly familiar perfume, the scent of alchemy. She closes her eyes, relaxing into her corner of the carriage, and waits for Miss Cottingsly's return.

The true work is about to begin.

* * *

No one and nothing else troubles them as they make the journey back to the house, the carriage riding lower with its full burden of bodies. A dead man weighs the same as the living, especially when that weight is put to carriage springs and horses, not grieving loved ones forced to carry the body to its eternal home.

The greenhouse in the back is the best place for them to work, near-abandoned since the rains returned and did away with the need to grow even basic kitchen seasonings in controlled conditions. There are still some pots of herbs and simples around the edges, things meant for use in alchemy rather than cooking, but those will be of more aid here than not.

The girl was not embalmed before she was given to the ground. This is both a gift and a trial. Her blood has long since congealed in her veins, and must be flushed out, replaced with a blend of saltwater, rainwater, and mercury, prepared by Asphodel as Miss Cottingsly works the bellows to push the rotten blood away. The smell of it is intense, and Asphodel pauses to rub an herbal liniment under her nose, blocking enough of it out that she can continue breathing despite her body's traitorous attempts to gag.

The man is fresher, his blood sweeter, but he was not their target tonight; Asphodel sees to him quickly, harvesting the organs she can use most efficiently, draining his circulatory system and harvesting a few veins. Excess to needs or no, nothing can be wasted.

After the girl's blood has been purged and the gashes made in her wrists to let it drain have been stitched closed, Miss Cottingsly cracks open her chest and abdomen, beginning to remove rotten, damaged organs. Asphodel is quick to replace them with the organs harvested from the dead guard, intermixed with sachets of dried herbs and twists of wire. They're constructing a body entirely inimical to life. That's an important part of the process. Auf are neither living nor dead. They shouldn't be treated like common resurrections.

Once the body is fully prepared, Asphodel moves across the greenhouse to the single electrical outlet connected to the structure. She has a large mechanical battery connected there, and she checks it before attaching the jumper leads to the metal bars along its sides.

If this works, this will be the first auf made entirely using electrical current, rather than requiring the use of a natural storm. It will modernize alchemy. They have observed the proper seals and sigils, have prepared the flesh according to the books of the masters, but the masters couldn't account for what they didn't have, and the exact applications of electricity will provide her Invention.

She will become a proper alchemist on the strength of this night's work. She attaches the jumper leads to the girl's wrists, turning to Miss Cottingsly. "The switch," she says. "Flip the switch."

Miss Cottingsly nods, serene as she crosses the greenhouse to flip the switch in question.

Electricity arcs and sizzles, and the light in the greenhouse goes out with a large popping sound, accompanied by flame appearing around the plug connecting the battery to the wall. And nothing else happens.

Asphodel swears, hurrying back to the table where their auf is waiting. She trips over the cable on the way, and falls into the body, cutting one hand on the jumper lead. Blood runs down the side of her palm, soaking the stitches on the girl's wrist. Outside, the storm screams, and lightning lashes down, hitting the frame of the greenhouse.

The electrical current is dead. Still, the lightning passes through the cables to the jumper leads, and into the body of the dead girl. Asphodel feels it brush across her skin, gentle as a kiss, sending her hair to stand on end before it dissipates and flows away.

And on the table, the girl opens her eyes.

* * *

Asphodel stands rigid before the members of the American Alchemical Congress, her creation by her side. Eliza—for that is what they call her even now, although she doesn't claim the name as her own, didn't even recognize it when it was first offered—shifts her weight uneasily from one foot to the other, squirming under the attention of these unfamiliar, much older men.

"As you can see, I have summoned life back out of death," says Asphodel, voice carrying and clear. "She is not an auf: her heart beats, her lungs expand, and while her wounds have healed, they did so only marginally faster than the human norm. There were components of her making which should have rendered life impossible for her to achieve. She is something altogether new, true life created by alchemical art."

"How are we to know that you didn't just bring us a child snatched off the street?" asks one of the alchemists.

"My uncle, John Baker, will testify to my efforts," says Asphodel. Miss Cottingsly would be better, but these are men of art and science: they have barely lowered themselves to speak with her. They will never lower themselves to hear the testimony of an auf. "He knows what supplies I commandeered, what my plans were, and what a mess I made of the greenhouse. He can tell you I speak truly. She is a masterpiece. She is my greatest creation."

"A woman making life is nothing new," says one of the alchemists. Others laugh, their agreement like acid in the back of her throat. Oh, how it burns.

"I brought back the rain," says Asphodel. "You promised me training and a fair assessment if I could do that much."

"So you did," says the man at the center of their number. "And so we have allowed you to be trained, as we had sworn we would never do. We have kept our side of the bargain, Asphodel Baker. We never promised you that you would be an alchemist."

"She breathes, she cries, she lives!" snaps Asphodel. "Eliza is a miracle. She can heal and grow. I believe she will age. Electricity is the answer. The modern world is waiting for our arrival, and you would rather sit there and play at godhood than pay attention to true progress when it unfolds before you!"

"And better minds than yours will make your future manifest," says the alchemist. "Your claim of Invention is denied, Asphodel Baker. Return to the kitchen and parlor where you belong. Take your 'creation' with you."

Asphodel turns away, tears stinging her eyes, and takes Eliza by the hand, leading her creation, her auf that isn't, away from the room of her greatest failure, which should have been her greatest triumph.

She doesn't look back. She doesn't see her uncle rise from his seat at the back of the quorum and begin screaming at the men who have always been his peers, doesn't hear the way that he defends her. It wouldn't change anything if she did, but it might lighten her heart in some small, essential ways. It might keep her from growing as bitter as time says she will, might spare some souls her fury.

But she doesn't look back, and all chances of changing the moment are lost, time repeating over again as it always has, as it always does.

* * *

Eliza is in the kitchen with paper and charcoals when John Baker arrives home, finding Asphodel in the parlor, tearstains on her blouse and tangles in her hair. Miss Cottingsly stands nearby, watching Asphodel's misery with an eagle's eye, and he goes first to her.

"Is the girl an auf?" he asks. Asphodel had kept Eliza from him, as was only proper when he was to be part of the judging committee measuring the validity of her work. There had been no opportunity for him to perform his own examination or draw his own conclusions.

Miss Cottingsly shakes her head. "No," she says, voice quiet. "Nor is she an urchin. She was dead. Exceedingly so. I cleaned her veins myself, and there is no way that child could have been restored to what she'd been before the fever took her. But she woke, and walked, and lives. Asphodel spoke truly: she has a heartbeat. If you stop her breath, she chokes and coughs and fights to have it back. She eats and excretes, and has no choice in either matter—hunger pains her, and while she's clearly been taught to manage her own bodily functions, she will begin to cry if not allowed to urinate for too long a period of time. She doesn't remember anything before she woke in the greenhouse, storm above and fire surrounding. Her resurrection was her recreation, but she lives. Your niece has created life. *True* life, not the theoretical twilight of the auf. And you have broken her heart."

"I fought for her," says John, sadly. "I did what I could do to show them the error of their ways. I *tried*. They refused to hear me."

"Then I will set myself against them," says Asphodel.

John jerks guiltily, pulling himself away from Miss Cottingsly. She looks less startled by Asphodel's appearance; as is almost always true, she is serene, impassive, as unbothered as the grave.

Asphodel looks like a witch out of a children's story, gaunt and disheveled, her eyes red and bright with weeping, her lips bitten bloody by her own anxiety. He looks at her and cannot imagine her an alchemist, composed in her ritual robes, content in her small corner of the world. She looks like she belongs among the alchemists of old, swinging wildly at the sun and changing the rules by which the universe functions.

"If you do, they will never forgive you," he says, through numbed lips.

"Who says I want their forgiveness?" she asks. "They should be the ones who beg for mine. They should bow before me and apologize for their weakness in every way their tongues know how, not expect me to ask them to forgive me for aspiring to something better than the station they would grant me. Does a storm beg forgiveness for raging? Does the rain beg forgiveness when it falls? I am going to be great, *Uncle*, and nothing they do has ever had the authority to stop me. I am going to change the world. My name will be remembered when their bones are ash and dust, too worn away to even fuel an auf."

"You're distraught, my dear; have Miss Cottingsly prepare you a cup of hot tea, and we'll talk about this in the morning—"

"*No!*" she snaps, and for a moment he can almost see the lightning in her eyes, almost see the storm that sparks and crackles inside her. He recoils, and she visibly composes herself, shaking her head. "No. I won't be here in the morning."

"Asphodel, what—"

"I can't stay here any longer. The Congress has spoken. They will not finish my education; you will not be allowed to train me. Eliza is a miracle—*my* miracle, born of my effort and my art. I won't keep her here where those hidebound little men can wrest her away from me and claim her as a part of their own studies. I'll take her far from here, to a place where I can educate and understand her. Miss Cottingsly will accompany me."

"Miss Cottingsly is my creation."

"And I have more than paid for her, with the blood and bodies of three incarnates. She was operational when I arrived here; as an auf, she can't have much longer before she begins coming apart at the seams. She'll do it with me, safely hidden from the world. You won't be forced to put her down before the public sees her dissolving. If that's not enough for you, I'll go with her to the graveyard and we'll build you a replacement before we take our leave of you. Only promise you won't pursue us."

"I can't leave the Congress," says John, looking profoundly uncomfortable. "They've been my allies for longer than you've been alive."

"I didn't ask you to leave them. I didn't ask you to come with us." Asphodel looks down her nose at him, and he wonders whether this is how the parents of prophets once felt: old and worn out, watching the children they raised become greater and more terrible than they could ever have dreamt they would be. She is a young woman, if old to be yet unmarried, and she is neither an alchemist nor a part of the mundane world around them, and none of that matters, because she is powerful and terrifying, and Miss Cottingsly—his Miss Cottingsly, the auf he crafted with his own hands to serve *his* interests, to work by *his* side—Miss Cottingsly is standing slightly behind her now, ready to serve. He didn't even see her moving.

The American Alchemical Congress has made a terrible mistake on this day, and John Baker is the first person to truly understand the scope of what they've done. They may never be forgiven for their trespasses, may spend the rest of their alchemically extended lives attempting to apologize, to make amends to one who has no interest in receiving them, but in the end, they will fail.

Whatever Asphodel intends, she was willing to be restrained for the sake of her art, perhaps—in some small way—for his sake, the uncle who wanted her as soon as he knew she existed, who lifted her out of a life of obscurity and placed her where she could reach for greatness. She was willing to stay small if only the people who controlled the golden gates of wisdom would be willing to open them for her, and when they refused her great and remarkable sacrifice, she became justified in rejecting them.

And reject them she has. He can see it in her eyes. She will never be tamed again.

"Will you write to me?" he asks.

"I will change the world, Uncle John. I will remake it in ways even I don't understand yet, and I will have your name on my lips as I do. I will study Eliza until I understand what I've made in her, and once I do, everything will be transformed. I will storm Olympus, by whatever name you care to call it, and I will have it for my own."

"How will you begin?"

"One step at a time," she says, and her smile is a terrible thing, brutal and cold. "That's how one walks a road, isn't it? One step at a time."

"My apologies for interrupting, but we came here to wake the child, and look." The Page gestured to Zib, who was leaning on Jack's arm, the tiny flame still burning at her breast. "The child is awake, and seems well enough for all that's happened to her thus far. The tower is dark. You *must* return to the Impossible City."

"And I can't go," said Niamh, finally turning around, with a look in her eyes like her heart was being broken.

"Of course you can go," said Soleil.

"Drowned girls are very possible," said Niamh. "I went the first time by the graveyard path, as I told you when the road was still with us. The path will not have me a second time."

"A drowned girl accessing the City a second time is entirely impossible," said Soleil. "It has never happened, not once in all the days of the Up-and-Under."

"Then I will stay here, in this dry and blasted place, until Fern returns from wherever the great owls go when they go missing, and then perhaps the Page and I can convince her to carry me back to the Saltwise Sea and let me go."

"You aren't *listening*," said Soleil, for the first time sounding ever so slightly annoyed. "Anyone dead can take the graveyard path when they want to visit the City. But if they want to visit the City again, they have to find something even more impossible than a dead person following a road. The City will let you in because you're with me, and because it's impossible for you to come in a second time."

"Even more impossible than following a road," said Niamh, with slow wonder. "Was it always that easy?"

"Not if you were looking the rules head-on, but once you step to the side, yes."

Avery's temper caught like the fire burning at Zib's breast. He whirled on Niamh. "You said all the way back at the beginning that you couldn't go with us into the Impossible City, and so we walked away, and all this has happened because we followed you! You could have gone there any time you wanted to!"

"No, Avery, she couldn't have," said Soleil. "She had to move far enough into impossibility that the gates would open."

"And if you hadn't gone on this adventure, so many things wouldn't have happened," said Jack. "You found Soleil's heart! You found the Lady of Salt and Sorrow, and let her be one person again, when she'd been trapped as two for so long! You found the Page of Gentle Embers and made sure she wasn't alone anymore! You found me. I would still be a captive in my mother's cage if you hadn't come along to make me fly for freedom."

Zib put a hand on his arm, steadying him as he was steadying her, and looked to Avery, her own face pale and drawn, especially when compared to how brightly she normally burned. "We had to walk the improbable road long enough to make the impossible things possible," she said. "Sometimes it's about taking the journey on your own. It's why my daddy gets mad at me when I don't want to do my homework. He says it doesn't matter if I'm bored, I need to go through all the steps, or the ending won't make sense when I get there. We couldn't go straight to the ending when we were first setting out. It wouldn't have made any sense."

"Soleil's the Queen of Wands, and has been the whole time," Avery informed her.

"Yes," said Zib.

"Doesn't this *bother* you?"

"Why should it?" She shrugged. "Royalty in disguise happens all the time in the fairy tales, and this is sort of like a fairy tale, if you squint at it and take a few steps backward. She didn't lie to us, if that's why you're unhappy. She didn't know. Someone who says something that's true when they say it doesn't become a liar just because that thing changes. . . ."

—From *Under the Smokestrewn Sky,*
by A. Deborah Baker

BOOK V

Mercury

Get down, Mama. Sleep your dark eyes down.
The scarecrow's a'comin' and he ain't no clown.
Cloak yourself in midnight; duck your head 'neath your wing.
Crazy things we're hearing are not meant to be seen.

Dead trees' bones on the hills
Wave at the tall rows of corn.
North wind howls and it chills,
Singing to the old things we mourn.

—Dr. Mary Crowell, "Get Down Mama"

Oh let me tell you cirromancy, cirromancy—
That cloud's for you. Is this cloud for me?
How can I bear this? Darling, it's just cirromancy.
Circe, can I look now? Can I look now?
And I will teach you cirromancy, cirromancy.
Sparklehorse knows where he has to go.

Your blood is my blood—telling it's still cirromancy.
Truth and lies and prophecy, and some we guess, and some we know . . .
Circe, can I look now? Can I look now?

—Talis Kimberley, "Cirromancy"

Mystery

TIMELINE: AUGUST 23, 2018.

Eventually, Lilianne gets tired of staring at the guest-room ceiling. Her shoulder doesn't even ache anymore, she's not hungry, and she feels, impossibly, like she had a full night's sleep, like she could challenge the universe to an arm-wrestling contest and stand a chance of actually winning. She sits up, giving the room around her a critical look.

This place can't exist. The physical space doesn't support it, and the light coming through the windows is oddly wrong, like it's being folded at right angles before it's allowed to flow into the room, compact and thick as honey. But whether it exists or not, it's a pretty nice room, and definitely beats the gloomy confines of the apartment she shares—shared—with David and the others.

Did he really mean it when he said one of them would be moving out by the end of the month? She doesn't want to leave. She's barely gotten unpacked, and the thought of moving again is exhausting. It shouldn't be, not when the alternative is incarnates and etiäinen and all the horrors she's seen since last night. She's not giving up on alchemy, but surely there's a way she can practice under more-controlled conditions? The safety of her room has never tried to rip her arm off, and self-transmutation doesn't require access to human flesh that belongs to someone else. She can find a way to do this. To study, to learn, and to know, all without taking the kind of risks she now understands she doesn't want to take.

This is where many of the self-taught alchemists she's known would choose to abandon their studies, retreating at the first sign of a trial, and if she's being honest, she wouldn't mind doing that herself. But that option has never been open to her, not really. Her parents being what they are means that she's been tangled with the alchemical world since she was born, unable to walk away without leaving her home and her family and everything she's ever cared about behind. Alchemy, for her, has only ever been a single part of the whole.

She just wants to fit properly within the world she was born into. She wants to be a part of something greater than herself. Is it really so unreasonable for her to wish for more than she's been given, especially when everyone around her has been given that "more" without even looking for it?

Lilianne crosses to the dresser Smita indicated, opening the top drawer and beginning to dig gently through its contents. They're a remarkable mixture of styles and sizes, everything from striped shirts intended for pre-teens to ruffled lace blouses that wouldn't look out of place at a retirement home. There's underwear as well, equally diverse in style and size. After some searching, she comes up with a butter-soft sweatshirt in a watered-wine shade of burgundy, and stretch jeans that manage to flatter her narrow hips while still extending the full length of her legs.

It's not the most fashion-forward thing she's ever managed to put together, but for cast-offs found in someone else's spare bedroom, she thinks it's pretty good. There's a brush on the dresser, and she uses it to perform quick repairs on her hair.

"My kingdom for an eyeliner," she mutters, studying her reflection in the mirror over the dresser. There are still dark smudges around her eyes, but they're less decorative than they are signs that she needs to go home and take a proper shower. She scrubs idly at one of them with the heel of her hand, then puts the brush down and turns toward the door. She half-expects it to be locked, keeping her prisoner inside this room, and is pleasantly surprised when the knob turns under her hand and the door swings easily inward, revealing a long, sun-soaked hallway.

No point in waiting around forever for things to get worse than they already are. She steps cautiously out of the room. No alarms go off. Shutters don't slam down to cover the windows, and she starts to think she might actually be a guest here, not just an unwanted complication.

Still moving carefully, she starts down the hall. She hasn't gone far before she hears the sound of cheery video-game music wisping from one of the nearby rooms. It's the only sign of life in an otherwise quiet house, and she turns toward it, lured by the sound like a sailor by the song of a siren.

When she finds the room the music is coming from, it's almost like stepping back into the house where she grew up, only with a less-polished floor: her mother would never have allowed the hardwood to get this dented and dingy. Everything else fits, however, from the canvas couch to the bookshelves with their eclectic assortment of titles. There's a large television, and a teenage girl with white hair is playing *Slime Rancher* from her seat on the couch, hands clenched so tightly around the controller that it seems like the plastic should crack and buckle beneath them.

Lilianne stops in the doorway, clearing her throat. The girl barely glances at her as she continues sending her avatar careening across the screen, sucking down chickens with a vacuum gun. "Hello," she says. "You're the alchemist Smita found in the sewer, right? All the adults are off getting ready for their field trip to Terror Town. I think Roger's in his office, and Dodger is wherever Dodger is. You probably don't want to bother her."

"I am," says Lilianne. "My name's Lily. I'm sorry to interrupt. I didn't know you were here. What's your name?"

"Not interested in talking to alchemists, thanks," says the girl. "You can go. I don't really have anything to say to you."

Lilianne blinks. "Sorry to bother you." This must be one of the teenagers Smita mentioned. She was right: babysitting would not be a swift route to sanity, even if it might seem like a low-effort way to convince the Doctrine that she's not here intending to do any harm. Assuming the Doctrine would allow her to babysit. Thus far, she hasn't seen anything to indicate that she'd be offered that sort of trust.

"I'm not bothered. Did I say I was bothered?" The girl pauses her game with the press of a button, then finally turns to look at Lilianne. "I'm just trying to be honest. I don't want to lead you on, or make you think that we're going to have a productive conversation."

"And I appreciate it. Do you know where Smita is?"

"I think she and Erin went out back, which probably means you shouldn't follow them. Erin doesn't like it when things upset Smita, and she normally reacts to things she doesn't like by getting annoyingly violent toward them. Stay in the house. Or leave via the front door. If they really cared about you not getting away, they'd have left more than just me to stop you."

"Are you?"

"Am I what?"

"Are you going to stop me?"

The girl snorts as she shakes her head. "Do I *look* like I could stop you if you wanted to leave? You're fourteen inches taller and thirty-seven pounds heavier than I am."

"That's . . . precise," says Lilianne. The girl's easy accounting isn't even insulting, just impressive: Lilianne can't be certain that she's accurate, but the way she rattled off the figures makes it sound like she must be, like she couldn't be so precise if she didn't know what she was talking about. "Smita told me about you."

"How's that?"

"She said there were designer cuckoos in the house who'd been built to hold the Doctrine, and that I needed to be careful if I didn't want to get slapped with babysitting duty," she says, still standing in the doorway. "Were you supposed to embody Math?"

"I was," the girl confirms. "How did you know?"

Because you should get a job as one of those carnival workers who guesses people's weight for them. "I just had a feeling."

"Huh." The girl turns on the couch, not putting down the controller, to properly focus on Lilianne. "Pretty specific feeling."

"You're a pretty specific person." Lilianne ventures a smile. "*Love* the hair. How does your stylist get that green undertone in there? I can't find a decent aesthetician in this city. Lots of people who think 'fashion colors' means they can get as sloppy as they want, but no one who has actual *artistry.*"

"You should talk to Erin," says the girl.

"I really, really shouldn't," mutters Lilianne.

"She's the only one of us who actually sees a stylist," continues the girl. "Something about maintaining her roots. Her hair color wasn't a part of her original blueprint, so it's not as consistent as it could be. So her roots grow in dark and even get streaks of gray sometimes. My hair's all the way unnaturally natural. The alchemists built me this way, and so this is how I am. I can't even dye it. When I try, the dye just runs right off, like my hair is hydrophobic." She makes a sour face. "I don't like it, but I didn't exactly get a vote when they were putting me together."

"That must be frustrating as all hell," says Lilianne.

"Dodger says it's because we're the Math kids. It's our job to draw attention, and by drawing attention, to draw fire. If we go down, the Language side of the Doctrine can still fix things. If they go down, we're fu—stuck. We're stuck without them. Or she is, anyway. I guess I'd be lost without Tim, because he's my stupid brother and I love him more than anything else, but I can't change the world just because he tells me to. I would if I could. I would have done it a thousand times over by now."

"Why can't you?"

"Didn't you hear?" The girl laughs, high and strained and a little bit shrill, like she's imitating a sound she heard someone else make once upon a time, and not making the sound for herself. "We're not manifest. We may never manifest. The Doctrine is occupied being other people than the two of us, and it's not natural like Winter or the Moon. It doesn't know how to be more than one person at a time yet. If it's ever going to learn. We don't know whether its current hosts *can* die, or whether they're just going to keep the Doctrine forever. Maybe this is one of the forces that don't like change, so it makes the people it occupies immortal."

"I don't know of any incarnates that work like that," says Lilianne delicately.

"There are a few," says the girl. "If the planets aren't immortal, they might as well be. Some of the really big gods. The sun. So I guess probably any stars that care enough to put on human bodies and walk around like they belong in skin and bone. They don't have to die unless they want to, and who wants to die, anyway?"

"I've never met anyone who was actually immortal."

"Of course you haven't." The girl looks down at her hands, still clutching the controller. "Once they get tired of the world the way it is, they pack up and head for the Impossible City. I wonder what they thought when it *became* the Impossible City. Whatever it was before probably looked a lot less like nineteenth-century Boston."

"Wait. You know what the Impossible City looks like?"

"Well, yeah." The girl shrugs. "I hang out with Lunars. Pretty sure Judy's trying to track down David so she can make him babysit us tonight. They visit the Impossible City monthly, and they come back here and tell us what it was like. So I've never seen it, but I have a pretty good idea of what I'd see if I *could* go there."

"About that . . . you seem a little old to need a babysitter. I didn't have a sitter when I was your age. Why do they need someone to watch you?"

"Roger can tell anybody to do anything. Did you know that? That when he gives an order, you have to do whatever he says. You don't get a choice, not like you normally would when someone says you should do something you don't necessarily want to do."

"I figured that out, yes. It's how the Doctrine is supposed to work, isn't it? The Language side of things keeps them moving in the right direction, and the Math side puts them in the right order."

"And when he gives an order, Dodger can rewind time enough to make sure that you follow it, even if you already did something else."

Lilianne is starting to get a painful sinking sensation in the pit of her stomach. She's heard people use that tone before, heard them talk flatly about how terrible things are, how there's no clear route from where they are to where they want to be. "Oh?"

"Yeah," says the girl. "But when Roger's not here, sometimes Tim and I can push past the orders he's given us. It's not easy—our thoughts don't want to go against him, even when he's not around to see—but we could have been the Doctrine, and so it's possible for us, if we work at it for long enough. Only when he's far away, though. And he can't always be here watching us so he can tell us not to kill ourselves as soon as he looks away, so they make sure there's always someone home to watch us. To make sure we don't do anything they'll have to take back. Dodger hates rewinding time without good enough reasons."

"I . . . Did you hurt yourself?"

"I don't know. Did I?" The girl looks up, shrugging as she meets Lilianne's eyes. "I don't have any scars. There aren't any bloodstains on the carpet, and I didn't have to have my stomach pumped. If you ask this timeline, no, I never did. Roger took even *that* away from me."

Lilianne flinches. She can't help it, and she sees the girl's eyes shutter at that reaction, some of the easy openness slipping away into silence.

"You know they're only watching you because they care," she says, and it's so awkward and useless and insufficient, she feels bad for the words as soon as they're out in the open.

"They don't care, they feel guilty, because they spent their whole lives running away from the Doctrine, and we spent our lives reaching for it, only it chose them when the time came, and left us perfectly prepared and positioned for an apotheosis that's never going to come," says the girl. "But sure, let's call that caring. There are worse ways to talk about guilt."

"Kim, are you chewing our new alchemist's ear off?" asks Erin from behind Lilianne. "You know you shouldn't trauma-dump on our guests before they've had a chance to get used to the way things work around here. Wait until she knows whether or not she's ever coming back."

"Sorry," says Kim, and there's no apology in her voice. She turns back to the screen, pressing the button to resume play, as Erin reaches out and puts her hand on Lilianne's elbow, guiding her away.

"Sorry," she says, and her tone is so much lighter than Kim's that it aches; it's a bruise, not an open wound. Lilianne wants to ask her if she can hear the difference, if she can understand how much the girl is hurting, how much she needs help. But the words die on her lips as Erin fixes her gaze with eerily blue eyes and says, "We've been waiting for you to wander into the kitchen. Didn't realize you fell into a tarpit. I probably should have."

"It's all right," says Lilianne, but it's not all right: it's a million miles and more from all right. That girl—that *child*—needs professional assistance, not video games and loving neglect. "I was just—"

"Kim's always like that," says Erin, and the dismissiveness in her voice makes Lilianne's teeth ache. "She took losing the potential to claim the Doctrine really, really badly. Like, I thought some of the other candidates had taken it badly, but she took the *cake*. It's not her fault. Reed raised her to believe that apotheosis was inevitable, and when it wasn't, well."

"I don't think this is her fault."

"No one here is saying that it is. But wow did we not need a suicidal teenager on top of everything else we're trying to deal with here. You ready to go?"

"Go?"

"Back to the lab. Smita told you we were going back, didn't she?"

"She did."

"We have shoes for you, and Roger's going to drive us over to the lab entry as soon as we're all ready to get moving. David's coming back to handle twin duty—Tim's up in his room, but I'm sure he'll come down as soon as he realizes that pizza is happening."

Lilianne frowns, looking at her more critically. "You're a lot nicer now than you were before."

"I still hate everything you represent, and I don't want you anywhere near Smita when this is all over, but she talked to me, she explained exactly what happened, and I no longer think you put her in danger on purpose. I'm a big girl. I can admit it when I'm wrong."

Lilianne's frown deepens. "That doesn't sound like admitting it when you're wrong."

"All right, let's try it this way: this is my family. It's big and it's weird and it's *mine*. When Darren died, I thought that was it for me and having a family I could call my own. Now that I have one again, I'm holding on to it if it kills me. Which it has, a few times. They didn't let those timelines stand, which I appreciate, since I like being alive better than I like the idea of being dead."

"This is . . . The way you people talk about dying, it's . . ."

"It's what the alchemists have been working toward this whole time. And the light shall guide us home," says Erin. "Isn't this what you wanted? Isn't this why you came to Berkeley? Because you wanted to hold the reins of creation in your hands and see where the ride would take you?"

"You make alchemy sound like magic."

"I guess I do." Erin looks at her levelly. "There have been a lot of words for the sort of things alchemy can do, across the centuries. Some places called it magic. But you know what other places called it?"

"No, what?"

"Miracles."

* * *

The kitchen seems to be where these people conduct most of their important business, maybe because the living room has been so conclusively claimed by video-gaming teens, or maybe just because half this household doesn't seem capable of surviving more than a few minutes without a cup of coffee in their hands. Kelpie and Artemis are there already when Erin and Lilianne arrive, both at the table, although it's clear that they've moved since the last time Lilianne saw them; for one thing, they're not as crammed together. For another, they both have drinks now, and Artemis has her bow resting on the table next to her coffee.

It shouldn't exist. Even the bright orange woman beside her is not as much of an offense to the laws of nature. The bow is translucent where the light hits it, sparkling silver-white, like moonlight that's been forced into a material form and turned solid. The sunlight should be enough to dispel a weapon made of moonlight, and Lilianne can't stop herself from staring.

Artemis sees where her attention is focused and smirks. "I'm the first Artemis in more than a century who's had her hind by her side," she says. "She runs the skies ahead of me, she gives me something to chase and be restored by, and her presence makes me stronger. I can pull my bow in the daylight when I need to."

"Or when you're trying to show off for some random alchemist," says Kelpie. "She wasn't part of the team that made me. Stop working so hard to scare her."

"I don't want to scare her. I just want her to understand that I could kill her without breaking a sweat if I needed to, and be respectful."

"Oh, is that what you're trying to achieve?" Kelpie sighs heavily and waves to Lilianne. "Hi. They tell me you're coming down with us to finish checking out the lab. I appreciate it."

"I didn't think I really had a choice in the matter," says Lilianne.

"Not if you ever want to see Smita again," says Erin.

Roger and Judy step back into the kitchen from the hall. Judy's hair is rumpled, and Roger's glasses are smudged, something he ignores as he makes a beeline for the coffee machine. "I wouldn't order you to stay away if you decided not to come with us," he says. "But I would strongly discourage you from coming around without a really good reason. We don't trust alchemists quickly here."

"I get that," says Lilianne. "I guess . . . I never thought all that much about what happens to cuckoos after their researchers move on."

"We set up communal housing situations in Berkeley," says Roger.

"Speak for yourself," says Artemis. "Some of us refuse to move in with the rest of the circus."

"Still your monkeys," says Judy.

"Only because you're hanging around here all the time, and I don't care enough about doing my job to help train up another senior Lunar I can actually tolerate," says Artemis. "You're the best available by default."

"Gee, thanks."

"Hey, no point in best behavior if the alchemist is thinking about sticking around," says Artemis. "May as well let her see us as we really are right from the jump, right?"

"Right," says Erin.

Smita, coming in the back door, asks, "Who's right about what?"

"It's nothing important," says Erin.

"I'll decide what is and isn't important, thank you," says Smita. She flashes a smile at Lilianne, and two things are immediately clear.

First, that she's still the most beautiful woman Lilianne has ever seen. All the chaos and complications have done absolutely nothing to change that. If anything, the fact that she can stand up in the face of all this alchemical nonsense has only made her lovelier.

Second, that this is the only place Lilianne wants to be. It's not just that Smita is beautiful, a fact so obvious and glaring that it feels almost strange to keep circling back to it, like dwelling on the self-evident is somehow a failing. It's also that Smita is stubborn enough to push past incarnates and embodied forces that were never meant to exist. She's fearless and determined, and it's impossible not to be drawn to that, like Smita has become the true magnetic north to which Lilianne must answer.

There are worse things in this world.

"David's nearly here," says Judy. "He's down to babysit as long as there's pizza and we bring him back a burger or something when we finish exploring the creepy-ass underground laboratory. I told him he was getting paid and that should be enough for him, and he asked if I wanted to trade and stay here while *he* wandered into unknowable dangers. Honestly, I'd take that trade if my stupid boyfriend weren't going with you lot."

"Hey, now," says Roger. "I'm very smart, you know."

"Mmm-hmm," says Judy. "Sure you are. I've seen you before coffee."

Roger halfheartedly swipes at her, and she leans away, smiling at him like this is an ordinary afternoon, like nothing bad is going to happen to anyone here. Lilianne wishes she could believe that.

The kitchen door swings open again, and Dodger steps through, scanning the room and taking note of each of them in turn. "All right, fuckos," she says. "David's in the living room with Kim and Tim, and he's good to stay until midnight. I gave him money for pizza, and then I gave him more money to take the kids to Ben and Jerry's after dinner. They'll be fine."

"I'm not sure I want them leaving the house while we're not here," says Roger.

"No one will be able to find the house while we're out, especially if none of us are home," says Dodger. "As soon as Kim and Tim go out, everything will fold down into sleep mode, and the whole place will seal itself off. It's fine. We don't have anything else to fret about. We have plenty of things to worry about, but not the kids, not the house, and not the cat."

"There's a cat?" asks Lilianne, seizing on the simplest part of Dodger's statement like a lifeline.

"Yeah," says Dodger. "Old Bill. He's been around since I was in grad school. Pretty sure he has the world record for oldest living domestic feline, or would, if we knew exactly when he'd been born. He's sort of immortal now."

"My bad," says Roger.

"Your wonderful," counters Dodger. "Who doesn't want an immortal cat? He's pretty happy. He was old enough when he got frozen in time that he mostly just sleeps and purrs and sometimes goes wandering around the neighborhood to drive all the outdoor toms into a screaming rage."

"That seems . . ." Lilianne stops. She can't even decide how it seems. It's too weird to be easily categorized.

"Outdoor cats are never really a good thing, between the casual murder of local wildlife and the risk of being hit by a car or eaten by a coyote or just fucked up by another cat. They aim for the face and throat, and when those injuries get infected, you can be down a cat before you've even had time to think about what just happened," says Dodger. She picks up and fills her own coffee mug. "But Roger ordered old Bill not to kill anything he finds outside the house—he can kill mice and spiders and house centipedes when he's *in* the house, we're fine with that, we just want him to leave the songbirds and lizards alone—and, well, the 'immortal' thing means the usual dangers just aren't as danger*ous* where he's concerned. So we let him do what he wants."

"It's a very odd approach to pet ownership," says Judy.

"Because everything else about us is so damn normal," says Dodger. "Everybody ready to go?"

"We were just waiting on you," says Roger.

"Then away we go." Dodger slams her coffee in one frankly impressive swallow. Smita moves to stand next to Lilianne, putting a reassuring hand against her wrist. Lilianne glances at her, barely managing to scrape up an uncomfortable smile.

"It'll be fine," says Smita. "This is the best group of people you could possibly go with into a potentially dangerous underground lab. Much better than going with just me."

"Dodger mentioned better shoes," says Lilianne.

"They'll be in the car," Smita reassures her.

Lilianne nods, and follows the rest of the group out of the kitchen.

* * *

They troop through the house to the front door. The sun is bright outside, bathing the whole block in deceptive summer brilliance. It's early fall, Lilianne knows; back home in Alabama, her mother is coming fully into her own, embracing her season and all its blessings, while her father is melting under the weight of inexplicable exhaustion and seasonal allergies. Because they're the incarnations of "shoulder seasons," rather than standing for the summer or winter, they can function mostly normally no matter what time of year it is, but growing up with them has left Lilianne deeply sensitive to the changing seasons. Seasons matter.

The porch is larger than makes any sense for a house this size, and even piling eight people onto it, they're not so cramped together that they're knocking against each other when they don't want to be. That, if nothing else, confirms that the house doesn't really exist. A house with a porch like that, this close to the university, would have long since been purchased and turned into faculty housing, something impressive for a dean or a department head.

Although Roger is a department head, so maybe he's just hedging his bets with the location of his ridiculous residence. And "ridiculous" is really the only applicable word. Lilianne's eyes widen as she takes in the walls and supports around her. Every board has been painted a different color, and not in a harmonious "pride-flag symbolism" sort of way. No. It looks like the painters were just given a list of colors the residents would like to see, and then told to do whatever they wanted.

Dodger is smirking at her. Lilianne forces her attention back to the mathematician, trying not to look totally appalled by what she's seeing.

"Something wrong, alchemist?" asks Dodger.

"I've just never seen a house that managed to clash with *itself* before," says Lilianne, too bewildered to be anything other than honest.

"That was the goal," says Roger. "I used to be colorblind. Like, on a genuinely distressing level. So once I could *see* colors, I wanted to see them all, all the time, no matter what. I don't care if they go together or not."

"Yes, she can tell that," says Dodger. "Everyone can tell that. The *birds* can tell that. People who are still colorblind can tell that."

"It's not that bad," protests Lilianne. "It's . . . definitely unique. It has character. I think it's fascinating."

"Lilianne," says Roger gently. "I am literally the living personification of language, spoken, written, or non-verbal. I hear what you're saying when you speak: not what you actually say, but what you mean. So trying to fool me by talking around whatever it is you really think is not going to work."

Lilianne pauses, pulling herself together. Roger's expression is grave but not unfriendly: he looks focused, like he's really paying attention to her, and not at all like he's preparing to turn her brain inside-out for his own amusement.

Fine, then. "It's hideous," she says. "Some of these colors were never meant to exist anywhere near each other. Honestly, I'm not sure some of these colors were meant to exist at all. Looking at them hurts my eyes. I feel like I'm still looking at them when my eyes are closed. I'm amazed your neighbors haven't accidentally burned the place down for what it's doing to the local property values."

Roger looks briefly surprised, then laughs. "Yup. That's what you really think. And you're not wrong, but the neighbors can't always see the house when we don't want them to, and there are ways around arson when you need to look for them. And we don't have to look at the house when we're inside."

"Speak for yourself," says Dodger, gesturing to the garden that takes up most of the front yard. It's filled with out-of-season fruits and flowers, and while they're as much a riot of color as the house is, they're not nearly as jarring to look at. "I can't avoid it."

"We all have our penance to pay," says Erin, and pulls a set of keys out of her pocket before loping down the porch steps, taking them two at a time, like a predator beginning the lazy pursuit of some small, unwitting prey animal. "I'll bring the van around. You lot come and meet me on the sidewalk."

Then she's gone, circling the porch to head down the side of the house. Lilianne shoots Smita a bemused look.

"The garage is behind the main house," she says, by way of explanation. "It's detached. There's a little workshop back there, but mostly we just use it for the cars."

"Which should be singular, since there's only one car," says Dodger. "We also have a van, which seats eight, and will get us where we need to go."

"There used to be two cars," says Smita.

"Yes, and persistence of forward continuity means the old car doesn't matter anymore," says Dodger. She descends the stairs, head swiveling to watch Lilianne as she does. "We only need to care about the things that are still in front of us."

Artemis and Kelpie trail down after her, followed by Roger and Judy, until Lilianne and Smita are alone on the porch. Lilianne sighs and runs her hands back through her hair, tugging a little as she does. The dull almost-pain centers her, returns her to the shape of her own skin, in a way that nothing else ever seems to manage.

When she lowers her hands, Smita is watching her, clearly anxious.

"What's wrong?" she asks.

Smita shakes her head. "I know this may not sound right, considering everything else that's going on, but we don't have new people show up here very often. The ones who do come tend to stick around, because there's a certain level of absolute weirdness that almost has to be achieved before you make it past the door, but . . . mostly when I make friends I don't already live with, they don't last long. I still don't know whether you and I are going to be friends, or whether this is going to be a short-lived association to get us past this whole thing with the lab, but I'm hoping you'll be able to stick around. Is that weird?"

"No," says Lilianne. "God, this was so much easier when we were kids. You just walked up to another kid on the playground, showed them your toy truck, and then you were besties going forward."

"For you, maybe," says Smita, holding up her forearm to show the shade of her skin. "It was a little harder for me, when all the kids I didn't already know were white. They were usually willing to play, but you never knew whose parents were going to come rushing over shouting about how they didn't know if I was clean, I probably smelled like curry, I probably had head lice. Those kids learned racism from their parents in the sandbox, and they carried it with them as we all went to school."

"That sounds awful," says Lilianne. "I would have played with your truck."

"I bet you would," says Smita, and she smiles, and there's nothing Lilianne wouldn't do for that smile. That smile is a promise and a prayer and she would follow it to the ends of the earth.

Which is what she's about to do.

A surprisingly mundane-looking van pulls up in front of the house, painted filing-cabinet gray, the side door already sliding open as Erin leans out the driver's-side window, beckoning the group forward.

"Shotgun," says Dodger, as she turns and hurries toward the van, bumping the garden gate open with her hip. Artemis is close behind her, rolling her eyes as she catches the swinging gate and stops it from closing. The others follow, one after the other, until Smita and Lilianne are the only ones left, still standing on the porch.

"Are you assholes coming?" calls Erin.

"Well. Are we assholes going?" asks Smita, turning to offer Lilianne her hand.

Lilianne lays her fingers across Smita's palm, and suppresses the thrill that runs through her when Smita grips them tight. Together they walk down the porch stairs and across the yard to the waiting van.

The interior is meticulously clean. Not unreasonable for a vehicle belonging to the living incarnation of order. The layout of the seats—two in the front, three each in the middle and back—means they have to split up, and Lilianne winds up sitting next to Judy at the very back of the van, while Smita joins Kelpie and Artemis in the middle.

Judy shoots Lilianne a sympathetic smile. Roger, meanwhile, leans forward so he can look around his girlfriend to Lilianne. "I know this is all a lot," he says. "But we really do appreciate you reminding us that we need to be worried about this lab. I guess it was easier just to pretend the whole thing had disappeared when the alchemists left, and that was a mistake."

"Yeah, it was," agrees Lilianne. "You're really going to let me go when this is all over?"

"We're not holding you captive," says Roger. "We just can't let you leave until it's been resolved. For your own safety as much as anything else. Those etiäinen got a taste of you. Until we know they've been neutralized, letting you go off on your own would be the same as feeding you to them."

"No one is feeding anyone to anything," says Smita firmly.

"Belts," says Erin, and pulls away from the curb without waiting to see if her command has been obeyed. She's an aggressive driver, but her turns are crisp and precise, and Lilianne knows without asking that she's obeying every law of the road, no matter how obscure or seemingly irrelevant. If anyone pulls them over, Erin will probably wind up writing *them* a ticket.

It's a humorous thought, but somehow it doesn't make her laugh, or even crack a smile. Lilianne leans back in her seat, belt tight across her middle, and watches the streets roll by outside the windows. Erin will get them there safely.

That may be the last safety any of them will see anytime soon.

Scrying

TIMELINE: AUGUST 23, 2018.

They don't drive far before Erin is turning off the surface streets and into a narrow alley that runs behind a large residential apartment building, heading for a wider alley tucked away out of sight, fenced in by brick on all sides. Once there, she wedges the van into an open spot half-concealed by a dumpster and kills the engine.

Even with the dumpster in the way, it's obvious that the van is the newest vehicle in this space by more than a decade, and it's also the only one with no visible dents or dings. Erin shoves the keys into her pocket and climbs out of the van, not looking back.

"Erin always finds parking," says Smita, apparently taking Lilianne's silence for confusion. "It's something about the way the streets order themselves. Honestly, it feels like a stretch to me, but nobody asked me whether I thought magic parking should come with being the incarnation of passive-aggressively rearranging the fridge magnets."

Artemis snorts, clearly more amused than the statement deserves, and everyone else starts getting out of the van.

Judy pokes Lilianne in the shoulder. "Hey," she says. "Get out. You're sort of trapping us in here."

Lilianne doesn't move.

Judy pokes her again, this time saying something irritated in Cantonese.

Roger snorts and responds in kind before leaning around his girlfriend and saying, "We really do need you to move, please. We can't go down to the lab until we all get out of the van. Getting out of the van is a pretty key first step."

"What if I don't get out of the van?"

"Well, eventually Erin will notice you're still in the van, and she'll come back to remove you." Roger says it like it's completely reasonable, and not the most terrifying thing he could possibly have said.

Lilianne gets out of the van.

"Great, thanks," says Judy, climbing out and moving away, Roger close on her heels. He pauses to give Lilianne a sympathetic look, then keeps moving, following Judy to the others, who have clumped up in the center of the alley. With a heavy sigh, Lilianne goes after them, catching up to the group just as Erin pushes the button on her keys to close the van door.

"All right," she says. "We know where the entrance is in this apartment complex, so we're going in through the front door. We're not going to talk to anyone, and if someone asks why we're here, we're just going to keep moving. It's rude, but it's also the best way to make sure no one else is in a position to get hurt tonight. Do you all understand?"

General murmurs of assent rise from the group.

"Until we're down, I'm in charge," says Erin. "Once we're in the lab, I'll hand things off to Kelpie and Lilianne, as our resident almost-alchemists, but until then, you listen to me, and you treat my orders like your own idea. Understand?"

Again, murmurs of assent. Even Lilianne joins in, too afraid of Erin's fierce glare to stay silent.

"Then we go. Be careful, be quick, and don't get dead."

"Some motivational speech, huh?" asks Smita, seeming to

appear at Lilianne's elbow. Lily manages not to jump, but only barely, and the two of them wind up at the rear of the group as everyone starts moving down the alley, following Erin's lead.

"I've heard worse," says Lilianne.

"That's terrifying."

Lilianne starts to laugh, then thinks better of it and clamps down. Smita bumps her shoulder with her own.

"Hey. This works better if we look natural," she says. "So laugh. Relax. We just need to get out of the open and this all goes much faster."

Erin is leading them into the apartment complex Lilianne noticed before; it's one of those open-air designs that only really seem to exist in places like California, where the weather never goes beyond a certain severity. The apartment doors face a central courtyard, shielded by small awnings but otherwise fully exposed to the elements. Some of the tenants have barbeque grills outside their doors, crammed in alongside window-mounted air-conditioning units.

It's the middle of the day, and the central courtyard is entirely deserted, although Lilianne can't stop herself from glancing at the open curtains of the windows they pass, waiting for someone who actually lives here to jump out and start chiding them for trespassing. Erin leads them unhesitatingly across the green central area to an apartment door sandwiched between a stairwell and a door marked LAUNDRY.

She tests the knob and, finding it locked, hisses between her teeth as she lets go and steps back, turning to Roger. "You're up," she informs him.

He steps forward, eyeing the doorknob sternly as he reaches for it. "I can see that you're a little stuck, but that's all it is," he says. "I know you're not locked against me. That would be unbelievably rude."

When he twists the knob, it turns easily enough, and the door swings inward, revealing an empty living room with white-painted walls and an industrial beige carpet. Erin nods to him.

"Respect," she says, and steps inside, heading for the hallway at the back of the room. One by one the others file after her, with Smita pausing long enough to close the door.

The air in the living room smells of fresh paint, cleaning solvents, and—very faintly, in the distance—alkahest. This place is definitely connected to the lab, no matter how distantly. Lilianne's mouth is suddenly dry, her heart beating too fast as she follows the others down the hall.

Past the open bathroom door, Erin opens what looks like a closet, revealing instead a flight of stairs descending down into the dark. "I tagged along the last time the management showed this apartment to a potential renter, and when they opened this door, they saw shelves. Or at least they acted like they did. They said it was plenty of room for all their linens, anyway. I sort of wonder what happens if they ever rent this place out, and the new tenants start just shoveling their towels into the abyss."

"They couldn't see the stairs?" asks Smita.

"Too much alchemy went into building them," says Erin. "It'll be years before anyone outside the alchemical world can see them. Longer if we don't clean up whatever's keeping the lab awake and active below us."

"What fun alchemy is," says Smita.

"What fun indeed," says Erin, and steps onto the stairs.

Again, they all follow her, like a little line of self-destructive ducklings willingly descending down into the dark.

The lab is definitely awake, and getting more awake by the minute. Once they're all on the stairs and the door is closed behind them, lights come on, pale and lambent at first, but rapidly brightening until they fill the entire stairwell with bright, sterile illumination, hurting Lilianne's eyes.

Kelpie sighs, shoulders slumping slightly. Artemis puts a hand on her back, right between the shoulder blades, and Kelpie flashes her a grateful smile. "Sorry," she says. "It's just that for the longest time, I thought this was what light was supposed to be. This was all that I knew until I got away."

"We can go back," says Artemis, voice low and urgent. "You just say the word and we'll go back. You and me. We can get the hell out of Berkeley for a little while, go and see the redwoods or something along the coast, whatever you want—"

"I want to finish this," says Kelpie firmly. "Whatever that means, that's what I want. I can't run away again. We all saw how that worked out the last time I did it."

Artemis looks pained, but she nods, and she descends the stairs a step behind Kelpie, the two of them staying close together. And the others follow, Erin ceding the lead to the Lunars, who seem to know where they're going, or at least have an idea of what they're going to do when they get there. The stairs are wide and relatively shallow, making it easy to descend. Lilianne stays near the wall, ready to brace herself if something happens or rises to attack them. She can't put it past this place.

This was all she was dreaming of when she came to Berkeley, and now it feels like she's descending back into a nightmare. They've gone at least three full flights down before they see the first real signs that the lab has truly been abandoned: the lights in the walls flicker and fail for a full twenty steps, leaving them to walk through a gray, grimy twilight zone lit only by the light radiating from above them and rising up from below.

Still they keep moving, and the unnatural channel the alchemists have opened in the earth rises up to swallow them all whole.

* * *

Lilianne loses count of the steps long before they reach the bottom of the stairs. Each flight is no more than twenty steps, followed by a short landing and a sharp turn to the next descending flight. About half the landings have doors, but Kelpie passes them all up, indicating that their destination is still somewhere farther down. The only thing worse than the thought of how far they've already descended is the thought of climbing back up them again.

"I can't feel my thighs," she complains to Smita, as they continue moving downward. "I'm starting to think the way through the sewer wasn't all that bad."

"Agreed," says Smita. "But whether we can use it or not is going to depend on what time it is when we're done here—and how many monsters we've encountered. Too many, and I'm not going into a sewer for anything, not even to avoid all these damn stairs."

"There's an elevator," says Kelpie.

Smita stares at her. "Why didn't you say so before?" she demands.

"Because there's no way we can use an elevator when we don't know whether the lab is safe," says Kelpie, tone reasonable. "If we got in and the cable snapped, I don't think even Roger could negotiate with the laws of physics fast enough to keep us all from getting splattered across the bottom of the elevator shaft."

"Or maybe we push a button and the elevator ignores it, takes us to whatever floor it thinks would be more fun to visit, and the doors open on a sea of monsters," says Erin, turning to look back at the group on the stairs. "This is the worst way to get down, but it's also the best way we have, because it's the safest."

"I still hate it," says Smita.

"Noted," says Erin, and keeps on walking.

The lights have continued to vary during their descent, sometimes on, sometimes casting them into temporary darkness. None of the dark patches have been large enough to make them stop and get out phones or flashlights; they're able to keep going, even when their footing is temporarily unsure. The air is temperate and smells of office building, a little dusty, a little tinged with cleaning products, but otherwise inoffensive, beyond the faint underscore of lingering alkahest. There are no hints of rot or glaring inconsistencies.

They've been going down for what feels like an hour when Kelpie abruptly stops, hooves clattering on the concrete landing, and looks toward the door on the wall with wide, unhappy eyes. "My room was through there," she says. "The place they kept me when I still had to belong to them. It's got my bed and my hairbrush and all the things that used to be my things but aren't my things anymore."

"Do you want to go get them?" asks Artemis.

"I want to burn this whole lab to ashes," says Kelpie. She looks toward the taller Lunar. "After we're done here, can we do that?"

"I don't . . . Judy?" Artemis looks toward Judy. "Can we burn down the lab?"

"No," says Judy. "Roman concrete doesn't burn. We could light everything else down here on fire, but then there's a decent chance that something in one of the workspaces would go up and just become some sort of fucked-up eternal flame."

"We're not turning Berkeley into Silent Hill, so no, we're not setting the lab on fire," says Roger firmly. "Kelpie, I'm sorry, and we'll try to find another way to make the place less terrifying for you. Maybe I can convince the molecular bonds in the concrete that they want to be flexible and turn the whole thing into mush. Or something. We'll figure it out."

"We better," says Kelpie, and starts moving again, clattering down the stairs toward the bottom.

Lilianne looks up. The stairwell is an endless concrete column between them and the surface, which is so far away at this point that she can't even say for sure where the ceiling is. The alchemists did this. They drove this spire of emptiness through the heart of Berkeley, and not long ago, she thought they were right to have done it: that anything could be justified in the endless quest for knowledge. Now she understands a little better. Now she can see that sometimes a void is just a void, and not a request to be filled: not everything needs to be codified. Not everything needs to be understood.

Not everything needs to be known.

From below her, Kelpie exclaims with what sounds like delight. Lilianne turns. Kelpie has reached smooth, solid ground, no more stairs descending, and is holding a white-painted door open on a gloomy space beyond. It's not totally dark on the other side of the door: some sort of auxiliary lighting is clearly still operational. That's about the only good thing Lilianne can say about the situation.

"This is the main lab," says Kelpie. "Through here is where I used to work with Margaret and the rest of her research team. That means hydroponics should be two levels up, and the menagerie is a level above that."

"The what?" asks Dodger, in a voice like ice.

"The . . . menagerie . . ." says Kelpie, voice going smaller with each word. "It's where they kept the animals for experimenting on. I hope someone got them out before the lab shut down."

"If they didn't, that's not going to be a very pleasant floor," says Erin.

"I'll go," says Dodger. She turns back to the stairs and lopes up several of them, Roger and Judy following after.

Kelpie is already moving toward the door Artemis holds open for her, and Erin hesitates, looking to Smita, who shakes her head and says, "I'll be fine," as she gestures at Lilianne.

A bubble of pride forms in Lilianne's chest—Smita trusts her to keep them safe—before bursting and leaving her awash in cold reality. Smita may trust her, but she has no special powers, no bow made of moonlight or capacity to command the laws of reality. She can mix a few simple potions, if she has the ingredients in front of her, and she can understand the way alchemists tend to look at things, the angles they use to approach the world. They have backup in the building. Will that backup be close enough to help them if the etiäinen decide to come again? If they get cornered?

She doesn't know, and she doesn't want to learn the hard way, but she's unfortunately concerned that she will.

"Hydroponics?" asks Smita brightly, and there's nothing Lilianne can really do but agree, and follow her back up two flights of stairs, to the closed door to the hydroponics floor.

She's not sure what she expects to find on the other side. Bodies, maybe, or auf still shuffling through their assigned tasks even as their unmaintained bodies begin to unravel; dissolution and decay. Instead, they step into a spotless, almost futuristic-looking space, which rapidly becomes a bright paradise of glass and chrome as the lights come on, only buzzing for a moment before they settle into a warm, steady glow. Even before the panel lights become active, the room is lit by a purple wash from the grow lights that are still visible through the forest of uncontrolled greenery that has consumed the various garden beds.

"If we told the stoners about this place, they'd move in and declare themselves an independent city-state," says Smita, sounding awed. She steps forward, wide-eyed as she tries to take everything in.

Lilianne follows more carefully, scanning the markings on the walls and around the bases of the contained growth tanks. She recognizes most of the sigils. They're for growth and stability, and while they've been combined in some truly innovative ways, they're not enormously surprising. She can absolutely see how these combinations would result in healthy, dependable growth.

"They must have some sort of irrigation system that's still running," says Smita. "Maybe it's tapping in to the water we had to wade through the first time we came here? Or maybe—do alchemists have a method for extracting water from the air? Normal people can do that with the right machines, so it wouldn't be all that surprising if alchemists could do it too."

"There are filtration systems that can be put in place when needed," says Lilianne. "This place looks like it was modeled on Reed's primary labs, so it would make sense if they were extracting water somehow. Or the plants may have just been held in functional stasis."

"I don't think so." Smita indicates a tank where the sides have been distorted and partially broken down by the vigorous growth of the bush inside. It looks like a raspberry of some kind, the individual canes of its central structure sagging low under the weight of ripe purplish-red fruit. It looks absolutely delicious.

Lilianne would sooner eat her own hands. She shakes her head as she turns away from the temptation.

"So they were still operational when the rest of the lab shut down," she says. "But where *is* everyone?" She's looking down in her effort to avoid the fruit. That's why she spots the first flash of white, and moves toward it, nudging vines aside with her foot as she reveals the discarded lab coat crumpled on the floor.

Finding one is like unlocking a hidden eye puzzle. As soon as she sees it and realizes what it is, she starts to spot other flashes of white buried among the greenery.

"I think . . . I found the alchemists," she says, in a small, tight voice.

"Hmm?" asks Smita.

Lilianne indicates the first coat, and waits for the horror of the moment to sink in. The silent plants suddenly seem less inanimate than they do poised, like predators that might strike at any moment.

"I don't think any of them made it out of here," says Lilianne. "We should go."

"Yes." Something falls over deeper in the lab, something small that makes a clinking noise when it hits the floor. Lilianne feels

Smita's hand questing for her own, and she takes it, interlacing their fingers. "We should go *now.*"

They hurry out of the lab, and nothing grabs them. The lights go out of their own accord as the two women reach the door. For a moment, the lab is nothing more than a purple-painted horror, and something definitely moves in the darkness, lashing toward the door even as Lilianne slams it shut.

She looks to Smita. "I am starting to have more sympathy for your position on alchemy," she says.

"I'm not asking you to throw your life's work away," says Smita. "Just to consider that maybe people who've already been hurt by alchemy won't be as enthusiastic about it as you are. Alchemy can make wonderful things. It made most of my friends. All you have to do is accept that there are other beautiful things about the world. Things alchemy didn't do."

"Like you," says Lilianne, and bites her tongue, cheeks flaring red. She stares at Smita, who looks like she's trying not to laugh. "I . . . That came out wrong."

"I can see you're pretty smooth," says Smita, and starts up the stairs, heading for the level Kelpie identified as the menagerie. "Come on. I'm sure we can catch up with the others."

Lilianne follows.

* * *

Dodger is the first to reach the menagerie door. Roger, following close behind with Judy beside him, doesn't comment on her apparent eagerness. It's all about his proximity, he knows, just like he knows that she wouldn't have been able to move with such confidence if he'd gone looking for some other danger of this strange, enclosed space. The nature of their entanglement is such that even now, when they're both fully manifest and virtually indestructible, she will always try to be the first into a dangerous situation, to stand where she can draw the fire away from him.

He understands and respects her reasons. Even if they were built into her by their creators, she's had plenty of time to make them her own, and she's not changing for anyone.

She opens the door, revealing a dark, narrow antechamber and releasing a gout of sour, musk-scented air at the same time. It smells like a place where animals are kept, like the secret back tunnels of a zoo, hot and vital and alive.

Nothing should be alive down here. Not after the amount of time that's passed since the place was officially shut down. Dodger hesitates, hand still on the doorknob, blocking him or Judy from getting past her.

"We sure about this?" she asks. "I know the alchemists are gone, there's no one down here to take aim at us or intend to do us wrong, but that doesn't mean they can't have left traps behind them. There could be something in here that we don't want to deal with."

This, too, is a part of her construction, and it makes the hairs on the back of Roger's neck stand on end: if Dodger is trying to make excuses for why they shouldn't explore the space beyond the door, it's because her probabilities are picking up a possible danger in the darkness. She doesn't have any extra senses, but the ones she does have are tightly honed for calculating risks. He's looked up the biology behind them, curious about how the alchemists were able to build such finely calibrated danger-detection into his sister, and whether that same apparatus might be sleeping within him, ready to be accessed; what he's found is that every attribute she displays is found in ordinary people, one way or another, just not at this intensity, and not all packed into the same skin.

There's something in there, and whatever it is, she doesn't want him facing it. He can respect and appreciate it. He just can't let her back down to protect him.

Judy has a peach pit in her hand and is flipping it across her fingers like a magician with a trick coin. It's something she does when she's nervous, and he knows the repetitive motion soothes her.

"I think we're sure, Dodge," he says, gently. She gives him a quick, sharp look, as interrogative as a question. He meets it with a nod, non-verbal reply to non-verbal query. "We need to find out what's going on with this place."

"The numbers don't add up," she says. "There's something wrong with this whole thing, and I don't like it. We should be going home and looking at the things we've learned with an eye to analysis."

"But we haven't learned anything yet," objects Judy.

"We've learned how big this complex is, and how much more Kelpie knows than she's been telling us," says Dodger. "That's something we should have been taking into account already, and the fact that we didn't means we're less prepared than we ought to be."

Roger looks at her and frowns. It can be hard, with the two of them, to tell when they're panicking: they don't tend to get red in the face, and their eyes are pale enough that it isn't obvious when the whites are showing around their irises. (And it wasn't always like this, was it? Not for him, anyway. He doesn't remember people reacting to his eyes as if there was anything strange about them when he was younger. There are no pictures to prove his recollection—artifacts rarely carry between timelines, and never without intent. On the few occasions when he'd needed something to endure, it had never been a picture of himself, never anything so small or petty as confirmation that he used to be something different than he is now.)

(They all used to be something different than they are now. Endlessly looping through time in pursuit of the perfect happy ending will change a person. It can't possibly do anything else.)

"Dodger," he says, in a voice pitched low and gentle, like he's trying to talk down a potentially dangerous animal, "what's wrong?"

"I don't *know*," she says, and she sounds frustrated enough to give him pause. She turns her face back to the open door and the dark beyond. "I know we've always been more inclined to player-versus-environment than player-versus-player, but normally when we're walking into danger, we've at least seen some indication that there might be another player on the board. Right now, it's just us and a bumbling baby alchemist from Alabama and this lab. It all feels too . . . too straightforward. We're moving in a linear line. We *never* move in a linear line. If we're doing it now, that means something must be going on that I can't see, and I don't like it."

"We won't find out what it is by standing around out here," says Roger. "Go on in."

Dodger nods, shoulders tightening as the command registers with her forebrain, and then she's stepping through the door, unable to stop herself any longer.

Roger and Judy are close behind, Judy still flipping the peach pit between her fingers, the small, ceaseless motion seeming to lend her some fragment of comfort. Then the dark closes around them, and the heavy, humid air is everything the world contains.

Slowly, the three of them inch along the antechamber. They're halfway to the point Dodger has estimated to be the next door when the door behind them swings shut and red runner lights come on along the base of the walls, filling the space with an eerie, horror-movie-adjacent glow. It's unsettling, and it doesn't get better when Judy takes a deep breath and begins to glow with a lambent silver-peach light. She seems to get a little taller at the same time, a little more than mortal. Roger turns to look at her, trying not to flinch from the way the mingled red and silver lights cast bloody shadows on her face.

"It's all right," she says. "I'm still mostly me. Chang'e just thought we could use a little extra muscle while we're walking around in here. She's close to the surface, but she's not taking the reins."

"If she decides she needs to, please try to tell me first," says Roger. He trusts and adores his girlfriend's divine alter ego, is aware that her presence is the only reason the two of them can ethically have a relationship like the one they currently enjoy; without Chang'e to elevate Judy slightly above the human baseline, he would feel like he was exploiting her every time he asked for anything, from a kiss to time to get his grading done. Chang'e creates a comfortable buffer between them. The Lunars, with their dual natures, are some of the only people who can actively defy him, by giving his commands to one half of their selves while the other half continues doing whatever it is they had wanted to do in the first place.

He trusts her, but he knows she isn't Judy, and unlike Judy, she isn't always willing to go along with preexisting plans. Which is not the same as "She won't follow orders," but is a close cousin, and not something he wants to risk when they're in a dangerous situation.

"I will," says Judy.

"Are you two done debating the nature of plurality back there?" asks Dodger, voice sour. Roger returns his focus to her. She has her hand on the latch of the door at the end of the chamber, which isn't a knob, but is one of those long crash bars usually found in theaters and public gathering spaces.

"We are," says Roger.

"Cool." Dodger pushes the bar inward, and reveals a chamber of horrors.

The room is large. That's the least offensive thing about it, and so it's the first thing that any of them take notice of. It's a good-sized space, big enough to host ten or fifteen people without becoming overly cramped. It's bigger than their kitchen, and they pretty regularly cram eight people in there. This was a working space before it was abandoned: even with the red runner lights painting everything slick and bloody, the various workstations and desks are obvious, although all of them have the same smooth, undifferentiated texture, like they've been wrapped in some sort of packing material by the people who used to work here.

Then the overhead lights crackle and come on, washing the red light out with white, and it becomes impossible to continue to deny what they're standing in the middle of. There are cages along the walls, most closed, all empty. The floor is springy because they're standing on top of a layer of what looks like pale human skin, waxy and bloated-looking, like a drowning victim. That same skin extends up the walls and over the workstations; it's been ripped loose where they came through the door, opening a wound like a picked-off scab. Layers of damage and recovery show there, and that manages to pierce Roger's horror with a new piece of information, which embeds itself even as his mind tries to reject it—if it's been hurt enough to already be healing in places, *they're not the first ones here.*

The rich, meaty smell of the space is explained. The skin has pores, little imperfections. Surely it also has glands, waxy patches, places where its essential animal nature can come through.

Judy almost drops her peach pit, eyes going wide with bemusement and disgust. "What *is* this?" she asks. "Roger . . ."

"We found the animals, and maybe the alchemists, too," says Dodger, top lip curling back from her teeth as she looks around. "I have no idea what could have done this to them. Something they probably thought was really clever right up until they felt themselves being absorbed into the greater whole."

"This is . . . wrong," says Roger, hollow horror in his voice. "We need to go."

"Yes, we do," says Dodger. She turns back toward the door, and stops dead. The torn skin is already sealing over, becoming just another flat section of the wall; it's happening so fast that she can virtually *see* it, see the muscle below the skin knitting itself back together.

(And what does a cavern of flesh need with muscle? The question is small, nagging, and terrible. If this is just skin and tissue made of liquified alchemists and their research subjects, it shouldn't need any muscle. It has no reason to move.)

"Roger . . ."

"Shit," says Roger. He freezes for a moment, clearly overwhelmed by the situation, then says, in a voice that leaves no room for argument, "You need to open for me."

The flesh over the door continues to heal.

Roger takes a deep breath. When he tries again, his voice has subharmonics the human voice shouldn't be able to convey, shadows and impossible distortions. "I command you to open, laboratory door. I am ready to leave."

The door keeps healing.

"I . . . That always works," says Roger. It doesn't matter that the door doesn't have any ears (or maybe it does, and that would be so much worse, somehow, than the alternative); the universe can hear him, and that means the universe should listen when he speaks. It always has before. People have come apart under his command, breaking down into their component pieces. Walls have fallen. Bullets have stopped, robbed of their kinetic energy.

"Maybe the rules are different here for some reason," says Judy. "Like when we're inside the everything."

"Or maybe this is where we need to run," says Dodger. She grabs hold of Roger's arm and whirls, running deeper into the cavernous depths of the fleshy horror.

Roger grabs Judy's hand in his own, dragging her along as Dodger pulls him in her wake, rapidly leaving the room where they initially arrived behind.

* * *

The door to the menagerie level is locked when Lilianne first tries the knob. She frowns before she tries again, wiggling it against the strange resistance she's feeling. It's not the feeling of a latch being thrown; there's too much torque for that. It's just like something is stopping it from turning, even when it naturally should.

"What's wrong?" asks Smita.

"I don't know," says Lilianne, and twists harder. This time the knob obliges, rotating until there's a strange popping sound, like a chicken bone being twisted out of its socket and finally ripping loose. The knob turns fully, and the door swings a few inches inward.

The smell that follows is bloody and carnal, carried by a gust of unusually warm, moist air. When it hits Lilianne's skin she recoils, briefly convinced that the next time she looks at her hands, she'll find them covered in a fine spray of bloody spots. Smita doesn't seem to notice. She pushes on into the darkened entryway, walking toward the door at the far end.

It doesn't resist her. When she shoves against the crash bar, the door pushes easily open, accompanied by a horrifying ripping, like someone has sliced halfway through a raw pork chop and is now tearing it in half. The room on the other side is bathed in white light, mingled equally with the warning red.

"Come on," says Smita. She steps through.

Lilianne follows.

The room beyond—the menagerie level proper—is *wrong.* Everything is clean and polished, the floor made of metal grating that opens onto a vast drop down into deeper darkness below them, the walls studded with chrome and metallic plates, all of which are perfectly spotless. It feels like something out of a science fiction movie, or—

"What is this, a Resident Evil remake?" asks Lilianne, voice low and bewildered. "If anything moans, I'm leaving."

"Noted," says Smita.

There are cages set into the walls, all of them empty, holding not even bones. Lilianne starts toward them, then pauses. She can see the metal grating underfoot. So why can't she feel it?

Every step she takes is elevated, just a little, just enough that she can feel the difference. It doesn't help that whatever she's actually walking on is softer than metal would be, yielding, like walking on the rubber matting that sometimes gets put down on convention center floors during trade shows or academic conferences. She stops and bends, reaching for the floor. She needs to feel whatever it is she's walking on top of. She needs to *understand*.

"Stop!" says Smita.

Lilianne looks sharply up, focusing on her companion. "What is it?"

"I don't . . . I don't think you should be touching that."

"Why not?"

"Because it's not safe."

Lilianne glances down again. The floor is glossy and unobstructed, no rugs or plastic sheeting to obscure the plain metal. "I'm standing on it," she says, trying to sound reasonable. "I'm already touching it, if you really think about it."

"Your shoes are touching it," says Smita. "Please . . . please don't."

Lilianne glances up again. Something about Smita's face isn't right. There's a lurking horror in her expression that doesn't match the situation in the slightest. "Smita, what's going on?"

"Can you really not see?"

Lilianne looks down for a third time. "I don't think so, no. Whatever it is you're seeing, it's not here for me."

"The floor is covered by what looks like a layer of skin. Not just skin: it's too plump and rounded to be just skin. There's tissue underneath it. It has *pores*, Lily. No hairs or freckles or anything like that, but it's alive. It's soft and squishy and *alive*. It's on the walls, too. And when you reach for it, it reaches back."

"How do you mean?"

"These little threads come up out of the pores and they stretch toward your fingers, like they're going to grab hold. I'm afraid if you touch it, you won't be able to pull your hand away."

Lilianne blinks then, and for just a moment, it seems like she can see what Smita's describing, a layer of pinkish flesh, the skin closer in shade to her own than to Smita's, skin that's never seen the sun before. She pulls her hand back as she straightens. "All right. Let's say you're right."

"So easy?"

"If I'm right and the floor is plain metal, I touch it and no one gets hurt. If you're right, anyone who touches skin that puts out feelers so it can touch them back could be in a lot of trouble. Do we turn back or keep going?"

"Roger and Dodger went this way."

The statement isn't the same as an answer, and it is at the same time, because out of all of them, Smita is the one who doesn't have to be here. She could have walked away as soon as the twins finished spinning the timeline into something that would let her stay away; she could have chosen freedom from the tangled web of the alchemical world. The fact that she didn't says more about her capacity for love and loyalty than anything else could possibly communicate.

If her people are here, Smita isn't leaving. That much is easy to see. Lilianne takes a deep breath. Logic says they should go and find Artemis and Kelpie, should get themselves some backup before they go any deeper into a space that is apparently trying to actively disguise itself from her. This isn't safe. And that doesn't matter.

"Alchemy has a lot of focus on transformation and healing," she says, haltingly. "Filling a room with flesh that lives despite not having a visible body is absolutely within the capabilities of a master. It would, however, require a lot of raw materials to set up."

"This was the menagerie, according to Kelpie," says Smita. "I don't see any animals, and there weren't any alchemists in here when we arrived. Not even dead ones. Maybe this was set up as a failsafe, in case the place was being evacuated? You can't spill anyone's secrets if you've been absorbed into a giant skin blob."

That isn't entirely true, but Lilianne doesn't think hearing that will make Smita feel any better. It wouldn't make *her* feel any better, and she doesn't have people lost somewhere inside this collection of horrors. She takes a longer look around.

In addition to the door they entered through, there are two halls leading deeper into the lab, one open, the other blocked by a door with a crash bar like the one they've already opened. Taking a guess, she points at the closed door: "What do you see over there?"

"Just wall, which means, just skin," says Smita.

Lilianne nods. She doesn't know why they're seeing two different versions of this space, but none of the explanations she can come up with are good ones. They range from the bad—everyone who comes here sees something different, chosen at random from a list of horrors—to the truly terrible—the lab doesn't want one of them, and is doing its best to get rid of the unnecessary body, whether by blocking out all the dangers so that they'll stumble into disaster, or by showing them everything to whet their curiosity. That option is worse in part because she can't decide whether it's trying to attract her or Smita.

She doesn't want to get hurt defending someone she barely knows. Her crush, while strong, is nowhere near that powerful. But she also doesn't want to stand idly by as Smita walks open-eyed into danger. She moves her finger, pointing to the second door.

"And there?" she asks.

"An opening. That's the way deeper into the lab."

"So we have two choices." Lilianne drops her hand. "Because I see openings in both spots I just pointed to. Either the lab really *wants* us to go the second way, or it wants me to go the first way alone."

"I don't like either one of those."

"Neither do I. I want to try something."

Lilianne turns and walks briskly toward the door Smita can't see. When she gets there she reaches for the crash bar, stopping before she can make contact, and looks back over her shoulder at Smita. "Anything?" she asks. "Any little threads or ripples?"

"No," says Smita. "What do you think it means?"

"I don't know." Lilianne takes a breath to bolster herself, then presses the crash bar, waiting for a stinging pain that never comes. She pushes hard, and the door swings open without any resistance, and when she takes her hand away, there's no resistance. Again, she looks to Smita. "What does this look like to you?"

"Like a cut just opened in the wall," says Smita, horrified. "I can see things dripping and pulsing inside. Fat and . . . and veins and . . . I think it's alive. How can it be alive?"

"I don't know," says Lilianne, grimly. "But I think this is the way we ought to go."

Smita nods, looking miserably anxious as she crosses the room (at once sterile and dripping in flesh) to follow Lilianne into the gaping maw of the open hallway.

Neither of them was present to see the skin grow back over the doorway, sealing them away.

* * *

"Are you sure you're all right?" Artemis walks a few steps ahead of Kelpie, bow drawn and arrow notched, ready to fire at the first signs of trouble. Her shoulders are locked, and her knees are slightly bent, lending a floating, dance-like quality to her motions. She's a huntress in the field, and whatever prey she finds to focus her anger on will surely regret attracting her ire.

"I'm fine," says Kelpie. She's following a few feet behind, stepping gingerly so that the echoes of her hooves won't alert anything that might be down here to their approach. She has her arms wrapped around herself, radiating discomfort even as she follows the faintly luminescent Lunar.

"You don't *sound* fine."

"Probably because I'm lying," says Kelpie. "But if I lie hard enough, I might start to believe myself, and if I can believe myself, maybe you can believe me too. Can you just pretend you believe me? At least until we're out of here?"

"I always want to believe you," says Artemis. "I want to believe you above everyone and everything else, even myself. I love you like I've never loved anyone in this world, and you're important to me. But that's why I can't believe you if I think you're hurting yourself, and the way you sound right now, it sounds like you're hurting yourself to make me happy. Again. Some of us weren't made to run naked through the midnight forests."

Kelpie grimaces. "I know, and you were really nice about telling me that I don't have to do that anymore. I was made to be your hind. I should be able to run beside you."

"Bipeds with hooves don't run as well as actual deer do. Who knew?" Artemis shakes her head, attention still focused in front of her. "I mean, besides everyone who's ever really looked at an ungulate. I don't need you to run through the woods with me. I'm happy with you just the way you are. That's what loving you means."

"I'm okay, really. I may not be fine, but I will be, once I know this place is well and truly dead forever, and we're not going to get dragged down here again." Kelpie slows to study a desk as she walks through the lab, exhaling when she sees the small framed photographs are still there. The computer being present means one thing; the personal effects of the alchemist who used it mean something else entirely.

Something heartbreaking and sad. The people who worked here were alchemists, yes, and since her escape from their custody and discovery of her strange, off-kilter little family, she's learned a lot about alchemists that she never knew before. She's learned they can't be trusted, that they lie and cheat and steal and even kill in the pursuit of their "Great Art." The American alchemists like to pretend they aren't the inheritors of Asphodel Baker, that they're more than her loves and hates and petty grudges all made incarnate in modern flesh, but her dreams and ideals and obsessions and cruelties have saturated the texts they study from: they are hers as much as the cuckoos are.

She was built as one of Asphodel's children and trained as one of her heirs, and now that she runs with the moon, she rejects everything she was intended to be. But these people were her friends before she had anyone else. They were her world when she thought the world was small and safe and contained within concrete walls. For them all to be gone, most likely victims of the same alkahest that brought her first friend, Margaret, to pieces before her eyes . . . it's a tragedy. So much more than alchemy was lost here. And there is still so much left to lose.

That's the worst thing about the world getting bigger. It gets more confusing and less linear with every piece that's added. But there is also so much more to lose now than there was when she called this place her home.

Artemis turns, making a slow sweep with her bow, then returns her attention to Kelpie. "I don't see any signs that there's been movement down here in a long time. But there's no dust."

"The filtration system cleans the air," says Kelpie. "And when I say 'cleans the air,' I mean that there are screens designed to attract and consume dust. They're technically alive. Just sheets of active biomaterial at regular intervals inside the vents. They eat spiders, too. Which is good, because any spiders that managed to make it down here would starve."

"Because the vents eat all the other insects."

"Exactly." Kelpie nods. "Since there's no dust, that means the biomaterial is still alive. It's probably grown since the alchemists left. I bet it completely fills the vents." She looks up at the ceiling, thoughtfully.

"We are not going into the vents to check," says Artemis firmly.

"I wasn't going to," lies Kelpie. "If you think this room is clear enough for us to move on, I can take you to Margaret's office. The man the Congress sent to relieve her may have ransacked it, but I doubt he had time to completely clear it out before everything went wrong."

"Margaret was your project leader?"

"Mmm." Kelpie nods. They've talked about Margaret before, but never in the kind of detail Artemis has tried to encourage. Margaret is hers, a pearl she carries in the treasure caverns of her heart, not meant to be carelessly spent. She'll never have another friend like Margaret was, and while that may be partially down to the fact that Margaret lied to her right up until the end, it's also true that Margaret died to save her. Without Margaret's willingness to stand up to the man from the Congress and keep lying, Kelpie would never have seen the surface.

Had she really been the lab accident Margaret claimed she was, the alkahest would have taken Kelpie apart bit by bit, leaving her to drip away like water. Alkahest is the universal solvent, and at the most basic level, it exists to dissolve everything it touches. But most American alchemists—even the Congress, who so despised her when she lived—use Asphodel's recipe to make the stuff, and Asphodel's alkahest recoils from the sympathy of her blood. Constructs and alchemists alike break down at the touch of her alkahest. Cuckoos don't. Cuckoos carry the philosopher's stone of Asphodel's genetics in their veins, and so her alkahest sees them as siblings, not entirely trustworthy, but undeserving of death.

Kelpie's feelings about Margaret will never be untangled, and maybe Margaret saw her as an owner sees a pet, but she still saved her life. Kelpie won't forget that.

"I think we can move deeper," says Artemis. She doesn't shoulder her bow, keeps it out and ready to fire at anything that moves.

Kelpie nods, and turns to start down one of the short halls that branch off the main lab like spokes of a wheel. Artemis follows.

They're almost to the door at the end of the hall when a voice speaks from the shadows, poisonously sweet and slightly lisping, like the speaker is trying to navigate a set of inhuman teeth.

"Little cuckoo, you've returned," it purrs. "I never thought to see you haunt these halls again. Come to join the other ghosts? We've saved a space for you in the depths."

Kelpie stops in her tracks, still looking straight ahead. Behind her, she knows Artemis has done the same. They're both too smart to look behind themselves. Anything that speaks out of the shadows like this is unlikely to attack as long as it remains unseen. That might not work with natural animals, but with alchemical creations, refusing to see them directly is often the surest means of survival.

"Did you take the bodies?" she asks. "If you've saved a space for me."

"There were no bodies," says the voice. "Of the staff of this lab, only the subjects walked as cuckoos do, and only they survived the purification. Of course, a cuckoo's flesh is flesh still, and they needed to eat if they wanted to survive. Sad for them, that they were all so well confined. They couldn't get out, couldn't get away, couldn't do anything but dwell and die where they were. You were our only loss, little cuckoo, our only survivor. Now that you're home, we'll have the full collection once again."

"And the other cuckoos?" She was never on the staff for those experiments, wasn't allowed to work around the cuckoos. Something she resented once, but now sees as the blessing Margaret intended it to be. She has no faces to put to the bodies the thing in the shadows describes. They're only shadows to her, and as long as they can stay that way, she doesn't have to mourn them.

"We took them when their eyes went dull, when their hearts stopped beating and the flesh began to cool. They were ours by right. We hungered, and the final alchemy they performed was to fill our bellies, for a time." The voice is getting closer. "Might you do the same?"

"No," says Kelpie. Her voice is strong and clear, and for a moment, she's proud of that. For a moment, she's untouchable. "I am not on the menu."

"Listen to the lady, beast," says Artemis.

"Lunar," hisses the voice. "We do not answer to you."

"No, but you'll listen to me, if you don't want to find out how much of you I have to ruin before the rest of your 'we' comes for lunch," snaps Artemis.

"Ruin?"

"Injury is no disgrace," she says. "Warriors bear scars. Losing a piece of yourself in the course of the hunt is unavoidable, and no one should shame you for it. But if I were to slice you bit from bit, little pieces of you dropping to the ground and severed from the whole, skin flayed and muscle exposed . . . I could ruin you. One cut at a time."

She makes it sound so reasonable that Kelpie stiffens, reminded what sort of woman she's welcomed to her bed, what sort of ageless authority she sleeps beside at night. She is a cuckoo and Artemis is a natural incarnate, but even apart from that, they embody forces of such dramatically different power that it's like comparing the sun to a candle.

The etiäinen that's been taunting them—for it can be nothing else—hisses wordlessly, and although she can't hear it moving, Kelpie has the distinct feeling that it's pulling away, moving farther into the shadows.

"I can mirror neither of you," it complains, tone turning sour.

"I'm supposed to pluck an image from your mind and make myself over in its image, and then anyone who doesn't share that face can be meat for me. But when I look into your minds, all I find is the shining of the moon."

"Then you should leave our minds alone," says Kelpie reasonably. "We're going into the office now. It was very nice to meet you."

"No, it wasn't," says Artemis.

"No, it wasn't," agrees Kelpie. "But it's important, when you're dealing with alchemical constructs, to maintain a veil of civility. If you're polite to them, they have to be polite to you, at least to a certain degree. So we play nicely, and then they do the same."

"That sounds like something out of the Up-and-Under."

"Of course it does. The Up-and-Under is something out of alchemy. The rules they follow there came from the rules as written here." Margaret's office door is unlocked. Kelpie opens it easily, looking back at Artemis for the first time since they entered this hall. Are the shadows behind her deeper than they ought to be? Is something hidden there?

"Everything changes so that it can stay the same," says Kelpie. She musters a frail smile for Artemis, who returns it and then follows her into the small office beyond the door.

Like the desks in the main lab, Margaret's personal effects are still in their original places, pictures tacked to the corkboards on the wall and adorning the edges of her monitor. There are a few small toys and pieces of art mixed in with the books and piles of papers. It looks like she just stepped out for a moment. It looks like she'll be right back.

"I was never allowed in here unsupervised," says Kelpie, walking over to the desk and resting her fingertips against the blotter. "Margaret didn't like it when people touched her things."

"Most people don't," says Artemis. She steps out of the doorway, closing the door behind herself, and freezes.

"Kelpie," she says, in a very carefully calm tone, "what was the order of floors here?"

"This is the main lab. It's at the bottom of the structure," says Kelpie, continuing to study Margaret's desk. "This was mostly used for theory and formulation. We mixed a lot of necessary solvents here. Which is a little odd, because it meant the fumes had to travel through the longest possible distance in order to clear the lab. We should have been mixing caustic chemicals closer to the surface, if we were going to mix them at all."

"Uh-huh. A base level," says Artemis. "And what's above us?"

"Directly above us? One of the secondary research libraries. It took up most of the level by itself, because that was also where they did the printing. Apart from that, the water filtration. Which should also probably have been below us, to prevent flooding." Kelpie is frowning now. "They don't seem to have put a lot of thought into things while they were building this place."

"Didn't they grow it?"

"Yes, but the Roman concrete would follow the sigils they drew. They got to decide what went where, even if some of the closets and shelving may have generated spontaneously."

"All right. Above the water filtration."

"Hydroponics."

"And above that?"

"The menagerie, and the incinerator. Why are you asking me about all this?"

"Do you know what happened above the menagerie?"

"The level above the menagerie was where they built the cuckoos. Arty, come on. You're starting to scare me. What do you see?"

Artemis steps to the side, gesturing to the colorful map pinned to the back of the door. It's drawn in the style of an old children's book illustration—may even *be* an old children's book illustration—and shows the various lands and protectorates of the Up-and-Under as a series of layers, beginning with the wall in the woods that leads to the Kingdom of Coins, where riches may be made out of common clay, and then wending its way slowly upward.

There were more than a dozen Up-and-Under books published before Asphodel's passing, but no one ever remembers them beyond the first four, with Avery and Zip and the lessons of the graveyard path. Kelpie looks at the map on the door, gravity slowly melting into horror as she traces the progression with her eyes, the journey through the levels of the Up-and-Under mapped out in the levels of the lab.

It's a tenuous connection. If it were drawn anywhere but in the temple of Asphodel Baker, she would think it was unrealistic. As things stand . . .

She turns to Artemis. "We need to find the others."

"Yes, we do," says Artemis. She finally slings her bow over her shoulder, grasping Kelpie's hand and squeezing it hard before she pulls her toward the door and out into the hall beyond.

They've only gone a few steps before Kelpie breaks into a run, hooves clattering as she pulls Artemis along behind her.

The etiäinen in the dark does nothing to interfere.

Movement

TIMELINE: AUGUST 23, 2018.

It's always been the Up-and-Under," pants Kelpie as she runs, not letting go of Artemis's hand. Her scramble up the stairs is unbalanced and unsteady, and might end with her on the floor if not for Artemis steadying her, providing a weight she can pull against and stop herself from moving too fast.

"Breathe," says Artemis.

"She *told* us it was always the Up-and-Under," says Kelpie urgently. They're almost to the top of the first flight of stairs. "From the moment she abandoned the Congress, she put everything she had into the Up-and-Under. All her secrets, all her plans, all her everything. She was writing a blueprint for her perfect universe. And we didn't see it."

"What are you saying?"

"I don't know, but I know that we need to figure it out fast, because whatever this is, we've walked straight into the middle of it."

The door opens easily, revealing a large library, the shelves still loaded down with books. The ceiling is, impossibly, cracked, the vines dangling down from above having conquered even the Roman concrete. Kelpie stops dead, staring open-mouthed at the hanging greenery.

"Nice jungle," says Artemis. The vines are dark green, their leaves spade-shaped and several shades lighter. She starts to step into the room, and Kelpie's grip tightens, stopping her.

"Fire an arrow," says Kelpie.

"What?"

"I want you to fire an arrow into the room." Kelpie's voice is hard, as unyielding as her grasp.

"Why?"

"Just do it."

"I'll need my hand if I'm going to do that."

Reluctantly, Kelpie releases her hand, pulling slowly back and stepping clear. Artemis watches her, then unslings her bow and draws an arrow, sliding it into place before turning to take aim at the opposite side of the room. She doesn't cross the threshold, just pulls back the bowstring and releases her arrow into the air.

It flies straight and true for a full second before the vines whip to life around it, wrapping tight around the wooden shaft and jerking it to a halt. Several leaves fall to the floor, shredded, even as the vines tighten around the captured arrow, constricting it. Artemis lowers her bow.

"Huh," she says. Then, turning to Kelpie: "How did you know?"

"Because this is the Up-and-Under, and it takes the help-kelp to travel between Earth and Water," says Kelpie. "The etiäinen downstairs, that was standing in for the Bumble Bear. You could argue your way out of the fight if you just said the right things and didn't look directly at the monster. Fairy-tale rules. I don't think it was something innocent before it was forced to become something terrible, but Asphodel was both Queens, and she made her monsters well." She looks down at her own bright orange hand, then balls it into a fist, nails biting into her palm. "Remarkably well."

"Well, at least we know no one came this way."

Kelpie turns to blink at her. Artemis waves her hand, indicating the floor, where only a few broken leaves mark the path of her arrow.

"If the vines had grabbed any of our people, there'd be a lot more mess. If they'd grabbed Roger, a lot more of them would be charred, and there would probably be a peach tree in here somewhere. Even Lily and Smita would have broken some vines before they went down. We know they left this room alone."

"We keep moving," says Kelpie.

"Yes," agrees Artemis.

They don't run up the next flight of stairs; they climb quickly and with purpose, and this time Artemis is the first to move toward the door, opening it to reveal the green room on the other side. "Now we know where the plants came from," she says. "That's a start."

"I don't know—oh, gods, Arty, look." Kelpie gestures, not stepping into the room, but her voice shakes as she indicates the bones tangled among the roots. "It ate them. This room *ate* them."

"Not our people," says Artemis firmly. "Those bones are old. It ate the alchemists who used to work here. Not anyone we care about."

Too late, she remembers that Kelpie may well have cared about these alchemists, may have called them her friends. But she's not Dodger; she can't take back her words once they've been spoken. They hang between them, free to do their damage, and she's relieved when Kelpie only turns her face away, not answering her.

After a few frozen seconds, Kelpie says, "We need to keep going up. We need to find them and get out of here before something terrible happens. To the people we *care* about."

"Kelpie, I didn't—"

But it's too late. The orange girl has turned and is heading back to the stairs. She's moving slower now than she was before, but still more briskly than she normally does, climbing to the next level without hesitating or looking back. Artemis follows, resisting the urge to draw her bow again, to ready herself to fight against an enemy she can't see and doesn't fully understand. She's a huntress, and more, she's an embodiment of a natural force of the universe. She doesn't have the freedom to act against what she was designed to be, not the way a true human would.

Because that's the thing that people like Asphodel and Lilianne always miss. She gets to be a goddess, yes, gets to run the forests and travel the sky above the Impossible City. She gets to be a part of something bigger than herself. But she never got to decide that she was going to do any of those things. She didn't even choose to occupy this body, the shell that once belonged to Annabelle Austin. That whole conversation was conducted between Anna and the moon, which was only the thinnest idea of Artemis while it was happening in the abstract. Once it was done, she manifested here, and now this is where she lives, and where she'll always live, until the day she's too slow or too careless and gets cut down, leaving her small fragment of the divine to return to the ruined hollows of Olympus and let Anna go on to whatever afterlife awaits her.

Most Lunars go to the Impossible City when they die, divinity and mortality remaining conjoined as both fragments enjoy their well-earned retirement. Given how much Anna has hated her on the few occasions when they've been forced to meet, she doesn't expect that to happen for her.

All she can do in the here and now is follow Kelpie, follow the woman she's come to love more than she would have believed possible after the amount of time she's spent running the moonlit roads alone, and hope that they're not racing toward their own destruction. The atmosphere in the lab was never comfortable; now, it's becoming oppressive, pushing down harder and harder against her skin, reminding her with every step that she was never meant to be here.

Asphodel only ever viewed the Lunars as useful tools, when she viewed them at all. There are old rumors about her being responsible for several deaths among their kind, long before her inheritors would figure out how to use the broken bodies of the Moon to build their grand designs in unbreakable concrete. She isn't a part of this plan, whatever that plan really is. Neither is Kelpie, or Judy, and that makes all three of them expendable—Kelpie maybe less than the other two, since she's at least a cuckoo, and that means she belongs to Asphodel on some level—and expendable things get discarded when their usefulness is spent.

Kelpie does at least hesitate when she reaches the next landing, looking over her shoulder at Artemis. There's a wild anxiety in her eyes, one that only intensifies as she turns and wrenches the door open, plunging through.

Artemis follows.

* * *

As she reminds the people around her on a painfully regular basis, Artemis is a hunter. She knows how to run and how to stalk, and she knows the smell of death. It permeates the forest, as omnipresent as the smell of life, but while the smell of life is green, bright, and growing, death is bruised purple-rot, thick and sludgy. Fresh blood is bright, torn between the two, but even that fades quickly into the decay of its inevitability.

The moment she steps into the space that was once the menagerie, the smell of death assaults her, so strong and immediate that it nearly eclipses the greater horror beneath it: the smell of life lingers here too. The space is alive. The ground turns soft beneath her feet, and she looks with revulsion down at the layer of skin and tissue covering the floor, tracing it up onto the walls and finally the ceiling.

Horror flooding her senses, she turns to Kelpie and asks, "What *is* this place?"

"The mosasaur," says Kelpie quietly. "The belly of the great beast that carries them from water into air, where they can make the passage into fire. We're moving through the layers of the Up-and-Under, and the story is laid out like a botanical walk. You have to go from one to the next, there's no reaching the ending if you don't. We started from the beginning and followed the opening chapters in the right order, and now we're in the middle of the story."

"Once you start things with 'once upon a time,' the only way out is through," says Artemis wearily.

"Yes," says Kelpie, nodding firmly.

"Is this a story or an alchemical working?"

Kelpie looks down for a moment, silent. Finally she says, in a soft voice, "We should keep moving. We need to find the others."

It's not an answer and it is an answer at the same time, and so Artemis counters with a comment of her own. "This is a hunt now. Follow me."

She leads Kelpie across the room of flesh, to a doorway like a sphincter leading deeper into the body of this impossible beast. The edges are red, irritated, and raw. She doesn't want to touch them. She knows, from the undefinable disturbance of the air, that their people went this way; there are no tracks, no trail to follow, but she is the goddess of the hunt, and she can see the signs of passage where no one else would.

So Artemis walks, and this time Kelpie is the one who follows, letting her open the way through the sphinctered door and into the tissues beyond. The next room is humid, the air rank with the smell coming off the impossible skin surrounding them, the temperature elevated by the unspeakable fluids, blood or otherwise, moving through the tissue. The sphincter closes behind them, sealing shut with a terrible squelching sound that makes Artemis's shoulders tense briefly. They are walking into the impossible unknown. There is no mercy to be expected here.

No mercy, but, as they continue onward, a hairclip, small

and copper-toned, the kind that come in packs of twelve. Artemis stoops, plucking it from the floor (which has, she notes with disgust, begun to pulse slightly; whatever terrible fluid keeps it suffused and moist, it is getting more plentiful, and stronger, something neither of them wants to consider much) and turning it over in her hand.

"This is Erin's," she says, after a moment of consideration. "She must have dropped it."

"How distracted would she have to be before she started dropping things?" asks Kelpie, anxiety painted loud across her words.

"She's the living force of Order. Losing your hairclips is disorderly. I'm going to say 'extremely,'" says Artemis. She tucks the clip into her pocket, finally re-drawing her bow and readying an arrow. She has no valid targets right now. That doesn't matter. She feels better with a bow in her hands, and if there's going to be some terrible danger lurking at the end of all this, she wants to be prepared to fight back. Even if it's only for a moment before they're all devoured by something much bigger than themselves.

Even if this is the end.

The thought is surprisingly grim, considering how much they've all been through. She's been here before, in the depths of this lab, and she survived: she not only survived, she came away with a lover and companion, someone to keep her endless nights from stretching on forever. They're not alone down here. It only feels that way, and even if they *were* alone, Kim and Tim are back at the house with David. Two unhatched cuckoos and a fully manifest Lunar aren't the best possible backup, but they're better than nothing.

Artemis just needs to keep telling herself that. If she can manage to halfway believe it, maybe the smell rolling off the walls won't make her throat so tight, and maybe the fear of something happening to Kelpie won't force her heart so high into her throat.

Maybe.

The second room is larger than the first, the shapes of the walls and equipment that used to be here obscured beneath the veil of skin that covers absolutely everything. It's been split in a few places, none of them particularly fresh, and red ropes of veins and lumpy muscular tissue bulge out of the slashes, wet and terrible. The smell is even worse here than it was before, and Artemis almost gags at the thought of how much worse it's going to get. There's a terrible moisture in the air, humid and heavy. Breathing feels almost like chewing.

Kelpie coughs, clearly struggling to keep herself from gagging on her own breath. She shoots Artemis a frantic, wide-eyed look, whites showing all the way around her irises. Her goat-slit pupils are narrowed, making them almost invisible.

"Hey, Kelp. Hey, baby. Breathe," says Artemis. "I get that you're freaking out right about now—I'm freaking about as bad—but you need to keep breathing. Please. If you pass out because you stopped, I'll have to carry you out of here. I can't carry you and aim my bow at the same time."

Kelpie visibly fights to calm herself, something that's hard to do when the air has become the enemy. She looks around, then back to Artemis.

"This was where they kept the live animals," she says. "Dogs and cats and pigs and monkeys and everything else."

"Does giving me a list help you feel better?"

"Yes. No. I don't know." Kelpie shrugs, looking momentarily helpless. "I know what should be here. I guess that makes it feel like I have to make sure you know, too, so everything that's lost won't be forgotten."

"What's lost is always forgotten, in the end," says Artemis, as gently as she can. "Would the animals we're not seeing have been enough to account for this much mass? If you added in the alchemists?"

"No," says Kelpie, with assurance. "This is—it's too much. Even if you liquified everything they kept in here, it wouldn't have been enough, and there's no channel to hydroponics, so whatever reaction caused this wouldn't have been able to obtain more r-raw materials." She stumbles at the end, apparently remembering that she's talking about her friends and colleagues, but recovers quickly.

"All right. Where does the next door lead?" Artemis swings her bow around so that her arrow points at another sphincter set into the wall, another hall presumably concealed beyond. "If we go that way, where do we end up?"

"The—the morgue," says Kelpie, voice small.

Artemis stares at her.

"Margaret always hated it when we called it that, said it was disrespectful to the human bodies we sometimes had down on the bottom floor, but the alchemists who worked up here said that all their subjects deserved to be remembered, and they didn't want to call it 'cold storage' like she wanted them to. So they put all the bodies in here once they were done running their tests, and supposedly the apprentices would take everything up to the surface every few months, but they never did. They just shoved it further and further back in the freezers, and counted on Margaret never coming in here to check."

"Was that enough to account for all this excess biomass?"

Reluctantly, Kelpie nods. "It could have been," she says.

"That's good. That means the lab hasn't somehow been sending runners out through the sewer and going *hunting*." Artemis shudders. "A place like this shouldn't hunt. It shouldn't be allowed."

"It's not just a straight line down here." Kelpie points to the other sphincter leading out of this room. "The personal labs are that way. I don't know what was kept there."

"Other than private spaces that we can hopefully ignore, what else are we likely to find here?"

"There's a dissection theater, and there's the cuckoo room, but it was shut down long before the man from the Congress came to tell us that we were being decommissioned—"

"Wait. Are you telling me that this is the level where they worked with Asphodel Baker's genetic material?"

"Well, yeah. Some people thought it was disrespectful to keep the samples on the same level as the animals, but Margaret overruled them. She said Asphodel was human and humans are the alchemical children of apes, and apes are animals, so it was only right for Asphodel's vital humors to be housed with the unevolved, at least until they were used to create cuckoos and could become human again."

"You know, it unnerves me when you recite the dogma with such ease."

Kelpie shrugs. "It unnerves me when you say that things I've always known are dogma. This is just something I've always known. That's all."

"How do we get to the cuckoo room?"

"It's on the other side of the morgue."

Artemis stares at her. It's easy to forget that this is the environment that shaped Kelpie's ways of looking at the world, of assessing the difference between "normal" and not. Even knowing that she's here with them—a kitten among the wolves, less dangerous and prepared than any of them except for maybe Lilianne and Smita—because this was once her natural environment doesn't make it any easier to remember that she grew up an alchemist among alchemists. Knowing it and internalizing it enough to keep it reliably in mind are two very different things.

"That's where we need to go," she says. "Can you get us there?"

"If the doors aren't locked." Kelpie gives the lumpy sphincter that has replaced the doorway a dubious look. "And if they're still doors."

"They're close enough for me. Let's go."

They start to move again, crossing the uneven floor to the

sphincter that will let them travel deeper into the lab. Kelpie pushes against it and it opens like an iris, showing a glimpse of an even-fleshier space, the skin there red and irritated, crisscrossed with bloody gashes. The air that rushes out, washing over them, is entirely free of decay. That would be a mercy, if not for what it *does* smell like: it smells like blood, nothing but blood, fresh and hot and terrible.

Kelpie seems to pay it no mind as she steps through the opening, Artemis close behind.

Here, there are signs that their friends, at least some of them, are close enough to find (alive if fortunate, still warm if not): the gashes in the floor still leak blood, unclotted, and someone has taken the time to try to cut a passage into one of the walls. They have clearly failed, and the skin around the room's other exit is bruised and battered, wounded by the drumming of hard hands and frantic feet.

There is no one here. But the bulky shapes of dissection tables loom out of the floor like fleshy mushrooms, their tops smoothed over with tightly drawn skin, their structures obscured. Kelpie moves to the middle of the room and looks up, at the dangling light structures likewise swallowed by the skin. It's the belly of the beast, and the final bruised sphincter illustrates that: all of them have looked like orifices inside some terrible, unthinkable creature, but this one is clamped tight, moist and unknowable, and it does not look inclined to yield.

"We have to keep going," says Kelpie, and it's half statement, half plea. She's begging to be told that she's wrong, and there's another way. She closes her eyes for a moment, then continues: "It wants us to keep going."

Artemis jerks in alarm. She hasn't seen or heard anything to indicate that this place is capable of *wanting* anything. "Kelpie . . . what do you mean?"

"I mean that whatever this place used to construct itself is still here, and it hurts, and it can tell it's almost done being forced to be whatever it is right now. In the stories, the travelers pick up the improbable road on the other side of the mosasaur, once they're on the shore again. They don't see another mosasaur until *Past the Pluvial Peaks*, and even then, it's not the same one. Once we're on the road, whatever that means, this whole thing can die."

"I don't like the idea that we're walking through something that can think," says Artemis.

Kelpie shrugs. "I don't like the idea that we're walking through an amalgamation of all my friends and the remains of every animal in this lab, but I'm here anyway," she says.

She turns and walks for the final sphincter, and Artemis follows, because there is nothing else to do.

* * *

In the final chamber, the animal nature of their surroundings is undeniable, painted in the wet moisture of the walls and floor, in the blood vessels as big around as adult human arms that spin their traceries across the ceiling. If they walked through skin and flesh before, now they stand in viscera, in the chambered space within the chest. They stand, no matter how they look at their situation, inside a nightmare.

A nightmare that has already claimed six people, all of them unconscious and seemingly unaware of their surroundings. Roger, Dodger, and Erin are webbed to the far wall by bonds of near-translucent skin, tied tight and held firm. Smita, Lilianne, and Judy are connected to the floor, red muscle tissue grown up around their feet and calves like terrible boots, holding them locked where they are. There is a half-grown peach tree about a foot away from Judy, close enough that she has collapsed halfway onto it, rather than to the ground. It holds her up, immature branches bending beneath the weight of her. Her eyes are closed; she does not move.

There is another figure here, wrought out of the same red, raw material as the walls, damp with mucus and internal fluids, almost invisible until it moves, turning toward the pair of them. It has a human face, flensed raw and bare of skin; when it smiles at Artemis and Kelpie, they can see every muscle and tendon pulling into place.

"My dears," it says, and it has a woman's voice, not only in timbre, but in pitch and intonation; it speaks like a kindly schoolteacher, like someone no one wants to disappoint. If Roger sounds like the platonic ideal of a college professor and Dodger sounds like a children's science educator, this figure sounds like a kindly woman in a patterned dress, the sort who exists mostly in memory and nostalgia-tinted stories for parents to recount around the dinner table. It speaks for a time that never was, an ideal that could never have been.

Artemis swings her bow around, taking aim at the center of the figure's chest. It continues smiling, lipless and terrible.

"We're all together now," it says. "A few of my children are missing, but enough of us are here. We can finally begin."

Dodger's eyes remain closed, but they move frantically behind her lids, the motion only obvious because the rest of her is so uncannily still. It's the first sign Artemis and Kelpie have had that their friends are in any way still aware of their surroundings. A muscle in her jaw twitches under the skin, sharp and staccato.

"Who are you?" asks Artemis, voice cold.

"I am the alkahest and the void," says the figure. "The alpha and the omega. The beginning and the end. I am the improbable road, and I am your doorway to the graveyard path."

"How did you take our friends?"

"As easily as a flower takes the petal," says the figure. "They were always mine. I only needed to remind them. The little Lunar isn't my property, but she comes close enough, and I pulled on the threads Avery had tangled inside of her to convince her to obey.

The rest were simple things. Their sympathies have always been mine to have and to hold."

Artemis is a hunter, but Kelpie, at her core, is a prey animal. When Artemis glances to her to see how she's taking this particular intro to a villain speech, she's standing so still that it barely looks like she's breathing. If not for the contrast between the vivid orange of her skin and the glistening red of the walls, she might well disappear, blending into the background through sheer force of will.

The flensed figure steps forward, and Artemis's stomach clenches, confronted with such an obvious sign of how *wrong* everything is here in this lab below the world, where the natural laws have somehow been warped and replaced with the outlines of the Up-and-Under, Asphodel Baker's wild reimagining of reality becoming manifest.

"You're not mine either, little Lunar, but you could be, if you stopped fighting and gave in to what I require," it says. "My son remade you in his own image. There are barriers in your flesh that have never been there for the others of your kind. I didn't tell him to take you. If it had been down to me, I would have set him stalking among the Hyades, to square this circle smoothly. But I was already gone by the time he came to court and claim you, and I had no way of telling him what to do."

"What do you mean, 'already gone'?"

"I've been traveling the graveyard path since my departure, and it's shown me so many things I didn't think I would ever have the luxury of knowing," says the figure. "It's taught me what I did right, and what I did wrong, and now that I understand it all, I can finally continue. Great sages have always died for wisdom. I have nothing of the god on the tree to claim as my own, but my father knew him once, and he was able to show me the path to descend and then return. They used to call it a katabasis, before they knew the name of the graveyard path. So many things are redefined when you name them, even if they remain otherwise entirely the same."

There's no more denying what—or who—this figure has to be, and still Artemis swallows the name, refusing to give voice to what she now fears more deeply than ever before. It's Kelpie, prey animal that she is, who overcomes her terror and steps forward, hooves muted against the flesh-covered floor, to look up at the skinless, raw-meat figure of their apotheosis come at long, terrible last.

"Hello, Asphodel," she says, and the word is spoken, the story is told: there is no longer any changing what comes next.

Death

TIMELINE: SEPTEMBER 5, 1896.

Miss Cottingsly is dying.

There's almost certainly another word for the process when entropy comes at last to consume an auf, making a victim of someone who has already been victimized by nature itself, winding down the artificial clock of the pulse and pulling the lightning from the lungs, but Asphodel doesn't know that other word. She only knows that Miss Cottingsly has been her companion longer than anyone else, that she never gave Asphodel away to an unfamiliar uncle or demanded she change her name for something more alchemically acceptable. Her memories aren't so rose-tinted as to paint Miss Cottingsly as her only ally, but in some ways, she feels the old auf is the only person who's always cared for her as herself, not as a useful tool or an alchemical potential. And now she's coming to pieces under Asphodel's hands, the immutable bonds that formed her fracturing and falling away.

And there's nothing Asphodel can do.

Eliza is still thriving. She talks and grows and changes and learns just like an ordinary little girl with no lightning in her heart or borrowed blood running in her veins. If Asphodel hadn't been there when it happened, she would swear the child had never been resurrected, that Eliza was perfectly natural in every way.

The nature of her resurrection makes her an auf, a useful tool with little free will of her own. The nature of her existence makes her something entirely new. In a world of scholarship, Eliza is her own field of study, her own specialization. Asphodel supposes the Congress was right about one thing: every mother, back to the beginning of humanity, must have felt in some way like an alchemist when they called life out of the void, when they walked the border of death and snatched a new soul from its cold hands. She didn't carry Eliza with her own body, but she may as well have done.

Eliza looks at her as she imagines normal little girls must look at their mothers, with love and trust and unearned faith that Asphodel can change the world in whatever way she needs it to be changed. And while Asphodel is more than willing to try for Eliza's sake, she finds that she still prefers to change the world to suit her own desires; she's more interested than ever in putting forth a version of the world that meets her needs.

And any world that meets her needs must by necessity have Miss Cottingsly in it. She supposes she came to love the old auf at some point in their relationship, imprinting on her as a cygnet swan may imprint upon a chicken. They're different in every way that matters, but Asphodel was a child in need of love, and Miss Cottingsly was a constant: sometimes that can be enough.

Her uncle could still find them if he wanted to. They haven't traveled so far from Boston as would be wise, but have returned to the village of Asphodel's earliest childhood, to the dilapidated house that was once her mother's. The villagers eye her with suspicion unallayed by the fact that some of them remember her—not so many as she would have expected. She's forgotten, during the long, safe city years, how dangerous it can be in the wild country. Father Clemence is more than ten years gone, stolen away by a fever, and a young priest who doesn't know her either by name or by history occupies his house. She will never walk those halls again.

She came here to decide what she's going to do next, now that the Congress has rejected her, now that she'll have to find a future for herself, rather than allowing them to hand her one. With every day that passes, Miss Cottingsly fades, Eliza thrives, and Asphodel becomes more determined to show those bastards in the Congress the error of their ways. She *will* be the greatest alchemist this world has ever known. She will earn and honor the storm inside her, and she will change reality to suit herself.

The American Alchemical Congress has made a terrible mistake in rejecting her. It wasn't their first, and it won't be their last, but it is the mistake that makes everything that is to follow entirely inevitable. Their deaths, when they come (in the far, far future, at the hands of a man she has not yet constructed, but is drawing ever closer to creating), will be entirely due to how they've treated her. They may never understand. It won't matter. They'll die either way.

It is late afternoon, the sunlight through the windows buttery gold even after passing through the dust that chokes the glass. (Miss Cottingsly would normally have scrubbed them clean within an hour of arriving in the house, but her decline began almost immediately after leaving Boston. Asphodel almost turned back when she realized what was happening; only Miss Cottingsly insisting that going back to her uncle would do nothing to change what was happening to her kept them moving forward, away from the Congress, seeking safety. The house is still a wreck. Asphodel has no skill at house-cleaning, and Eliza is too young and too recently returned from the dead to have the knack.) Eliza is somewhere out in the fields behind the house, running wild through them even as Asphodel once did. Miss Cottingsly is resting in the single narrow bed, not seeming to mind the dust or the smell of mouse droppings.

"There must be something I can do," says Asphodel.

"There isn't."

"But there is. There always is. I can . . . I can go hunting for the current incarnate Winter. The seasons don't die, they cycle. They come back again."

"You can't steal me a seasonal crown, and I wouldn't wear it if you could. I've been dead longer than you can imagine, sparrow, and I'm ready to rest. I'm ready to see my families again."

Asphodel pauses. "Miss Cottingsly . . . do you remember who you were?"

"Not as complete pictures. I'm more like . . . like a patchwork quilt, bits and pieces sewn together, remembering the colors of the whole they once belonged to. I remember three distinct wedding days, to three different men. I remember the births of what I believe were all my children. I remember two of my deaths. And I remember other things, little scraps of all those women. They would never have been friends, when they were alive. They had different religions, different ideas about the world . . . but they learned unity, when they woke up and they were me. They're fading away now, one by one, like candles blowing out in the night. Soon they'll all be finished, and I can rest."

"I don't want you to go!"

"Oh, sparrow, we all have to go in our time. Some of us get a chance to come back, in one way or another. I did. I've lived more than any ten women could wish for, and I've seen things change in ways a hundred women couldn't even begin to dream. I've seen you come, and you're going to remake the world. I know you are. Maybe what you make will be kinder. Maybe it will be crueler. Either way, the men who make monsters like me will burn, and that's all I can really hope for."

"Why— Was my uncle doing something special to sustain you that you never told me about? Do you need a new heart? New lungs? Human blood? Gods'-blood?" Asphodel hasn't summoned a god since Phaesyle. She knows enough of divinity to fear the wrath of Dionysus should she ever remind the pantheon that she exists. Her father may have been enough to buy her a single indulgence, but that mercy won't extend to a second sacrifice.

And she doesn't care. If Miss Cottingsly says a sacrifice will sustain her, Asphodel will lure any god her companion chooses down from the heavens and slit their throat with a smile. She'll do anything to stop the inevitable from unfolding.

"It's not so simple, child," says Miss Cottingsly.

"So *make* it simple," snaps Asphodel. "I've created life itself! I've reshaped the world according to my own desires. I can keep you here with me."

"It's the life you've created that's allowing me to die."

Asphodel freezes, feeling her heart go cold. "What?"

"I lied to you when I told you all my grandchildren were already gone. Eliza—the one who lived before the grave—was my last grandchild. Surely you guessed we were connected in some way when I led you directly to her body. I already knew that losing her would let me go. The sympathies have been snapped. Her father is dead. Her mother's blood is none of mine—I would have called her a daughter had I lived to see their wedding, and maybe that would have been enough, but I was dead and gone before they even met. I never knew her, and so she couldn't feed into the universal affection it takes to stabilize the ordinary dead in this world."

"Why did you . . . ?"

Miss Cottingsly turns her face toward Asphodel, and there is a kindness to her expression that violates a hundred years of common wisdom regarding the auf. Even with the sympathies broken, she looks at Asphodel like she cares about her.

"You needed a fresh body, and you needed something to strive for," she says. "I could offer you both, and I've seen the storm raging in your heart. I already knew some of what you would be capable of. I may never have known the girl in life, but I still cared for her in death, and you were her best chance at coming back."

"You drained her veins yourself. You pushed the blood from her body."

"I did. It was necessary for the resurrection to succeed. You made something new, Asphodel. You *created* life. You didn't just write about it. Your quill was dry when you set it to the paper, and still, you scribed a symphony. Let the rest of them play. Those inkpot gods are going to regret shunning you."

"I still don't understand what I did."

"You bled, Asphodel. The lightning in the storm and the lightning inside you came together, and like a cuckoo laying its egg in a cowbird's nest, you made something new. Eliza is gone. The girl who lives inside her skin now has no memory of her. But that doesn't make your achievement any less brilliant."

"If I'd managed to bring her back as an ordinary auf, could you stay?"

Miss Cottingsly sighs. "I know you too well, sparrow. Killing the girl won't restore Eliza's sympathy, and even if it did, I've lasted this long because of the living. An ordinary auf wouldn't be able to anchor me here. Let go. Fly free, and be brilliant—and don't offer to kill gods for anyone else. You did it for the Congress. That was a time too many."

Asphodel glances away, and doesn't mention Deborah, little moon goddess bleeding silver and scarlet beneath the stairs. Lunars are barely gods, anyway. They've traded away most of their divinity in their endless bid to remain manifest in a world that's rapidly outgrowing them. Lunars don't count. No more than the seasons do.

"The girl is all you have now," says Miss Cottingsly. "She's your first cuckoo. Watch her, study her, understand her—and for the love of the art, don't lose her. Do you know where she is now?"

Normally, Asphodel would see the trap in Miss Cottingsly's question. But right now, she's exhausted and she's grieving—not just the impending loss of her companion, but the loss of the life she had planned for herself for most of her life. She'll still be an alchemist, but she won't be a Congressional alchemist. She'll have to forge her own path, unsupported and alone.

She's been unsupported before. She's been alone. She killed a goddess with no one beside her but an auf, she brought back the rain, and she can do this. She *can*.

Asphodel rises. "I'll go find her," she says. "Rest. We'll talk more when I return."

Miss Cottingsly nods approvingly, but doesn't say anything, only watches as Asphodel walks away, plucking her shawl from the chair beside the door as she makes her exit.

Once she's alone, the old auf closes her eyes. "It's time to fly, sparrow," she says. "It's time to burn everything those terrible men have done to ash and dust, and see it scattered before you."

Then she sighs, one final time, and exhales.

She doesn't breathe in again.

* * *

Asphodel steps into the sunlight, blinking rapidly as she waits for her eyes to adjust. The air is crisp and chill, September's weather all too aware of its position in the hierarchy of the year. Winter will be here soon enough, and her memory of the winters of her early childhood, while fuzzy, tells her it will be even more brutal than the snows that fall in Boston. Without the brick walls and gas heaters to break the back of the cold, the winds are free to rage, the snows to sear.

She hasn't heard anything about a coronation since she served her young lover up like a lamb for the slaughter. The old Winter King still sits astride the throne, and he's unlikely to hold her killing of a potential heir against her. Given the way in which the seasons keep their house, he may honestly have seen it as a favor, something done to court his good graces. He's unlikely to target her for special torments just because she baited the trap.

Still, Eliza has very little experience with anything. She remembers speech and some of her letters, can move and play and curtsey as prettily as any child, but she remembers nothing of her life before the lightning. She's a blank slate waiting to be scribed, and she'll be a perfect canvas for what Asphodel intends.

Or will she? Asphodel herself illustrates the problem Eliza will face: the world is still balanced against the feminine sex, is still inclined to see them as lesser due to the accident of their birth. Eliza will make a poor apprentice-heir, because the doors that are closed against Asphodel will also be closed against her.

If Asphodel wishes to plan for the future, she'll need to make herself a more-fitting avatar, a man with the same cuckoo's nest inside his soul, who can carry her alchemy into the bright and distant world to come. She walks around the house, consumed with thoughts of everything he'll need to be, everything he'll need to do in her service.

His body won't be assembled for another month, pieced together from what corpses she can cobble, what slivers she can steal, but in many ways, this is the moment when James Reed is born: he will be her first intentional cuckoo, her first studied creation, and he will be the one to show the Alchemical Congress the scope and severity of their errors. One day.

Not this day. On this day, Asphodel hurries around the house and out into the meadow, where she sees Eliza in the distance, standing at the edge of the open space, in the tangled shadows of the trees. The child has a stick in her hand, and is using it to prod at something unseen. Asphodel heads unhesitatingly toward her, gathering her skirt in her hands to keep herself from treading on the hem.

As she draws closer, she sees what the girl has found: a rabbit, its neck clearly broken and its gut ripped open, stirred up by some predator's claws. Eliza is poking her stick into the remains, watching the flesh and organs move around it, a look of intense focus on her face.

"Eliza," says Asphodel.

The child raises her head and slowly blinks, catlike. There is no guilt or confusion in her expression: her knowledge of good and evil have been lost along with everything else, and she has no cause to question what she's doing. Not until Asphodel teaches her she should.

Asphodel intends no such thing.

"What do you have there?"

"A rabbit."

"Did you see what killed it?"

"A hawk."

"Some of the organs are missing. Would you like to know the names of what's still there?"

Eliza nods.

Asphodel reaches for her stick. "May I?"

After only a moment of hesitation, Eliza gives it to her, and Asphodel begins using it to indicate the organs remaining inside the bodily cavity, laying a name to each of them. Eliza listens intently, as a normal child might listen to a bedtime story. When Asphodel finishes, Eliza reaches out a hand, silently requesting the return of her stick. Asphodel gives it to her, and watches as Eliza begins to indicate and name the organs, following Asphodel's lead.

She doesn't get a single scrap wrong. When she's done, she looks to Asphodel for approval.

I can do this, thinks Asphodel. *I can raise up a full intrusion of cuckoos and set them on the Congress, and they'll regret that they ever turned me away. I can make their world my own.*

"Very well done, Eliza," she says. "I think you've earned an extra serving at supper tonight, don't you? You're a growing girl."

"Can we eat the rabbit?"

"No," says Asphodel. "It's been dead on the ground long enough to cool, and we've stirred its guts up with a filthy, filthy stick. I can set some snares tomorrow, and we'll have rabbit for our supper later in the week, but this one, I think we leave to the forest as a thanks for giving us such good shelter."

Eliza considers her words, then nods gravely and tosses the stick aside before reaching out for Asphodel's hand.

Asphodel allows it, twining her fingers with the girl's own, and they walk side by side through the field behind the house where Asphodel was born, together as she was never able to be with her own mother, silent in their respective thoughts.

The first sign that something is wrong comes when Asphodel opens the door to the house and is met with a silence so profound that she can't pretend there's anyone else there. The comforting presence that even an auf can generate is gone, replaced by stillness. Letting go of Eliza's hand, she walks alone to the bed where Miss Cottingsly has been declining, holding her breath and her tongue alike as she waits to see what she'll discover.

When she steps around the end of the bed and sees what awaits her there, a small sound escapes her lips, even as tears cloud her eyes. She claps a hand over her mouth, simply staring.

"Del? What is it?" asks Eliza.

Working hard against instinct, etiquette, and grief, Asphodel forces her hand down. "Miss Cottingsly has gone," she says.

"Oh. Will she be back soon?"

"I don't . . . I don't believe so," says Asphodel. The remains in the bed are not those of a singular woman, but a horrific patchwork of five different women in varying stages of decay, mixed with pieces of animals, stitched together with a practiced hand. She didn't know auf reverted to their component pieces when they died. Presumably, that was one of the secrets she would have learned in the last two years of her apprenticeship, the things that would have grounded her in her art and granted her the title of alchemist in the eyes of the Congress.

Miss Cottingsly, the woman and the working, is no longer with them. What she's left behind is what's unneeded, ready for disposal.

"Oh. What are we going to do now?"

The question gives her a moment of pause. Asphodel raises her head, looking at Eliza, and slowly, terribly, she smiles.

"Whatever we decide," she says. "But first, fetch me a shovel from the shed. It seems I've something to dispose of."

"I have something better than Earth," said Jack, and reached into his chest like a man reaches into a cupboard, his arm sinking through flesh and bone to vanish into the very substance of his self. When he pulled it out again, he was holding a bird in his hand. Not a jackdaw or a crow, either of which might have been expected, but a black-and-white bird whose feathers gleamed oddly blue in the light. It cocked its head, looking around itself with bright, keen eyes.

"I stole this from my mother's cages before we fled her kingdom," he said. "She's never been a part of anyone before, but she would be glad to have a flock. She told me so, while she slept in the aviary of my heart. If Zib hasn't traveled too far down the graveyard path by now, we might be able to call her back."

"Just get her back," commanded Avery.

Fern hooted in distress, still prisoned in the cage where the Page of Frozen Waters had sealed her. The King of Cups moved toward her, reaching for the bars with his newly youthened hands. Fern shied away, hooting again, even as Jack bent toward Zib, the bird still firmly in his hand.

"Getting her back won't free her, you know," he said, with one last glance at Avery. "She's a burning girl now, and she'll be a Magpie if this works, and either way, she'll be a creature of the Up-and-Under always and ever more. When you go home from here, you'll go on alone, and all of this will be a strange story you'll tell to your children someday, in the far-off country where you have them for your own."

"No," protested Avery. "I can't go back without her. I can't—she lives on my street! If I go back without her, they'll know something bad happened!"

"Were you friends, then, before the wall?" asked Jack, as he leaned closer still to Zib's unmoving shape, as he slipped the bird in his hand into her breast, letting it roost and settle there. "Did you play in the fields together, build snowmen, while away your hours?"

"We met at the wall," said Avery dully.

"Then the Up-and-Under brought you together, because it needed one of you to learn a lesson, and one of you to *be* a lesson. It seems the roles are set." Jack stepped back, away from Zib, straightening as he went. "I would have done it the other way around, if anyone had asked me. Let *her* carry the truth of what we are and what we serve back to your America. Let you walk the graveyard path and stay forever down among the dead and the drowned."

Zib took a great, shuddering breath and rolled onto her side, hacking and coughing like her lungs were preparing to burst. Avery cried out, a low, wordless sound, and moved to steady her. She turned her face away from him, and when this tilted her eyes toward Soleil, she screwed them shut, denying the sight of any of them.

"No," she said. "I didn't mean it. No, no, no." And between each word she spat out either a cinder or a feather, a burning thing or a tiny slice of sky.

"Drowning is hard," said Niamh, walking over and reaching down to guide her off the ground. "Drowning without water is harder."

Zib let herself be lifted. "No," she said again.

"You made the choice, Hepzibah. You could have chosen to let the light in the tower blow out in exchange for your own candled heart, but you chose the Queen. You chose the regent who will see us all protected over the one who would see us washed away."

The remade King of Cups looked briefly ashamed at that, and said nothing, only produced a key from inside his shirt and bent over the lock of Fern's cage.

"Choices have consequences, and they can't always be taken back."

"I didn't know," said Zib.

"But you did. Even if not all of you knew, part of you did, because part of you told the rest of you what to do. You listened when it spoke. You chose, Zib, and now you get to see what happens next."

"What do you . . ."

"Look for the path. It's waiting for you."

Zib frowned at Niamh, then turned around, squinting at the grass around them. The door to Fern's cage was swinging open, and the great blue owl was stepping out, shaking the fear from her feathers like dust, or ashes.

And Zib saw the path.

If the improbable road was a rainbow ribbon, this was its dark twin, a twining twist of black-and-gray iridescence stretched across the landscape. Upon seeing it, she could think of nothing she wanted more in all the world than to walk it, to see where it would take her if she followed to its dim and distant end. She took a step forward, and then another, and then another after that, and the others watched her go, Jack moving to hold Avery back so he couldn't grab her arm, couldn't stop her.

The graveyard path beckoned, and Zib, finally able

to see it for what it was, to understand its sweet allure, went willingly. It gleamed in the fading sunlight, and she stepped up onto it, onto the dark beauty of the road that called the dead, and she faded from the view of the living, disappearing into the space where only the dead can go.

Niamh, who was still a drowned girl, even if the graveyard path was no longer open for her, watched in silence, and if some of the moisture running down her ever-damp cheeks was from tears and not the memory of the sunken city where her heart belonged, who would ever know? Who would ever tell.

Zib walked away, into darkness. . . .

—From *Under the Smokestrewn Sky*,
by A. Deborah Baker

BOOK VI

Antimony

When you go, take your nettles and flowers.
When you go, take the girl with no voice.
When you go, take your long hair and your tower.
You are going; you say it's your choice.
As you go,
I'll be watching and waiting.
As you go,
You'll be walking alone.
As you go, there's a tale they're relating.
You are leaving the stories you have known.
—Dr. Mary Crowell, "When You Go"

This night, stay home
Don't go out alone there's
Blood on the Moon and the river is running with
Sweet sweet wine.
Stay put—don't stir

Gods' sakes don't run out after her
Blood on the Moon and the sky is ringing.

Sacred this night (the gods are hunting)
Sacred this rite (they are not always kind)
Sacred this fever (blood on the Moon and the sky is
ringing)
Burns on forever! Bacchanal!

—Talis Kimberley, "Bacchante"

Freedom

TIMELINE: AUGUST 23, 2018.

Hello, Asphodel," says Kelpie, and Artemis stumbles where she stands, balance shocked away by the simple truth of her companion's words. This figure—this construct—this flensed horror out of nightmare is Asphodel Baker, long dead and buried, yet somehow here returned.

"You're dead," says Artemis, and her lips are numb, the words lightly slurred by the effort of forming them.

"I was," says Asphodel. "As I told you, I've been walking along the graveyard path. I would have returned sooner, but Dionysus wanted to have words with me over a friend of his, who I'd treated poorly but with the best of intentions. I understand his anger. I still say I did only what I had to do."

"Why have you restrained our friends?"

"Your friends? Why, little moon, they were mine long before they were yours, and they'll remain mine long after you've waned and been forgotten. All cuckoos belong to me. They were born of me, and they'll return to me when they're unmade. I've taken only what's mine to have."

"They're not all cuckoos. I'm not a cuckoo."

"No," allows Asphodel. "But the alchemist is mine, by teaching, and the reborn girl is mine, by proximity. She stinks of failed experiments and rewritten methodologies. A layer of wax covers her flesh in every way of seeing without the eye, marking the number of times she's been used to make a Hand of Glory. They aren't bone of my bone as the cuckoos are, but they're mine all the same."

"And Chang'e?"

"Allows my Jack, my beautiful Jackdaw, to wander the labyrinthine corridors of her mind and take what he pleases. He rewrites her at her own request, and she shines, immortal and shackled in her own impossible way. They're all mine to claim. They all belong to me. *You* belong to me, because of what my boy did to your mind. He stopped up the very passage between mortal blood and moonlight, and made of you something closer to the old gods than the diminished Lunar creatures of my time, much less of *this* time. Everything here is mine to have and use as I desire."

Asphodel moves closer. Her feet never fully leave the floor; when she lifts them, red threads of viscera and tissue connect her to the greater mound of flesh surrounding them. Artemis thinks she can see the answer in that connection: if they break Asphodel's connection to the lab, they may break whatever terrible power she's using to control their friends.

Dodger, at least, is aware of her surroundings. If she could open her eyes or speak, she would. The fact that she doesn't means she can't, which means she's being suppressed somehow, forced down below the surface of herself.

"It's all about sympathy," says Asphodel. "That's the *real* magic in this world. Not divinity, or blood, or any of the other things people try to pin power to. Sympathy is what connects us, what keeps us from unraveling into the void. I walked the graveyard path for decades. My Up-and-Under was enough to anchor me there, until dear James began to succeed with his own experiments, began to birth new cuckoos into the world. Their sympathy gave me an immediate tether back to where they stood, and as their number grew, that tether got stronger. Even losing

James wasn't enough to sever it through. Other alchemists began mirroring his work, using what I'd left behind to craft their own cuckoos—but they were always mine. Every cuckoo is mine, no matter who has the making of them, because they carry my storm within them."

"You just said it wasn't about blood," says Kelpie. She steps forward, closer to Artemis, so that their shoulders almost touch, but not close enough to interfere when Artemis decides to draw her bow. "How can it be about the sympathy with you when it isn't about blood?"

"Because it's not blood. It's lightning," says Asphodel. "I was born of a storm, nestled in the womb of a woman who had never known the touch of a mortal man, and every cuckoo carries my lightning inside them, a fragment of a segment of a storm bound inside their bones. They belong to me."

"You'd belong to him, if he cared to claim you," says Artemis, voice going sharp. "I'm an Olympian. I know what it means to serve a storm. You're toying with dangerous forces, alchemist. You're not going to have the ending you're aiming for."

"Maybe. Maybe not." Asphodel continues moving closer. "But I'm here now, and I'll have an ending, and that will be enough. I can see that you won't yield to me. That doesn't matter much. You have something of mine." She snaps her skinless fingers and Kelpie crumples, collapsing to the wet, sticky floor without making any effort to catch herself. She lands in a tangle of limbs, hair fanned wide, one hoof twisted beneath her body at a painful angle.

"Kelpie!" cries Artemis, lowering her bow as she moves to kneel by her companion.

"I don't understand why they wasted the lightning to make her," says Asphodel, turning back toward the others. "An artificial moon, I can see the purpose, but to embody the *hind*? To make a form with elements of human and deer intermingled, so that it can never walk normally in the world? It's a waste of resources and of power. I've no further use for her."

She waves her hand, and Kelpie begins sinking into the floor, the flesh dragging her down inch by inch, opening around her limbs and, as she settles into the space this creates, closing again around her. Artemis gasps in horror and drops to her knees, trying to yank Kelpie free.

"You can't *have* her!" she wails, as the floor fights back and drags Kelpie ever more steadily down.

"I already do," says Asphodel. She continues onward until she stands in front of Judy, Lilianne, and Smita—the three she has the loosest claim over. Leaning forward and reaching out with skinless fingers, she caresses Judy's cheek.

"Yes," she says. "I think this will do."

And the skin begins to slide from Judy's face onto her hand, leaving raw, gleaming muscle behind. There is no blood. If there's any mercy in this, it's that there is no blood. But when her eyelid slides away, Artemis can see her eye rolling frantically. Like Dodger, Judy is awake.

And Kelpie is still sinking. Artemis has other things to worry about. Frantic, she reaches foe her belt and draws the knife she always keeps there, only hesitating for a moment before she drives it into the floor all the way to the hilt and begins to cut.

Blood wells up where she slashes through the flesh, hot and steaming and turning everything around her into a sticky mess in seconds. Judy's stolen skin slithers around Asphodel, wrapping around her own exposed muscles and concealing them. She doesn't look back at Artemis or the still-sinking Kelpie, only continues to allow the skin to cover her, one terrible inch at a time.

"You've lost, little moon," she taunts. "This was never a fair fight. My alchemists brought together everything I needed, built me the perfect cocoon and left the sympathies to resonate until they were enough to call me out of the Up-and-Under and back into the world. All I had to do was wait. I'll take what's been embodied for my use, and then I'll take the City, and no one will stop me."

"What do you mean?" snaps Artemis.

"I mean, a natural incarnation is deep and rooted in the bones of the person who carries it. But a cuckoo? Stop the storm, sever the strand. Snatch the strand, braid it into your own sympathies, and continue on. I just needed to wait until all the tools I was going to need had been prepared."

Asphodel pulls her hand away from the now-flensed Judy, turning her stolen face back toward Artemis and Kelpie. She smiles, lips pulling back from straight white teeth, and she could be any woman walking naked down the street, she could be an ordinary person and not a nightmare brought back from the dead by some implacable working set in motion more than a century ago. She could be anyone.

She is Asphodel Baker, and she is beautiful, and she is terrible, and she keeps smiling as she hooks her finger toward Kelpie, who cries out—the sound practically a bleat, more animal than human—and sinks fully into the hole that surrounds her, going entirely limp. Artemis fumbles for her wrist, checking her pulse, then picks up her bow and stands, turning to aim an arrow at Asphodel's chest.

"You can do that, if you think it might do you any good," says Asphodel, with evident disinterest. "Can you kill a dead woman with an arrow made of moonlight? It sounds like something out of a story, and I'm more story than scholar right now: it might fell me. But it might not, and in the time it takes to draw, your friends will die. You can kill me, or you can save them. Choose."

Roger, Dodger, and Erin are limp in their cocoons of meat and sinew; Lilianne and Smita are still unconscious; Judy hasn't made a sound, but her uncovered eyes are wild and staring, while tears leak from the corners and run down her naked cheeks. Artemis lowers her bow.

"Good choice, little moon," says Asphodel. "Now, if you don't mind, I have business beyond the Up-and-Under. Shine as you like, but shine not on the City. That passage has been closed."

She walks away then, and when she reaches the flesh-sealed portal out of the room, it opens for her, allowing her to pass through into whatever waits beyond.

Courage

TIMELINE: AUGUST 23, 2018.

Judy, can you hear me?" Artemis rushes to the other Lunar, dropping her bow on the fleshy floor. Judy makes a terrible, guttural sound deep in her throat, and Artemis knows the screaming will come next: if she's recovered enough to react, she must be in pain. "Drop down. Descend, and let Chang'e come forth."

Judy can't blink, but her eyes roll back in her head as a peach-colored glitter begins to consume the air around her, filling it with a divine brightness. She sags, then straightens, turning her face to Artemis. Her eyes, now peachy-gold, roll back into their normal position, and she looks at Artemis, gaze clear and steady.

"Can you finish your peach tree?"

"Why?" croaks Chang'e, the word rendered odd by her lack of lips.

"The peaches heal. They restore. They grant us immortality, for a time. Judy needs one now, or she's going to die of the shock as soon as you let her come back to the surface. This version of you will die, and every other version of you will have to contend with the Doctrine of Ethos realizing that you couldn't save the woman he loved. Please."

Chang'e nods. "Good enough," she says, and lays a skinless palm flat against the trunk of the half-grown tree. It shudders and straightens, growing rapidly toward maturity. Its limbs put out branches, which put out flowers that swell and ripen into fruit.

Chang'e plucks the ripest peach within reach and brings it to her mouth, biting delicately down. With each nibble, a bit more of Judy's skin regrows, thin as rice paper and equally as fragile, and Chang'e continues to bite and swallow, consuming the peach a fragment at a time.

Artemis grabs another of the peaches and whirls, dropping to her knees beside Kelpie. She presses the peach to Kelpie's mouth with one hand and recovers her knife with the other, cutting the flesh, which is no longer actively growing, away. Kelpie takes a bite of the peach, automatically, and chews, swallowing before she opens her eyes.

When she does, she squeaks and scrambles to her hooves, unsteady as she rarely is. "Asphodel!" she gasps. "She's going to— She can— Where is she?"

"Gone," says Artemis grimly. "Are you all right?"

"My head hurts, and it feels like there's a hollow where something's meant to be, but I think I'm okay," says Kelpie. "Where did she go?"

"The Impossible City, I assume," says Artemis. She moves back to Chang'e and the two human women, kneeling to begin cutting their feet free of the floor. Smita and Lilianne remain sprawled insensate on the floor. "It's a big place. I don't know how much damage she can do there."

"So let's not find out," says Kelpie.

Chang'e's skin is mostly back where it belongs, if still thin and half-translucent. It looks less like rice paper and more like she's stitched an entire human skin out of peach-blossom petals, impossibly delicate, impossibly easy to destroy. She takes another dainty bite of peach, then exhales, slowly. "They were walking deeper into this mess of a maze when the walls attacked. They threw out strands of flesh and nothing could be done about it. Roger commanded them to stop; they disobeyed. Erin tried to weave between the ropes, and they continued to reach for her. In very little time, they were all caught, and then the floor split open and Asphodel emerged." She sighs. "What an unpleasant woman. We were better served when she was dead."

"None of us authorized her coming back," says Artemis.

"But she did." Chang'e looks at her. "I am not safe here. Neither are you." The glitter fades out of the air around her, and Judy staggers. The transition is rarely so clear.

"We need to get the others down," says Artemis, and turns away from her. This isn't the time for hysterics, and Judy just had her skin stolen and regrown. She's earned a few.

If Judy wants to break down as badly as Artemis suspects she does, she doesn't allow herself the pleasure. Instead, she brushes past Artemis, heading for the wall, where she leans up and begins yanking on the sheets of skin holding Roger in place. Her own skin splits with every yank, too fragile for this sort of treatment. Artemis is there a moment later, cutting him free, and Judy catches him before he can fall. He sags against her, but there's tension in him: he's awake, just oddly limp, wrung-out and weakened.

"Judy?" he asks. "Where are we? Where's my sister?"

"We're still in the lab. And she's right behind you. Artemis is helping her down," says Judy. "It's all right, Roger. We're all here."

"No," he says. "I don't think we are."

Artemis cuts the others down. Erin falls without a sound. Artemis is able to catch Dodger, if only barely, and lets go of the gawky redhead when she pushes her away, allowing Dodger to huddle against the wall.

All of them look terribly traumatized, like they've just been subjected to something beyond imagining. Lilianne and Smita are still unconscious. Erin lifts Smita, while Judy and Artemis together hoist Lilianne, holding her under the arms.

"We have to get out of here," says Erin, looking around them. The flesh on the walls is starting to sag, softening and dripping down like candle wax. "I don't like the way this looks."

"Neither do I," says Artemis. "Come on."

She leads them back the way they came, moving as fast as she can while not outpacing the others. Kelpie is still walking unsteadily, like she doesn't quite understand her own legs, while Erin is burdened with Smita. Judy is doing an admirable job of keeping up with Artemis despite her strained and splitting skin, although part of that may be being pulled along by their shared custody of Lilianne.

Nothing rises up to stop them as they flee the fleshy chambers for the stairwell. There, they're faced with a new horror: cracks are forming in the walls, spreading rapidly.

"Do we go up?" demands Judy.

"We'll never make it," says Kelpie.

"We go down," says Artemis, and tries to sound like she means it. Dodger still hasn't spoken; Roger is moving with quick efficiency, but he seems closed down, sucked into himself like he's barely aware of his surroundings. No one argues with her, and so, together, they descend.

The cracks get wider as they go deeper, and Kelpie almost falls several times, barely catching herself on the rail. Artemis is so busy focusing on her that she almost drops Lilianne. Then they're on the lowest floor, and she turns to Kelpie. "We need to get out of here," she says. "Take us to the back door."

"What back door?"

"The one Smita and Lilianne used to get in here in the first place."

"The little Lunar doesn't know the way," says a sibilant voice from the shadows. Artemis jerks around, and watches as the etiäinen slips out of the shadows. It's wearing Dodger's face, red-and-white hair a shock against the gray walls of the lab. "I remember her from when she served here. She was never meant to go outside. They didn't tell her how."

"We have to get out of here," says Artemis.

"Yes," says the etiäinen, unblinking as a snake as it stares at their little cluster. "You have to go, or else you'll die here."

"Which way?" demands Artemis.

"Why do I care if you die here?" counters the etiäinen. "I can't leave this lab or I'd already be free. I'm going to die. No matter what becomes of you, I'm going to die. But her . . ." It turns slowly to look at Smita, hanging limp in Erin's arms. "She helped me before. She had no cause to, but she helped me all the same. For her, I'll show you the way out."

"Thank y—" begins Artemis.

"But you, bow-woman, Lunar who gives orders, you will stay behind, and you will fight me." The etiäinen looks perfectly content with this declaration. "The others may go, but you will have to earn your survival. That is my price for the way out."

"We don't have time to bargain," says Artemis. "Fine. Show us the way, and I'll fight you."

"Fool," says the etiäinen smugly, and moves to the front of their group. It moves quickly after that, forcing them to follow as fast as they can. In not much time, it leads them to the cafeteria, gesturing toward the door that they've been looking for. "Your exit," it says.

"Thank you," says Artemis. She waves the others through, releasing her half of Lilianne's weight to Judy, and remains at the rear until they're all through. She sees Kelpie turn like she's going to rush back to the door on her unsteady legs, then moves as if she's going to follow them, grasping the edge of the door.

The etiäinen's clawed hand closes around her bicep. "Your exit, my price," it says, mouth suddenly very full of teeth.

Artemis turns back to face it. "Very well," she says, and slams the door shut as she turns to face her bargained battle.

* * *

The sewer is dark as midnight, and the water is so cold it's like a slap. Smita and Lilianne both jerk upright as they're pulled into it. Behind them, Roger and Judy are pulling Kelpie away from the closed door in the wall. She's scrabbling at it, frantic, trying to pry it open even as they pull her toward the water.

"Kelpie, no," says Judy. "She made her bargain. She's Artemis. She'll be fine."

She doesn't sound like she believes it, but under the circumstances, it's not like she could say anything else.

Kelpie, crying, allows herself to be tugged into the water, and they begin to wade through the sewers, letting Lilianne lead the way. Smita moves to walk beside her, and they all stay close together, not talking as they wade toward safety. After everything that's just happened, silence feels safer.

They're halfway to the ladder when a wave of water rushes up from behind them, driving them briefly forward. Judy loses her footing, going under with a splash, and flails until hands find her arms. She opens her eyes to find Roger and Dodger holding her out of the water, and blinks as she realizes she can *see* them. The wave has been followed by light, thin and pale, but light. She looks up.

The ceiling above them—the ceiling that is also the street—is riddled with cracks, some wide enough to let considerable shafts of light through. She gasps, then says the only word she can think of: "Run!"

For good measure, she repeats it in Italian, Mandarin, and German—all languages she's heard Roger and Erin use, if not the others—before she turns and starts running as fast as the thigh-high water will allow.

Two more waves follow, but all of them hurry toward the ladder as fast as they can go, and they manage to reach it before the street begins to fall inward, collapsing in slow motion. A wave of water catches them when they're halfway up the ladder, and Kelpie is swept loose, carried down the length of the sewer by the rush. Judy watches helplessly, but there's nothing she can do; all she'd do by following the other Lunar into the water is drown with her.

In the end, they all climb out of the sewer, two less than they were when they descended, and into chaos.

The nearby street has collapsed in on itself, creating a giant broken hole where a large square of downtown Berkeley should be. Emergency vehicles are already swarming, authorities securing the edge of the hall. Somehow, no one takes notice of them climbing free, and why should they? They can't have caused this disaster, which is too big and too dramatic to have been anything but a massive infrastructure failure.

Shivering and soaked, they limp back to the spot where they left the van, no one saying a word as they pile inside. There's nothing to be said. Even the linguists have been struck silent, a silence which grows thicker and heavier as Erin drives them toward home.

When they finally turn down the correct street, for a moment none of them can make sense of what they're seeing—or what they aren't seeing.

The house is gone. Where it should be is a much smaller structure, painted a peeling eggshell color. David, Tim, and Kim are sitting on the porch, the twins huddled together, David looking deeply perplexed—and a little uneasy, as he's suddenly a visibly Black man with two white teens, in a very predominantly white neighborhood where some of the neighbors have no idea how to mind their own business. It's never been a concern here before, not with the house effectively invisible to anyone uninvited. But now, he has to be aware.

Erin parks and gets out of the van, eyes wide as she approaches the gate. The others follow, more slowly, Roger and Dodger seeming to hold each other up while Judy trails along behind them, blood dripping from her many wounds, remaining equidistant between the pair and Smita and Lilianne.

"What *happened*?" asks Erin.

"Can't you tell?" asks Dodger, speaking for the first time since Asphodel. She steps away from Roger, who staggers but stays standing. "She took back what she gave us. Every bit of it. She drained us dry, like a vampire or something, and she left us to deal with what she didn't need."

"I don't understand," says Judy.

"Of course you don't," says Dodger. "You're a natural Lunar, and I'm just a woman alone in her own head for the first time in her damn life."

"Asphodel wrote the formula every alchemist has used to construct their cuckoos," says Roger, voice gone dull and dead. "She didn't make us, but she told other people how to do it. She laid the groundwork. And when she finally woke up, she took it all away. She's won. It's over."

Silence falls then, all of them looking at one another, none of them quite certain what to do.

* * *

Asphodel walks along the rainbow-ringed corridor of Kelpie's slice of the everything, moving toward the window into what she's wanted ever since she knew it was a thing that could be desired.

"Ah," she says, and swings the window open wide. "The Impossible City."

Acknowledgments

From the beginning, the Alchemical Journeys have been a voyage through the classical alchemical elements, and it has been incredibly important to me that I don't cheat: no shortcuts to the Impossible City. But this has meant that every flower I intended to gather was first a seed that had to be planted, and those seeds began with A. Deborah Baker, the author of the Up-and-Under books, and the woman at the center of so many of the things that have happened over the course of the series. Without Asphodel, none of this would have happened, and so it felt important to me that we spend some time with her as a person, to truly understand how she got us all into this mess.

Thanks, Asphodel. You are, and remain, the worst.

I would never have been able to make it this far without my agent, the endlessly patient Diana Fox, and my editor, Lee Harris, who speaks the language of British pantomime and modern musical theater as fluently and ceaselessly as I do. Between the two of them, I can mostly be kept on task the majority of the time, and I appreciate them endlessly. I would be in much worse shape without them.

At the end of the day, this entire series is for Shawn Connolly, my self-proclaimed stupid brother. He is the sibling I was always searching for, and his acceptance of this fact brightens my days and eases my nights. We live very far apart, but he is always with me, especially when I'm working on these books. I'm going to miss them at least in part because I'll miss how many midnight phone calls they've justified, and how much closer together they've been able to bring us.

Kate Secor and Natalie Cardinali have been some of the best support I could possibly have asked for through this complex and convoluted process; Natalie has been especially understanding of canceled plans and late nights when I couldn't really explain what I was doing without a flow chart.

Thanks to Chris Mangum, Tara O'Shea, and Alec Fowler for being the best pit crew and general support system I could ever have wanted. Thanks to Jennifer Brozek for being a shoulder to lean on, and someone who understands the way I jump from one thing to the next. Thanks to Ruby for kindness, to Amy King for cleverness, Amy Mebberson for reliability, and Olivia Youngers for being the smartest sweetheart I know. And thanks to the entirety of Team Starkid for giving me something else to do.

Amy McNally . . . I love you. Thank you for being patient, and I'll see you in the corn soon enough.

Finally, thank you all for continuing to read. I couldn't tell these stories without someone who wanted to listen. We've almost reached the Impossible City at this point, and I can show you a shortcut, if you like. Just take my hand, close your eyes, and trust me.

I know the way.

About the Author

Beckett Gladney

Seanan McGuire is the author of the Hugo, Nebula, Alex, and Locus Award–winning Wayward Children series; the October Daye series; the InCryptid series; and other works. She also writes darker fiction as Mira Grant. McGuire lives in Seattle with her cats, a vast collection of creepy dolls, horror movies, and sufficient books to qualify her as a fire hazard. She won the 2010 John W. Campbell Award for Best New Writer, and in 2013 became the first person to appear five times on the same Hugo ballot. In 2022 she managed the same feat again!